KU-432-537

Lynda Page was born and brought up in Leicester. The eldest of four daughters, she left home at seventeen and has had a wide variety of office jobs. She lives in a village near Leicester. Her previous novels are also available from Headline, and have been highly praised:

'You'll be hooked from page one'   *Woman's Realm*

'Cookson/Cox aficionados who've missed her should grab this. Romantic and gripping.'
Peterborough Evening Telegraph

'Filled with lively characters and compelling action'
Books

'As always with Page, the text is rich in Leicester dialogue, there's a wealth of well-drawn characters and a happy ending'   *Leicester Mercury*

'It's a story to grip you from the first page to the last'
Coventry Evening Telegraph

Also by Lynda Page

Evie
Annie
Josie
Peggie
And One For Luck
Just By Chance
At The Toss Of A Sixpence
Any Old Iron
Now Or Never
In For A Penny
All Or Nothing
A Cut Above
Out With The Old

Against the Odds

Lynda Page

headline

Copyright © 2004 Lynda Page

The right of Lynda Page to be identified as the Author of
the Work has been asserted by her in accordance with the
Copyright, Designs and Patents Act 1988.

First published in 2004
by HEADLINE BOOK PUBLISHING

First published in paperback in 2004
by HEADLINE BOOK PUBLISHING

1

Apart from any use permitted under UK copyright law, this
publication may only be reproduced, stored, or transmitted, in any
form, or by any means, with prior permission in writing of the
publishers or, in the case of reprographic production, in accordance
with the terms of licences issued by the Copyright Licensing
Agency.

All characters in this publication are fictitious
and any resemblance to real persons, living or dead,
is purely coincidental.

ISBN 0 7553 0112 9

Typeset in Times New Roman by
Letterpart Limited, Reigate, Surrey

Printed and bound in Great Britain by
Clays Ltd, St Ives plc

Headline's policy is to use papers that are natural, renewable and
recyclable products and made from wood grown in sustainable
forests. The logging and manufacturing processes are expected to
conform to the environmental regulations of the country of origin.

HEADLINE BOOK PUBLISHING
A division of Hodder Headline
338 Euston Road
London NW1 3BH

www.headline.co.uk
www.hodderheadline.com

For Laura

Wherever you are, whatever you are doing, our love and thoughts are with you.

Acknowledgements

Sharon and Everal Dawkins – thank you so much for the welcome into your home and for the great evening we spent reminiscing over your past experiences. I hope you feel that my character Everal and my portrayal of the times as they were in sixties Leicester does justice to you both.

Jim and Mandy Reid (Ma and Pa Larkin) – for being such wonderful neighbours. Who else would provide a 'meals on wheels' service for a starving writer who forgets to cook for herself because she's so engrossed in her work?

Everyone at Headline – for your faith in my abilities, your total support and commitment. I just hope I deserve it.

Chapter One

At the sudden clanging of a fire-engine's bell close by, the two women facing each other over a front garden gate abruptly stopped their gossiping and watched in silence as the engine careered past them to speed off down the road.

Tess Potts turned her attention back to the woman with whom she was in mid-conversation. Tess was a huge woman, her monstrous rolls of fat covered by a bell-shaped Crimplene dress of vivid orange heavily patterned with psychedelic swirls of brown and cream. The dress, having been worn continually for well over a fortnight, was dirty and stained, particularly down the front with amongst other things the greasy remains of fish and chips covered in dollops of tomato sauce that had been eaten out of newspaper the previous night. Personal hygiene was something Tess did not practise personally or insist upon from her family, and consequently all the Pottses emitted a powerful stench. Behind her back Tess's nickname hereabouts was Piss Pot; her equally as filthy husband was known as Cesspit, and the four unfortunate offspring of this foul couple all had names prefixed with the handle Stinker.

Tess unburdened herself of several parcels she was carrying, putting them down on the grimy pavement, and made to lean on the rickety gate then thought better of it, realising it was falling to bits as it was and her hefty weight pressed on it might just finish it off. She didn't want to risk a verbal exchange which would inevitably lead to flying fists as they argued the toss over who was responsible for repair. Normally Tess loved a good fight, was usually the one to instigate it, but at this moment she had some stuff she was in a hurry to offload and was hopeful that her neighbour, one of her best customers, would oblige so the last thing she wanted to do was antagonise her.

'My guess is bleeding kids have set fire to one of them abandoned wrecks on the green again,' Tess matter-of-factly announced.

Avril Downs gave a superior sniff, folding her arms under her flat chest. 'One of your bleeding kids most probably.'

Pursing her fat lips, Tess nodded almost proudly. 'More than likely.' Then before she could stop herself, she barked defensively, 'But they ain't doing n'ote your lot have never got up to. Your Colin ain't the little angel you mek him out to be, your Caitlyn's definitely no saint, and as for your Ray . . . well, what can I say about him? 'Cept it's a pity he wasn't just a little bit cleverer and then he wouldn't be in jail.'

Avril's thin lips tightened into a murderous scowl,

the wrinkles on her face forming deep crevices around her mouth. Her extremely hard life and inherited thinness from her mother's side gave her the appearance of someone at least ten years older than her actual forty-two. 'My Ray had no idea that telly was stolen,' she snarled.

Tess's piggy eyes danced maliciously. 'No idea, my arse! 'Course he knew. Ray's as guilty as sin and you know he is. He's lucky he's got away with what he has. You should count yerself fortunate that the judge who passed sentence on him for handling that stolen telly hadn't a clue about all the rest of the stuff that's been through his hands too or he'd have been put away for a damned sight longer than a year.'

Normally Avril would have lashed out at anyone daring to speak in such derogatory terms about any of her children, especially her beloved son Ray, but Tess hopefully had some items she was interested in purchasing – at the right price, of course – and she didn't want to upset her and risk losing her chance of first pickings. Tess might stink to high heaven, and keep a house best avoided by people who cared about their health, but when it came to making a bob or two on the side, her acquisitions were as good as the next person's. Besides, although Avril would never admit it even on her death bed, Tess spoke the truth. Her eldest son Ray had shown flair for being light-fingered from an early age, and that skill had proved to be her salvation on more occasions than she cared to remember, doing much towards helping feed and clothe the rest of the family.

The father of her children, Daniel Downs, had been a good-looking, raven-haired Irish navvy. She had fallen head over heels for him the moment she had set eyes on his rippling muscles while he dug a huge hole in the road so the Water Board could repair a burst main. It had been 1940, Daniel was twenty-four and Avril then sixteen years old, ripening very nicely into womanhood but as naïve as a newly appointed choir boy. The terrible war raging in Europe had brought with it hardships on an unprecedented scale. And on top of everything else they'd had to endure, their carefree youth cruelly stripped from them, the young women of Leicester were suffering from a dire shortage of eligible young men. A find like Daniel was a rarity.

As she had gingerly negotiated a plank of wood spanning the hole, Danny, who had avoided being called up to do his bit for the war due to Ireland being neutral, and if they hadn't been he would have found some way to get out of it, leaned on his shovel and fixed his eyes on her then shapely legs. Liking what he saw very much, he cockily shouted up to ask if she fancied going out for a drink with him. Within weeks he had persuaded Avril's widowed mother to allow him to marry her only daughter. She hadn't really any choice by then anyway unless she wanted her first grandchild arriving in the world illegitimate.

Not long after their wedding day Avril discovered that her husband was only charming when there was something to be gained. Otherwise he was a wastrel and a bully who had deliberately set out to get the innocent girl pregnant in order to ensure his own residency in England and all the home comforts Avril's mother's crumbling terraced house afforded him, which was still better than the squalid lodgings he'd lived in before. Besides, he'd reached a stage in his life when he wanted to be taken care of, and Avril and her mother were just the types he felt he could bully into doing so.

Their marriage was extremely turbulent and during the nine years it lasted Avril produced seven children, of whom only five survived infancy. For the rest of her life she would carry the scars of the vicious beatings her husband awarded her whenever the mood took him, while her mother stood helplessly by. It was a great relief when finally, after a violent row one Saturday night, he left Avril, then some weeks pregnant with her seventh child, and raged out of the house with the contents of her purse and the smashed gas meter. Not a word had been heard from him since.

Avril lurched from one financial crisis to another as she struggled single-handedly to feed and clothe her surviving offspring of four boys and one girl as well as her ageing mother whose meagre widow's pension barely fed her let alone paid for anything else. They had to scrape by on the couple of pounds Avril earned from her job as an early-morning cleaner at a local factory, donations from kindly souls who lived nearby, handouts from charitable organisations, and on what her elder children managed to swipe on their daily foraging sprees around local shops and late-evening visits to the market.

The massive slum clearance project that Leicester City Council had begun in the 1930s plucked the Downses out of their uninhabitable two-up, two-down terrace and deposited them in a modern three-bedroomed house on the North Braunstone Estate, a sprawling council development on the edge of the city bordering countryside. Carrying what they could of their few threadbare possessions, the rest piled haphazardly into a rusting coach pram, the bedraggled family had arrived in front of their new abode and stared at it in wonder, all unable to comprehend that this palace was their new home. In fact, it was far from luxurious with an outside lavatory, and inside only one cold-water tap set over the square pot sink in the kitchen which often froze in winter. Hot water had to be laboriously heated in the gas-fired copper.

Unfortunately, providing better housing for the poor of the city did not do anything to lift them out of the poverty trap and they were still forced to live by their wits, supporting themselves by any means they could find, and often only barely getting by.

Jobs were plentiful in post-war Britain, especially in industrial Leicester. For the skilled workforce a prosperous lifestyle was possible, but for the unskilled it was a different matter. For those who did want to find work, wages were still appallingly low, and conditions in many cases not much improved from those their ancestors had worked in at the turn of the century.

Regardless, the majority felt it their right to have decent furniture and modern household equipment, whether they could afford it or not. As a result unpayable hire-purchase debts were the bane of practically every household on the North Braunstone Estate, as were unpaid debts to the tally man, loan sharks, even the bread and milk man, and consequently acquiring what you wanted by illegal methods was commonplace. The North Braunstone Estate became infamous, known as 'Dodge City', and the corporation bus that ran through it 'The Dodge Stagecoach'.

Avril had long ago lost any sense of shame for the petty misdemeanours her family were forced to commit in order to survive. Her conscience vanished after her tyrannical husband left her penniless with five young children to raise as well as the care of her arthritic mother. She knew that what the Downses did to get by was not right, but neither could she condemn it as wrong if it kept food on their table and the children dressed and shod, albeit shabbily. Indeed, she felt proud that against the odds she had managed to keep her family together.

Now she glanced down at the parcels Piss Pot had dumped on the pavement, then fixed her eyes enquiringly on the unsavoury woman. 'What yer got then?' she asked.

Upstairs in the box room Caitlyn Downs glanced over the rooftops towards a cloud of black smoke billowing skywards.

'Looks like there's a good fire blazing across by Hand Avenue way. I bet kids have set fire to one of the wrecks on the green.' Her face clouded over. 'I hope for his sake our Colin ain't involved. Mam says if she gets the police knocking on the door for anything else he's got up to this week then she personally will kick his legs from under him and he won't see daylight for a month of Sundays. She's worried that if the coppers are constantly on our doorstep, one of these days they're going to catch us with something in the house that shouldn't be and it'll be her in jail next.

'Mind you, fat lot of good her threats are. Colin doesn't take a blind bit of notice. You wait 'til our Ray gets home, he'll sort that little tyke out with no by your leave. Our Ray might be some things but he's always respected our mam. He'll knock our Colin's block off when he finds out how much trouble he's been in while he's been inside.'

Then she glanced down to the scene by the garden gate.

'I see Piss Pot has collected the catalogue parcels. It makes me laugh! Mam can't stand Piss Pot, usually avoids her like the plague, but whenever she's got something to offload me mam suddenly becomes her bosom buddy.'

She turned around and looked across at her friend Shirley Haggar who was sitting on an old piano stool by the dressing table, peering at herself in the mirror, pursing her lips as she tried on Caitlyn's new lipstick which had treated herself to from Woolworth's cosmetics counter on her last half-day off work.

The small room at the top of the stairs was just big enough to hold a single bed, wardrobe and dressing table which Caitlyn, or Lynnie as she was affectionately called by all who knew her, had actually constructed herself using two piles of old house bricks as side props and spanning them with a piece of chipboard. Covering the bricks and concealed hole in the middle which Caitlyn used as a place to store her most personal items, not for her brothers' inquisitive eyes, was an offcut of pink gingham material held in place by intermittent drawing pins.

The walls of the room were still covered with the gaudy cheap floral paper the council had slapped up when the house was first built, which after fifteen years of the family's occupancy – like the rest of the walls in the house – was badly faded and torn in places. The original cheap white gloss on the woodwork was now a dingy cream. An old strip of lino, salvaged from an unlit bonfire not long after the Downses had moved in, covered the floor. Without the luxury of central heating, Lynnie's room was stifling hot in summer and bitterly cold in winter.

'The catalogue company is surely going to cotton on to what Piss Pot is up to one of these days,' she remarked.

Shirley gave a chuckle as she sat back and admired herself.

'Yer've gotta admire her though, ain't yer?' she said, turning to look at her friend. 'I mean, it's hard work keeping a check on people moving out of houses, then ordering stuff in their name and lying in wait for the delivery man to drop it off. Even when they do eventually cotton on to what's going on when the weekly payments are called for and they find the house empty, they'll never be able to pin this scam on Piss Pot unless they catch her red-handed and she's far too clever for that. Besides, half this street wouldn't have blankets on their beds or clothes on their backs if it wasn't for Piss Pot and her scams . . .

'I like this shade, Lynnie. It suits me, dunnit? Can I have it?'

'No, you can't. I haven't used it myself yet and it cost me one and six! If you like it that much, I'll get you one for your birthday.'

Shirley's face fell. 'That's months away.'

'Well, you'll either have to wait or buy your own.'

She issued a forlorn sigh.

'I can't buy 'ote for meself at the minute, Lynnie. Any spare money we scrape together is spent on baby stuff for this little blighter,' she said, patting her swollen stomach.

Lynnie flopped down on her bed, folding her arms under her head and stared up at the ceiling.

'Shirley, do you ever dream of walking into a shop and buying anything you want?'

Her friend gawked at her, surprised.

'Doesn't any woman? But yer can get anything yer want anyway, by getting it on tick.'

'No, I don't mean on tick. I mean, paying for it in

cash. Money that you've earned yourself and not borrowed. Spare money that's not supposed to be for bills.'

Shirley pulled a wry face.

''Course I do, but that ain't ever likely to happen on the paltry wage I get for slaving eight and a half hours a day making sausages in that stinking meat factory. No wonder I can't stand the sight of sausages after I've seen what goes in 'em.' Her face filled with a look of utter disgust and she gave a violent shudder. 'Neither would you if I told yer. I bleddy hate my job and I'll be glad when I leave it in a few weeks' time, though God knows how we're gonna manage without the money I earn. I can see us living with me mam for ever, and believe me, that thought terrifies me to death. You know as well as I do that she ain't the easiest of women to get along with.'

'Mmm,' Lynnie murmured. Her own mother could be very trying at times, but Shirley's was just downright lazy and expected her children to run after her in every way, her reasoning being that since she had raised them they could return the favour by looking after her and their equally lazy father now. 'The council will allocate you your own place soon after the baby's born. They know your mam's house is bursting at the seams as it is with all your brothers and sisters, and you and Pete having to sleep on a mattress behind the table in the living room.'

'Our own house,' Shirley uttered wistfully. 'That would be just heaven. You know as well as I do that it's purgatory in ours. Always someone bellowing for summat or me mam and dad arguing, telly blaring out from the minute transmission starts to when it shuts down at night. I ain't bothered for meself but because me dad don't work himself, he doesn't seem to consider that Pete's to get up at six in the morning and can't get to sleep until he's switched it off and gone to bed. We've no privacy at all. We have ter wait until the coast is clear before we can even consider a *bit of the other*.' She gave a miserable sigh. 'But even if we were given a house, without my wage coming in we'd really struggle to pay the rent and feed ourselves. And getting some furniture together is another matter.'

Lynnie smiled across at her reassuringly.

'Well, when you do get a house maybe you could get a neighbour to watch the little one while you do a part-time job. I bet a woman with a few kids herself who can't get out to work would be glad of the chance to earn a couple of bob and what you've left would help towards yer bills. And I shouldn't worry about furniture. Our Ray will be out of prison soon, and as my closest friend he'll see you right. He knows people who can get whatever you need for a fraction of its real worth.'

'That'd suit me, Lynnie, but Pete . ... well, he won't hear of it. He's that honest if he's given too much change he hands it back, no matter how much of a godsend those few coppers'd be to us. He says it'd frighten him senseless if every time someone knocked on the door it could be the rozzers on the other side, waiting to pounce, and he could land up in jail. Since his dad got put away for twenty-five years for being involved in that armed robbery, and he saw his mother work herself into an early grave raising him and his sisters, Pete won't have anything to do with 'ote that ain't above board.'

'Well, I admire your husband for his principles, Shirl, but when all's said and done, needs must. As well as you Pete's got a baby to think of now, and he'll soon realise when it arrives that if he's to provide for you both half-decent, which he'll be hard pushed to do on his dustbin man's wages, then some of his conscience will have to fly out of the window. No use clinging on to it when the baby's crying out in hunger 'cos you can't afford to buy any national dried milk. If someone offers him milk cheap then he'll snap their hand off for it, believe me he will, if the alternative is letting his child starve.'

'I expect yer right, Lynnie, but as it stands now it don't matter how much I reason with him, Pete puts his foot down. What we have, we have legit or we don't have it at all. If we ain't got the money for it, we go without. I love him dearly but that trait in him can be a bloody pain at times, especially when yer get the chance to buy summat you'd otherwise never be able to afford.'

Lynnie eyed her knowingly.

'Believe it or not, my mam and grandma were as honest as daylight once, would never have dreamed of doing anything even a little bit crooked. After me grandad died and money was short, me grandma often went without food herself so she could feed me mam, and she'd sit in the dark at night to save a few coppers on the gas. But when me dad went off like he did it was a different matter. Mam was left on her own with seven mouths to feed and no trade behind her because me dad got her pregnant with me so young any jobs she could get were so badly paid it was hardly worth doing them. When he'd gone, though, she had no choice but to accept any offers that came her way. Without what we kids and especially our Ray brought home, we'd definitely have ended up on the streets and more than likely starved. Some people, who don't have a clue how hard it's been for people like us, just see us as petty criminals, Shirl, but we see what we do to earn a few extra coppers as the difference between life and death. And how can that be wrong, eh?'

Shirley nodded. 'I agree with yer, Lynnie, and I've said as much to Pete but he won't budge, said he'd die sooner than resort to anything underhand. He gave me the third degree over that set of pans I bought for our bottom drawer off Winnie James whose husband got hold of all that fire-damaged stock from the warehouse that went up in smoke the other week. Those pans are ever such good quality, Lynnie, far better than I could afford if I had to buy 'em from a shop, but Pete didn't care about the quality – he just wanted to know if I'd bought them honestly. I lied to me back teeth and managed to convince him the pans were kosher, but if he'd had any notion I knew that Win's old man was one of the arsonists hired by the owner of that warehouse to torch the place, and the stock was part of his pay off, Pete'd have hit the roof.'

Lynnie looked surprised. 'Win's husband was behind that, was he? I didn't know that.'

'I only know meself 'cos I heard her bragging to our neighbour when I was hanging out some washing. You should have heard what she's bought with her share of the proceeds! Mind you, knowing Win's old man, I doubt she saw much of what he made. Regardless, she's kitted out all her kids with shoes and new coats, and twice last week they had frying steak for dinner.'

Lynnie frowned as a memory struck her.

'The night watchman of that warehouse got badly burned in the blaze, didn't he, trying to stop what was going on?'

'Well, more fool him. He should have made a run for it when he realised what were happening instead of trying to defend the place.'

Lynnie sat bolt upright and glared across at her friend, appalled.

'I'm surprised at you saying that, Shirl. The man was just trying to do his job. Look, I know me and my brothers will never go to heaven after some of the things we've got up to to help me mam out, especially our Ray, but even *we've* got morals. Nothing we've ever done has hurt anyone, except maybe dent the pockets a little of those that can afford it.

'Okay, our Ray got sloppy over his handling of that telly and is paying for his mistakes now. He's lost his job through his own stupidity – but the ironic thing was that the money he expected to make from it was going to be used to buy our Colin some new trousers and an anorak for school that he badly needed. I think it's dreadful that Win can go about bragging like she has when someone was hurt in the process and decent people lost their jobs through the owner being greedy. That's wrong, Shirl. When they set fire to that warehouse they should have made sure the place was empty. At the very least got the watchman out of the way on some pretext or other before they did what they did. I'm shocked you bought those pans off Win, knowing that innocent old man will probably never work again after what happened to him.'

Shirley's face clouded over in shame.

'Yer right, Lynnie. I should have refused them but I was so glad to get 'em cheaply I forgot meself.'

'Well, it's done now so there's no point in beating yourself up over it.'

Shirley looked across at her. Lynnie was her best friend, had been since coming to her aid and punching a girl at school on the jaw for bullying her when they were both twelve years old. From that moment on their friendship had flourished, but it didn't stop Shirley from being envious of Lynnie sometimes because she was taller than Shirley and very shapely, possessing an arresting face, the kind that people looked at twice, framed by brunette hair so dark it was almost black.

Poor Shirley was short and dumpy despite permanently dieting, and her round face barely drew a second glance from anyone except for her husband Pete. She felt herself fortunate to have met him. He might not be the handsomest of men or the most intelligent but he loved his wife and couldn't wait to be a father, was desperate for the day when they could move into a home of their own and he could look after his family without Shirley's parents' constant interference. Pete wanted to do right by her, and although sometimes his high principles went against her upbringing and could be very frustrating, Shirley couldn't fault his motives. He didn't want his wife to have to live like his mother had, and would do anything to avoid that.

She suddenly realised the time and struggled to get up off the stool.

'I'd best be off, Lynnie. I promised me mam I'd get the tea tonight, and I might be married and expecting a baby but she still clouts me lugs if I don't pull me weight. What time is Ozzie due?'

'About two hours ago,' Lynnie replied tersely, easing herself off the bed to stand next to her friend.

'Oh, I wonder what's keeping him?'

Lynnie eyed her meaningfully.

'I'll give you two guesses, and he'll bear the full brunt of my annoyance when he does finally get here. We were supposed to go and see the Vicar this afternoon to discuss wedding dates, but I should have guessed from past experience he'd no intention of showing. I wonder what his excuse will be this time?'

'Oh, but maybe he's ill or summat, Lynnie.' When she gave a disbelieving look, Shirley continued, 'I hope yer gonna wait to get married 'til after me baby's born? I don't fancy the idea of waddling down the aisle with me waters breaking. Can't you just imagine me, giving birth on the altar?'

Lynnie giggled at the thought, then her laughter faded and her face clouded over. 'I should think you'll have had your fourth child and be planning no more by the time me and Ozzie finally make it up the aisle.' Her voice lowering, she added distractedly, 'That's if we ever do get married.'

Shirley frowned at her quizzically.

'What d'you mean, Lynnie?'

'Oh, just that if I ever get Ozzie to set a date, it'll be a bloody miracle. He's forever telling me he loves me, wants me to be the mother of his kids, reckons he's saving to buy us a little terrace down off the Hinckley Road. But . . .'

'But what, Lynnie?'

She gave a shrug.

'Oh, I dunno, I sometimes have a feeling it's all just words with Ozzie to keep me sweet. I've lost count of the number of excuses he's thrown at me for letting the Vicar down after we've made an appointment to see him. Considering the time it is now that's probably going to be the case again today. It wouldn't surprise me if the Vicar flatly refused to make another appointment with us.' She gave a deep sigh. 'I used to believe Ozzie's excuses, Shirley, 'cos I wanted to believe them, but I'm beginning to wonder if maybe he's terrified of losing his freedom. I tell you, Shirl, I'm getting a little fed up of his false promises. I'm twenty-four and close to being on the shelf. If he doesn't watch out, I'm in danger of going off and finding someone else.'

Shirley laughed at the absurdity of her friend's statement. 'Yer don't mean that! You and Ozzie have been an item since you met at the youth club when you were both fourteen years old. He worships you, Lynnie, and you do him. He'd be devastated if you left him.'

'Then he should do more to show me that he cares.' She scraped her hands through her hair. 'I can't imagine life without Ozzie, Shirl, but I've started wondering whether that's just because I've been with him so long. Well, he's the only serious boyfriend I've ever had. But I do know one thing: he takes me for granted. He's absolutely convinced I'd never carry out my threats to leave him, and he's right, isn't he? I never have.' Her dark blue eyes narrowed resolutely. 'But one day, if he's not careful, he's going to get a shock. And I've a feeling today's the day unless he gets his act together.'

Shirley frowned. 'I wouldn't like to be in his shoes when he does finally stroll in.'

'Well, he should have thought about the consequences before he let me down once again. I warned him last night that I'd be far from pleased if he didn't show at two o'clock like he promised. If it was his mates he'd made the arrangement with it'd be a different matter. He'd be there, boots blacked, before the clock struck the hour. But not for me. Like always, he knows I'll be waiting, knows I'll be annoyed and give him hell, but thinks all he has to do is turn on the charm and I'll be putty in his hands. Well, I think I've come to the end of my tether, Shirl. I just feel that if I don't make some sort of stand now then this situation between us will just carry on and I'll end up a withered old spinster.'

Shirley laughed again at her friend's determination then eyed her sharply. 'I ain't never heard you talk like this before, Lynnie. What's the matter with yer, do you reckon?'

She shrugged. 'I dunno, Shirl. I just feel restless, have done for a few days now.' She paused and frowned in thought, then said distractedly, 'I've felt like this since I bumped into Pauline Babcock in Lewis's last Wednesday afternoon.'

'Pauline Babcock? Who's she when she's at home? Oh, yer mean that stuck-up cow that always had a nose in a book at school? We used to call her Professor, didn't we?'

'Yeah, and I'm ashamed to remember some of the stick we gave her. We were always taking the mickey out of her. But I tell you, Shirl, she's made something of herself, which is something we can't say. She did a course in accounts at the technical college and works as a clerk for an office in the city centre. She was telling me she's up for promotion. She was on her way to see a client and cutting through Lewis's as a short cut. She was wearing a smart suit and had herself a nice leather handbag, not plastic like ours.'

'So what if my bag is only plastic?' Shirley said defensively.

'Mine's plastic too,' Lynnie shot back at her. 'I'm not saying there's anything wrong with having a plastic handbag, but let's be honest, Shirl, both of us would prefer leather if we could afford it and we'd be liars if we said otherwise. I felt so humiliated when Pauline asked me what I did for a job. I lied, Shirl. After the way we treated her at school, always acting superior to her, I just couldn't bring myself to tell her what I actually did.'

'So what *did* yer tell her?'

'That I was a manager in a posh clothes shop with several staff under me.'

'Oh, Lynnie, you fibber!'

'Oh, don't start being all righteous with me, I know you'd have done the same in my position. To make matters worse, I had to change the subject quickly when she asked what shop it was so she could come and see what we stocked. But let's face it, Shirl, if we'd spent more time listening to the teacher like Pauline did, than mucking about being far more interested in catching the boys' eyes and talking about the new releases, I might really have ended up the manager of a posh clothes shop.'

Shirley sniffed haughtily.

'Well, yeah, I suppose you've a point. But regardless of the fact me and yer family were shocked when yer gave up yer job at the Three Sisters to take the one yer did, and did our best to talk you out of it, you like that job, Lynnie.'

'Yes, I do. Naughty of me, I know, but to be honest I

think I was hell-bent on getting it *because* of your reactions. I never know why people think that working for a turf accountant is only for the lowest of the low, and that such places are dens of iniquity unsuitable for a young woman like me to work in considering the foul language some of the punters use. In fact, it's no worse than you hear from some of the neighbours around here, and you know I had the devil's own job persuading Cigar Sid to give me a try out when he really wanted a bloke. Even so, I don't think I ever believed for a minute I'd be taking tuppenny ha'penny bets from people barely able to afford their stakes for the rest of my life.'

Her eyes became distant. 'I always fancied myself as a switchboard operator for the GPO, but my mam thought I was mad to be aiming so high. She said people like us don't talk posh enough for the likes of the GPO, and besides once they found out I was off the North Braunstone Estate it wouldn't matter whether I talked as posh as the Queen herself, my application would be laughed at and I wouldn't get a look in. She said she didn't want to see me hurt by a rejection. That's why I landed up in a haberdashery shop in the first place. But maybe I shouldn't have taken so much notice of my mam, Shirl. Just maybe the GPO might have given me a chance and now I might have a proper career like Pauline and be able to afford good clothes and leather handbags. Still, it's too late. Have to content myself with working for a back-street betting shop and get on with it.'

'I shouldn't let Cigar Sid hear yer talk like that, Lynnie. He's proud of his establishment. Me dad says he's the only honest bookie he's ever come across in his life and he wouldn't trust his bets with anyone else – and that's saying summat considering me dad is as crooked as our back fence.'

Lynnie sighed despondently.

'Yes, Sid is an honest man, too honest sometimes, but he's a smashing bloke to work for. It's just that . . .'

'What?'

She looked at her friend blankly. How could she explain to Shirley the way she was feeling when she wasn't sure herself? Until she had bumped into Pauline she had been for the most part happy with her lot, but after their conversation she suddenly realised that beyond the boundaries of her existence was a world full of opportunities and experiences she would never taste. And it was all down to her own lack of ambition. She could have been like Pauline and ignored the masses at school, got herself a decent education which would have enabled her to get a job with better prospects, but at the time she hadn't had the foresight to look further than that very minute.

As she had stood facing the woman she had mocked as a young girl at school, Lynnie had seen her own future laid out before her. She and Ozzie would eventually marry, and like Shirley and Pete would live with her mother or his. When children began to arrive they'd get a council house of their own, probably around the corner from where she lived now, and grow old together, scratting from week to week to make ends meet. As much as she loved Ozzie and could not see her life without him in it, the thought of that kind of future together suddenly did not appeal. In fact, it terrified her. Trouble was, she felt she was stuck with it now.

She forced a smile to her face.

'Oh, nothing's the matter, Shirl. It's just one of those days when I wish my life was something more than it is, and I'm sure you have plenty of those too. No one is ever completely happy with their lot, are they? I expect even millionaires find something to grumble about.'

'Yeah, but I'd sooner be grumbling about how to spend me millions than grumbling about not having any. Still, I can always live in hope me dad comes up on the pools.'

Lynnie shook her head.

'If he did, do you really believe your dad would share some of it with you and Pete? I doubt your mother would see any of it, let alone anyone else.' Just then Lynnie heard her name being called and pulled a face.

'Now that's either my mam wanting to show me what she's bought off Piss Pot or else she's after borrowing money to pay for it. Most probably both. I'd better answer her before she charges up and gives me hell for ignoring her,' she said as she pulled open her bedroom door. 'And you, gel, need to get home before your mother comes around here brandishing her frying pan, ready to clock you one 'cos you're not back yet to run after her.'

Chapter Two

Lynnie glanced disinterestedly over the bright turquoise Bri-nylon sheets her mother was showing her.

'I like the colour, Mam, very trendy, and I know those type are all the rage, but I know someone who got an electric shock from sleeping on them and they said the sheets snag your toe nails.'

'Well, as they ain't for you, you ain't got ter worry about any of that, have yer? I'm taking these down ter the pub tonight as I know I can get more there than what I haggled Piss Pot for 'em. Cheeky sod wa' expecting me to pay ten bob for the pair and *she* got 'em for n'ote. I offered her five, take it or leave it 'cos I was offering her no more.'

'Piss Pot took all the risk, though, Mam.'

'Eh, whose side are you on?'

'Yours, of course. I was just pointing out a fact.'

'Well, keep yer points and facts to yerself. When all's said and done I'm doing that stinking old bag a favour by taking this lot off her hands.' Avril's face screwed up disgustedly. 'Mind you, *stink* is a mild word for the pong coming from her today. I don't know about her house wanting urgently fumigating, *she* certainly does. You'd think she'd tek the hint when everyone uses any feeble excuse they can not to invite her into their homes, but as she doesn't then it's obvious her skin is as thick as the tide mark around her filthy neck.

'Anyway, Piss Pot wa' desperate to get rid of the catalogue stuff 'cos she needs the brass herself, and she got as much from me as she would anyone else around here.' She looked at her daughter enquiringly. 'Look, are yer sure you don't want these sheets, Lynnie? I'll let you have 'em for ten bob. And there's pillowcases and a bedspread to match, if yer interested. Tell yer what, being's yer me daughter, I'll let yer have the lot for thirty bob – and that's a lot less than you'd pay in that cheap shop Aladdin's Cave on Belgrave Gate.' She pulled a disapproving face. 'The chap that owns that place is a downright crook, charging the prices he does, considering practically all his stock fell off the back of lorries. *And* he fiddles his books. I know all this 'cos one of the women I work with, her daughter is the one he pays highly to doctor his books and keep her gob shut.'

Lynnie stared at her, flabbergasted.

'Mother, you've a bloody cheek calling the chap who owns Aladdin's Cave a crook when you've just bought stolen goods yourself! Even worse, now you're trying to make a profit from them out of your own daughter.'

Avril raised her hand and before Lynnie could dodge out of the way, had cuffed her around her ear.

'What have I told you about swearing at me? You ain't too big to have yer mouth washed out with soap and water so be warned. I was trying to do you a favour, me lady. I have ter cover me own costs. Oh, that reminds me, can yer lend me a quid to give Piss Pot? I hadn't got quite enough on me to cover all I had off her. I'll pay yer back when I get rid of this. She's waiting at the gate for yer.'

Still rubbing her smarting ear, Lynnie opened and closed her mouth fish-like at the audacity of her mother, but knew there was no point in voicing her displeasure. Avril didn't see anything unethical in what she was doing. Without a word Lynnie spun on her heel and went to sort Tess out with money she had planned to put in her Post Office savings out of her wage the previous week, but which luckily for her mother, she hadn't had time to do. Presently she returned.

'Piss Pot said to tell you she's hoping to get some more stuff next week.'

Avril eyed her keenly.

'Did she say what?'

'No, and I didn't ask 'cos I was in too much of a hurry to get away from her. You're right, she stinks worse than a sewer.'

Avril had turned her attention back to the items she had just purchased. 'Look, Lynnie, it ain't like you to turn down a bargain. A' yer sure yer don't want this bedding?'

She shook her head.

'I thought I'd already made my feelings clear, Mam. I don't like the idea of sleeping on Bri-nylon, whether it's all the rage or a bargain.' Her eyes suddenly twinkled in amusement as a thought struck. 'Anyway, it's already my bedding as I've just paid for it. I should be asking if *you* want to buy it from *me*.'

Avril glared at her.

'Very funny, clever clogs. Well, you can maybe afford to be choosy but there's others around here who'll jump at this lot and those towels I got.' Her face clouded over. 'I was only thinking of you and Ozzie's bottom drawer.'

Lynnie smiled at her warmly.

'I know you were, Mam, and I appreciate it. But I've got enough bedding in my bottom drawer to last us years, same as everything else I've collected since he and I got serious. That's if we ever do get married,' she added as an afterthought.

Avril, who was bundling her ill-gotten gains out of sight behind the shabby burgundy moquette settee, turned and looked at her daughter sharply.

'Wadda yer mean by that? 'Course you and Ozzie will tie the knot, it's a foregone conclusion.' She scrutinised her daughter for a moment then frowned in concern, eyes narrowing questioningly. 'Is that lad backing out of his obligations?' she accused. Without waiting for an answer, her face darkened thunderously as she reached her own verdict. 'I'll sort that beggar out if he thinks he can jilt a daughter of mine! After courting you all these years, coming around here and treating this place like his own . . .'

'No, Mother, it's nothing like that,' Lynnie urgently interjected, feeling trouble brewing, knowing that as soon as Ozzie finally did show his face, her mother would immediately pounce and then he wouldn't know what had hit him.

'Well, what is it like then?' Avril demanded.

'Well . . . er . . . Look, just forget what I said. I didn't mean to say it anyway. It's just . . . oh, I dunno, Mam, I sometimes wonder if I want to get married, that's all.'

''Course yer want to get married. All gels do. When you was a little gel you were always throwing one of yer granny's old patched sheets around yer shoulders, pretending it was a veil and playing weddings.'

'That was when I knew no better.'

'Knew no better?' Avril stared at her daughter blankly. 'Oh, now, Lynnie lovey, Ozzie's nothing like yer dad. Why, that lad wouldn't lift a finger to you, let alone walk out leaving you to raise five kids and yer mother by yerself – and that after robbing yer blind. Just 'cos I happened to be fooled into landing meself with the devil, don't mean ter say that's gonna happen to you.'

'Mam, I know. I know Ozzie wouldn't hurt a hair on my head, it's just that . . .'

Lynnie stopped abruptly and spun around to see the man they were discussing framed in the doorway. He was swaying slightly. Normally just the sight of his slim six-foot frame and handsome features would have sent her racing into his arms, but today she was annoyed at

31

his lateness and also that he was the worse for drink.

'Oh, I see you're not dead then,' she hurled at him.

He looked startled for a second then his face split into a silly grin.

'Oh, come on, Lynnie, don't be mad with me,' he slurred. 'Just 'cos I'm a little late . . .'

'A little late?' she snapped, cutting him short as she advanced on him, wagging a finger angrily. 'Two hours is more than a little late. You promised me, Ozzie. You swore on your grandfather's grave that you'd be here on time.'

He tried to take her in his arms, and when she stepped out of reach, looked at her, hurt.

'I said I'd be here at three.'

'Ozzie, we arranged to meet at two o'clock, not three. We'd an appointment with the Vicar at three. Besides, it's four o'clock now.'

His eyes widened in shock. 'It's never four!' he exclaimed. He pulled up his sleeve and looked at his watch, shaking his wrist and raising it to his ear. 'Oh, God, Lynnie, me watch has stopped.'

Her lips tightened. 'Don't come that one, Ozzie. It might have worked in the past but not today. And don't bother giving me any of your cock and bull 'cos I know damned well where you've been all afternoon. You've been in the Shoulder of Mutton with your mates.'

'Hardly, Lynnie. Pubs shut at two on a Sunday.'

'Stop treating me like an idiot, Ozzie. I live around here, remember, and I know all that goes on. That landlord never throws anyone out who's still got the price of a pint in his pocket. He's had a lock in and don't deny it. And you felt it was more important to stay and booze with your mates and discuss football than to honour your arrangement with me. That's the truth of it, isn't it?'

Ozzie shuffled uncomfortably on his feet, eyeing his fiancée apprehensively. He'd expected Lynnie to be cross with him, after all she'd every right to be, but he hadn't anticipated her being quite this angry. He'd seen her cross many times, had in fact usually been the cause of her annoyance, but there was a deeper edge to her displeasure today that he had never witnessed before and he had a dreadful feeling he wasn't going to worm his way out of this episode so easily as he had done others in the past. His eyes were darting, brain whirling as he frantically sought to come up with a more plausible excuse for his lateness. Lynnie was right. He had been drinking with his mates but all the time had been well aware of the passing hours. Ozzie had never had any intention of keeping their arrangement to see the Vicar but knew better than to admit that.

'Well, *Oswald*, answer me daughter,' demanded Avril, now standing at the side of Lynnie, arms folded, face tight.

Ozzie glared at her. He detested being addressed by his proper name and knew damned well that his future mother-in-law had done it to annoy him. He gulped in trepidation. Facing up to Lynnie he could handle as he had done many times in the past. She never stayed angry with him for long once his charm broke down her defences. But facing up to the two of them was a different matter. Avril Downs was a formidable opponent at the best of times, but when she was upset over something, especially a matter that involved one of her children, she was frightening and to be avoided.

'Er . . . I've just remembered, Lynnie, I promised our Owen I'd . . . er . . . tek a look at his motorbike with him. Summat to do with the brakes or summat.' His excuse was a lame one but he prayed it worked. 'I'll see yer later, yeah?'

Avril grabbed his arm.

'Oh, suddenly become an expert in mechanics, have yer, Ozzie? Bleddy miracle that, considering it was only last week yer told me yer hadn't a clue about 'ote with a motor attached to it when I asked yer to tek a look at me Hoover 'cos it wasn't picking up properly.' She scowled at him darkly. 'Yer a master of excuses, Ozzie lad, I'll give yer that. But you ain't going nowhere 'til yer explain yerself to me and our Lynnie.'

Her daughter spun to face her.

'Have you not got anything to do, Mam?'

'Nothing that can't wait,' she snapped. 'I wanna hear what the lad has ter say for himself.'

'Mam, I can deal with this.'

Avril scowled at her in protest. This situation promised to turn into a good showdown and she very much wanted to be part of it.

'But . . .'

'Mam, please give me and Ozzie our privacy,' Lynnie insisted.

'Huh!' Avril huffed, indignantly. As she made to depart, she shot Ozzie a warning glare and thrust her face into his. 'I hope fer your sake, me laddo, your story's a good 'un else I've a feeling it's yer cards for you.'

'Well, Ozzie, I'm waiting,' Lynnie urged after her mother's very reluctant departure.

He smiled at her winningly.

'Come on, Lynnie. So I was having a pint or two with the lads and forgot the time. The Vicar will understand and give us another appointment.'

'Like he has done before, you mean,' she shot back at him tartly. 'Ozzie, the Vicar might be understanding, I'm not. You're always doing this to me, and like a prat I've always swallowed your cock-and-bull excuses. Now I've had enough. You promised me faithfully you wouldn't let me down this time.'

She tilted her head and looked at him questioningly. 'Or is it that you really don't want to marry me, Ozzie, and just agreed to set a date to keep me sweet?' She held up her hand in warning. 'Don't bother answering me 'cos I already know. You want to marry me but only when *you're* good and ready to give up your freedom, and that could be in ten or maybe twenty years' time, or maybe never. Well, I'm ready *now*, Ozzie. I want a home and a family and all that goes with it. If that's not what you want too then . . . then it's better we call it a day.'

Ozzie inwardly groaned. His drink-fuddled brain wasn't sharp enough to deal with this situation right now and come out on top. He had to try and steer Lynnie off this interrogation until he was better equipped to deal with it. He gave a helpless shrug, purposely forcing a look of utter bemusement to his face.

'Oh, come on now, Lynnie, what's got into yer?' He made to take her in his arms again but once more she stepped out of reach. His heart plummeted then as it hit him full force that she wasn't easily going to drop her line of questioning.

'Nothing's got into *me*, Ozzie,' she snapped, her voice rising angrily. 'It's *you* that's got the problem. If you never intended to marry me, you shouldn't have proposed. I know you were drunk when you asked me after Leicester City won the League cup, but that still counts as a proposal.'

He scraped his hand through his hair, blowing out his cheeks.

'Of course I want us to get married, Lynnie. It's just that . . . just that . . .'

'Just that what, Ozzie?'

'Well . . . er . . .'

He fixed his eyes on her, staring at her blindly. What on earth was he to do? It wasn't that he didn't love Lynnie: he did, worshipped her, and had done since their eyes first met across the ping-pong table at the local youth club when they were both fourteen years old. She had been a popular girl and he the envy of all the other lads in their age group when she'd made it clear she fancied him. Even all these years later he knew he was envied by many other chaps and had no doubt that should Lynnie become free they would not hesitate to play their hand.

But in truth the whole commitment of marriage frightened him witless. He liked his life the way it was. Having his freedom to come and go and do exactly what he wanted. Having his mother cook and clean for him in exchange for just a pound a week, the rest of his wage from his job as a warehouseman for the British Shoe Corporation his to do with exactly as he pleased. And, the icing on his cake, the lovely doting Lynnie hanging on his arm. This situation suited him perfectly. He was quite happy and content to keep it this way for a long time yet.

He'd witnessed his own brothers and many of his mates change dramatically the minute they got hitched. Marriage to them had been an automatic step, blindly taken when they had been courting for a certain amount of time. Ozzie had seen so many steered towards their fate by a sweet-natured girl suddenly transformed into a formidable force as soon as they'd popped the question, spurred on relentlessly by her army of family and friends, the groom rushed down the aisle before he knew what had hit him. As soon as the wedding was over, to Ozzie's way of thinking, his brothers and mates had become old, aged before their time by the huge responsibility of having a wife and all the baggage that went with it. He wasn't ready for that yet.

Lynnie was right, he had proposed in a drunken stupor, overcome with excitement that his team had won the trophy. Afterwards, realising just what he had done, he had been conceitedly of the opinion that he could string her along happily until such time as he was himself ready to take the plunge. Completely sure that Lynnie idolised him, he'd never thought for a minute that she would challenge him to honour his obligation. How badly he had underestimated her.

His heart thumped painfully. He didn't know what terrified him most: marriage or losing Lynnie.

He realised she was talking to him.

'What?'

'I said,' she snapped, 'you obviously think I'm stupid and don't realise that as the youngest of five brothers you have always been your mother's baby. You're her favourite, Ozzie. She does things for you she never did for the others. She couldn't wait for your brothers to leave home, encouraged them out, but not you. She wants to keep you at home for as long as she can because with you gone, what has she left except for your dad? And let's face it, Ozzie, he's never been a model husband, has he? He does nothing for her. Never takes her out or does anything around the house. He comes home from work and sits on his fat arse all night, watching the telly and stuffing himself with his packets of crisps and bottles of beer. That's when he's not off down the pub.'

'Now, Lynnie, just a minute, that's my dad yer talking about.' He looked at her for a moment before adding, 'Well, yeah, yer right about him. He ain't bin much of a husband to me mam, and neither has he been much of a father to his sons, but he's still me dad. And are you saying I'm a mummy's boy?' he demanded, insulted.

'In a manner of speaking, yes, you are. Don't get me wrong, Ozzie, I'm quite happy to have your mother as a mother-in-law, but she's always spoiled you. You click your fingers and she comes running. You've got it all, haven't you? Between me and your mother, you've got yourself the perfect life.'

Lynnie was right, he had. But right at this moment that perfect life was in danger of disintegrating. He fought to fathom a way to keep it intact. There were plenty of other women who would happily settle for what he was offering, but he didn't want any other woman. He'd known from the minute he set eyes on Lynnie that she was his ideal, and his opinion had not changed all these years later. Trouble was, he wasn't ready to settle down with her yet but this time it was clear that Lynnie meant business. His luck had just run out. The one thing he was absolutely sure of though, was that the idea of parting from her was unbearable, so he had no choice but to agree to set a date and honour it. A surge of absolute dread raced through him, then miraculously a happy thought struck. Hopefully the Vicar wouldn't have a slot free to marry them for at least a year, maybe longer if Ozzie was lucky, and during that time he could come up with a good plan to stall matters further until such time as he was ready to do the deed.

He heaved a loud resigned sigh.

'All right, you win, Lynnie. Next Sunday I promise we'll go and see the Vicar. I won't even meet me mates beforehand. That please yer?'

She looked at him searchingly. 'Do you really mean it this time, Ozzie? Because if you let me down again . . .'

'I won't, I promise on me mother's grave,' he insisted. 'Now just come here and give us a kiss.'

Cradled in his arms, she looked up at him and a warm glow filled her. Ozzie meant it this time, she felt sure he did. She reached up to respond to his demand and as she did so there was a shuffling noise behind her and she sprang away from Ozzie, spinning around to see her grandmother entering the room.

'Hello, Nan,' she addressed her beloved grandmother, somewhat embarrassed by the intimate situation the old lady had just caught her in. 'Had a good sleep?'

'Hardly, ducky,' the old lady gruffly responded. 'What with the noise of that fire engine and kids screaming roundabouts, I barely scraped three winks let alone forty.' She paused and eyed the young couple, then fixed shrewd faded-blue eyes on Ozzie. 'Just back from seeing the Vicar, are yer? When's the date then?'

Lynnie hurriedly took the old lady's arm. 'Come and sit down, Nan, and take the weight off your legs. Want a cuppa?'

'Love one, ta,' she said, easing herself down into one of the shabby armchairs either side of the grey and maroon tiled fireplace. 'And a couple of me painkillers if yer don't mind, Lynnie lovey. Me ryetist is giving me such gip today. Oh, and if there's any Yorkshire pudding left over from dinner, I wouldn't mind a bit of that spread with jam. That's if Colin ain't scoffed it all. It'll just help tek the edge off me hunger pangs 'til tea time.' Having settled herself comfortably, she looked at them both. 'Now what date did yer say yer'd fixed up?'

Lynnie could tell by the twinkle of amusement in her grandmother's eyes that she strongly suspected no date had yet been set.

'We never got to see the Vicar, Nan. He got called away urgent. Definitely next Sunday.'

'That's the excuse yer used last week, wasn't it, ducky, and the time before?'

'Now, Nan, stop it,' Lynnie gently warned. 'Come hell or high water, next Sunday I'll have a date for you.' She shot a meaningful glance at Ozzie. 'Won't we, Ozzie?' Then she turned her attention back to her grandmother, smiling at her affectionately. 'You just can't wait to have a good knees up, can you?'

'What I'd like is to see you finally settled before I pop me clogs.' She looked sternly at Ozzie who was hovering nearby. 'You need a rocket up yer arse, young man. In my day we'd never have put up with the excuses you've thrown at my granddaughter. She's too tolerant of you, to her own detriment. Another woman would have hung you out to dry long before now. Yer wanna watch out someone else don't just snatch Lynnie away from you while you're dilly-dallying. She's a good catch, yer know.'

'Ah, now come on, Nan . . .'

But Freda Bates cut him short. 'Oi, Nan's the title yer get the privilege of using when yer proper family. Until then it's Mrs Bates to you, *Oswald*.'

Ozzie cringed and would have commented on her use of his detested Christian name when Avril strode in, her face wearing an expectant expression. She addressed her daughter as though Ozzie wasn't present.

'Well, what's the verdict? Has he been hung, drawn and quartered and given his marching orders, or do we still have a wedding to look forward to?'

Ozzie thought it was about time he made his escape and butted in before Lynnie could respond.

'I'd best be off. Me mam will have me tea about on the table. See yer tonight . . . er . . .' He paused, about to say he would call for her as usual, but thought he'd better steer clear of the Downs household until something else other than his and Lynnie's nuptials occupied their minds. 'You wanna call for me when yer ready? About seven-thirty as I told Matt we'd meet him and his new girlfriend down the Mutton about eight. Apparently, she's a right corker.' And he had the cheek to add, 'Don't be late, will yer?'

Before Lynnie could respond Avril barked, 'Not so much of a corker as my Lynnie.'

Face reddening, he blurted, 'No, I never meant that.'

'You'd better go, Ozzie, before you really stick your size tens right in it,' Lynnie said. 'I'll be around when I'm ready.'

He made a thankful escape.

Before either Avril or Freda could say another word, Lynnie addressed them both.

'Like I've already told Nan, we're seeing the Vicar next Sunday – that's if he can manage to see us then – and I don't want another word said on the subject by either of you, thank you. I'll make a start on the tea, Mam.'

Chapter Three

A short while later Lynnie was rinsing a head of lettuce under the kitchen tap when the back door opened and a tall, well-set, dark-haired youth of fourteen sauntered in. He had an air of self-assurance aided by the glaring fact that he was an extremely good-looking boy and already an object of desire for most of the young girls in the area.

'Tea ready yet, Sis?' he casually asked, pinching a slice of tomato out of a small dish.

She glared at him.

'Wouldn't have hurt you to come in earlier and given me a hand with it, would it? Then it might have been ready.'

Leaning back against the door frame, he eyed her scornfully.

'No chance, that's women's work.'

Before he could avoid it she had given him a slap around his ear.

'Cheeky beggar!'

'Ah, Lynnie,' he yelped. 'That hurt.'

'It was meant to. Now set the table, and if you know what's good for you, you'll do as I ask.' She dried her hands and picked up a sharp knife to cut some bread. Suddenly she paused, glanced at her brother quizzically, then pushed her face close to his and sniffed. 'Is that paraffin I smell? It is,' she accused, waving the knife at him. 'Oh, Colin, please don't tell me you were responsible for that visit by the fire brigade today?'

'Weren't just me,' he responded cockily. 'Corky Murphy and Stinker Bill were involved as well.' His face lit up in sheer rapture. 'Ah, Sis, yer should have seen it go up! Warra blaze.'

She stared at him worriedly.

'I hope it's a wrecked car you're talking about and not anything else?'

'Not one wreck, Sis, two,' he proudly announced.

She shook her head in utter disbelief.

'Mam warned you to keep out of trouble, Colin, especially after that episode last week when you were responsible for breaking the school window and the cops got involved.' She kept her voice down, conscious that their mother could walk in at any minute. 'I suspect you and the rest of those silly boys you knock around with were planning to rob the tuck shop, and how you got away with convincing the police you were only playing football and kicked it too hard beggars belief. You were lucky to get away with a caution. Didn't you take any heed of what the sergeant said to you about what would happen if they caught you again? And don't you listen to Mam at all? She warned

46

you that under no circumstances were you to get yourself into any more trouble or she would personally knock your block off, and I can assure you she meant what she said.'

He gave an innocent shrug. 'But I never got into trouble today. We scarpered before the brigade arrived.'

'Oh, Colin! And that makes it all right, does it?'

'Well, don't it?'

'Don't act stupid with me,' she fumed. 'You might think you're the big I am, but if you aren't careful you'll be joining your brother. Aren't you scared of landing up in jail?'

He sniggered, 'Ain't old enough to go to jail.'

She clipped him across his ear again. 'Well, bloody borstal then, you cocky little sod.' She suddenly noticed a bulge in his trouser pockets. 'What's that?' she demanded.

He eyed her shiftily. 'Er . . . n'ote, just me handkerchief.'

'I don't believe you. Show me.'

'Bugger off, Sis. What's in me pocket's my business.'

'Bloody show me and now, and less of your lip else I'll call Mam in and tell her what you've been up to today. Then you'll really be for it.'

At that threat he complied.

She looked at the empty Mars bar wrapper and half-eaten packet of Spangles then fixed his eyes with hers. 'Did you pay for those?' she asked suspiciously.

He avoided her gaze. 'Yeah.'

'Liar,' she hissed. 'I know for a fact you had no money because you tried to cadge some off me this morning. You nicked those sweets, didn't you?'

'So what if I did? I'm getting in training for when Ray gets out then hopefully he'll let me help him. And you've no right to lecture me, Lynnie. Everybody knows you were the best tea leaf around here when you were little.'

She glared at him, wagging the bread knife.

'I swiped stuff to eat because we were hungry, or something that Mam could maybe sell on to help pay the rent or put a penny in the gas meter – never just 'cos I wanted some sweets. I didn't enjoy doing what I did. Half the time I was so bloody scared I'd get caught, I wet myself. Since I started work and could help Mam out with my wages, I haven't stolen a thing.'

Before she could add anything else he erupted. 'You do still steal!' he vehemently accused. 'You're always getting knock-off stuff through people down the bookie's and bringing it home for Mam to sell on if you can't yourself.'

She looked at him, startled. 'That's different,' she hissed.

He gave her an 'Are you stupid?' look. 'Is it? How?'

''Cos it just is,' she snapped tersely. 'For a start, we aren't stealing the stuff ourselves, just buying it cheap from people who are glad to be rid of it. If me and Mam didn't buy it then you can bet your life someone else would. Now I've had enough of this conversation. I'm warning you, Colin, for God's sake keep out of trouble for the time being because if you don't you'll regret it in more ways than one, believe me. You'd better set the table now like a good little boy or I'll personally put you across my knee and smack your bum.'

He scowled fiercely at her but thought better of any retaliation for this slighting way of addressing him, knowing that although he now surpassed her in weight and height she could still pack a good punch should she choose to.

Just then Avril arrived in the kitchen. 'Oh, yer home, a' yer?' she addressed her youngest son. Narrowing her eyes, she wagged a warning finger at him. 'I hope that fire engine weren't anything ter do with you?'

Without batting an eyelid, he gave an innocent shrug. 'No, Mam.'

She thrust her face into his. 'You sure?' She gave a sniff. 'Is that paraffin I smell?'

His response came off pat. 'Yeah, Mam, it is. I've bin with Stevie Tilly all af'noon helping his dad tidy their garden. That's why I'm in a mess 'cos we was burning rubbish and had ter use paraffin to get it going.'

She stared at him, taken aback.

'Tubs Tilly was gardening? Well, wonders will never cease. And you helping him, eh? Well, that's a bleddy miracle. Right, me laddo, being's you're such an expert now and so willing to help the neighbours, you can tidy ours. Mek it nice for when our Ray comes home.'

His face fell in utter dismay.

'Ah, Mam, it's like a jungle out there!' he wailed.

'Well, sooner you get started, the sooner you'll stop it from getting any worse. Lizzie Coombe has got a mower. You can pop over after tea and ask her if we can borrow it. I'm sure she won't mind, she hardly uses it herself. Now give us a hand in setting the table,' she ordered as she picked up a stack of plates and disappeared off with them.

Lynnie chuckled. 'That'll teach you for telling such a whopper, our Colin.'

Just then there was a tap on the back door and a woman entered. Her clothes were rumpled, face red and blotchy, hair a tousled mess. It was apparent she was deeply upset.

'Whatever is the matter, Charmaine?' Lynnie asked her. 'Is it one of the kids?'

She shook her head. 'No the kids are fine, they're round me mam's. I . . . I just wondered if you'd seen your Jimmy in the last couple of days?'

Lynnie pulled a thoughtful face. 'Come to think of it, I ain't seen him for about a week. Unless Mam has.' She looked at the woman searchingly. 'Oh, God, what's our Jimmy gone and done?'

Charmaine took several shuddering breaths. 'He's . . . he's left me, Lynnie, that's what he's done.'

'Left you?' Lynnie mouthed, shocked.

The other woman sniffed hard and wiped her runny nose using the back of one hand. 'He never even told me he was going, Lynnie. I got home after collecting the kids from me mother's after work on Friday evening and found all his stuff gone.'

'He never left you a note?'

'Nothing. I ain't no idea where he is. I was hoping you might have?'

She gave a helpless shrug. 'I haven't a clue.'

'Hello, Charmaine,' Avril greeted her as she arrived back in the kitchen. She flashed Lynnie a look as if to say, 'Oh, God, this is all I needed', then turned her attention to their visitor. 'My Jimmy and the kids with you? Come for some tea, have you? Colin,' she shouted, 'set four more places.'

'Mam,' Lynnie said, moving over to her mother, 'Charmaine's on her own. It seems our Jimmy has left her.'

Avril seemed unsurprised by this news. She folded her arms under her bosom and eyed the younger woman knowingly.

'Well, Charmaine, I did try and warn yer when our Jimmy moved in that it wouldn't last. I'm surprised meself it's lasted this long. Fer a start you're nearly ten years older than him and your kids, besides not being his, well, they're hardly angels, now are they?'

'I know they ain't but I thought he'd grow to love 'em just like he would his own.' Tears of distress filled her eyes and rolled down her face. 'He said he loved me, Mrs Downs,' she blubbered.

'Listen, lovey, all men say that when they're getting a bit of the other on a regular basis. Look, I don't wanna hurt you more than you already are but you must have realised that this moving in with yer business was just a bit of fun as far as our Jimmy was concerned. He's hardly twenty, still a kid himself. You're gonna have to put it down to experience, gel. Next time, mek sure you get someone nearer yer own age who wants the responsibility of a ready-made family.'

'But if I could just talk to him, Mrs Downs,' she pleaded. 'I know I could . . .'

'Begging and pleading ain't the answer, gel,' Avril cut in. 'It might bring the men back for a short while but only 'cos they feel sorry for yer, and even if you did persuade our Jimmy to come back, you'd never be at peace, wondering if the next time you came home you were gonna find him gone. Look, tek my advice and count yerself lucky yer've had a bit of fun for a while. Concentrate on your kids instead. And, by God, they could do with it,' she added scathingly.

'Are you saying I ain't a good mother, Mrs Downs?'

'You don't need me to answer that, ducky. You already know you ain't. Your own mother is closer to those kids than you are. Now when I do see our Jimmy I'll tell him you wanna talk to him, but don't count on him coming round. We're just about to have our tea so if there's n'ote else, will you excuse us?'

'Oh, Mam, you were hard on her,' Lynnie said immediately the distraught woman had left.

'Hard on her be damned! I let her off lightly. She's no more than a slut and I was shocked our Jimmy took up with her, you know that, Lynnie. She enticed him with what she's got inside her brassiere and knickers. Young men of our Jimmy's age are mesmerised by a big chest, and they don't come much bigger than

Charmaine's. The only decent meal he ever got in all the three months he lived with her was what I gave him when he came around here. I personally ain't sorry to see the back of her or her kids. I'm just glad my boy has come to his senses at last. But I tell you this, I'm gonna paste the little bugger when I do catch sight of him for not telling his own mother what's going on. Have you sliced up that tin of York ham yet?'

'I was just doing it.'

'Well, hurry up, Lynnie lovey, yer nan reckons she's about to pass out with starvation if she don't get her tea soon. And, Colin, give our Dec a shout. Lazy bleeder he is, lolling in bed all day. He thinks this is a doss house, so he does. He's already missed his dinner, I'm damned sure he ain't gonna miss his tea.' She looked at Lynnie enquiringly. 'Did you hear what time he came home last night?'

She shook her head.

'I saw Ozzie out at just past one o'clock and he hadn't come home by then. I fell asleep as soon as my head hit the pillow.'

'Mmm,' Avril mouthed disapprovingly. ''Cos he's turned eighteen he thinks he can do what the hell he likes. Well, that young man has a shock coming to him, same as our Jimmy has when he condescends to show his face, thinking he can just stroll back in here and pick up where he left off until the next time he decides to shack up with some tart. I've had enough! I'm gonna start laying down some rules in this house and woe betide you if they ain't adhered to.' She cast a warning look in Colin's direction. 'Especially you!' With that she grabbed up the dish of salad and stalked off.

Lynnie made to complete her task of cutting the ham when it struck her that Colin was standing ram-rod straight by the back door. As she turned her head to look at him, the look of total horror on his face sent a surge of terrible foreboding racing through her.

'Whatever is the matter, Colin?' she demanded. 'Colin?'

'Eh! Oh . . . er . . .'

'Spit it out, will you?' she snapped agitatedly.

He shuffled uncomfortably on his feet, staring blindly down at the chipped red tiles covering the kitchen floor. 'It's . . . er . . . er . . . our Jimmy, Sis, and our Dec.'

She frowned. 'What about them?'

He delved in his back pocket and pulled out a crumpled piece of paper which he thrust at her. 'It's a note for Mam. Dec asked me to give it to her this morning. Only I forgot.'

'This morning?' she queried, taking it from him.

'Yeah, about five it was. Well, it was still dark so it could have bin earlier or later but I think it was about that time. I was asleep. He woke me. I was terrified, our Sis, 'cos I thought we'd got burglars, then I saw it was just our Dec packing his bag. When I asked him what were going on, he warned me to keep me trap shut or he'd wring me neck. Just before he left he gave me the letter and told me to give it to Mam when I got up.

Then he said to go back to sleep.'

'And did you go back to sleep?'

'Well, yeah, I was tired.'

'You should have woke Mam at once and told her what Dec was up to! Colin, I can't *believe* you just went back to sleep. You must have realised Dec was sneaking around for a reason.' She opened up the letter, scanned it and gasped. 'Oh, my God, Mam is going to go mad when she reads this and finds out what they've done.' She folded the note back up.

Colin didn't enquire what that was. He was far too worried about the telling off he was going to receive for forgetting to hand the note over.

'Don't tell Mam I forgot about the letter. She'll skin me alive.'

Lynnie looked at him hard.

'Wash the dinner pots for a week and I won't.'

'Ah, Sis, that's blackmail!'

'Blackmail is the only way we ever get you to do anything. Now, dishes for a week or do I tell?'

He scowled at her fiercely. 'I've got no choice, have I?' he muttered, then proceeded to curse her under his breath as he stalked from the kitchen.

A few seconds later Avril was staring at the letter, eyes wide in shock.

'What's it say?' demanded her mother, picking a tomato seed out of her denture with the tip of her knife.

Avril ignored her. 'You found this stuffed at the back of the packet of Omo on the window ledge, Lynnie?

Strange I never saw it when I did some washing this morning.'

From under her lashes she stole a glance at Colin who sat looking at her intently across the table, then gave the contents of her plate her full attention.

'Well, it was more behind the milk bottle with the plastic roses in than the soap powder,' she fibbed, then hurriedly changed the subject by saying, 'Oh, by the way, Mam, Colin's offered to do the dinner dishes for a week.'

'Has he? Oh, there's a good lad,' Avril said distractedly, then scraped back her chair and raced from the room. Presently she returned with a look of great distress on her face and slumped back down on her chair. 'I'll kill the little buggers,' she cried. 'They've really gone and done it this time.'

'Done what, Mam?' Lynnie asked, knowing very well what she meant.

'Who's done what?' Freda asked, looking at them in confusion.

'It's our Jimmy and Declan, Mother,' Avril responded. 'They've sodded off down to London to make their fortunes. Dozy buggers have got more chance of finding oil in our back garden than they have of making their fortunes down the smoke. What do my boys think they're playing at? They've both good jobs on that building site, especially considering the bit they make on the side.'

Lynnie flashed her mother a meaningful look.

'Mam, you know as well as I do our Dec and Jimmy

make more on the side than ever they do in wages. And some of the risks they take are brazen. Last week our Dec bragged to us that when the foreman was out of sight they'd walked off in full view of everyone else with a bag of sand and cement and a barrowload of bricks which they flogged on to that chap near where I work who's mending his garden wall.'

'They took the barrow back,' Avril defended them. 'Besides, most of the lads they work with are at it, so our Dec and Jimmy ain't doing n'ote the others ain't.'

'Oh, Mam,' Lynnie said, giving a chuckle. 'That may be so but the foreman is going to cotton on sooner or later and then someone will be for the high jump. Maybe our Dec and Jimmy felt it best to get out while the going was good.'

'And I don't blame them for that, but there's plenty of other sites in Leicester. They didn't have to go to London, did they? The note says they know someone already down there who reckons he can help them get work and lodgings so I suppose that's summat.' Lynnie watched as her mother's eyes filled with tears. 'Oh, Lynnie, anything could happen to my boys so far away. London's a dangerous place. All those gangland killings yer hear about and . . .'

'My grandsons are more than capable of looking after themselves, Avril, as you well know. Now stop fretting, they'll be fine,' interrupted Freda matter-of-factly. 'It's about time they spread their wings 'cos if you're honest they give you more strife than peace. Besides you've still Colin and Lynnie at home to fanny about after and worry over, plus our Ray will be back in a couple of months so it's not like all yer kids have flown the nest, now is it?'

Lynnie rose from the table, rushed around and gave her mother a comforting hug. Although she was as upset and fearful as Avril about what her brothers could be up to, she didn't want to show this and cause her mother more anguish than she was already suffering.

'Nan's right, Mam. Dec and Jimmy will be fine, and if not they'll be on the first train back. They just didn't tell you because they knew you'd try and stop them going.'

'And they'd have bin bloody right! I'd have chained them to the wall and thrown away the key if I'd had an inkling what they were up to.' She swallowed hard. 'I know yer both right,' she said, giving a big sniff. 'But I'll miss 'em, so I will.' She took several deep breaths then and raised her head to look at each of them in turn. 'Well, without yer brothers' board money and bits and pieces they helped out with, we'd all better get used to the idea that things are gonna be a bit tight around here. No more York ham, it'll be luncheon meat for the foreseeable future. Anyway, life goes on for us Downses left here, so let's get on with it. Christ almighty, what's that?' she exclaimed as the distant sound of breaking glass could be heard, followed by an eruption of screaming.

Lynnie was first to reach the front door. 'Something's happened at the Johnsons',' she announced, noticing a gathering of neighbours on the pavement outside a house several doors down. In the distance she could see a gang of skinheads running away, shouting obscene abuse as they did so which none of the gathering seemed at all concerned about.

Squeezing in beside her daughter, Avril poked out her head and quickly appraised the situation. 'Get inside,' she ordered Lynnie. 'Best we keep outta this.'

Colin arrived then and fought to get between his mother and sister so he could see what was going on. When neither of them would allow it, he jumped up and down, trying to see over their heads. 'What's going on?' he demanded.

Avril turned on him. 'Get back to the table and finish yer tea,' she instructed. 'This is none of our business. The Johnsons are getting what they deserve.'

Lynnie looked at her mother, astounded. 'Oh, Mother, how can you say that? They haven't done anything to anyone. They keep themselves to themselves and have done since they moved in three weeks ago. That's the third brick they've had through their window, plus dog dirt through their letter box, on top of all the taunts they receive whenever they go out. Why can't people leave them alone? They just want to get on with their lives, that's all.'

Avril was staring at her, gob-smacked. 'We don't want *their kind* around here, and the sooner they move out the better.'

'*Their kind?* What do you mean by that? Colin, will you stop pushing me, there's nothing to see. Now do as

Mam says and get back to the table. If you've finished your tea, go and make a start on the pots, then you've the garden to get cracking on. Go on, skedaddle.'

She made to rush out of the door herself but her mother pulled her back.

'Where do yer think you're going?'

'I'm going to see if I can help.'

'Yer not,' Avril erupted furiously. 'You're staying put. I won't have a daughter of mine associating with the likes of *them*, especially *him*.'

'Him!' Lynnie gave a heavy sigh then eyed her mother defiantly. 'It's too late for that, Mam.'

'Whadda yer mean?'

'I've already been inside their house and had a cup of tea. As I was coming home from work the other night, Mrs Johnson was tidying the front garden. She smiled at me and said hello, and out of politeness I stopped to chat to her. She invited me in to meet her husband and children. It would have been blatantly rude of me to refuse, and besides, after I saw how nice Mrs Johnson was, I wanted to meet the rest of her family. I didn't tell you because I knew what your reaction would be.

'You're wrong, Mam, to take this attitude, and to be honest I can't understand why you and others round here have. Sheila is a lovely woman, and her husband's very polite. Their two kids have more manners between them than most of the tykes around here put together, and that's saying something as they're only toddlers. Now I'm going to see the Johnsons to see if there's anything I can do, and don't try and stop me.'

Avril was too flabbergasted to restrain her daughter, just watched in silence as she left the house.

A few minutes later Lynnie looked at her deeply distressed neighbour, feeling ashamed.

'I'm so sorry, Sheila, really I am. People around here can be such an ignorant lot.'

Sheila pushed a stray strand of long carrot-red hair behind her ear and gazed protectively at the two little girls cuddled on her lap. Then, through deeply grieved eyes, she looked at Lynnie. She was a petite woman, not much older than Lynnie, and extremely pretty, her large jade-green eyes heavily fringed with dark red lashes, almost filling half her tiny oval face. Her creamy skin was dusted with a fine coating of freckles, reminding Lynnie of a fairy cake covered in chocolate-flavoured hundreds and thousands. Lynnie knew Sheila would not have been short of male admirers before she had made her choice of husband.

'It's not just people around here who are narrow-minded, Lynnie,' Sheila said sadly. 'Since we married we've lived in four sets of rooms in completely different areas of Leicester, some so bad you'd be loath to put a dog in them let alone human beings, but securing lodgings for the likes of us was so difficult we had no choice but to accept what we did get offered. Each time we hoped we could live in peace, and each time we got the same reaction as we've had here. When we were allocated this house by the council it was like a gift from God. We knew the area had a . . . well, dubious reputation but we so hoped the people round here would be more accepting of us.' Her face filled with deep sadness. 'As soon as we moved in we knew we were wrong to have had such a hope.'

She looked over at her husband who was busy trying to board up the broken window and her face filled with unashamed adoration, voice falling to a husky whisper. 'We've done nothing wrong, Lynnie, except fall in love. Why is that so bad, just because my skin is white and Everal's is brown? He's a good man, Lynnie. Honest, caring, treats me and the children like we are his most precious jewels. He works hard to support us. How many women can say they've a husband who worships the ground they walk on and would lay down and die for them? Yet we're looked on as scum and hounded wherever we go because of his colour.'

Lynnie's heart bled for this woman's plight. 'I feel ashamed to be white,' she murmured.

Sheila reached over and patted her hand. 'Oh, please don't,' she urged. 'It's not just white people who treat us like lepers, Lynnie. Everal's own kind don't approve of mixed marriages either. Everal's had it tough from his own friends and family. We've been married for five years and his mother still won't allow me into their house or acknowledge her grandchildren. She had a nice Jamaican girl lined up for him and was furious when he refused to have anything to do with her because of me. My own mother and the rest of my family and friends too won't have anything to do with me either. But I refuse to be beaten, Lynnie. Everal and

I love each other and we'll not let anything force us apart.' Her face screwed up in defiance. 'We are not moving again. It's not fair to keep shunting the girls around. They need roots. People around here can throw as many bricks as they like, taunt us as much as they like but they're eventually going to have to accept us and that's all there is to it.'

Everal came over to join them then, perching on the arm of the shabby armchair, putting his arm around his wife's shoulders and giving her a reassuring squeeze. He was a tall slim man, whose skin reminded Lynnie of a cup of milky dark cocoa, eyes large and twinkling. His broad smile showed a row of large glistening white teeth and when he spoke his accent was thick Jamaican which fascinated Lynnie.

'It's not a perfect job I've done boarding up the window, but it will do until I can repair it properly.' He looked tenderly down at his wife. 'You okay, honey?'

She smiled up at him.

'I'm fine, Everal. I'm just so relieved that none of us was in here when the brick came through, especially the children.' She turned her attention back to Lynnie. 'I appreciate you coming to see if you could do anything. You don't know how much it means to me and Everal. It's good to know that at least one person around here isn't against us.'

Lynnie gave her a weak smile, hoping she could hide a surge of guilt from these lovely people. When the couple had first moved in, although not having a clue why, she had automatically sided with the majority who had lost no time in voicing very strongly their opposition to this mixed race family residing amongst them. Lynnie hadn't herself participated in any action against them, but hadn't done anything by way of welcoming them into the neighbourhood either.

She suddenly felt an urgent need to do something for the Johnsons by way of getting them accepted into the community. There must be some way she could make the neighbours see the error of their ways. Lynnie knew that if she could only get them to meet the new arrivals and spend a few minutes getting to know them then like herself they would soon change their opinions and warm to the Johnsons like she had done. Suddenly an idea came to her. She didn't know whether it would work but she'd give it a try. She decided not to contemplate her mother's reaction or to feel guilty for the lie she was about to tell.

'Sheila, my mother asked me to ask you if you'd like to come in for a cup of tea tomorrow night, that's if you've nothing else on? You, Everal and the kids.'

Sheila eyed her in shock. 'She did?'

Lynnie nodded.

'Oh!' She looked at Everal then back at Lynnie and the hope that filled her eyes was unmistakable. 'We'd love to, wouldn't we, Everal?'

The beam lighting up his handsome face was a delight to witness. 'Be nice to meet your mother, Lynnie. I have no doubt she'll be as nice as you.'

Her heart pounded erratically. She dearly hoped her mother *would* be nice. She rose and smiled at them warmly. 'We'll see you tomorrow night then, about seven?'

They both nodded eagerly.

When Lynnie arrived home she ignored her mother's frosty greeting and dashed straight upstairs to get herself ready for her date with Ozzie, knowing she was going to be at least an hour late as her visit to the Johnsons had delayed her. Plus, in order to put her plan into operation, she had several other visits to make before she set off for the pub.

Ozzie was far too engrossed in a game of darts with several of his mates to notice Lynnie's arrival. She got herself a drink and looked around for a seat. Most nights the Shoulder of Mutton was busy as it was the only public house that served the estate. Tonight was no exception. As Lynnie squeezed her way through the crowds towards the tables near the dartboard she spotted one occupied by a girl of around her own age and wondered if this was Matt's new girlfriend. Hoping her assumption was correct, she made her way over and sat down on the vacant stool next to her. The girl was very attractive, dressed fashionably in a pastel blue mini-dress and white, shiny, plastic knee-length boots. Her stony expression struck Lynnie then. This girl obviously wasn't happy.

Slipping off her coat which she draped across her knee, Lynnie flashed her a smile. 'Are you Matt's girlfriend?' she enquired.

The girl looked her over before nodding. 'I take it you're Lynnie?'

She nodded back, then glanced over to where Ozzie and his friends were gathered. He still hadn't noticed her arrival and she tried to catch his eye but failed so turned back to face the girl. 'They seem to be enjoying themselves,' she said, by way of making conversation.

'I'm glad someone is,' came the sharp response. She looked at Lynnie enquiringly. 'Does Matt always treat his girlfriends like this?'

Lynnie looked at her nonplussed. 'I'm sorry, I don't understand.'

'Abandons them. When he asked me out in a four-some tonight, I didn't realise we women would be sitting on our own while the men played darts. I've been here nearly an hour by myself.'

'Oh, well, I'm sorry I got held up.'

'It's Matt I came out with, him that's abandoned me, it's not you that should be apologising.' She looked over at the lads and tutted disdainfully before bringing her attention back to Lynnie. 'Your boyfriend hasn't even noticed you've arrived. Don't you mind him treating you like this?'

Lynnie looked at her blankly. 'I don't get what you mean.'

'Well, it's very bad manners to ask someone out for the evening then ignore them.'

'Oh, they're not ignoring us, they're just enjoying themselves playing darts.'

'While we sit here like good little girls and wait

patiently until they decide they want to join us? By the looks of it this game will go on for quite a while yet.' She picked up her glass and downed the remains of her drink, then rose and put on her coat. 'Well, you might not mind being treated like a door mat, Lynnie, but I have no intention of becoming one. It was nice to have met you.'

With that she walked off.

It was a good while later before Ozzie and Matt finally sauntered over.

'That's a pint you owe me,' Ozzie was saying to his friend as he sat down on the stool next to Lynnie and put his half-empty glass of lager on the table. 'I'll have a pint of me usual when yer ready.' He turned and grinned at Lynnie. 'Never learns his lesson, does he? He's never beat me at darts yet. You wanna drink?' Before she could respond he said to Matt, 'Lynnie'll have a half of lager when yer ready, Matt,' picking up his glass and downing the remains.

Matt took the glass from him, then his face clouded questioningly. 'Where's Pam, Lynnie? Gone to the lavvy?'

She shook her head. 'Oh, Pam's her name, is it? She's gone home, I think, Matt.'

'Home! Why?'

'Because you were ignoring her, that's why.'

He gawked in shock. 'I wasn't ignoring her, I was playing darts.'

'Obviously the bossy sort,' Ozzie commented, pulling a wry face. 'Best off without her type, mate. That

67

sort want to rule the roost and it's only a wimp who allows that to happen, not proper men like us. Men are the bosses, ain't that right, Lynnie?'

She looked at him blankly. Men certainly seemed to think they were, particularly Ozzie. But to her Pam hadn't come across like the bossy sort at all. As she had rightly pointed out, Matt had asked her out for the evening and quite justifiably she'd expected him to stay with her, not go off with his mates, leaving her to her own devices until he saw fit to pay her some attention.

'Well, maybe Matt shouldn't have asked her out if he didn't intend being with her. Some women don't like being taken for granted. Obviously Pam is that sort, rather than bossy.'

Ozzie looked at her, taken aback. 'Wadda yer mean?' he questioned. 'Are you saying a man's not entitled to his game of darts?'

Lynnie sighed. 'No, I'm not saying that at all but . . .'

Before she could finish he erupted, 'Well, that's all right then. For a minute I was worried you were turning into one of them women's libber-whatsits. Get those drinks in, Matt. And, eh, there's a bird over there that's giving you the eye,' he said, winking at him knowingly.

After Matt had departed Lynnie took her fiancé's hand and asked him, 'Ozzie, do you love me?'

He eyed her awkwardly. 'We're in the pub, Lynnie, yer don't ask a man things like that in front of his mates.' He lowered his voice. 'Yer know I do,' he said huskily. 'So why ask?'

She gave a deep sigh. 'I just wonder sometimes, Ozzie. It would be nice if you didn't take me so much for granted.'

He flashed her a look of bemusement. 'Eh? When have I ever taken you for granted?'

All the time, she felt like saying. 'Ozzie, I was sitting here for at least an hour before you even noticed, and you only came over to join me then because you'd finished your game.'

'You've never minded me playing darts before,' he said sulkily.

'You've never asked if I minded. That's what I mean by taking me for granted, Ozzie.'

He gave a shrug. 'Well, I couldn't ask yer as you weren't here for me to ask, was yer?' His face suddenly lit up as a thought struck. 'Eh, I nearly forgot to tell yer, Lynnie. Biz has asked me to join the pub's darts team. You know how long I've wanted to be in it.' He jumped up from his stool. 'Best get a copy of the fixture list so I can mek a note of when all the games are. Won't be a tick.'

It was a good fifteen minutes before he returned and meantime Lynnie was left on her own, Matt now busy chatting up the girl Ozzie had pointed out to him.

'Me first game is tomorrow night,' Ozzie announced, sitting back down. 'So I'd better get here early and get some practice in. You come down when yer ready, Lynnie, but before eight-thirty 'cos that's when the match starts and I need you here cheering me on. Oh, and Biz asked if you'd mind giving a hand with making the sandwiches for the eat up afterwards. I said you'd do it.'

She looked at him, dismayed. 'I've something else planned for tomorrow night, Ozzie, and I really wanted you there.'

'Well, whatever you've planned can't be as important as me playing in the darts team, can it? In future you'd better check with me before you arrange anything else in case it interferes with a fixture. Oh, and don't forget, Wednesday is me billiards night.'

And Friday evening is lads' night, Saturday afternoon football when Leicester City play at home, and Sunday lunchtime Ozzie set aside for a pint with his dad and brothers, she thought. Now darts matches were going to have to be fitted in plus, she suspected, practice sessions, and Lynnie wondered how much of his time would be left to spend with her?

Much later he was doing his best to kiss and cuddle her in the seclusion of the Downses' back porch by the outside toilet.

Her indifference was noticeable. 'What's up with yer, Lynnie?' he snapped, releasing her.

'If you must know, I'm upset that you could practically ignore me all night, and now you're ready to show me some attention expect me to be all over you. But then, you've always been like that with me, Ozzie, so why should I expect any different from you now?'

He nodded knowingly. 'Oh, I get it, you're still mad

with me, ain't yer, for not seeing the Vicar? Well, I've apologised for that and I've promised yer I'll go with yer next Sunday, so what more d'yer want me to do? Look, I can't cope with yer when yer in one of your moods.' He leaned forward and gave her a peck on her cheek. 'I'll see yer tomorrow night. And remember, the match starts at eight-thirty so don't be late.'

With that he turned and strode away.

Inside the house her mother was just making a cup of hot chocolate.

'Hello, ducky,' she greeted her, putting a cigarette out under the tap, chucking the stub on top of another pile of household rubbish which before going to bed she would wrap up in newspaper to put into the dustbin. 'Ozzie not with yer?'

'No, we were both tired so he's gone home to get an early night.'

Avril chuckled. 'Don't fib, Lynnie. He ain't come in 'cos he's feared of getting the third degree from me and yer nan again about not setting a date for yer wedding. I know Ozzie, and we won't see his face in here again until he thinks the heat is off him. I'm just making a cup of hot chocolate. Would you like one?'

She shook her head. 'No, thanks.' She leaned back against the door and asked distractedly, 'Does any man put his woman first, do you reckon, Mam?'

'In my experience, no, not unless they want some-thing, ducky. Yer've bin with Ozzie long enough to know that. What's he done now?'

'Nothing in particular. I just wish sometimes he'd

pay me a little more attention.'

'And you could wish to win the Pools, Lynnie. That's just as unlikely to happen as getting any man to put you first.' Avril smiled at her daughter affectionately. 'I know Ozzie's ways are sometimes enough to test the patience of a saint, Lynnie, but the lad does love you in his way. And, believe me, you could do a lot worse than him. What more do you want, eh?'

She sighed. She supposed that compared to her mother's experience of men Ozzie was a saint.

'You're right, Mam, what more could I want? I really am tired so I'll just say goodnight.'

'Goodnight, lovey. Eh, don't forget to pop in the front room and say goodnight to yer nan.'

'I won't, Mam. Night, night.'

Chapter Four

The sudden pungent aroma of urine hit Lynnie full force. 'Oh, God,' she groaned, pulling a disgusted face. 'Old Willy Noble has weed himself again.' Through the haze of thick cigarette smoke swirling around the dark wood-panelled interior of the betting shop she glanced across at the tattered eighty-eight-year-old figure hunched in his usual spot on the long wooden bench that ran the length of the side wall underneath the Tannoy, ear cocked so he could hear every word that crackled from it. 'Don't worry, Mrs Crane,' she addressed her colleague. 'I'll do the honours with the mop and bucket.' Lynnie had no choice but to volunteer, knowing very well Madge Crane wouldn't.

'Dirty bugger!' the older woman exclaimed, wrinkling her nose in utter disgust. 'I dread to think what his house is like.'

'However bad it is, it can't be as awful as the Pottses' who live near us. Theirs is so filthy even rats refuse to live there,' Lynnie said matter-of-factly, easing herself off her high stool and lifting the flap of the counter so she could pass through. 'I feel sorry for old Willy. He's got no family and I think his brain is fuddled now 'cos sometimes he comes in here and he's forgotten to put his clothes on underneath his coat – and it ain't a pretty sight, believe me.'

'He wants locking up in Carlton Hayes nut home,' Madge Crane said, her voice full of disdain. 'He'd better not show his bits to me especially if I've just had me dinner. And no family doesn't excuse him being so filthy,' she declared. 'My mother always said a bar of carbolic soap is cheap enough and water costs nothing. Anyway he can't be that fuddled, he certainly seems to have his wits about him where the horses are con-cerned, and it might not be much but he wins more times than he loses. Pity he didn't put his winnings towards cleaning himself up sooner than back on the horses.'

She gave a loud tut.

'I was so glad to get this job yer know, Lynnie, after being retired from the bakery after working there over forty years, but little did I realise then the types I'd have ter deal with. Tek Duggie Craven over there,' she said, nodding her tightly permed grey head in a cus-tomer's direction. 'I know for a fact he spends nearly all his wages on no-hope bets while his wife and kids go around practically threadbare. There were a few times today when I felt like shoving bets back at our customers and telling 'em not to be so senseless as to waste all they have to their name in such a stupid way. Don't you ever feel guilty taking their money, Lynnie?'

'If we didn't, they'd find someone else who would. It's our job, Mrs Crane,' she snapped. 'Something we are paid for doing. We shouldn't really be criticising our customers, now should we? After all, it's them that pay our wages, and it ain't our place to give them a lecture on the evils of betting.'

'Huh, I suppose yer right.'

'Oi, Lynnie,' a gruff male voice erupted. 'Old Willy's peed himself again.'

'Yeah, I know,' she called back. 'I'm just about to mop it up.'

'He should be banned,' another man insisted. 'He pissed all over me shoes last week.'

'And you spewed up all over the walls last Friday when you came in here so drunk you could hardly stand, but we didn't ban *you*,' she responded tartly.

The man eyed her sheepishly before turning away to study the board on which were chalked the odds on the horses running in the next race, which in this case was the two-thirty at Sandown.

Before she could pass through the counter flap to collect the cleaning utensils the shop door opened and a man dressed in a bloodied brown coat came in, carrying a large parcel under his arm. He strode up to the counter and put the parcel in front of her. 'Got you a couple of nice joints this week, Lynnie, besides the usual,' he said, his voice hushed, giving her a meaningful wink.

'How much extra do I owe you?' she asked, smiling and grabbing the parcel. She hurriedly secreted it under the counter before her boss witnessed what she was up to, knowing very well what his reaction would be to her using his premises as a place to have her knock-off stuff delivered to.

'To anyone else it'd be two pounds ten shillings, Lynnie ducky, but to you we'll call it two quid plus five shillings for delivering it personally.'

As she settled up, she smiled to herself. Her mother would be pleased. The meat Wilf Warren had pilfered from his job at the abattoir nearby would, even after they had fed themselves, fetch double again what she had paid for it.

Before he hurried off, Wilf took a half crown out of the money Lynnie had given him and said, 'Put that on Sonny Jim to win the three-thirty at Sandown.' He added confidently, 'I'll be back before you close to collect me winnings.'

'You'll be lucky,' a man standing nearby piped up, obviously a mechanic by trade judging from his oily dungarees. 'You're about to back a donkey. You'd have more luck with Will o' the Wisp in the two-forty-five at Ayr.'

'I've had this tip from a good source so I'll stick with me instincts, ta very much, Rob.' He took his betting slip from Lynnie and grinned. 'If I win, I'll divorce me wife and marry yer, Lynnie.'

She laughed. 'Sorry, but you already know I'm spoken for, Mr Warren.'

'Ohhh,' piped up an excited Madge. 'You saw the Vicar yesterday then and set a date?'

Lynnie looked at her enquiringly. 'How did you know I was seeing him yesterday, Mrs Crane?'

Madge gave a haughty sniff. 'Well, I just happened to hear yer talking to Mr Mallin about it last Sat'day.'

Earwigging more like, she thought, annoyed, and wondered what else Madge had overheard that she wasn't supposed to. Not that Lynnie had any secrets as such but she didn't want details of her personal life that she let her boss in on becoming common knowledge. 'Well, for your information the Vicar was busy and got called away.'

'That Vicar got called away urgently the last time you had an appointment with him too, didn't he?' Madge commented with a hint of sarcasm. 'I heard yer telling that to Mr Mallin last week as well.'

Lynnie looked at her knowingly.

'Either you have exceptional hearing, Mrs Crane, or else the walls in this shop are very thin as I always chat to Mr Mallin on personal business with the door shut. Now, please hold the fort for a minute while I go and clean up the floor.'

Just before she left that night, Lynnie made her way into her boss's office and put a bag on his desk.

'Not a bad day for takings, Mr Mallin. A few small wins but nothing over a fiver today. Did the runners do all right?'

Her portly sixty-eight-year-old boss leaned back in his chair and smiled at her.

'One of Terry's punters from Jones and Shipman's where he collects won a bull's eye on the three-twenty at Alexandra Palace. I bet it's made the chap's week-end, planning how he's going to spend his fifty quid when Terry teks it to him on Monday. Bet he ain't told his wife neither for fear of her getting her hands on it. Probably planning to leave her, having a good amount like that to do what he likes with.' Sid gave a chuckle. 'It's laughable really, me being a bookie and making me money on people backing losers, but yer know summat, Lynnie lovey, I still get quite a thrill from the odd punter winning a substantial amount, even though it slices through me profits.'

He picked up the bag and, swinging around in his large leather chair, placed it in a safe in the recess behind his desk. After making sure the door was locked properly, he swung back to face his employee.

'Take the weight off yer feet for a minute, Lynnie,' he said, indicating a chair placed in front of his desk. 'Tell me, what's yer opinion of Madge Crane? You know I took a gamble in putting a woman behind the counter when I moved this business from my back room into licensed premises after the law changed three years ago, and ain't never regretted letting you persuade me to take you on. But I'm not so sure I've done the right thing with Madge Crane even though you need the help since we've got busier.'

Lynnie settled herself in the chair and took a deep breath. It was her opinion that Madge was totally unsuited to the job she was doing. She was intolerant of the type of man who frequented this kind of establishment; incessantly complained about the smoky atmosphere and the continuous clearing up of fag ends and other debris that littered the floor, while her mental arithmetic left much to be desired. Lynnie was forever being asked to help her work out quite simple calculations of the bets on the slips while simultaneously trying to deal with her own queue of customers. And never yet had Madge volunteered to make a cup of tea though she greedily accepted all those Lynnie made for her.

Lynnie was well aware that her kindly employer had not only agreed to give Madge the job so as to provide female company for her but also out of pity, knowing the older woman desperately needed the wage to supplement her meagre pension. With her constant badgering of him to give her the job when she had learned the vacancy existed, he just couldn't bring himself to refuse Madge's pleas.

Before she could respond he spoke up.

'Yer don't need to answer me, ducky. I can tell by yer face what yer answer is. She's not suitable, is she? I knew when I agreed to tek her on I was making a mistake. A bookie's ain't the kinda place for the likes of Madge Crane. I'd be blind not to notice that our customers ain't all that keen on her either.' He scratched his balding head. 'What to do now is the problem. Well, I can't just sack her, can I? That'd really hurt her feelings. Can you put up with her for a bit longer, Lynnie, 'til I come up with a nice way of getting rid of her?

'Maybe I could have a word with Bert Simmons who

owns the greengrocer's around the corner: I heard he was looking for an assistant. The customers he gets will suit Madge much better than the types we get here. I know I shan't miss her coming into my inner sanctum and hassling me to tidy it up. Even me own wife never dares do that and I've bin married to her over forty years.' He gave a rueful shake of his head. 'I should never have let her talk me into taking her on. It's my own fault.'

He gave Lynnie an affectionate smile, eyes twinkling merrily. 'I never made a mistake with you though, did I? Best day's work I ever did was giving you a job here. Yer never regret leaving the Three Sisters haberdashery shop, do yer, Lynnie?'

She looked at him for a moment, remembering the conversation she'd had with Shirley the previous afternoon and how she had described her job as taking tuppenny ha'penny bets off people who hardly had it to spare. She suddenly felt guilty. Her job at Mallin's Turf Accountants was far more interesting than anything else she could envisage doing, and she couldn't wish to work for a better boss who couldn't be compared in any way to the sour-faced Miss Victor who'd been in charge of her at the Three Sisters Haberdashery. The customers she dealt with here might not have much but they treated her well and she had a laugh with them. It struck her that she had landed on her feet and not many people were as fortunate as her workwise. She would remember that in future.

'Not one bit,' she said sincerely. 'I love working for you, Mr Mallin. I was never really cut out to sell big pink knickers to fat old ladies. Oh, don't get me wrong, some of the old dears were lovely – but some you could have stuck your foot up their backside and kicked out the door, they were so nasty. On the whole I found the job boring and was desperate to find something else. I was lucky to get this. Until I started I never realised how involved racing was, and the different characters we get in – well, where else would a customer treat you to an iced bun 'cos he's won two bob on a horse? It's your night for the Hinckley dogs, isn't it, Mr Mallin? Hadn't you best be going?'

Sid looked at the clock on the wall and nodded. 'Yes, I had.'

She looked at him thoughtfully, then her face lit up. 'I'd love to come with you down the track sometime, Mr Mallin. See how it all works.'

He shook his head. 'Letting you persuade me to have you work behind the counter was enough of a decision to make, Lynnie. Let me tell you, there is no way you'll persuade me to take you down the track. It is most definitely not a place for a young girl like you. If yer were a bloke I wouldn't hesitate to take you. But, well, the women yer get there are as rough as they come, and the blokes . . . the language they can use would be enough to make a navvy blush. Believe me, you're best off behind the counter, Lynnie, your pretty face keeping my punters happy.'

His eyes glazed over as he leaned back in his chair

and hooked his thumbs into the pockets of his bright yellow waistcoat.

'As yer know, I took the business over from my father who operated out of our back room at home. Betting was illegal then and if you were caught it could involve a sizeable prison sentence, but mostly the police turned a blind eye to what was going on.' He laughed. 'Some of them weren't averse to a flutter themselves, others wanted a back hander to keep quiet and paying that was well worth it to keep yer business going. Anyway, me dad started off very small by keeping a book on the odd race for his workmates in the brush factory, but by the time he handed the business over to me at the beginning of the forties he had over a dozen runners collecting his bets from all around Leicester and made himself a good living from it, enough to give us a nice house and car. He loved it all, he did really. But the best part for him was when he was down at the tracks along with the other bookies, setting the market odds.

'When I officially took over after he finally retired I operated the same as him, kept all the old traditions alive until they legalised betting a couple of years back and we bookies were allowed to operate from proper premises. 'Course it's been good for the punters, them having somewhere to go to, to place their bets themselves and hear the commentary over the radio as the races are run. But the downside for me was having to let go of several of my loyal runners when they weren't needed any more. I've only a handful of them now, collecting from the factories and from me regulars that can't get into the shop, but I do worry that in time when more shops open near the places me runners serve then I'll have no choice but to let them go too.' He shook his head sadly. 'They call it progress, don't they, and I suppose it has its good points.' He gave a sudden smile and mentally shook himself. 'Goodness me, I do go on about the past sometimes, don't I? You'll forgive an old man's ramblings, won't yer, Lynnie?'

She smiled.

'You can tell me the story of how all this started as many times as you like, Mr Mallin. I never get fed up with hearing about it. It helps me understand my job better. But I'd still love to come to the track, and I will turn a deaf ear to the bad language, promise.' After all, she already heard all there was coming from the types she lived amongst. 'So please won't you change your mind about taking me?'

He fervently shook his head.

'My decision is final even though I know you'd be fascinated by what goes on. You get a thrill there I could never explain to you. The whole atmosphere is charged with excitement. And some of the things the racing fraternity get up to trying to sway the odds in their favour defy belief, but it's all part of the game. I can't take you, though, Lynnie, not unless the types I deal with at the course change dramatically, and I can't see that happening, so please accept my decision.'

She sighed, 'All right, Mr Mallin. Can I just ask,

though, if the same things happen at the greyhound track as at the horse racing meetings?'

He took his thumbs out of his pockets, leaned forward and eyed her meaningfully.

'Oh, yes, me duck, and more besides. There's the usual doping and feeding up of dogs before races, and running them hard beforehand so they're tired out and have no chance of winning.' He gave her a grin. 'Of course yer can't bribe a jockey to lose a race as hounds don't have jockeys, do they?' he said, chuckling at his own joke. 'But then the hounds are much easier to substitute than the horses, and punters are more readily duped into thinking they're backing a winner and bet heavily when in fact the dog's been swapped for one with very similar markings or which has even been dyed to look the same, without having a hope in hell of winning the race. Owners have made tidy sums doing that, and bookies have come out of it smiling too. And traps are sometimes fixed, yer know, if the master in charge can be bribed by a back-hander to turn a blind eye.'

'How do they do that?'

'Well, my dear, the springs are tampered with so the trap takes longer to open. A precious second or more lost can mean the difference between a dog getting off to a good start or not. But let me assure you, Lynnie, if I have any doubts about a race I never participate because it's not worth losing my reputation should I be found out. I like being known as honest, just like my father, and I'll do me best to keep it that way.'

'Do people complain if they suspect foul play, Mr Mallin?'

''Course they do, but when race track managers, bookies and dog and horse owners are in each other's pockets, what chance has the man in the street got of proving anything?'

'It really is a mug's game gambling, isn't it, Mr Mallin?'

'It can be, lovey, unless you're extremely clever and know your runners better than yer know yer own wife, and every trick in the book that can be got up to – but don't ever let our clients hear you say that. I should apologise as I've just made the whole business sound thoroughly bent and it isn't. There are a lot of crooks in racing, Lynnie, but then there are also lots of honest people like me. It's just that the handful of dubious ones bring the whole game into disrepute. But then, yer get that in every walk of life, not only in our field. Just remember that some people will go to extreme lengths to make a fast buck so always be on your guard. But I'm sure you know that already, having experienced at first hand what some of our customers get up to and expect us to fall for.'

She gave a nod. 'I've lost count of the number of times Bernie Lawson has altered his slip after a race, substituting a winner's name for the old nag he put his money on and demanding to be paid out. I wouldn't mind but his alterations are so noticeable, yet he still swears blind the slip is in its original state even though we'd never accept it like that in the first place.'

'Well, yer can't blame 'em for trying. Gamblers are driven by their hopes and dreams of having that one big win, and for us bookies that desire makes our profits. But for the majority of punters it never happens. To make a fortune you need big money to put on a runner with long odds, and a whole lot of luck.' He ruefully shook his head. 'I've seen a family almost starve because the last penny they have to their name is put on a bet. I've witnessed fortunes lost on the turn of a card. Seen marriages break up; acts of extreme violence ending in death. But once a gambler, always a gambler, Lynnie. It gets in the blood and if yer not careful it becomes a craving so deep that placing a bet is more important to you than anything. I have ter say, rightly or wrongly, I'm glad people like a flutter or let's face it I wouldn't have a business and you wouldn't have a job you love doing so much. Now, lovey, I must get off and I'm sure you have to as well.'

Her heart thumped painfully at the reminder of what lay in store for her this evening. She prayed that what she was about to do would go the way she hoped or else she feared she was in for terrible trouble.

'Yes, I do, I want to get off sharpish if I can. I hope you do well tonight, Mr Mallin.' And she added with a twinkle of amusement in her eyes: 'I hope you get lots of losers.'

'Me too, Lynnie lovey. My wife, God bless her, has set her heart on a new three-piece suite and it's an expensive one too. Not that there's anything wrong with the old one, but if it makes my wife happy then I'm happy.'

She made to rise then paused, feeling a great urge to ask her boss a question which had mystified her since the very first day she'd begun working here three years ago.

'Mr Mallin, I hope you don't mind me asking, but why do people call you Cigar Sid? Because in all honesty I've never seen you smoke one in all the years I've worked for you.'

His eyes twinkled merrily at her and he gave a chuckle.

'And you never will, my dear. I was fourteen years old and not long started working full-time for my dad as one of his runners. He wanted me to learn the business right from the bottom up and, boy, did he make sure I did. Well, he might have been hard on me then but I have much to thank him for. As you know, there's nothing worth knowing that I don't know about this racket.

'Anyway, I'd taken a shilling bet on a rank outsider which my dad laughed at when I handed it over to him. Well, against the odds the horse romped home at 150/1 and the chap was so ecstatic when I went back with his winnings, which I must say my dad cried over when he handed them to me, he fetched two cigars out of a box which he'd been keeping for an extra-special occasion and rammed one in my mouth and one in his own. He insisted I join him in celebration and wouldn't let me leave until none of the cigar remained. Well, I was so sick I had to take to my bed for over a week and I've never touched a cigar since. The very thought makes my stomach churn. But the nickname had stuck. I shall have it put on my gravestone, I think. "Here lies Cigar Sid, The Cigarless Honest Bookie". Wadda yer think, Lynnie?'

She grinned. 'A perfect epitaph for you, Mr Mallin. I couldn't think of a better one to describe you.'

Avril looked at her daughter, puzzled.

'What on earth are yer doing?'

Without looking at her mother, Lynnie replied, 'Mashing a pot of tea.'

'I can see that, yer cheeky beggar. But that's me big pot I keep 'specially for when the whole family is here. You ain't broke me smaller pot, have yer?'

'No.'

'Then why are you using me big one?'

'Because . . .' She hesitated, took a deep breath and turned to face her mother. 'I've invited a few neighbours in for a cuppa.'

'Yer've what? What in God's name did yer have to go and do that for?'

'I thought it would be nice.'

'Nice! Lynnie, I've just had a hell of a day doing an extra shift cleaning at the school after the kids ran rampage through the art room, and a bigger flipping mess you've never seen in yer life. All I want to do now the dinner is cleared away is put me feet up. And it's a good night on the telly tonight . . .'

'Well, you can put your feet up and watch telly when they've all gone, Mam.'

'Lynnie, what's going on?'

'Nothing's going on, Mam,' she fibbed. 'I just thought it'd be nice and friendly to invite a few of the neighbours in for a cuppa, that's all. I thought the company would be good for Nan.'

'I don't believe you. You know as well as I do your nan gets more than enough company from her daily trawl around all her old cronies. And what's in this bag?' demanded Avril, grabbing at a brown carrier which Lynnie had put by the door when she had arrived home from work a while earlier. 'Why have yer bought all these biscuits? Garibaldis, fig rolls, custard creams, ginger nuts . . . oh, and a jam *and* a chocolate Swiss roll. Are we celebrating summat I ain't aware of?'

'Oh, great, cake,' Colin said, smacking his lips as he arrived in the kitchen. 'Can I have a slice now?'

'Get your mitts off!' snapped Lynnie, slapping his hands. 'I thought you were going out?'

'I am.'

'Well, get going then.' She waited until her brother had left before saying to her mother, 'Mam, I've told you, I've just invited a few of the neighbours in for a cuppa and thought a biscuit and a slice of cake would make it a bit special.' She heard the front door knocker. 'That'll be the first of them. Can you do the honours, Mam, and let them in while I finish making the tea?'

Avril scowled hard. 'I've a feeling there's more to this than you're letting on, my girl. Well, I hope for your sake a cuppa and a biscuit is all it is or you're for it, be warned.'

The front room was soon filled with several of their neighbours, a couple of women had even dragged along their husbands, and all were armed with cups of tea and biscuits, several greedy ones with a handful which they were stuffing into their mouths like they'd never seen a biscuit or a piece of cake in their life before. The atmosphere was sociable as they all chatted amongst themselves but Lynnie was well aware they were all wondering just why this unusual party had been organised.

They were about to find out.

The whole room fell into a shocked silence, all eyes riveted on Lynnie, as a few minutes later she led the Johnsons through.

Without waiting for any kind of response, her heart pounding painfully, she announced to the gathering: 'Now that Mr and Mrs Johnson have had time to settle in I thought it would be nice for them to be properly introduced to some of their neighbours. Why don't you budge up, Mr Murphy, and let Mr Johnson sit down next to you?'

Ignoring the look on Donal Murphy's face, she continued, 'Everal, this is Donal Murphy. Mr Murphy, please meet Everal Johnson. You have a lot in common, you know. You both work for the council. Mr Murphy works for the roads department, Mr Johnson.

Mr Murphy is part of a crew that travels around doing repairs.'

She fixed her eye on Donal Murphy and gave him a winning smile. 'Mr Johnson was telling me that back in Jamaica he worked for his family's building firm but there wasn't much to do as there isn't much money out there. That's why his family came over here in the hope of making a better life for themselves. That's the same as your family, isn't it, Mr Murphy? When you all came over here after the potato blight struck and you nearly all starved to death.'

Without waiting for a response she shot back to Sheila who was hovering anxiously by the door, her hands clutching those of her two daughters, mortally uncomfortable before the sea of faces staring back at her.

'Now, Sheila, why don't you bring the children over to meet Mrs Farmer?' Lynnie suggested. 'She has children of their age and I'm sure they'd all play well together.' They arrived before the chair where a stony-faced Joan Farmer perched. 'Mrs Farmer, this is Sheila Johnson,' Lynnie introduced them. 'Sheila is marvellous at sewing and I understand you want a hand with the finishing touches to a special dress you've been making?'

'I possess many skills, Lynnie, but my sewing . . . well, it leaves much to be desired,' Sheila whispered to her.

'Oh! Well, now would be a good time for it to improve,' she whispered back. 'Joan Farmer has a lot of influence with the young mothers around here and if she befriends you then others will too.'

After Sheila was settled and a stilted conversation began taking place between herself and Joan, Lynnie escaped into the kitchen to pour the new arrivals a cup of tea, praying she'd done right. Next thing she knew her mother had stormed in, her expression thunderous. She grabbed Lynnie by her shoulders and shook her so hard her head wobbled.

'What the hell you playing at?' she demanded. 'To bring those . . . those . . . people into my house, and invite the neighbours too! You're instigating World War Three, gel, and any minute now it's about to start.' She shook her again, then with the flat of her hands pushed Lynnie from her. 'Did you see Des Haggar's face?' she snarled, wagging a menacing finger. 'And you his daughter's best friend. Well, yer can kiss goodbye to that friendship, Caitlyn Downs, after yer mindless actions of today. Des will never allow his daughter to associate with you again. And what the bleddy neighbours are gonna say about me now, I dread to think. We'll probably start getting bricks through our windows now and be called nigger lovers. I can't believe you did this to us, Lynnie, really I can't.'

Her face set. 'Mother, stop it! People around here, including us, are making the Johnsons' lives a living nightmare and they've done nothing to any of us to deserve this treatment. Someone has to put a stop to it, and as no one else seems likely to then I will. And . . .' she paused, looking at her mother searchingly, '. . . I'm hoping you're going to help me.'

'Help you!' Avril exclaimed.

'Mam, come on, you're well respected in this area and how you act with the Johnsons could go a long way to bringing about their acceptance around here.'

'But I don't approve,' Avril barked. 'Far from it.'

'Why not?' her daughter demanded.

'Why not? Well . . . because . . . because . . .'

'Everal's black, Mam, go on say it. And Sheila's white. So what?'

'So what? Why, it's disgusting so it is.'

'No more disgusting than you marrying Dad.'

Avril glared at her, shocked. 'How dare yer say that? Why, there's no comparison.'

'Isn't there? You were English, Mam, like Sheila, and Dad was from a foreign country like Everal is. Ireland is a foreign land, Mam, whether you like it or not. But the Irish, like the Welsh, the Polish, Hungarians and Italians to name just some of the other foreigners who live around here, are all easier accepted 'cos they're white. That's about the size of it, ain't it, Mam?'

Avril was struck speechless. Her daughter spoke the truth.

'Mam, Everal is black because he comes from a hot country. Underneath his skin he's the same as every other man. He and Sheila fell in love and I've never known that be a crime. They have every right to raise their children in peace in their own home without the fear that folks around here are going to hound them out simply because of their own ignorance. Now,

Mam, you have it in the palm of your hand to make a huge difference to the Johnsons' lives by showing a little charity, and you ain't the mother I know and love if you can't find it within yerself to stand up to the lot around here and do it. Whether you help me or not, Mam, I'm going to do my best to help them. Now excuse me while I pour Sheila and Everal's tea and get their children a drink of pop.'

Avril stared at her, stunned, then jumped as she felt a presence by her side. She turned her head to see that her own mother had come through.

'My granddaughter is right, God bless her,' Freda said, patting her daughter's shoulder. 'As a mother myself, I think I'd be right in saying that that young couple have enough to contend with, coping with their families all fighting over their marriage, let alone having to deal with those they live amongst braying for their blood. You, my gel, should be proud of our Lynnie trying to do something for them, 'cos I know I am. Now hand me that plate of biscuits so I can pass them round.'

Just then the back door opened and Colin sauntered in. He saw the frozen expression on his mother's face and asked worriedly, 'What's up, Mam?'

'Eh? Oh, nothing, son, nothing.' She flashed a searching look at her daughter then brought her attention back to her son, taking his arm. 'Lynnie's invited some of the neighbours in to meet the Johnsons. Now you come with me and you can meet them too.'

Colin looked at her, shocked. 'Eh, but Mam, he's . . .'

'A very nice man,' Avril interrupted, cutting him short as she dragged him off.

Lynnie gave a deep sigh of relief.

It was over three hours later when the last neighbour but the Johnsons finally left.

Sheila looked down tenderly at her two little girls, cuddled up together fast asleep in an armchair covered by the eiderdown from Avril's bed, then looked up again at Lynnie, Avril and Freda who were sitting like three wise monkeys in a row on the sofa, Colin leaning over the back of it.

'I don't know how to begin to thank you all for what you've done tonight. I know it's not been easy,' Sheila said.

'No need to thank us,' said Avril gruffly. 'Neighbours help each other. I can't promise yer it's gonna be plain sailing from now on but we've made a good start tonight in getting some of the neighbours on your side.'

Sheila gave a deep sigh. 'And that is such a relief.'

Avril looked at Everal and gave a chuckle. 'I wish I could understand all that you say, lad, but I expect I'll get used to yer accent given time. I expect you have the same trouble with ours.'

He grinned at her broadly.

'I do. The Leicester slang takes time, doesn't it? I know now that *'ote* is not what you make porridge with but a shortened version of "nothing", and *me duck* is not something we have roasted for dinner. Now, Mrs Downs, please don't forget you've promised to come and listen to me ska music over a drop of rum punch? I'll have you dancing around our front room better than a Jamaican mama. You'll enjoy it, I know. And you, young man,' he said to Colin. 'If you'd like to come along, you're more than welcome. Be something to brag to your friends about 'cos none of them would have heard the music I'm gonna play yer.'

'I'd like to come too,' said Lynnie who was thrilled that the evening had gone much better than ever she had hoped it would.

'And me,' erupted Freda. 'I can't promise to dance as good as a mother in Jamaica does, but I'll promise to do justice to the rum punch.'

An exhausted but very gratified Lynnie was about to shut the door after waving off the Johnsons when the front gate burst open and Ozzie came charging up the path. 'Where yer bin, Lynnie?' he breathlessly demanded. 'All the other wives and girlfriends but you were there cheering us on.'

She stared, bemused, then her hand went to her mouth as it suddenly struck her that she had completely forgotten her promise to cheer him on at his darts match.

'Oh, Ozzie, your match! I'm so sorry, I forgot.'

'You forgot! Lynnie, how could yer? You knew how important this was to me.'

'Yes, I did, Ozzie, and I really meant to be there, but I did have something important to do and it went on for much longer than I expected it to.'

He looked hurt. 'What was more important than supporting me at the darts match?'

'I was introducing Everal and Sheila Johnson to some of the neighbours, to help them get settled in. They're the ones that moved into number thirty-four after the Smiths emigrated to Australia.'

He frowned. 'The Johnsons?' Then his face clouded. 'But he's black, ain't he?' This sounded like an accusation, not a statement.

'Yes, that's right. A nice man too. You'll like him, I know.'

He glared at her, appalled. 'I bleddy won't! Coming over here, stealing our jobs and our women. I don't want nothing to do with no blackies, and no girlfriend of mine will either. A' you listening, Lynnie?'

Her hackles rose. 'I'm listening, Ozzie, but I don't like what I'm hearing.' She folded her arms and took a stance. 'I don't think there's much chance of Everal stealing your job as he has a perfectly good one which you would never have got even if you had applied for it because you've no skills as a builder. And I can assure you, he won't be stealing anyone's woman as he has one of his own that he totally adores and she him.' She looked at him hard. 'Ozzie, don't you think it's about time you got your facts right before shooting your mouth off? It's people like you that've caused the Johnsons unnecessary suffering, and the reason why I didn't get to your match tonight was because someone had to show them that not all white people are bigots.'

'I ain't no bigot,' he cried, deeply wounded. 'And are you accusing me of having anything to do with what's happened to the Johnsons?'

'No, Ozzie, I'm not, but you've never even met Everal yet you've just accused him of things he hasn't done. Saying stuff like that is what causes trouble. It gets around, people who haven't got the sense to think for themselves believe these things, and before you know it, all black men are labelled a bad lot whether they are or not.'

He was looking at her uncomfortably. 'Well, it's not just the blacks. I ain't particularly fond of the Scots neither,' he blurted defensively. 'Or the Irish come ter that.'

'I'm half-Irish.'

He gawped at her. He had totally forgotten that fact. 'Oh . . . well, I didn't mean to say Irish,' he shot back hurriedly.

'So what have the Scots done to upset you?'

He gave a shrug. 'Well . . . er . . . nothing in particular. But they're all drunks, ain't they? Everyone knows that.'

'Jocky McVie who comes into the betting shop isn't. He's a teetotaller. And anyway, Ozzie, you can talk being's you like a drink yourself and have been known to get so drunk on more than a few occasions you couldn't remember a thing that you did the next day.'

He held up his hands in mock surrender. 'All right, Lynnie, all right,' he said sheepishly, and with extreme difficulty added sulkily, 'I admit I was wrong to say what I did about black men and the Scots.'

'What about the Irish?'

'I never said anything about the Irish.'

'You were about to until I reminded you that I was half-Irish,' she accused.

'What's this about the Irish?' a voice demanded. 'Oh, it's you,' said Avril, squeezing herself between Lynnie and the door frame. 'I came to see what the raised voices were all about. Trying to wheedle yer way out of seeing the Vicar on Sunday, a' yer, Oswald?'

'No, I ain't. I promised Lynnie I'd go and I will, Mrs Downs.'

'You'd better this time, lad, or you'll have me ter deal with.'

Lynnie jabbed her hard in the ribs. 'Mam, do you mind? Ozzie and I are having a private conversation.'

'N'ote private from yer family,' Avril tartly responded. 'So what are yer having words about? Why don't yer come in, Ozzie, and have a cuppa? Then Nan can join in too. Be a proper family discussion then, won't it?'

'Mother!' At the innocent look that Avril gave her, Lynnie sighed. 'I think it's best you go home, Ozzie, as my dear mother is obviously not going to grant us any privacy. I'll see you as usual on Wednesday night.'

He didn't need a second invitation to escape an obvious grilling from the matriarchs of the Downs family. Within three seconds flat he had rushed up to Lynnie, pecked her goodnight on her cheek, nodded goodbye to Avril and disappeared down the street.

Chapter Five

The look of horror on Ozzie's face was readily apparent.

'Are you all right, Mr Matthews?'

'What!' He eyed the Reverend Jackson blankly. 'Er . . . yeah, yeah, I'm fine. Just a bit hot under me collar, that's all,' he said, running his finger between the edge of it and his neck.

'Yes, it is a bit warm in here. I'll open a window for you,' the Vicar said, getting to his feet.

Ozzie felt a nudge in his ribs.

'What's the matter with you?' Lynnie hissed. 'You're acting like a condemned man about to face the gallows.'

That's exactly how I do feel, he thought. 'I don't feel well, Lynnie. I think I'm sickening for something,' he complained, putting on a pathetic face.

In concern she put her hand on his forehead. 'Well, you don't feel hot.' Then her face screwed up knowingly. 'There's nothing wrong with you, is there, Ozzie?'

'Yeah, there is, honest,' he insisted. 'I really think I'm

going down with something. Maybe you should tek me home and we'll do this another time,' he appealed.

'We will not go home,' she snapped. 'It's taken me months to get you here and I'm not leaving until we've set a date. You promised me, Ozzie. Now you can hang on for a few minutes longer, and then you can be as sick as you like and I'll carry you home if necessary.' She acknowledged the Vicar as he sat down again.

'That better?' he asked Ozzie.

He sighed resignedly. 'A bit, Rev, thanks.'

The Vicar smiled at them both. 'Shall we proceed? Now as I was saying, I do have a cancellation for the twelfth of November then I'm afraid I have solid bookings for over eighteen months and the earliest I can offer is June sixty-eight.'

Lynnie looked at Ozzie eagerly. 'That would be all right, wouldn't it? Give us plenty of time to do what we have to.'

He breathed a sigh of relief. He had inwardly panicked that Lynnie was going to try and talk him into the slot the Vicar was offering in two months' time. He couldn't cope with that, but eighteen months would give him a chance to get used to the idea of becoming a married man – if ever he could, that was. 'Yeah, that's great. Look, I really don't feel well, Lynnie, so d'yer mind if I leave you to it and get a blow of fresh air? You can finish dealing with the Vicar by yerself, can't yer?' he pleaded.

She tutted, annoyed. 'Well, it would be better if you were here, but if you're really not feeling well then I can't object, can I? I'll be as quick as I can then we'll get you home. I'm sorry about my fiancé,' she apologised to the Vicar after Ozzie had rushed out.

'Oh, that's all right, my dear. I'm used to that kind of behaviour. I've had men struck dumb with fear and more than one pass out. It's just pre-wedding nerves, that's all.'

A short while later Lynnie found Ozzie leaning on the Vicarage gate smoking a cigarette. He threw it down as soon as he spotted her and ground it out with his foot. 'All fixed up then?' he asked.

She nodded then looked at him, bothered. 'How are you feeling now?'

'Eh? Oh, bit better, thanks. I could do with a pint.'

She looked at him questioningly. 'You're not having second thoughts, are you, Ozzie?'

He shook his head. 'Nah, 'course I ain't.' Which was true. His opinion of the state of marriage had not changed.

She beamed, hooking her arm through his. 'Let's go and tell my folks the good news. Then afterwards we'll tell yours. They'll all be so excited.'

I'm glad someone is, he thought.

Avril rubbed her hands in delight. 'Well, I had begun to lose hope this day would ever come but now I can't wait to start planning this wedding. Where's your husband-to-be?' she asked Lynnie.

'He bumped into one of the lads from the darts team at our gate and they're talking tactics. I came on ahead 'cos apart from the fact darts bores me silly – but don't tell Ozzie that, Mam – I couldn't wait to tell you our news.'

'This is a red letter day for you, Lynnie, and it's natural you're desperate to tell your own family, especially me. We ain't got much time though, have we?'

'How much time do you need to plan a wedding then?' asked Ozzie as he walked into the room, sitting down next to Lynnie and putting his arm around her. 'I mean, Lynnie's only got to pop to C&A to get a frock, and the florist next to the bookie's will do a bunch of flowers. Eh up, they might do 'em cheap being's they know yer, Lynnie.'

'Ozzie!' she exclaimed. 'I'm having a nice do not a cheapskate one. And I certainly won't be going to C&A for my dress. And it's not just *my* dress . . . there's the bridesmaids too.'

'Bridesmaids!' he exclaimed. 'They buy their own dresses, don't they?'

Her look gave him his answer.

'I ain't gonna have to wear a suit, am I?' cried Colin, aghast.

'You'll wear what I tell yer,' Avril harshly responded. 'And, yes, it will be a suit. Eh, Lynnie, maybe Piss Pot will order one out of the catalogue and we can rig Colin out reasonable – that's unless her scam's been scuppered by the catalogue company by then.'

'We'll keep our fingers crossed it hasn't,' said Lynnie. 'I want the best wedding we can afford, but we'll still have to watch our pennies.'

'Not on the reception though, eh, Lynnie?' Ozzie piped up. 'Me mates'll be expecting a good booze up. I could ask the landlord of the Mutton if he'll sell us a couple of barrels cheap. Still, we've bags of time for organising that yet.'

'Leave the booze ter me,' said Avril, tapping the side of her nose. 'I know a bloke who'll get it much cheaper than the landlord of the Mutton will sell it us for. He works for Davenport's brewery delivering around the houses and I know for a fact the odd crate or two goes astray. Maggie Stimson at the off licence will sell me some spirits at cost price. She owes me a favour for getting her out of a sticky situation a while ago.'

'What sticky situation was that, Mam?' Colin asked.

'Never you mind,' she snapped at him. 'You're quiet, Mother,' she said, looking across at Freda.

'Can't get a word in edgeways, that's why,' she grumbled. 'Where yer having the reception?' she asked Lynnie and Ozzie.

'Oh, we haven't thought about that yet.'

'I could see how much a room at the Braunstone Working Men's Club would cost,' Avril said.

Ozzie frowned, worried. The pounds were beginning to mount already and this fact seriously concerned him; he was wondering how much he was going to be expected to contribute. 'Er . . . I'm sure me mam wouldn't mind us having the reception at our house. Well, seems pointless paying good money out to hire a room, dunnit eh?'

Lynnie turned on him. 'Ozzie, I've said I want a

proper wedding. We can at least enquire how much it costs. If it's too expensive for our pockets then we can ask your mam.'

'If she's not keen you can have it here,' said Avril. 'I don't mind at all.'

'And where you gonna be living?' was Freda's next question.

Lynnie beamed happily.

'Well, the money Ozzie's been putting past since we got engaged should have built to a tidy sum by now for a deposit on a house. There is enough for a deposit, isn't there, Ozzie?' she asked, looking at him expectantly.

'Oh, er . . . I ain't sure how much is in the account. Depends how much we need,' he answered cagily. 'But I've bin giving this house-buying business some thought and I can't see the point when we can rent somewhere and not have all the solicitor's bills and such like. It's just my hard-earned money in their pockets paying towards their flash cars and big houses. Anyway, we've got plenty of time to discuss this later.'

He gave a sigh, fed up already with wedding talk. And he still had his own parents to tell yet and they would want to know all the details so he'd have to go through this all over again.

Lynnie looked at him strangely. 'You keep saying we've plenty of time, Ozzie, but there isn't. Weddings and getting ourselves somewhere to live don't happen overnight. And one of the first things we must do is make out our invitation list so we give everyone as much warning as possible. I'd hate one of our friends not to be able to make it because they'd something else on on that day.'

His face screwed up in bewilderment. 'How much warning do people need?'

Before Lynnie could respond Avril said, 'Ozzie's right that buying a house is an expensive business. Even a little terraced one will cost yer an arm and a leg. Five hundred pounds or thereabouts they're asking these days. Downright disgraceful for a few bricks and mortar, if yer ask me. Then you'll need at least fifty or sixty quid to cover yer deposit and the solicitor's fee. And a mortgage is such a big millstone for newly weds to have. You could have a smashing honeymoon in a posh hotel for that plus have enough left to pay for some furnishings to go in a nice little rented flat. Why don't yer think about renting, Lynnie? I wonder if there's any flats coming vacant over the shops where you work? That'd be handy for you, wouldn't it, and not too far for you to get to work either, Ozzie. And not too far away from us. Or there's nothing wrong with yer both staying here and getting yer names put down on the council list. Yer could be lucky and get one close by. I'd like that. I wouldn't be losing yer then, would I, Lynnie?'

She ignored the look that Ozzie gave her and turned to address her son. 'Colin, go and get a piece of paper and a biro so we can start making a list of what's to be done. There's no time to be lost, yer know. Go on, Colin, move when I tell yer.' A broad smile of happiness lit her face. 'Oh, isn't this just the best homecoming present we could give our Ray? His only sister getting married. You are going to ask him to give you away, ain't yer, lovey?'

'Yes, of course I am, Mam. I just hope he's home by then. I mean, we haven't had his exact date of release yet.'

Ozzie was looking puzzled. 'Has Ray had his sentence lengthened?' he asked.

They all looked at him, puzzled.

'What makes you say that?' asked Avril.

'Well, he's due out at the end of October, ain't he? Or that's what I thought. Now you're worrying he won't be out in time for our wedding in eighteen months.'

'Ozzie, what are you going on about?' Lynnie asked him. 'We're getting married in two months' time, not eighteen.'

He stared at her, stunned as her words sank in. When the truth hit home a sickening churning began in his stomach and his throat felt dry. 'But . . . but I thought . . .'

'Thought what, Ozzie?'

'That . . . that . . .' He felt the room closing in on him. 'Look, er . . .' he said, jumping up. 'You don't need me here to discuss all this wedding malarkey. That's women's stuff. I . . . er . . . might go for a pint. Tell the lads the good news, eh? Yer don't mind, do yer, Lynnie?'

'But the pub isn't open for another hour or so, don't forget it's Sunday and they don't open until seven. And we ought to tell your parents before you tell anyone else, Ozzie.'

'Let him go off and do what he wants,' said Avril. 'He's right, we don't need him here, men just get under yer feet when weddings are being organised.' She grabbed the pen and paper that a sulky Colin had brought through. 'That includes you as well, Colin. Bugger off and annoy the neighbours for a while. Eh, I didn't mean that literally. If I hear you've been up to 'ote that yer shouldn't then yer know what to expect, lad, don't yer?' she warned severely.

As soon as the males had shot out, Avril, pen poised, said, 'Right, let's get down to business.'

Chapter Six

'You all right, Lynnie? Only you're very pensive. I thought brides-to-be were supposed to be all glowing with excitement.'

'Yeah, Sheila's right,' said Shirley in concern. 'You're not your usual bubbly self, Lynnie.' She handed Merrily, Sheila's youngest daughter, a dolly she had redressed for her. 'There yer go, Merrily, don't your baby look nice now I've put her best dress on? That's right, you go and put her in her pram 'cos I think she's tired, don't you?' As the child happily toddled off Shirley's face softened. 'She's so cute, Sheila. Both your little 'uns are. I hope my baby is as good-natured as your two.'

'Oh, they aren't always such little angels,' she replied, laughing. 'They both have their moments. It's when they have a moment together that I question why I wanted to be a mother in the first place.'

'Oh, but you don't ever regret it, do yer, Sheila?'

'No, not a bit of it. I wouldn't be without my girls for all the tea in China. They can be a handful but it helps when you have a good husband. I can't fault Everal's fatherly qualities. He dotes on his daughters, and they in turn have him wrapped around their little fingers.' She pushed forward a plate of custard creams. 'Help yourself,' she offered. 'Is your Pete looking forward to being a father?' she asked.

Shirley helped herself to a biscuit and bit into it. 'Oh, he's driving me mad. He can't wait for this little tyke to be born. In fact, he reckons he wants to be present at the birth. But I told him, he can take a running jump. Husband or not, he's not looking at my southerly regions when I'm in such an embarrassing predicament. I'm so glad the hospital won't allow husbands in the delivery room else I'd have a real fight on me hands.'

'How long have you got to go now?' Sheila enquired.

'My due date is a week after Lynnie's wedding. Part of me wants it to come now 'cos I'm so uncomfortable, but the other part of me prays not yet 'cos I'd hate to miss me best friend's wedding. Mind you, if I get any bigger I'll never get a dress to fit me. The one I hope to wear is like a tent and I only just fit into it now. These days I feel like I've been pumped up with a bicycle pump. I worry that if anyone stuck a pin in me I'd go bang.'

Both women giggled and when Lynnie didn't join in, looked at her askance.

'Lynnie, what's wrong?' Sheila asked.

'Pardon? Oh, nothing, I was just thinking, that's all.' She gave a sigh, then gazed at her friends searchingly.

'Were Pete and Everal . . . well . . . what were they like just before you got married?'

'In what way?' asked Shirley, helping herself to another biscuit.

'Well . . . did they seem as though they wanted to?'

Shirley tutted. 'You must remember what Pete was like, Lynnie? He was like a big kid waiting for Santa to pop down the chimney. He wanted to be involved in everything. In the end me mam gave him what for 'cos he was getting on her nerves and he sulked in the corner like a child whose sweets you'd took off him. I was told afterwards that he was at the church an hour before the ceremony was due to start, pacing up and down like someone demented, worried I wouldn't turn up.'

'I remember,' said Lynnie. 'He was so anxious, bless him.'

'What was Everal like, Sheila?' asked Shirley.

'Oh, well, we had lots of problems to contend with, both our families and friends being so against us, so you can't compare our wedding to most people's. I have to say, I had no doubts. Everal wanted to get married or he'd never have gone through the hell that he did when it would have been easier for him to walk away from me. Ours was a very quiet affair with just us and a couple of witnesses who very kindly agreed to help us out. One was the newspaper vendor whose stall is on the corner of the street where the register office is, and the other was a woman on her way to the market to do her shopping.' Sheila gave a wistful sigh. 'I'd have loved a big do with all the trimmings. Both families getting on and wishing us well, and friends too. Still, never mind. I married the man I love and we're happy, so that's what matters, isn't it? Why are you asking us both this, Lynnie?'

She sighed heavily again. 'It might just be me but Ozzie's going around like he has the weight of the world on his shoulders. When I ask him what's wrong he shrugs me off, says it's my imagination, but he's hardly showing any interest in the wedding preparations. He keeps saying it's women's stuff.'

'Ozzie's right, it is. Men ain't comfortable around women when all the talk is of frocks and flowers. They'd sooner be down the pub talking football with their mates. Unless yer get one like my Pete, of course, and I don't know if that's not worse. But when all's said and done the actual day is really for us women, innit? The men take a back seat.' Shirley leaned over and gave her friend's hand a reassuring pat. 'You're just getting paranoid because the big day is getting close.'

'Shirley's right, Lynnie,' said Sheila. 'You've got pre-wedding nerves.'

She stared at her friends thoughtfully then grinned. 'Yes, you're right. I'm just worried something is going to go wrong.'

'Well, it's not, Lynnie, so relax. Between yer mother and grandmother everything's organised like a regimental ceremony. Any news on where yer gonna live yet?' Shirley asked.

She gave a sigh. 'Looks like with my mother for the

time being at least. I hope it's not for long as I really didn't want to start married life living with either of our families. I know Ozzie isn't happy at the thought of living with my mother, but she's so insistent even though it's going to be a hell of a squash we've no choice but to grin and bear it. And I have to say, as much as I like Ozzie's mam, I'd prefer to stay with mine. I know his mam would find it hard to relinquish her motherly role and we'd both be fighting over the right to look after him. Ozzie would love all the attention, of course, but it wouldn't do my relationship with his mother any good.'

'Oh, yer didn't take the flat yer went to see then?' Shirley said.

She shook her head. 'I'd sooner camp out under the arches on Grand Central Street where all the tramps and vagrants live than live in that flat, Shirley. I can assure you that living with my mother or even Ozzie's until we find something is a far better prospect than that flat.'

'Oh, that bad, eh?'

'Yes, it was. I don't think the people who lived in it previously had a clue about cleaning. It was filthy and it stank so bad it took my breath away. I'm sure I heard rats scratching in the attic. To get to the toilet you had to cross a yard which had so much rubbish in it that the staff from the shop below had discarded you'd be lucky to reach the toilet in one piece, and on a dark night . . . well, you risked serious damage, believe me. And the toilet itself was worse than I can imagine Piss Pot's is, and that's saying something. Ugh! It was disgusting. I can't believe the landlord was expecting us to pay two guineas a week for the privilege of living in that place. He seemed really surprised that we didn't snatch his hand off for it. The only decent thing I can say about that flat was it was a good size and if it had been in better condition we'd have been happy living there.'

'You'll get summat, Lynnie, don't worry.'

She gave a wan smile. 'I would have preferred to before we got married. Still, it's only a small setback, and as soon as possible after the wedding we're going to start looking for something suitable as a matter of urgency. Anyway, let's give the wedding talk a rest for a while. It's all giving me a headache. Sheila, how are things now?' she asked, looking at her meaningfully.

'Oh, much better, Lynnie, thanks. Of course we still get stares in the street and the whispering and nudges, but that's something I expect we'll always have to live with. It upsets me when some people look at the children as though they're lepers or worse, but thankfully they're both too young to notice at the moment. Maybe by the time they go to school things will be different. I hope so anyway, for their sakes. We haven't had any bricks through the windows or anything else since that night your mother invited us round to meet the neighbours, and I pray it stays like that. I still don't know how I can ever thank her for that gesture, Lynnie.'

She smiled warmly. Sheila and Everal were still both of the opinion that that evening was all Avril's doing and Lynnie preferred to leave it like that because it made her mother look good.

'There's no need for thanks. In truth people should never have treated you like that in the first place.'

She felt guilty for a moment, remembering that before she had come to know Sheila and Everal she herself had been one of the ignorant multitude who'd condemned a white and black union as against all common decency, their offspring as freaks of nature. Thank goodness she now knew this attitude to be utterly misguided and she sincerely hoped that those still harbouring such bigoted opinions soon wised up and allowed Sheila, Everal and others in their situation to live their lives as they should be allowed to.

'There's n'ote so queer as folks, as my nan is always saying.'

Sheila laughed. 'You can say that again! But some good has come out of this, Lynnie. We've become friends, haven't we?'

Lynnie smiled. 'Yes, we have.'

'And me too,' piped up Shirley.

Lynnie gave a sudden grin as a thought struck. 'I can't believe our Ray's due home next week,' she said excitedly. 'I can't wait to see him and ask him to give me away. It's been awful for us as he wouldn't let any of us visit him in prison. Mam was furious but there was nothing she could do if Ray refused. He's going to be in for a big telling off, I can guarantee that. Anyway, Mam can't wait to get him home and is planning a surprise welcome home party for him.

Nothing elaborate as it's so close to my big day. A few sausage rolls and sandwiches just to give him a welcome back. Probably a few bottles of beer if we can manage it. She asked me to ask you and Everal to come, Sheila. Said not to worry about a babysitter. If it goes on longer than expected, as these kinda things tend to do and the girls get sleepy, you can pop them into one of our beds and lift them before you go home.'

Sheila's face lit up. 'Really? Oh, we'll be delighted to come.'

'I hope me and Pete are invited too?' said Shirley, helping herself to yet another biscuit.

'Of course you both are, that goes without saying.'

'Any chance of another cuppa, Sheila?' Shirley asked her. 'All this talking is making me thirsty. Mind you, I am drinking for two, ain't I?'

'And if you eat any more biscuits you really will burst, Shirley,' Lynnie giggled. She suddenly caught sight of the time by the clock on the fireplace. Picking up her handbag, she stood up. 'I'd best get home as I promised Mam I'd give the downstairs a going over in readiness for Ray's homecoming. Some Wednesday half-day off, eh? See you soon, girls. And you, little ones,' she said, going over to give them both a peck on the cheek before she departed.

Lynnie arrived home to find her mother bent double in the meter cupboard under the stairs and immediately knew what she was up to.

'Another burglary, I see, Mam?'

'Yes, that's right, ducky.' She emerged carrying a jemmy and a chipped bowl full of shillings. 'Got to pay for our Ray's homecoming party somehow. Then there's your wedding . . . I'm far short of what I need for that. Well, we ain't had much warning, have we? Eh, and before yer start offering ter chip in out of yer savings, you need all of that to put towards furniture and suchlike when yer get a place of yer own. It's a mam's dream ter mek sure her daughter has a good send off and I ain't no exception. Hopefully I'll get a good deal coming my way next week.

'Now pop to the phone box and call the rozzers. Tell 'em I came home to find the house has been broken into again.' She looked thoughtfully at her daughter. 'Apart from the gas meters and electric being robbed, what else can I say's gone missing to corroborate our story?' She clicked her tongue. 'Oh, never mind. We ain't got n'ote of value that a burglar would think worth the bother and the cops know that as they were only here for the same thing a couple of months ago. Spin 'em the usual cock and bull about the meters. The fact we've reported a burglary will keep the gas and electric inspectors off our backs.'

'I doubt they're gonna believe us so soon again, Mam.'

'They can believe what they like, it's their word against ours. They'll have no choice but to believe us as they can't prove it's an inside job, especially since the back-door window is broken anyway where our Colin got locked out and smashed it to get in. That reminds me, I need to get on to the council again about fixing it. Maybe Everal might have some clout in getting us moved up the repairs list, being's he works for them. Oh, hang on a minute, Lynnie. Before yer telephone, nip next door and tell Ada to empty her meters, and Phyllis next to her. The rozzers and the inspectors can't argue the toss with three of us in the street telling the same story, can they?'

Lynnie looked at her worriedly. 'Are we really so hard up, Mam?'

'When are we not boracic? And even more so now yer brothers have buggered off. I miss Dec's board money sorely, and I know Jimmy weren't exactly living here just lately but he did bung me a few quid now and again when he was flush. Eh, and before yer start blaming yerself 'cos of yer wedding, don't. Yer my only daughter and if I can't push the boat out to give you your big day then it's a poor do. Yer brother's homecoming party ain't helping matters, but I don't begrudge that either.' She looked pained for a moment. 'I just wish it was a proper homecoming for our Ray with all the family present. Won't be the same without Dec and Jimmy here. I s'pose I should be thankful they took the trouble to bother writing me that note telling me they'd arrived safely and had found lodgings and work, but as they ain't replied to the letter I sent back informing 'em of yer wedding I've no idea whether they're coming or not. Oh, Lynnie, what's happening to us all, eh?'

It pained her to see tears of distress glisten in her

mother's eyes. She stepped forward and put an arm around her shoulders.

'Mam, I'm sure they'll do their best to come but we have to realise they might not manage it if they can't get time off from their new jobs. I'll be devastated if they don't turn up, but if it came to a toss up whether they came to my wedding or kept their jobs . . . well, Mam, come on, even Dec and Jimmy have to be sensible sometimes. They wouldn't miss my wedding for anything else, you know that, Mam, so I bet they'll move heaven and earth to get here, you'll see.'

Avril gave a sniff. 'I suppose yer right. Sons! Who'd have 'em? Now go and see the neighbours then ring the cops, there's a good gel, or they'll be asking me why I took so long to call and it could look suspicious.' Her miserable expression lightened. 'Oh, I can't wait to see our Ray. This time next week I'll be sitting in the kitchen with him and it'll be like he never went away. Oh, I have missed him, so I have! Mind you, I hope he's prepared for the bollocking he's gonna get for not allowing us to visit.'

Lynnie tightened her arm around her mother's shoulders and gave her a comforting hug. 'I know, Mam. I've missed him too.' She released her and made a grab for her coat. 'I won't be long.'

Chapter Seven

Avril glanced worriedly at the clock on the fireplace, then cast her eyes around the packed front room. Although the crowd she had invited in to welcome her son from his long absence appeared to be enjoying themselves, she was conscious that everyone was wondering where the guest of honour had got to.

She made her way into the kitchen to collect another plate of sandwiches and flashed a forced smile at Lynnie who was mashing another pot of tea for those who preferred not to partake of the beer and sherry that had been provided courtesy of the gas and electric board.

'Don't worry, Mam, I'm sure there's a good reason why he's not here yet,' she said, although she was increasingly concerned herself about where her brother had got to.

Despite her daughter's efforts to allay her worry, Avril frowned. 'Oh, Lynnie lovey, I can't stop being worried. It's hours since Ray was released and how long would it have taken him to get home? An hour,

123

two if I'm being generous. So where is he?'

It distressed Lynnie greatly to see tears in her mother's eyes. 'He's probably gone to see a mate.'

'All his mates are here. Well, all the ones I know.'

'Well . . .' Lynnie was stumped, unable to come up with another plausible excuse. 'He's not the only one who hasn't arrived. Ozzie's not here yet either.'

'Ozzie never arrives anywhere on time,' her mother scoffed. 'He's a master when it comes to excuses. Me watch stopped,' she mimicked. 'I had ter stay late at work. Me dad got stuck in the outside lavvy and we had to tek the door off to get him out. And the rest he's flannelled yer with over the years! I doubt any of 'em was the truth, Lynnie. More than likely he either fell asleep after his dinner, was watching summat on the telly, or else popped for a quick one with his mates. But that's Ozzie and you have to accept that's how he is. Right now he's probably having a couple of pints before he comes here, just taking advantage of his last days of freedom.'

'You make it sound like . . .' Her voice trailed off. She had been going to say like he was heading for a prison sentence, but thought that the wrong thing in the circumstances. She gave a deep sigh. 'Yes, you're right about his excuses. I know he's more than likely spinning me a line but he puts that cheeky grin on and I can't help but forgive him. And I suppose I can't blame him for enjoying his last days as a bachelor.

'Look, Mam, I'm sure there's a good reason why our Ray's been delayed. If anything had happened to him, we'd have heard by now. You know he's more than capable of taking care of himself.'

'Yes, I do, but yer'd have thought he'd have been desperate to get home and see us and have a bit of home comfort after being locked up in that place for a year. I'm upset too 'cos the banner we spent ages painting and nearly broke our necks stringing across the front of the house . . . well, he'll hardly mek it out now it's dark.'

Sheila arrived then. 'Anything I can do for you?' she asked.

'We invited yer here to enjoy yerself, gel, not act as waitress,' said Avril.

'I don't mind really.'

'Well, I do.'

'Okay, but give me a shout if you do need anything. Oh, Everal has brought some records and they're great for getting people dancing.'

'Later, when our Ray's arrived, Sheila, eh? I'll thank Everal when I come through.'

As she departed Colin dashed in. 'Nan's asking where the sandwiches are, and Mrs Frakes wants ter know if you've any bottles of barley wine, Mam?'

She spun round to face him. 'What's she think this is, a bleddy public bar? Bleddy hell, we do our best to throw a little party to welcome home our Ray and people are never satisfied. Tell her to mek do with the beer or sherry else go without. Cheeky cow, she is.'

Lynnie chuckled. 'She asked me if it was best ham we'd used in the sandwiches as according to her she gets awful dyspepsia if it's cheap stuff she eats. When I told it was pork shoulder she pulled a face and settled for cheese.'

Avril's face contorted furiously. 'Anyone else gets an attack of wind but Josie Frakes has to act posh and call what she gets dyspepsia. Considering she's from Wharf Street, I wouldn't have thought she'd have known the proper medical term. I'll give her best ham,' she fumed. 'I bet she's never had best ham in her life, well, not what she's bought herself at any rate. And as fer barley wine, she has half a bitter down the pub and meks that last all night unless someone is fool enough to buy her a drink 'cos I've never known her yet get her purse out and buy anyone a drink back. Who does she think she is? I never invited her anyway. She heard through the grapevine what was going on tonight and invited herself. Well, I'm not standing for . . .'

'Mam, leave it,' Lynnie urged, grabbing her arm. 'She's not worth it. And it wouldn't be good for our Ray walking in and finding his mother thumping hell out of a neighbour over a piece of ham, now would it?'

Avril's shoulders sagged. 'Yer right, Lynnie lovey. It wouldn't. I'll thump hell out of her next time she opens her gob out of turn, though, yer can bet on that. Besides, everyone around here knows Josie Frakes acts like the Queen of Sheba when in truth she ain't got a pot to piss in.' She suddenly raised her arm and smacked her hand across the back of Colin's head.

'Ow!' he wailed. 'That hurt, Mam,' he cried, vigorously rubbing his smarting scalp.

'It was meant to, you little sod. I saw you picking the icing off our Ray's cake. It took me and Lynnie nearly all last night to ice it and I've asked yer several times not to touch it. If yer think that slap hurt, yer in for much worse if yer don't keep yer mitts off. Now go and mek yerself useful and hand these sandwiches round.'

Colin had no choice but to accept the piled plate his mother thrust at him. As he departed he called out, 'Oh, Lynnie, Ozzie is in the living room. He told me to tell yer to bring him through a clean glass for his bottle of beer.'

Lynnie gawped. How dare he? she thought. To arrive late and not seek her out to inform her he was here, not even bother to fob her off with one of his excuses, but instead make himself comfortable and demand her to serve him!

'Your Ozzie's starting as he means to go on, Lynnie. Tek yer mam's advice and put him right before you end up running after him like his mother does.'

'Oh, I will, Mam, don't worry,' she said, annoyed at his audacity. 'I've no intention of taking him through a glass. If he wants one that badly then he can get it himself.' She suddenly felt an overwhelming desire to have a few minutes by herself to calm down before she faced her intended. The last thing she wanted this late in the proceedings was bad feeling developing between them; she'd avoid that at all costs. She wanted her wedding day to be one to remember for the rest of her life, and she and Ozzie being at loggerheads wasn't any way to ensure that. 'Do you mind if I pop out into the garden for a bit of fresh air, Mam?'

''Course I don't, ducky. Put yer coat on though 'cos it's cold and I don't want you catching 'ote before a week on Sat'day. Be just the ticket, you walking up the aisle with yer nose streaming, wouldn't it? Shall I send Ozzie out to yer?'

'No, Mam, I just want a couple of minutes to myself.'

Avril looked at her knowingly. Her daughter was having pre-wedding jitters and Ozzie's behaviour tonight hadn't done anything by way of soothing them. 'Hopefully by the time you come back, Ray will be here.'

Lynnie flashed a smile at her as she unhooked her coat from the back door, opened it and slipped through.

Her mother was right, the early-November evening was decidedly chilly and as she reached the edge of the cracked slabbed path where the brick coal house ended and the grass patch began, she shuddered, digging her hands deep into her pockets as it struck her that today's short fashions were fine in summer but winter proved hard on the exposed legs. She wished she had put on thicker denier tights instead of the lighter ones that went better with the daringly short pale pink sleeveless dress she'd decided on for the party.

A full moon shone down from a cloudless sky and bathed the garden in an eerie light. There promised to be frost come morning. Absently she scanned her eyes across the uneven tufts of weedy grass and smiled to herself. Colin would never make a gardener. Or maybe she was being hard on her young brother. The grass had been too long for the blunt blades of the borrowed mower to do the job even half-decently and in the end even his mother took pity on him and told him to give up, joking about getting a goat in to do the honours.

Suddenly a sound reached her ears and automatically she spun around. Eyes darting, she cried out, 'Who's there?'

Without warning a hand clamped over her mouth from behind and stifled her scream.

'Shush, Lynnie,' a deep voice ordered. 'For God's sake, keep quiet. It's only me.'

The grip loosened and she spun round to face her assailant. 'Ray!' she uttered. 'Oh, Ray,' she cried, falling on him to hug him tightly. 'What on earth are you skulking out here for?'

'Lynnie, please keep yer voice down. Come over here where no one can see us,' he urged, grabbing her arm and pulling her into the gloom behind the back of the brick shed.

He sat down on one of several upturned plastic crates embossed with *Property of Hoyes Minerals Please Return* and motioned her to join him.

'Ray, what's going on?' she whispered, bewildered, squatting down beside him. 'Mam's in the house worried sick about you. We've organised a welcome home party. Apart from Mam, Nan, me and Colin, there's most of your mates and some neighbours too. Quite a gathering. We've plenty drink and food.'

At a sudden blare of music, Ray said, 'Sounds as though everyone's enjoying themselves.'

'Not as much as if you were in there. Why aren't you, Ray?'

'I just couldn't, Lynnie, I'm so sorry. I saw the banner when I walked up the street a few hours ago and guessed what was going on.'

'A few hours ago? But . . .'

'Lynnie, please let me finish.'

'I'm sorry.' Then, unable to stop herself, she blurted delightedly, 'Oh, Ray, it's so good to see you!' She flung her arms around her beloved brother again so tightly he could hardly breathe. 'I've missed you so much. We all have.'

'I've missed you all too,' he replied, his voice thick with emotion, and returned her embrace.

She pulled away from him to scan his face. 'Then why didn't you come in?'

'I couldn't face it, Lynnie.'

She looked at him, baffled. This tall, stunningly handsome brother of hers whose marked resemblance to the film star Tony Curtis had women of all ages swooning, and whose charisma commanded attention wherever he went, was telling her he couldn't face a simple homecoming party? It didn't make sense. Ray had never shied away from anything, especially not a party held in his honour. The brother hunched passively at the side of her was certainly not the same man she'd witnessed walking cockily away in handcuffs to begin his sentence.

He turned his head slightly, moonlight bathed his face and to her shock she saw the black circles under his eyes, the hollows in his cheeks. Mortified, she cried, 'Oh Ray, what did they do to you?'

'Made me see sense, Lynnie. Made me see sense.' He gave a deep sigh and from out of his coat pocket pulled a baccy tin, and from that a roll-up which he stuck in his mouth and lit with a petrol lighter. Taking several deep draws from it, he blew a plume of smoke into the air then fixed his eyes on hers.

'It was bad, Lynnie, and I'm not just talking about the terrible conditions inside. The strict rules, the disgusting food, the humiliation of doing my business in a bucket and slopping it out every morning I could cope with. But the other inmates . . .' His voice trailed off and he took another deep draw from his cigarette and stared down at his feet.

'What about the other inmates, Ray?' she probed.

He took a deep breath. 'Most of them were okay, Lynnie, men like me serving time for petty stuff, but just a few were in there for far more serious reasons. About as serious as you can get. They weren't rational, Lynnie. Nut cases is the only way to describe 'em. They should've been locked up in a psychiatric hospital not a prison. I thought I'd been in the company of hard men before but they had nothing on them inside the nick.' He lifted his head and looked at her. 'These were mean men, Lynnie, hard as nails with no remorse whatsoever for the terrible things they'd done. The sort that'd take a gun to a man's head and laugh when they pulled the trigger. Even the screws were scared of them. So was I, bloody shit scared, I ain't afraid to admit it. Me, Ray Downs, the big man around here that was looked up to, admired . . . well, I was nothing compared to them. To those men, Lynnie, I was just another soft lag to push around at their bidding, replacing the one who had just been released. When they clicked their fingers you jumped, 'cos believe me if you didn't you risked a fate worse than death, either in there or back outside. 'Cos they could get you, Lynnie, one way or another, if they took a fancy to.'

He paused to take another drag from his cigarette and stared out across the gloom of the garden.

'The showers was the favourite place. I hated going in there, dreaded it, wondering all the time if it was my turn. I witnessed many beatings, some so savage it was a wonder the men survived, but what sickened me beyond words was seeing a man stabbed to death with a bit of metal stolen from the machine shop. His crime, Lynnie, was that he dared tell one of the big shots what he thought of being expected to hand over two-thirds of the things in his parcels from home. A couple of bars of soap, three packets of tobacco and some chocolate. That's what his miserable life was worth. And not one of us witnesses to his murder said a word, 'cos we knew if we did it'd be our turn next.

'I spent the whole of my time doing my best to avoid contact with any of those types. It was a daily nightmare, and a miracle I got out in one piece. I used to watch the clock, willing lock-up time to come so that at least for a few hours I didn't have to watch my back. I spent most of my free time in my cell reading anything I could from the prison library. Me who's never read more than a comic in his life before, praying I wouldn't be disturbed, if yer get me meaning.'

She was staring at him, stupefied. 'Oh, Ray, Ray,' she uttered, distraught, tears of anguish trickling down her face.

He turned to look at her, grabbed her hand and squeezed it tightly. 'Don't cry for me, Lynnie. It was my own fault I was in there in the first place.'

'But we had no idea you were suffering like this,' she uttered, deeply distressed.

'And I didn't want you to. I couldn't stand the thought of Mam, you, any of yer, visiting me in that hell hole. If the authorities put yer in places like that in the hope of teaching yer a lesson then it bloody worked with me. I ain't going back, Lynnie, never!' he spat. Then his shoulders sagged as if a heavy weight was being pressed upon them. 'It was the old lags that brought me to my senses.' He shook his head ruefully. 'When we were young, we took what we could to help Mam out, and without that I dread to think what would have become of us. I have no regrets about any of it because, as they say, needs must. When I left school and got me first job, I know the pay wasn't great but at least I was able to give most of it to Mam – and that's when I should have stopped me criminal activities. But no, I didn't, 'cos I liked the buzz it gave me,

Lynnie, not to mention the extra that went in me pocket. And I can't deny I liked the way most people around here acted towards me, like . . . well, like they respected me. I was big-headed enough to think I could get away with anything.

'Out of all I've got up to, to get caught over that worthless telly! It didn't even work but when I was offered it for next to nothing, I knew a bloke with a second-hand shop who'd buy it off me for a couple of quid and repair it and make a few quid more when he sold it on. Yer know me, Lynnie, never turned anything down I could mek a few bob on. I never suspected for a minute the police were keeping their eye on me. Besides, I was big Ray Downs, I was too smart for the filth. Well, I was proved wrong, wasn't I? And no one was more shocked than me when I was caught. When I was being led away to start me sentence all I thought was that I'd have to be more careful in the future.

'Then inside I met the wizened old men who all their lives had drifted in and out of prison for petty crimes, nothing worth the penalty they paid. Along the way they'd lost families, had no homes to speak of, and if they didn't die in prison would end their days in an old lags' hostel with no one mourning them. That's how I could end up, Lynnie. More than likely will if I carry on the way I was. When that hit me it shook me to the core. Few criminals escape the law in the end. In truth, hardly anyone gets rich on a life of crime. That was forced home to me big-time in prison.

'And then it struck me – as the eldest male in the

family, just what kind of example was I setting the rest of you? Jimmy and Dec are already heading for trouble. I got a letter from them – well, a scribbled note really – telling me they had decided to try their luck elsewhere, but they don't fool me. I know the real reason why they've scarpered off there and that must be 'cos they've been in some kind of trouble here. They've gone down south until the heat dies down. Colin, now, he's showing more of a talent than any of us did at that age for being light-fingered. But it's you and Mam I'm most frightened for, Lynnie. What you both do ain't big-time by any means but it's still enough to warrant sending you to jail should you be caught for knowingly receiving stolen goods. I can't bear the thought of any of you going through what I just have, but especially you and Mam. It's got to stop, Lynnie. Here and now. All of it,' he implored.

He took a deep breath and looked at her hard. 'I've shocked you, ain't I? You and everyone else was expecting the old Ray back: breezing in, great big grin, full of himself. That man's gone, Lynnie, gone for good.' He threw his cigarette down and ground it out then immediately took another out of his tin and lit it, drawing on it deeply. 'I don't know what the future holds for me but one thing I do know, and that is whatever I do from now on will have no risk attached of ever landing up where I've just been. I'm a free man and I intend to stay that way. I know I'm going to have trouble getting any kind of decent job now I've a record but I will, Lynnie. I'll prove to people somehow that I can go straight and they can trust me.

'Now do you understand why I couldn't face all those people Mam's invited round to celebrate my release? They'll be badgering me to know what big plans I have for me future, especially me old mates who'll want to know what's in it for them. As soon as it's around that I'm home, I know certain people will be beating a path to the door, wanting to do me a deal. I can't explain all this to them, Lynnie. I can't have them look at me as though I've gone mad. 'Cos I haven't, just the opposite in fact.' He eyed her worriedly. 'Do you think I've gone mad?'

She vehemently shook her head. 'No, Ray, not at all. Not after what you've told me. You've shocked me. You were right when you said we expected the Ray who went inside to be the same coming out. Oh, Ray, we all know prison is no picnic but none of us had any idea it was as bad as that. I don't know how you survived, but I'm so glad you have.' She swallowed the huge lump in her throat and uttered, 'I'm proud of you.'

He released her hands and tenderly stroked one side of her face. 'Are you, Lynnie?'

'Yes, I am,' she said fervently. 'It takes a big man to do what you're about to and turn their life around.' She looked at him, shame-faced. 'I'd never really considered what we do as bad, Ray, not when men rob banks armed with shotguns and in comparison to all the other terrible crimes that happen. I suppose we've been doing it that long it's just become a way of life – we never really think of ourselves as criminals. And it's not like we've ever made much from it. A few bob here and there – a couple of quid if we were lucky. Even when you got caught and we were so upset, none of us seriously considered we could get caught too.'

'Whichever way you look at it, what you do is still thieving, Lynnie. That meat you get from that bloke who works at the abattoir – he steals it, you know that. And the same for the clothes and shoes and whatever else comes your and Mam's way. I got a year for receiving that telly and you'd get the same, maybe longer depending what mood the judge was in.' Ray gave a violent shudder. 'I hate to think what I'd have got if the police had known I'd sold a stolen car the week before they nabbed me, and they'd taken that into consideration when they prosecuted me. I could have ended up with a five-year stretch. One was bad enough – I can't imagine surviving prison any longer.

'I tell you, Lynnie, the sentence ain't worth the money you make, really it's not. I can't stress that enough to you.' He gave a harsh laugh. 'If you'd told me a year ago I would have been talking like this, I would've laughed in yer face. People are going to have trouble getting used to the new Ray, but they'll have to lump it because under no circumstances am I going to be swayed back to my old ways. Never again.'

'I'm with you, Ray.'

He looked at her earnestly. 'Really, Lynnie? So I don't have to worry about you possibly ending up inside and going through what I did? 'Cos women's prisons are just as bad.'

'No, you don't,' she said with conviction. 'I can't say it's going to be easy managing without the extra bits I earn on the side, but I will. What you've told me tonight has scared me. You've made me realise that the rest of us have been lucky not to have been caught before now. Very lucky.'

He looked troubled. 'I hope the others are so easily persuaded. Jimmy and Dec aren't going to be easy nuts to crack.'

'They'll listen to you, Ray.'

'Do you think so?'

'You're their big brother. They look up to you.'

He gave a forlorn sigh. 'Yeah, they do, and look what I helped teach them, Lynnie.'

'I'm as much to blame. I'm their big sister. Between us we taught them all they know, so it's up to us to stop them before they decide to really start chancing their arm doing bigger stuff. And you're right about our Colin. I caught him with some sweets on him last week that he'd lifted from a shop, and he told me he was practising to be your partner when you got out. Like Dec and Jimmy, if we don't stop him now there's no telling what he's going to end up like. We'll stick together on this, Ray, and make the others listen to us.'

'How, though?'

'Tell them exactly what you've told me. Scare them witless like you've done me, Ray. Jimmy and Dec see what they get up to as one big joke. They won't think it so funny when they hear you tell them what it's really like inside.'

He said worriedly, 'I hope yer right, I really do, Lynnie. How d'yer think Mam's gonna take this? She relies on the extra money she makes. Until I get a job, I won't be able to chip in and help make up for what she's losing.'

'Mam loves you, Ray. Out of any of us she takes most notice of you. Just tell her what you told me and the rest you held back, 'cos I'm sure you haven't told me everything. You haven't, have you, Ray?'

He looked at her grimly and lowered his head to avoid her eyes. 'Some things that went on in there I'll never talk about with anyone,' he said softly.

Her eyes filled with sadness for what her adored brother had suffered. Some would say he well deserved what he had got, but he wasn't a bad man, not cruel or evil, and although he deserved to be punished for what he'd been caught doing, he hadn't deserved to live for the past year in fear for his life. But maybe what Ray had been through had been in its way a blessing and would turn out to be the salvation not only of him but the rest of the Downs family too. What he had described so graphically to her had turned her cold, frightened her more than anything had ever frightened her before, enough to make her want to put an immediate end to her unlawful sidelines. She would stick with Ray on this and between them they would unite the family in one aim: to live on what they legally earned, and no more ducking and diving.

'Mam needs to know you're here, Ray. She's going mental worrying why you're not.'

'I can't go in, Lynnie,' he insisted. 'Not 'til everyone's gone.'

'I understand why now. But you know what that lot in there are like. A few drinks down them and they'll be partying until we eventually chuck them out. You need to get indoors, Ray, you're freezing.' She stared at him thoughtfully. 'Look, I'll get rid of them somehow, but first I'll get everyone into the living room and you can slip upstairs then I'll send Mam up to you. I'll make sure you get your privacy with her until you've told her what you have to.'

He put his arms around her and gave her a bear hug. 'I love you, yer know that, don't yer, gel?'

A flood of tears filled her eyes. The old Ray would never openly have admitted such a thing. 'I love you too,' she whispered emotionally. She suddenly realised neither of them had mentioned her forthcoming wedding though she had written to him about it. But at this moment her own big day, although hugely important, was not as imperative as getting Ray back where he belonged.

Lynnie was gratified to have her prayers answered when both the kitchen and the passageway leading to the stairs were empty of people. Motioning to Ray that the coast was clear, she made her way into the living room and shut the door behind her. Despite the music no one was dancing but all stood huddled together in groups, and it wouldn't have taken a genius to guess what the main topic of conversation was: Ray's absence. As she entered they all looked at her expectantly. She ignored their questioning eyes and sought out her mother.

'Mam,' she said, beckoning her over, 'can you pop upstairs and get my cardi for me, please? I'm a bit chilly.'

'But it's stifling in here,' Avril responded, frowning.

'Where yer bin, Lynnie?' said Ozzie, joining her.

'Not now, Ozzie,' she snapped, and to his utter amazement turned her back on him and addressed her mother again. 'I'm cold, Mam. I left my cardi on one of the beds in the boys' bedroom. *Please can you fetch it for me?*' she said, trying to put emphasis on her words so that her mother would understand she was trying to get her to go upstairs and that the cardigan was just a pretext.

But Avril was too worried about her son to cotton on that Lynnie was trying to tell her something. 'I ain't yer hod carrier, fetch it yerself. What's your cardi doing in the lads' room anyway? Oh, no matter, I've too much on me mind as it is without being worried over why you left yer woollie in the boys' room.'

'Mam, please,' Lynnie said, almost begging now. '*Please* fetch me cardi for me. I swear I'll never ask you to do anything for me again, but please just do this for me.'

'Watch out, Avril,' a female voice boomed out at the side of them. 'Lazy cow will have yer cleaning her shoes next.'

Avril scowled hard at the person responsible for this slight. 'My Lynnie is anything but lazy, and I'd keep yer comments about any of my family to yerself if yer know what's good for yer. If my Lynnie wants me to fetch her cardi then I bleddy well will.'

With that she spun on her heels and stormed from the room.

Lynnie clapped her hands to get everyone's attention and shouted loudly over the noise of the music: 'Look, I'm sorry to break the party up but it looks like we've got our Ray's release date mixed up somehow. Me mam's really upset so I think you'd all best be off.'

'Ah, Lynnie, we're just getting going,' slurred Harry Grimly, taking a swig out of a bottle of beer.

Murmurs of agreement came from the others. Lynnie sighed. Getting rid of them all was going to be no easy task.

Colin came across to her. 'Ah, Lynnie! I was just about to ask Jackie ter dance with me and I'm well in there.'

'Colin, you're fourteen,' she hissed at him, sisterly protectiveness rearing up. 'You're too young to be *well in there*, and I don't want to hear you talk like that again for at least another five years or so. Now, help me get this lot out.'

She began walking across the room towards the record player, meaning to turn it off. As she passed by the chair where her grandmother was sitting, Freda caught her arm. 'What's going on, Lynnie?'

'In a minute, Nan.'

Everal, who had been closely watching the proceedings, instinctively knew that something wasn't right.

With his deepening regard for all the Downses he wanted to take Lynnie aside and offer his help, but felt that would be intruding too much and he didn't want to jeopardise this new friendship for anything. It was apparent, though, that Lynnie desperately wanted the house clearing, and also that the majority were not going to leave easily. It was up to him to aid her. Without further ado he turned around and switched the record player off.

'Come on, Sheila.' He spoke loudly so all could hear. 'Let's give Avril some space. You collect me records up, darlin', while I gather the girls. A lovely party, Lynnie,' he said, going up to her and kissing her cheek. Then, lowering his voice, whispered, 'I'm sorry yer brother was delayed but I'm sure you've nothing to worry about. If you need me and Sheila for anything, you know where we are.' Then, raising his voice again, he added, 'Thank yer mam for inviting us. Goodnight, everybody.'

The others looked at each other then reluctantly gathered their own belongings and followed Everal and Sheila out.

As the room was slowly emptying Ozzie came up to Lynnie, his expression showing that he was not at all happy. 'Yer've avoided me since I got here,' he sulked. 'What's up with yer, Lynnie? I might as well not have come.'

She glared at him and despite knowing she should keep matters harmonious between them before the wedding, couldn't help but snap: 'Sooner have spent the evening with your mates, would you, Ozzie?'

'No,' he replied mardily, then followed that by, 'Well, yeah, if yer want the truth. When yer in this mood.'

Before she could stop herself she blurted, 'Then sod off! And I don't want to see you again until you promise to treat me like your future wife and not your slave.'

He looked astonished. 'Eh?'

'Don't look so innocent, Ozzie. Having the cheek to arrive late, then not even bothering to come and find me but ordering our Colin to tell me to get you a glass.'

He grinned cheekily at her. 'Well, that's what women do, ain't it? Look after their blokes.'

His flippant comment was an attempt at a joke but Lynnie took it as anything but. She reared back her head and, hands on hips, retaliated: 'There's looking after and there's becoming a drudge. I ain't your mam, Ozzie, and I don't intend turning into her.'

He was staring at her now. 'What's got into you, Lynnie?'

She stared back for several long moments, then her shoulders sagged and she gave a sigh. Ray's terrible story of his stay in prison was still upsetting her and added to that was her deep concern over what was happening now upstairs and how her mother would take Ray's pleas for all of them to stop their illegal activities. Lynnie knew she was taking out her feelings unnecessarily on Ozzie.

Before she could respond to him he'd put his arms around her and pulled her close. 'Ray will be here soon, Lynnie, you'll see. He's probably . . . I dunno . . . bumped into some old pals. I'll go and have a look for him, shall I? I'll go around his old haunts, he's bound ter be in one of them.'

Ozzie's rare moments of thoughtfulness always came when she least expected them and now his offer to find her brother touched her deeply.

'Yer mam's teking a long time fetching yer cardi, Lynnie,' Freda piped up, her eyes narrowing shrewdly. 'Now I might be old but I ain't lost me marbles yet. Summat's going on and you'd better tell me what it is.'

'Lynnie won't but I will,' said Avril as she entered the room. 'Now sit down, all of yer. Yer might not like what I'm gonna say. Yer gonna be shocked, that I promise yer. But first of all let's welcome Ray home properly.'

A while later Colin was staring at his brother, appalled. 'But all me mates are gonna think I've gone soft, Ray. I won't half get some stick!'

'I don't care what yer mates think, Colin, like I don't care what mine do. If I ever catch you with anything on yer yer shouldn't have, or involved in anything yer shouldn't be, then I'll personally kick yer legs from under yer.' Ray looked at him earnestly. 'Do yer think I've been telling yer a fairy story, Colin? 'Cos I assure yer I ain't. If your mates think yer've gone soft or give you any stick then it's about time you found yerself some new ones.

'We're all going to find this hard. What do you think Piss Pot or whoever else is going to think when Mam

145

tells 'em she ain't interested in their stuff no more, however cheap they're offering it? How d'yer think she's going to manage, not getting the money she makes selling it on? Lynnie too? But we're all going to *have* to manage, Colin, and learn to do without what we can't afford. I can't bear the thought of any of yer going through what I have and I'd kill yer all first than risk you facing that, that's how strongly I feel.'

A subdued Avril rubbed a hand over her face as she listened to her son. What he had told her in the bedroom upstairs had shaken her rigid, frightening her more than anything had ever frightened her in her life before. She'd had no idea that during his time away her beloved son had been going through such an ordeal, terrible enough to bring about this huge change in him. A surge of guilt reared up, almost choking her. What her son had suffered during his stay inside was all her fault. She had turned a blind eye to everything he and the rest of her brood got up to because she was so desperately glad of the rewards, and when opportunities for herself had come her way, had readily participated. After all, what they brought in in this way had at times made all the difference to whether they ate or starved.

As the years passed and the family's monetary burdens were gradually eased with the wages earned by the elder children, it never even crossed her mind to stop her little sidelines. Now the extra made allowed them all the little luxuries their collective wages would not. But all the time none of them had passed more than a joke between themselves on the possible repercussions of getting caught. Not even Ray's collar had taught them that. As the head of the family Avril should have taken stock then, seen her boy's prosecution as a warning of what could happen to them all, but she hadn't because like the rest of them she'd chosen to view his incarceration as rotten luck, vowing like the rest of them to be more vigilant in future so as not to end up the same way.

And if Ray's account of what he had witnessed and endured himself at the hands of the hardened criminals wasn't bad enough, it was his stories of the plight of the old lags which hit her hardest. The thought of any of her family ending up lonely and penniless like them terrified her more than the thought of going inside herself. It wasn't even as though what they did brought them riches, just a few luxuries now and then: butter instead of marge, or a cream cake for tea; new shoes occasionally instead of constant repairs.

After what Ray had told her these luxuries suddenly seemed paltry compared to the price they could pay for having them. He was right. All their unlawful activities must stop here and now. Even scrimping along was a far better prospect than landing up like those old lags. It wasn't going to be easy but she'd stand by Ray and Lynnie and do her best to ensure the rest of the family complied.

She looked across at Colin. 'Listen to yer brother, son,' she firmly ordered. 'This is no cock and bull he's spinning yer. From this minute on we're all going straight. When we next see Dec and Jimmy, which I pray is gonna be fer yer sister's wedding, then they're gonna get the same talking to and woe betide them if we get any back chat.' She looked at Ozzie who was sitting dumbstruck to one side of Lynnie. 'You'll become part of this family on Sat'day, lad, so the same goes for you too.'

He looked at her innocently. 'I don't get up to 'ote I shouldn't so I don't have ter make no promises.'

'Oh, come on, Ozzie, we all know you regularly walk out of your workplace with a pair of shoes under yer coat and then flog 'em down the pub,' said Ray.

'But that's nothing! What I make on them only pays for a few pints. Lots of warehouse workers do it. It's a perk of the job.'

Lynnie looked at him, startled. 'I never knew you nicked shoes from work.'

'Some things you do, you don't tell me about,' he accused.

'Yes, I do,' she snapped back, hurt. 'I tell you everything. In future we're honest with each other about everything, okay, Ozzie?'

'Yeah, all right, Lynnie, stop going on.'

Ray eyed him sternly. 'You could get away with what you're doing for ever, Ozzie, but then yer might be one of the unlucky ones who get caught. Even if you didn't get put inside, you'd lose yer job and have a police record so you'd find it hard to get another decently paid job. How would yer support our Lynnie then? See sense, man, pack it in before it's too late. Besides, if we're stopping all that kind of thing then, joining our family, you will too or yer'll have me ter deal with. Understood, Ozzie?'

He gave an off-hand shrug. 'I suppose.'

'I'm glad that's settled,' said Avril. 'Now to let you see how serious I am, I'm gonna see about getting some extra cleaning jobs. And you, Colin, can look for a Saturday job until you start full-time next April.'

Freda, who had been sitting patiently listening to all that had gone on, piped up, 'Well, I for one won't be sorry. I shan't be jumping out me skin when the door hammers in future, terrified it's the coppers on the other side. I don't mind us having to cut back one bit. I'm too old to get a job, and besides me ryetist wouldn't let me, but I can help more around here while yer all out at work. Apart from our Ray you've all bin lucky up ter now, but luck runs out, yer know. Any road, if you all land up being put away, who'll look after me?' Her remark, although outwardly selfish, was said to make them think, they all knew.

Avril smiled warmly at her mother, glad she was showing her support, then turned to Lynnie who was sitting beside her and took her hand, squeezing it affectionately. 'This means we're gonna have to cancel some of the extras we were going to have for yer big day, lovey, and cut back on the rest.'

'I don't mind, Mam,' she said sincerely.

Ozzie gave her a nudge. 'Would it be better if we put the wedding off 'til we can afford a proper do? I know how yer'd set yer heart on a posh send off, Lynnie.'

All eyes turned to him.

'This your way of trying to let our Lynnie down gently?' Avril accused him.

That's exactly what he was trying to do, had seen a glimmer of opportunity and dived right in. 'No, honest,' he lied. 'I was just thinking of her, that's all.'

She smiled at him lovingly. 'It's the vows we make that are important, Ozzie. I'd marry you wearing a sack. And yes, I'd have liked a posh do, what woman wouldn't, but I'm not bothered if we can't manage any sort of reception. Not when we're trying to band together and set this family on the straight and narrow. Cutting down on my wedding celebrations is a small sacrifice to make, don't you agree?'

'Yeah, yeah,' he murmured, his heart sinking. In just over a week he'd be a married man and still hadn't come to terms with all the commitment entailed.

Ray looked across at his sister. His face, although showing marked signs of last year's ordeal, was still breathtakingly handsome. 'I'm sorry, Lynnie. With all this being uppermost in me mind I ain't congratulated yer yet in person on getting Ozzie to make an honest woman of yer.' He winked at the other man. 'You are going to ask me to give you away, ain't yer?' he asked his sister.

'You bet,' she replied enthusiastically. She got up and fetched over a handful of glasses from the top of the sideboard and the remains of a bottle of sherry, putting them all down on the well-worn coffee table. 'Let's drink a toast to the Downses' new beginning,' she said, filling the glasses and handing them round, ignoring Colin's look of dismay when the glass he received contained just air.

'To the Downses,' Avril toasted, raising her glass. 'Absent ones included.'

They all held their glasses up. 'To the Downses,' they said in unison.

No one noticed that Ozzie's voice held a reluctant tone.

Chapter Eight

From under her lashes, Lynnie flashed a look at Ray who was absent-mindedly pushing food around his plate. Deep concern filled her. Since his return home from prison a week ago and his declaration of the plan to change his life around, true to his word he had not gone back on his decision. Almost every minute of his time had been spent pursuing work, from traipsing the streets calling on the off chance on firms in the hope that they had something to poring over the job vacancies in the *Leicester Mercury*. He was willing to take anything, but nothing as yet had been offered and Lynnie was beginning to worry that if this state of affairs continued her brother might have no choice but to revert to his old ways. She knew that Ray was well aware when he'd persuaded them into managing solely on their legitimate earnings that the family's resources would be stretched to their very limit, without the added strain of supporting him too.

'If you're not enjoying your dinner, Ray, can I get you something else?' she asked him.

'There ain't n'ote else,' said his mother. 'My dinner not up to prison grub, eh, son?'

Her comment was made in jest but received a stony glare. 'That isn't funny, Mam. You wouldn't give pigs what we got in there.'

'I'm sorry, I didn't mean ter say that,' she uttered, mortified. 'I opened me gob before I got me brain in gear.'

'You always have done,' remarked Freda, looking suspiciously at the plate of food her daughter had put before her. 'And age ain't improved yer. Is this lamb's liver?'

'It's ox,' Avril shot back at her. 'I could do yer egg and chips, Ray?' she offered.

'Mam, this liver and onions is fine. I'm just not hungry, that's all.' He pushed his plate away and gave a despondent sigh.

'Huh, well, that's a lie for a start, son. This liver is far from fine. It's as tough as old boots,' Avril said, pulling a face.

'Yer can say that again,' said Freda. 'It's that tough chewing, it's worn me denture plate down.'

Avril glared at her mother. 'Well, in that case yer'd better get yer dentures sharpened 'cos for the time being it's the cheapest cuts for us, that's when we can afford meat, otherwise it's the old saviour of a pan of vegetable soup. And woe betide any of yer,' she said, looking at them all meaningfully, 'who moans over what I put before yer in future. Now we ain't getting Lynnie's meat parcels I had to go back to the local butcher and it's well known the meat Rolly Smythe sells comes from old milking cows, that's why it's so tough and that's why he can sell it so cheap. But if we're gonna succeed in our aim to go straight then that's the way it's got ter be. Fer the time being at any rate.'

Ray looked at her, bothered. 'You are keeping to our agreement okay, Mam?'

She gave a snort. 'I wouldn't say okay but I'm doing me best. 'Tain't easy this being honest business, is it? For a few weeks before we decided to go straight I had hardly 'ote worth getting excited about coming my way. This week I've had some great offers, can yer credit it?'

'It's called sod's law, Mam.' A worried frown knotted Ray's brow. 'But you weren't tempted, were you?'

''Course I was, yer daft beggar, especially as we've a wedding ter cater for, but I didn't succumb because I made yer a promise, son, and I won't let yer down.' She gave a sudden grin. 'Piss Pot thinks I've got the arse with her. She couldn't believe it when I told her we Downses weren't in the market for knock-off stuff no more. The look she gave me, yer'd have thought I'd suddenly sprouted a witch's wart on the end of me nose, long black hairs coming out of it an' all. She didn't believe that we'd gone legit and stalked off, muttering under her breath that if she found out who we was using now instead of her, she'd stab their eyes out with a hot poker. Well, I was one of her best customers after all and she'll miss my custom badly. Warrabout you, Lynnie?'

'I agree, Mam, turning down good offers is hard.

But I haven't wavered either,' she replied.

Ray smiled proudly at her. 'Good gel. Keep it up, Lynnie, and you too, Mam, and if either of yer do get tempted, remember what I told yer.' He looked across at his brother. 'You've bin behaving yerself, ain't yer, our Colin?' he asked.

The boy sulkily nodded. 'I won't have no friends left soon.'

'Then get some new ones like I told yer. It's harder staying out of trouble than it is getting into it, but it gets easier, Colin.'

'If yer say so,' he muttered, scraping back his chair. 'Can I go out, Mam?'

'Where yer going?' she demanded.

'Just over to Mick's to see if he'll let me have a go on his new bike.'

'Don't be late,' Avril warned him, then when Colin was out of earshot, added, 'It wouldn't tek much for me to guess where that bike came from. Knowing Big Mick Mason as well as I do, some posh kid came out of a shop or whatever ter find his bike had disappeared.' She forked the last bit of mashed potato into her mouth and pushed away her plate. 'Can't say as I enjoyed that. There's some spuds left in the pan, Mam, if yer fancy them, and some gravy left?'

Freda shook her head. 'No thanks, ducky. The lot I've already eaten is sitting like a brick in me stomach. I'll have a dose of Liver Salts in a bit, that should shift it. I judge by yer face you had no luck today, Ray?'

'Not a bite, Nan. Plenty of vacancies for jobs I could

do, but as soon as I mentioned what I'd been doing for the past year, the door was slammed in me face.'

'Don't tell 'em then,' advised his mother.

'There's no point in trying to go straight if I start off by lying, Mam. Even if I did chance my arm, I doubt the job would be mine for long before my record came to light and then I'd be dismissed on the spot and my prospects would be worse than they are now, if that's possible.'

'Oh, come on, son. It ain't like yer a murderer.'

'No, I know, Mam, but not many people want to risk having a thief on their premises. Once a thief, always a thief, that's people's belief. I want the chance to prove them wrong, but it's getting that chance that's so hard. I knew it would be, it's come as no surprise.'

Avril reached over and patted his hand. 'Summat'll turn up, you'll see, and when yer least expecting it.'

'Yer mam's right, our Ray,' said Freda. 'Life has a funny way of surprising yer. I'll have a cuppa if anyone's mashing, and I'll have it in the living room,' she said, pushing back her chair. ' "Z Cars" is due on and I don't wanna miss the start. Besides I know yer want a word with the youngsters, Avril, and as I already know what it's about I'll leave yer to it.'

As her mother made her way into the front room, Avril tutted. 'Don't tell her I told yer but yer nan's got a fancy for that Stratford Johns who plays the Inspector. She forgets she's sixty-seven and stiff with arthritis, and he wouldn't look at her. I suppose it doesn't hurt for her to have her day dreams, though.

Now, if I can have yer attention, I've some good news ter tell yer.'

Lynnie and Ray looked at her eagerly. 'Oh?' they said in unison.

Avril puffed out her flat chest proudly. 'Well, I don't mean ter brag in light of your rebuffs on the job front, Ray, but I've got meself an afternoon job at the factory where I do me morning cleaning. It ain't n'ote fancy but the couple of quid a week I'll get for it ain't to be sneezed at. I hope this'll mek yer realise I'm serious about being good, Ray.'

'What is it doing, Mam?' Lynnie asked keenly.

'Scrubbing the canteen out after it shuts at three. A couple of women have been doing it for years but one of 'em broke her leg and it looks like she'll be off for a while so I said I'd fill in for her. Hopefully she'll decide not to come back and I can have it permanent. The added bonus is that usually there's food left over that can't be used the next day and the cleaners get a share in it same as the canteen staff do. It all helps, dunnit?'

Ray's shoulders sagged. He was so proud of his mother's efforts but the downside was that the family was being reduced to relying on handouts. Hopefully, though, this situation was just temporary until he got himself a job, which he prayed would materialise soon or he worried that in time his mother might be lured into taking a risk because she was so desperate for money. Trouble was that that one risk could land her right where he was fighting hard to keep her from. 'That's great, Mam, I'm proud of you.'

'Yes, me too, Mam,' echoed Lynnie.

Avril beamed. 'I thought yer both would be. I start Monday. Me and yer nan have had a chat and she's volunteered to prepare the weekday dinners in future. Well, as much as her arthritis allows. She'll manage simple meals. I've told her we'll prepare most of it the night before to make it as easy as possible for her.'

'Well, I don't mind a bit Nan cooking the dinners, 'cos she's far better than you, Mam,' Ray said tongue-in-cheek as he took a roll-up out of his baccy tin and lit it, drawing deeply on the smoke.

She reached over and slapped his hand, pretending annoyance. Then she stood up. 'Right, I've a daughter getting married in two days' time and a reception that needs tackling. Is Ozzie coming round to give us a hand?' she asked Lynnie.

She tutted. 'You are having a joke, Mam. He went pale when I mentioned it. Says he's things to do, packing and such like for when he moves in here. He might pop in later and bring some of his stuff, but I won't hold my breath because I have a feeling Ozzie is going to take full advantage of his last two nights of freedom.'

'Typical man,' Avril scoffed. 'Leaving the work to the women. Well, I suppose we should be glad he's keeping his distance. He'd just be a bleddy nuisance and get in our way. Yer'd have thought his mother would have offered to come and help with the cooking tonight or at least chip in with something towards the cost when I went around ter see her to explain we had a few problems moneywise at the moment and had to cut back. But did she hell! All she said was, "Oh, dear, what a shame. Well, I'm sure what you do will be lovely." Condescending cow she is! I know what her problem is. She's miffed yer taking her son off her, Lynnie, and she's livid 'cos yer staying here with me 'til yer get somewhere of yer own, and not with her. She should be bloody grateful her Ozzie has landed someone like you 'cos he won't get no one better.'

Lynnie could see her mother was getting herself worked up over Ozzie's mother's attitude and thought it best to try and defuse the situation. 'You're going to Ozzie's stag do tomorrow night, aren't you, Ray?'

He shook his head. 'I don't think so, Lynnie.'

'Oh, but you must,' she urged. 'I need you to keep an eye on him and make sure he doesn't drink too much. I want him to enjoy himself but . . . well, I'm worried he'll drink himself into a stupor and collapse in a heap somewhere and not make it to the church on time. Or else his mates'll do something like chain him naked to a lamp post in town so he ends up in a police cell for the night.'

'I'm sure neither Ozzie nor his mates are that stupid, Lynnie,' Ray fibbed in an attempt to alleviate his sister's fears. He knew very well that those Ozzie chose to mix with were just that type, and come to that so was Ozzie too. 'Don't worry, Dec and Jimmy will be there to keep an eye on him and make sure he gets home at a decent time.'

Lynnie's face filled with alarm. 'Oh, Ray, we aren't

even sure if our Dec and Jimmy will get here for the wedding yet. We've heard nothing from them. And besides they have trouble enough looking after themselves without a drink, let alone themselves and Ozzie with more than a bucketful down them.'

Avril looked at her, horrified. 'Oh, God, don't start me worrying about our Dec and Jimmy not being able to look after themselves, Lynnie. I'm worried enough about them as it is, them being so far away where I can't keep me eye on them.' Then she looked at Ray. 'I'm still bothered about how they're going to take our pact and if they'll agree to do the same. Yer know what a pair of buggers they are.'

'Don't worry, Mam, by the time I'm finished with them they won't dare disagree.'

She sighed. 'I hope yer right.' Then her face set. 'Those pair are in for it when I see 'em. One scribbled note I've had since they went off two months ago, and they hardly said a word in it really. Job okay, lodgings okay. What kind of letter is that to send to a mother?'

'Give over, Mam, lads don't write.'

'Not that you told us much now we know what really went on, but at least you did write when you was away,' she snapped at him.

'That's 'cos I had nothing better to do,' he said quietly.

Her face filled with shame. 'Oh, yes. I'm sorry, Ray.' She hurriedly changed the subject. 'Why ain't yer going to the stag do?' she asked him. 'You ain't been out since yer got back, lovey,' she said, eyeing him in concern. 'Well, not socially, and you was out every night before yer went inside. When anyone's called here yer've told us ter tell 'em yer indisposed. They ain't gonna believe that for ever, and if yer don't watch it yer'll end up with no mates at all.'

'I'll go out when I'm ready, Mam,' he said shortly. 'Besides, the kinda mates I had before ain't my type any more.'

'All right, all right. No need ter lose yer rag with me, son. I just mean it ain't natural fer a young bloke like you to be hanging around the house of an evening, that's all. I bet the gels are missing yer,' she said, her eyes twinkling mischievously.

'Mam, I'm concentrating all my efforts on getting meself a job before I do anything else. Besides, I can't exactly pay me way at the moment. I might have had bad habits in the past, but I always paid me way, yer know that.'

'I could sub you a few bob for tomorrow night, Ray,' Lynnie offered.

He smiled appreciatively at her. 'You need every penny of your money for yer married future, but thanks for the offer.' He scraped back his chair and stood up. 'Well, I've a speech ter write that's giving me nightmares so best get cracking. I'll be upstairs if anyone wants me.'

'Oh, it's so good to have our Ray home again but he is worrying me,' Avril said a while later as she and Lynnie made a start on preparing the food for the reception. 'It's one thing turning yer life around, another becoming a hermit. I'm just praying I can persuade our Dec and Jimmy not to go back down the smoke. Our Ray needs his brothers around him right now to help him adjust back to life outside. Maybe the three of them could get a job on a site somewhere. Ray'd be able to keep an eye on Dec and Jimmy then and make sure they're behaving themselves.' She sniffed hard and turned her back so Lynnie couldn't see she was crying. 'I want all me family back together under this roof.'

Lynnie was busy opening a packet of flour. 'I miss them too, Mam, but don't build your hopes up too much about Dec and Jimmy coming back, 'cos I'd hate you to be disappointed if they've decided they like it down there, especially if they've both managed to get decently paid jobs. Anyway, when they lived here you were always moaning that they got under your feet and saying it was about time they moved into a place of their own. Now they've done just that you want them back. They can't win with you, can they? As for our Ray, he's been through hell, Mam, and he needs time to get over it before he faces the world again. *Then* you'll be complaining that he's never in. Now, how much flour do you want me to measure out?'

Avril knew that her daughter was talking sense. Quickly composing herself, she turned and looked at her thoughtfully. 'Er . . . enough to mek a mountain of sausage rolls.'

'A hundredweight then?'

She giggled. 'Yer daft sod! Weigh a couple of pound out for starters and we'll see how far we can eke that out. I'll start grating stale bread to add to the sausage meat to bulk it out further.' She paused and looked at Lynnie then issued a forlorn sigh, her shoulders sagging despairingly. 'Oh, lovey, why couldn't we have started our new regime *after* yer got married? This ain't the kinda wedding I wanted to give yer, us having ter mek do with sausage rolls and cheese and egg sandwiches. I wanted yer to have a proper sit-down affair with waitresses serving us.' Her eyes became dreamy. 'A topside of beef, leg of pork and ham on the bone, all carved by a chef in his whites, us in our finery sat at tables being served by waitresses in a lovely room all decked out with pink and white flowers and matching balloons.'

She looked across at the wedding cake she had attempted to make. 'There's no beating about the bush, Lynnie, that cake I made and tried to decorate ain't fit to be seen in public, let alone in pride of place in the middle of the table. The fruit all sank in the middle.' Her eyes glinted with tears and her voice fell to a choked whisper. 'Oh, I didn't want this for you, Lynnie, really I didn't. I wanted you to have a wedding to remember.'

She gave a sniff, wiping her hand under her nose. 'My wedding was . . . well, the sort yer don't want to remember. A rush job at the register office and a drink in the pub after. And I spent me honeymoon night terrified me mam could hear us in her bedroom next door. But I needn't have worried 'cos yer dad was that drunk he collapsed spark out on the floor and I spent it in my bed alone, crying me eyes out because it was slowly dawning on me what a terrible mistake I'd made. I know Ozzie's not a bad chap and I'm sure you'll whip him into shape once you're married. He'll turn into a decent enough husband for yer once he settles down to it so I've no worries on that score, but I so wanted me only daughter to have a real grand send off, Lynnie.'

She put down the bag of flour she was holding and ran around the table to throw her arms around her mother and hug her tightly. 'I *am* getting a grand send off, Mam. The cake you made is wonderful and the best of it for me is, I know you made it with love, same as the food we're about to do now. It's going to be great, Mam, you'll see. The best bloody wedding I could wish for. Now come on, we've work to do. Sheila, Phyllis and Ada should be here any minute to give us a hand and we've hardly made a start yet. It was so kind of them to offer to come and help us, wasn't it?'

Just then there was a tap on the door and Sheila bustled in. 'Sorry I'm late. Those girls of mine just would not go to bed. I did tell you they weren't always angels. Anyway, I've left Everal reading them a story.' She carefully put a large biscuit tin on the table, and from out of one of three heavy bags she'd placed on the floor took out an apron and tied it around herself.

'Oh, Phyllis and Ada said to tell you they'll be around to help as soon as they've finished washing their dinner pots and settled their husbands in front of the television.

'Now you might not know this but I'm a dab hand at doing all sorts of tasty bits and pieces for parties because when I was young I used to help my mother who entertained a lot. So have you any idea what you'd like me to do?'

Avril put her arm around Sheila's shoulders. 'I'd like you to mek every fancy thing you know how to, Sheila, but I for one will be surprised to see what fancy things yer can make out of cheese and bread besides sandwiches. I hate ter disappoint yer but since we started this drive to keep on the straight and narrow that's all we can afford.'

'And you're to be commended for what you're doing, Avril. Obviously some of your neighbours think so too because when they heard you were doing Lynnie's reception yourself as money was tight, they wanted to help out. They knew I was coming to lend a hand and gave their donations to me in case they offended you.'

'They what!' exclaimed Avril.

Sheila smiled at her. 'Don't you realise there's quite a lot of people around here who admire this family? They know how hard it is to try and manage on what you earn. They do it themselves. Those that scoff at you, Avril, aren't worth knowing. Anyway, Mrs Newman sent over four tins of salmon and couple of corned beef, sardines and mackerel. Mrs Green a dozen eggs, two huge jars of home-made pickled onions and three of piccalilli. Mrs Williams has made three bowls of trifle but said she'd bring those around tomorrow morning along with a batch of fairy cakes. Oh, what else? Ah, Gladys Ormond sent a cucumber and apologised for it not being much but she's not well off, is she? We can cut that thinly to eke it out and make cucumber sandwiches with the crusts cut off, like royalty has. There's tins of cocktail sausages and other things but for the moment I can't remember who gave me those. It'll come back to me, though. There's another bag outside on the door step. That's got a huge cooked ham in it from Mrs Dickson who told me to tell you, Lynnie, that it's your wedding present. Well, I think that's it, but I can assure you we'll make a wedding feast fit for a queen with all that.'

Both Lynnie and Avril were staring at her. 'Oh, Sheila,' Lynnie cried. 'Why, this is just . . . Oh, Mam, this is just great, isn't it?'

'I'll bleddy say,' Avril erupted. 'I'm having trouble teking all this generosity in.' Then she spotted the tin on the table. 'Er . . . yer never mentioned what was in that, Sheila?' she said, pointing at it.

She looked at her hesitantly, gnawing her bottom lip. 'Well . . . please don't take offence but I knew you were struggling with the cake. I mean, you said yourself, Avril, that baking isn't one of your gifts. Well, if I say it myself, I'm quite good so I thought I'd see what I could produce and surprise you with it. It's my gift to you,

Lynnie. I'm just sorry it's not a three-tiered cake but I never had the time.' She eyed Avril worriedly. 'I hope you're not offended?'

Avril opened the tin, looked down into it and gasped in shock. 'Oh, Sheila, you made this and iced it yourself?'

'Yes. It's got plenty of rum in it courtesy of Everal. Do you think it will do?'

'Do!' Avril exclaimed. 'It's better than I'd ordered and had to cancel from Kinton's the bakers. I'll say it'll do!'

Lynnie was looking at it in awe. Marvelling at the delicate pink iced rose buds surrounding the edges. In the centre, carefully piped, was lettering congratulating herself and Ozzie on their marriage. Around the cake was a thick matching pink ribbon tied with a bow. Tears of gratitude pricked her eyes and she looked at her new friend happily. 'It's beautiful, Sheila. Thank you so much.'

They both heard a thud and looked around.

'Well, that's ended up right where it belongs,' said Avril, laughing down at her own dismal effort which she'd just thrown into the bag on the floor containing rubbish to be put in the dustbin later. Eyes sparkling with happiness, she threw her arms around her daughter. 'Yer right, this is going to be a grand send off for yer, Lynnie, just bleddy grand.'

Then Freda shuffled through. 'Right, that's me programme finished so I've come to lend a hand. Stratford Johns weren't in it tonight, more's the pity,' she grumbled. 'Good God,' she exclaimed, spotting the overflowing bags Sheila had brought in plus the tin with the cake in it. 'Has someone robbed a shop?'

She couldn't understand why they all burst into laughter.

Chapter Nine

'Can I have a word, Lynnie?'

'Yes, sure, Mr Mallin,' she said, easing herself off her counter stool. 'Can you manage for a minute, Mrs Crane?'

'S'pose I'll have ter,' Madge mumbled, pursing her lips indignantly.

Lynnie ignored her colleague's disagreeable attitude and followed her boss into his office.

'Shut the door behind you and sit down, lovey,' Sid told her as he sat down in his own chair, leaned back and eyed his employee in concern. 'You look tired, gel. Yer getting married tomorrow, yer should be all bubbly and excited.'

'Oh, I am excited, Mr Mallin, but I was up late last night helping prepare the wedding reception food and I'm getting edgy about tomorrow going well. I didn't get much sleep.'

'And I expect yer won't get much ternight either. Having a hen do, I expect?'

'Not as such. I thought the money it'd cost me could

171

be put to better use and we've still things to finish off. A few girl friends are coming round, though, but I'm hoping they don't stay late so I can get my beauty sleep.'

He smiled at her. 'You look to me like you could do with a good night's sleep but not to aid your beauty, Lynnie. You're a cracker. Look, I'm concerned that apart from tomorrow yer not having any time off for a honeymoon.'

'Well, our wedding has been a bit of a rush job due to the fact the Vicar could slot us in so quickly as you know, Mr Mallin, but also . . . well, money's a bit tight and we've got to look for somewhere to live and furnish it so we've decided to do without a honeymoon just now. We might take one next year all being well. I'm not bothered at all. I'm marrying Ozzie and that's the main thing, isn't it?'

'Yes, of course it is, ducky. But yer could still take a week off, Lynnie, even if yer not going away. You've holidays due yer.' He looked at her knowingly. 'I know the real reason why yer not taking time off. It's her, isn't it?'

She gnawed her bottom lip anxiously. 'I can't leave her on her own to cope with the counter, Mr Mallin. I'd never rest easy if I did. She's still not got the hang of the job properly yet and . . .'

'Her attitude stinks. Yes, I know, Lynnie. I also know how much you cover for her mistakes. I know I've got to do something about her or I'll risk you leaving, or worse still me business going down the pan 'cos me customers stop coming. Punters spend time in here to escape nagging wives and place their bets in peace. The last thing they want is Madge Crane giving them the same as they get at home.' He ran his hand over the top of his bald head, his face set grimly. 'I have approached a couple of other shopkeepers around here and asked if they're looking for any assistants. A couple were but as soon as I mentioned Madge's name I was laughed at. Seems her reputation precedes her.

'I was hoping she'd leave of her own accord but it doesn't look like she's going to, does it? Yes, I've been a coward, Lynnie, I don't mind admitting it. But no more. I'm going to take the bull by the horns and finish her tonight. Now I totally appreciate yer loyalty to me, Lynnie. It's good for an employer to know that his employees have his best interests at heart like I have yours, but now and again it's only right you should think of yourself. This is one of those times, Lynnie. You only get married once. Well, hopefully. Now I want . . . no, insist you should have the rest of the day off and Monday at least, if not the rest of the week.'

'But with no staff, how will you manage, Mr Mallin?'

'That's not for you to worry about. I want you to enjoy your break. By God, gel, you deserve to after all the hard work you've put in here. And hopefully the next person I choose as an assistant will be far more suitable than the last. I'll set about finding a replacement as a matter of urgency.'

An idea suddenly struck Lynnie and her heart thumped in anticipation. If Mr Mallin would agree it could be the solution to all their problems. 'What about our Ray, Mr Mallin?'

He looked at her, taken aback. 'Your brother!' His face fell. 'Lynnie, this job involves handling lots of money and . . . well . . .'

'Yes, my brother has a record as a thief, Mr Mallin.' She eyed him beseechingly. 'But Ray has learned from his mistakes, really he has. He's vowed never to get into trouble again. If you'd just agree to talk to him you'd see that for yourself. I'll vouch for him, Mr Mallin. He'd be great behind the counter, especially when we get fights breaking out between the customers which we regularly do, and he knows quite a bit about betting as he used to have a flutter himself before he went inside.'

Sid leaned forward. Placing his elbows on his desk, he clasped his hands prayer-like and looked at her hard. 'Your word means a lot to me, Lynnie. I've learned to trust you completely, and if ever I have to go out on business I know the shop is safe in your hands. Under normal circumstances I'd be glad to give anyone a try on your recommendation and if they proved ter be half as good as you then I'd be absolutely delighted.

'But I've deep reservations about yer brother. What if temptation does prove too much for him? I won't stand for anything underhand going on here, Lynnie, yer know that, and if I found your brother up to something he shouldn't be and had to sack him, or worse still get the police on him, then how would you feel about me doing that? I know yer love yer brother,

174

Lynnie, but I wonder if yer faith in him is misguided. Don't forget I've met him when he's been in here. I've met all three of yer older brothers. They're not bad lads in the big picture of things but I'm a pretty good judge of people, yer have ter be in my game, and I wouldn't put me trust in any of them. They're all what I call chancers. Thank God you're not in their mould else yer wouldn't still be employed here, Lynnie. I'm sorry to say that but it's how I feel.'

She felt herself blushing and lowered her head. Sid Mallin wasn't as good a judge of character as he thought he was. She *was* in the same mould as her brothers. She felt a surge of guilt, knowing that Sid's good opinion of her would dramatically change should he learn that on more occasions than she cared to remember she had accepted stuff cheap from many of his customers and hidden it under his counter. Luckily he had never discovered what she was up to. Sid would never know that this practice had benefited him too because the money she had paid over for the goods had gone straight back into his till on bets.

'People can change, Mr Mallin,' she implored. She wanted to add that as well as Ray, she and her mother had but knew it would be best not to. 'They can, really. But they need a chance first. You're just the chance our Ray needs, Mr Mallin. Oh, you should see how demoralised he's getting through not finding any work just because as soon as he tells a possible employer he's got a record they slam the door in his face. He could have had a job by now if he hadn't been honest with them, but he won't do that because he wants to be all above board in everything he does in future.

'Mr Mallin, our Ray is really desperate for money and if he was going to go back to his old ways he would have done so by now, especially to help towards giving me a better wedding. Ray is well aware that the odds are stacked against him but I know, against those odds, he'll prove himself. Just talk to him, what harm will that do you?'

He sighed deeply. He didn't want and couldn't really afford to make another mistake in his choice of employees. But he liked Lynnie, had grown to respect her, and her pleading was wearing him down. And she was right, everyone deserved a second chance. He just hoped Ray's wasn't at his expense. He supposed it would do no harm to talk to him. 'All right, you win. I'll see him, Lynnie, but more I won't promise.'

'Oh, Mr Mallin, thank you!' she cried. 'You won't regret giving Ray your time, I know you won't.'

'We'll see. Now I want you to have the rest of the day off and I don't want to see you on Monday either. Just give me a telephone call to let me know about the rest of the week as yer might change yer mind about taking it off. If I do give yer brother a go – I'm only saying *if*, mind – you're going to need to be in fine fettle when you return to help with his training.'

She jumped up from her chair, face wreathed in delight. 'I'll go straight home now and if Ray's there I'll send him down immediately. If he's out job hunting I'll send him to see you as soon as he can make it.'

Sid clamped his hand to his forehead in a fed-up gesture. 'Lynnie, go home.'

'Yes, Mr Mallin, and thank you. Thank you so much.'

'Oh, just a minute,' he called, urging her back. 'I nearly forgot to give you this.' He held an envelope out towards her.

'What is it?' she asked, taking it.

'Yer wedding present. Yer know I can't come tomorrow being's Saturday is my busiest day but I hope it all goes well for yer. Me and Mrs Mallin pondered what to get yer and both agreed that being's you needed most things like young newly weds do then we'd give you the money and you could choose what yer wanted yerself.'

Her eyes widened in shock when she saw the two five-pound notes inside. 'Oh, Mr Mallin,' she uttered. 'I don't know what to say.'

He laughed. 'That makes a change. Now go home, will you, before I have you thrown out.'

Several hours later the back door burst open and Ray charged through. Lynnie was sitting at the kitchen table putting the finishing touches to a plate of salmon sandwiches before she covered them up with a damp tea towel to keep them moist until the next afternoon. Before she could ask him how he'd got on in his chat with Sid he'd leaped over to her, grabbed her arm, pulled her out of her chair and begun spinning her round, whooping in delight.

Avril, who was washing up at the sink, spun round

and stared at them, mystified.

Freda appeared, rubbing sleep from her eyes, and exclaimed, 'What on earth . . .' Her voice trailed off when she witnessed what was taking place.

Ray let go of Lynnie, threw an arm around each of the older women and gathered them to him. Eyes shining, he blurted, 'Cigar Sid's took me on. I convinced him I was kosher and he agreed ter give me a go. I start Monday. It's all thanks to you, our Lynnie. I won't let yer down, gel. I won't let Sid down either. Ain't this just flipping great? I'll be earning now, Mam, not a bad wage either, and I can earn extra if I want to do some bookie's running so I'll be more than able to pay my way.'

All the women gave screams of sheer rapture.

'Oh, Ray, that's fabulous!' Lynnie cried, jumping up and down with excitement and clapping her hands. She dived at her brother to give him a bear hug. 'Oh, I'm so pleased. We'll be working together and a great team we'll make, I know we will.'

Suddenly a male voice boomed, 'Someone won the Pools? Seems like it with all the racket yer making. We could hear yer down the street.'

All eyes turned to see Jimmy and Dec framed in the kitchen doorway.

Avril raced over to her sons and gave them each a slap round the ear. 'That's fer going off without telling me! Now give yer mam a hug, yer pair of bleeders.'

A while later, all sitting around the table in the breakfast room, Dec and Jimmy looked at their elder brother expressionlessly as they listened to what he had to tell them.

When he had finished a surprised Dec scratched his head. 'By God, this is a turn up for the books.' He looked at Jimmy. 'Whadda yer think, broth?'

'Well, I dunno,' he replied non-committally. 'What do you?'

'Oi!' snapped their mother. 'Yer act like yer deciding whether to have a cheese and onion sandwich or cheese and pickle. This is bleddy serious, yer know. Now, are you going to toe the line or what?'

'What happens if we don't?' Jimmy asked nonchalantly.

Avril scowled at him warningly. 'You teking the bleddy mickey? 'Cos if yer are . . .'

'No, Mam, no, we're not, honest,' Dec insisted. He turned his attention to Jimmy. 'We can't let the family down, broth. They need us back up here to help 'em.'

Jimmy nodded in agreement. 'No, yer right, we can't let 'em down.'

Dec smiled at each of them in turn: Avril, Ray, Freda, Lynnie and Colin. 'We're both willing to mek the sacrifice. 'Course I doubt we'll have it so good up here as we had down there, but . . . well, after all, family is family.'

Avril looked at her sons remorsefully. 'Oh, lads, I can't deny you'd make me the happiest mother alive if yer didn't go back 'cos I ain't half missed yer. And I can't deny either that I could do with yer board money sorely at the moment, but if things are that good down in London I can't ask yer to give it all up.'

'It's okay, Mam, really . . .' Dec began.

'No, really, sons,' she cut in. 'I'm being selfish asking yer to give up yer new lives. It ain't easy getting yerselves settled in a new place, making new friends, but most importantly getting yerselves good jobs. All I'm asking for is yer'll promise yer'll not misbehave yerselves in future and risk ending up in jail. That's all we're bothered about, ain't it, Ray?'

'But you need us, Mam,' said Dec resolutely. 'If we can't give up what we are for our family, we can't do it for anyone. Can we, Jimmy?' he said, looking at him meaningfully.

'No, we can't,' Jimmy insisted.

'Right, we'll say no more on the matter. We're with yer one hundred per cent.' Dec grinned cheekily at his mother. 'Besides, we've missed getting our washing done, and yer lumpy custard.'

Avril choked back a lump in her throat. 'I'm a lucky woman. Thanks, boys.'

Their grandmother was looking at them questioningly. 'So just what was so good down there that's such a sacrifice to give up?' she queried.

Dec rose and grabbed his heavy holdall. 'If we don't get a move on, Jimmy, we'll miss the start of Ozzie's stag do. And we've gotta unpack yet. You're coming tonight, ain't yer, Ray?'

He looked at them thoughtfully then grinned. 'Yeah, I think I will. Got plenty to celebrate now, ain't we?' he said, rising to slap each of his brothers on the back. 'I appreciate what yer doing, boys. As the males of this family we'll mek sure the women are looked after as best we can.'

'Don't forget me,' erupted Colin.

Ray laughed. 'How could we? Yeah, you're included too.'

Lynnie beamed as a wave of relief flooded over her. She had prayed her older brothers would be present at Ozzie's do to keep an eye on the proceedings and she had got her wish. 'You'll all make sure Ozzie gets home safe and at a decent time, won't you?'

'Oh, come on, Sis, 'course we will,' said Dec. 'Is there hot water for a wash down, Mam?'

She nodded. 'I put the copper on earlier. Have as much as yer like.'

'See, Mam, I told yer it'd be all right,' said Ray after Dec and Jimmy had gone upstairs.

She leaned over and patted his hand. 'Yes, yer did, ducky. Oh, this is just wonderful, ain't it, Mother? Having all the family back under me roof again. Mam, where yer going?'

'Ter get me cardi,' she said, heading for the stairs. 'I've gone a bit chilly.'

'I'll get it for you, Nan,' offered Lynnie.

'It's all right, ducky, I'll manage meself, ta. Then I'll be back down to help yer finish off the reception food. Won't be a tick.'

Upstairs in their room Dec and Jimmy were unpacking their holdalls.

'Well, we've come out of this smelling like roses,

Dec,' said Jimmy, giving him a grin.

'Sure have. The family, especially Mam, will be treating us like royalty for a good while if we play our cards right. Mind you, warra turn up! Them going kosher. How long do yer give 'em all?'

Jimmy frowned thoughtfully. 'I dunno, Dec, they seemed pretty adamant on keeping it up.'

'Oh, don't be soppy, Jimmy. It's a nine-day wonder.'

'D'yer reckon? I dunno. What Ray told us bleddy frightened me, I can tell yer.'

'Yeah, it bleddy scared me too, but we're too clever to be caught.'

'That's what Ray thought.'

'Well, we ain't been caught yet,' Dec said smugly.

'Only just. We've had some pretty close shaves. I can't believe how lucky we were to get clean away from the smoke.'

Dec stopped ramming his underwear and socks into the top drawer of a well-used old-fashioned tall boy. 'Well, how the hell were we supposed to know we were being set up and that the bloke whose crazy paving we agreed to lay was actually the owner of the building site we nicked the stuff off? We both thought he was just a bloke off the street asking us to do a cash-in-hand job for him. I'm just upset 'cos we couldn't go back and collect the wages we were owed.'

'And risk getting the beating of our lives from the site-owner's heavies?' scoffed Jimmy. 'I just hope they don't find out where we live and come after us. We made a good few bob before we were sussed. Then there's the landlady. I wonder how long it's going to take her to cotton on we ain't going back? We left owing her two weeks' rent, and you loosened the sink on the wall when yer were leaning too heavily on it washing yer feet. And don't forget that woman's husband who's out for your blood. He's gonna kill you if he ever catches up with yer . . .'

'Well, he won't think ter look for me up here, will he? And nor will any of the others who are after us 'cos we never told anyone the truth about where we came from. Clever move that, brother, if I say it meself. Now in future we're just going to have ter be more careful. Have eyes in the back of our heads, so to speak.'

'Eh? But we've just promised . . .'

'Don't be soft, Jimmy. Yer don't think I meant any of that downstairs, do yer? Listen, they can all say they're going to be as honest as they like but I know it won't last. It's a five-minute wonder. As soon as our Ray meets a gel and can't afford to tek her to a fancy restaurant on the pittance he's getting at that bookie's then mark my words, he'll be tempted back into doing a deal. Same goes for Mam. Sooner or later either Piss Pot or whoever else Mam got her stuff from will tempt her into buying something. Lynnie too. Her and Ozzie are just about ter start married life and there's bound ter be summat they need but can't afford . . . I don't need to go on, do I, Jimmy? Before you know it, everything will be back to normal. In the meantime we just keep a low profile and what we're doing to ourselves. What the eye don't see . . .'

'Ah, that's yer game, is it? I bleddy knew you two were up to summat!'

They both almost collapsed in shock to see their grandmother standing in the doorway. It was apparent to them she'd heard every word they'd said. She shuffled further inside, waving her walking stick at them.

'You might have pulled the wool over the rest of 'em's eyes but not yer old nan's. You boys have always been chancers, and yer don't change, do yer? Well, let me tell yer that yer *gonna* change. Yer gonna become that squeaky clean we could eat our dinner off yer. Now, yer mam's downstairs under the impression that her two doting sons have given up well-paid jobs and lots of friends to come back home and unite the family. You've made her a happy woman and she's gonna stay that way, 'cos I tell yer, from this minute on, if you two put one foot wrong, I'll be down on yer like a ton of bricks.

'I'll tell the others how yer lied to 'em and the truth of it is yer scarpered back up here 'cos half of London's after yer. Yer mother won't be pleased, believe me, not to say how the others will react to you deceiving them. And if *that's* not enough of a deterrent, I'm sure one of the poor sods you crossed down in London lodged a complaint with the police so a word in their ear about your whereabouts could be of interest.'

Both of them gawped at her, terrified.

'Yer wouldn't, Nan?' said Dec, finally.

'Try me,' she warned. 'This family is making great

strides to go straight, and you'll do the same. Now, yer not getting another warning. Is that clear? I said, is that clear?'

They both looked at her sheepishly, then their shoulders sagged in defeat.

'Yeah, Nan.'

'What, I never heard yer!' she barked.

'Yes, Nan,' they said louder.

Ray suddenly appeared. 'Everything all right, Nan?' he asked, putting his arm around her shoulders in an affectionate gesture.

She looked at Dec and Jimmy. 'I dunno. Is everything all right, boys? Lass, I asked yer a question!'

'Yeah, Nan. Yeah, it is,' they answered sulkily.

'What was all that about?' Ray asked his brothers when their grandmother had departed.

They both gave a helpless shrug. 'No idea,' said Dec. 'Have you, Jimmy?'

He vigorously shook his head. 'No, not a clue.'

Chapter Ten

With tears of pride glistening in her eyes, Avril stood and stared at her daughter. 'Oh, darlin', yer look just beautiful,' she uttered emotionally.

Lynnie smoothed her hands down her plain satin dress. 'I'll do, will I, Mam? It's not the dress I planned on wearing . . .'

'It's better, ducky,' she interrupted. 'That dress might not be as fancy as the one you'd set yer heart on, but by God you don't need lace and diamonds, Lynnie. You're beautiful enough without all that frippery and that's the truth of it. Shirley and Sheila between them have done a great job with yer hair. All those twists and loops pinned at the back and twirly bits hanging around yer face really suit yer, lovey. And the dainty crown thing on yer head . . . what's it called? A tiriara . . . that yer borrowed from Ada's daughter next door finishes you off just perfect.'

'Oh, Mam, thank you.' She appraised her mother admiringly. 'You look lovely yourself.'

Avril cast her eyes down over her fitted lemon shift

dress, the hem of which finished just above her knees. 'Between yer nan and me we've not done a bad job of running this up on the old treadle, if I say it meself. It turned out far better than I thought it would. It's ages since either of us has made anything to wear for a posh do like this. If ever, in fact. I've never been to a posh do.' She eyed Lynnie, bothered. 'You youngsters wear yer clothes almost to yer bum these days but yer don't think it's too short for a woman of my age, do yer?'

'No, Mam, not at all. It's hardly showing your knees. You've a great pair of legs and should be proud to show them off.' And she added, her eyes twinkling mischievously, 'For your age, that is. Those pearls finish your outfit off just perfectly.'

Avril took a look at herself in Lynnie's full-length wardrobe mirror. 'It's a long time since I've worn these,' she mused, fingering them. 'They ain't worth nothing else they'd have been hocked a long time ago. I bought them from Woolie's costume jewellery counter to wear on me first date with yer dad. Oh, I did think I was grown up! And I was so excited about that date that if I went to the toilet once, I went a dozen times before I set off to meet him.' Her face soured. 'If I'd realised what I was getting into I'd never have spent me savings on these or turned up to meet him either.' She smiled at her daughter lovingly then. 'Still, I wouldn't have had you lot, would I, so what I went through was worth it.'

Tears pricked Lynnie's eyes. 'Oh, Mam . . .'

'Now, now, don't you start blubbering. Yer'll smudge

yer makeup and get mascara on yer dress. I'm sorry, lovey, I shouldn't have mentioned yer dad, especially not on a day like today.' She gave a dismissive flap of her hand. 'That's all past, gone, done with. I just pity the poor bugger who's landed up with him now.' Avril came towards her and took her daughter in her arms, hugging her lightly so as not to disarray her in the slightest. Then she kissed her lovingly on her cheek. 'I know I keep saying this but Ozzie is a very lucky man. I just hope he realises how lucky.'

Ray appeared, looking extremely smart in a dark blue suit and pink shirt. 'Oh, God, Lynnie, what a picture you look,' he enthused. 'Best-looking bride ever.' He addressed his mother. 'They're all getting ready to walk across to the church, Mam. I'll take care of Lynnie now.'

She took a deep breath. 'Right then, I'd better leave yer to it and see yer there.'

'Mam!' Lynnie called after her.

Avril turned back to face her. 'Yes, me duck?'

'Thanks, Mam. Thanks for everything.'

Avril smiled warmly at her before she turned and left.

'How do yer feel?' Ray asked his sister.

'Like I've a swarm of bees in my stomach.'

He grinned. 'Yeah, well, yer bound to be nervous. Not every day a girl gets married, is it?' His eyes scanned her admiringly and he said huskily, 'Not one as beautiful as you look anyway, Lynnie.' He smoothed his hands over his own suit, looking in the wardrobe mirror to straighten his tie. 'I don't look bad meself either,' he said, giving a lock of hair that had fallen across his forehead a tweak back into place. Then he hooked his fingers into the waistband of his trousers and adjusted them. 'I musta lost a bit of weight in prison; this suit is quite loose. Never mind, a few more of Mam and Nan's dinners will soon have me filling it out.'

He turned his attention back to Lynnie. 'Colin made me roll up earlier, causing such a stink about wearing that suit Mam got him from the second-hand shop on the Narborough Road. He reckons he looks a right nancy in it and his mates are gonna tek the mickey something rotten. If Colin had got his way he'd have worn his jeans and denim jacket. Mam won, though, as if any of us had any doubt she would, and I have to say our little brother is going to break a few hearts before he's much older. He looks really smart. He knows he does but is in too much of a sulk to admit it.'

'All my brothers leave a trail of broken hearts in their wake,' she said, eyeing him fondly. 'If Dad did nothing else, he fathered handsome boys. It used to cross my mind at school that I only had so many friends because then they all had an excuse to call at our house and eye you lot up.'

Ray smiled cockily. 'You might have a point.' He looked at her seriously. 'But Dad also fathered a cracker of a daughter, Lynnie. Ozzie's a lucky man, 'cos if he hadn't snapped you up you'd have had no trouble getting anyone yer wanted.' He took a look at his watch. 'Right, sister dear, Mr Bevins will be here any minute in his old jalopy to drive us to the church. So shall we go down?' he said, offering her his arm to escort her out.

A little earlier, in a house a few streets away, washed, shaved and dressed in his light blue wedding suit and bright yellow shirt with frills down the front and edging the sleeves, Ozzie was prowling his bedroom. A couple of hours before he had been rudely awoken by his mother at what seemed to him the crack of dawn, especially when suffering a raging hangover after the celebrations of the night before.

She put a cracked mug of weak sweet tea on the floor by his bed before going over to the window. 'Rise and shine, son.' She spoke briskly, whipping the curtains open, allowing rays of weak November sun to flood the room which only accentuated its shabbiness. 'Today's the day.' She tweaked aside a square of dingy netting and peered out. 'Looks like it's gonna stay dry too so that's summat to be thankful for, I suppose.'

'Ah, Mam,' he groaned, rolling over and pulling the bedcovers up over his head. 'It's still the middle of the night.'

She turned to face him. 'It's just after nine and you get married at twelve,' she barked. 'Today of all days you ain't gonna be late, Oswald Matthews, not even by a minute, 'cos I ain't having us do n'ote those Downses can have a swipe at us for.' She folded her arms and leaned back against the window sill, her face screwed up smugly. 'I know Avril Downs is smarting 'cos I never offered to put anything towards the reception, and after her giving such a strong hint that they were feeling the pinch 'cos of them supposedly going all righteous. Well, I couldn't offer what I ain't got, could I? Besides, I wouldn't even if I could have, it's the bride's family's job to give her a good send off.'

From under the bedclothes Ozzie fought to drown out the sound of his mother's monotonous voice droning on and on. But he knew she was on a roll now and wouldn't stop until she had said her piece. He only hoped she hurried up so he could go back to sleep.

'And I don't believe for a minute this cock and bull that they're going all moral,' she continued. 'Huh! Even if they are it won't last fer long. And if they did have to, why couldn't they have waited 'til after the wedding? Damned inconsiderate, if yer ask me. Bearing in mind their Lynnie's landed herself such a good catch in you, the least they could have done was pull out all the stops to give yer a decent wedding reception. 'Cos let's face it, son, Lynnie's a nice enough gel and I like her well enough but you could have got yerself someone from a much better background than she comes from. It's well known her dad was an Irish waster and a bully at that, and let's be honest while we're at it, you are marrying the sister of a convicted criminal.' She gave a deep sigh. 'Still, yer've made yer bed so there's n'ote yer can do but lie on it.

'Now get yer backside off that mattress while I go and mek yer breakfast. All yer wedding outfit is pressed ready and I've hung it on the back of yer wardrobe. Yer clean Y-fronts and socks are in yer drawer, and I polished yer shoes 'til yer can see yer face in 'em. Yer brothers and their families will be here soon and I want you all spruced up to greet them, then we can have a drink of sherry together to toast yer happiness before we set off for the church.'

It all went quiet for a moment and from under the bedclothes Ozzie heard his mother sniffing. He cringed, praying she wasn't going to start crying. He couldn't cope with women crying, especially his mother. Despite being close to it, thankfully she didn't.

'Oh, son, I can't believe me last baby is leaving home ter get married.' Her voice was thick with emotion as she stared sadly at his packed belongings piled by the wall. Despite being asked several times by Lynnie why he hadn't moved them into the Downses' house, Ozzie had avoided doing so, feeling that would be finally shutting the door on his old way of life. 'I never thought yer would get married. Right from a little boy you've always told me yer'd never leave me 'cos yer loved me too much. I ain't half gonna miss yer. Now yer must promise me one thing. If any of those Downses mistreat yer in any way you're to get yerself straight back here, understood, son? Just 'cos yer married to their Lynnie doesn't mean ter say yer at their beck and call.'

She pulled a dingy-looking piece of ripped sheet from out of her shabby cardigan sleeve and blew her nose long and loud before saying, 'Right, I'd better go and get yer dad up.' And she muttered under her breath, 'Let's just hope he doesn't get too drunk today and cause a fight.' As she reached the doorway, she stopped and turned, looking back at the bed. 'Oh, I don't suppose yer know anything about three strange chaps I found unconscious in our front room this morning?' When she received no reply she added, 'No, somehow I didn't think yer would. Anyway, I woke 'em up and sent 'em packing. I had ter fling the windows wide as the room stank of stale beer and other male smells,' she said, wrinkling her nose disgustedly.

Ozzie, now wide awake, allowed a decent enough interval of time to pass for him to feel sure his mother had left the room then slowly pulled the covers away from his head and forced open his eyes, wincing as the light flooded in, almost blinding him. Tentatively he sat upright to lean his head against the wooden headboard. It pounded painfully, like a herd of rhinoceroses were running amok through it. He shouldn't be so surprised by the way he felt, though, considering the amount of beer and several rum and blacks he'd tossed back in an attempt to enjoy himself on his last night of bachelorhood.

Through the thumping pain memories crept back of the raucous time they had all had and his mouth curved into a silly smile. Almost twenty males made up of friends, work colleagues, his own brothers and Lynnie's, had descended upon the town centre hell-bent on giving Ozzie a send off to remember. And they had succeeded admirably. It was just a pity, he felt, that Lynnie's brothers had been present. Although inebriated themselves they'd still had enough of their faculties left to ensure they dragged him home at a reasonable hour, much to the annoyance of himself and the girl he happened to be entangled with at the time, secreted in a secluded corner of the Adam and Eve night club. Ozzie himself hadn't seen the harm in having an innocent kiss and cuddle with a pretty woman on his last night of freedom. Still, he supposed he couldn't blame Ray, Jimmy or Dec for unceremoniously prising them apart. After all, he was marrying their sister today.

Marrying Lynnie today! The day he had done his best to put off had finally dawned and he suddenly knew what a trapped animal must feel like with no means of escape.

His mother's head appeared around the doorway. 'Oh, at least yer awake,' she said, surprised, and as he raised his head and looked at her, added, 'Good God, son, yer look like death. Well, that'll teach yer for drinking yerself stupid. You'll feel better after yer've eaten the sausage, bacon, fried bread and eggs I've cooked yer. Now come and get yer last breakfast as a single man before it gets cold.'

The thought of all that fatty food, which normally he would have wolfed down after a night on the beer, made his stomach churn today. It was a hair of the dog he needed most not food, but he doubted even a couple of pints would make him feel better able to face the demon he was about to confront.

Finally, and only because he was continuously nagged by his mother, he had readied himself. Satisfied with his appearance, he then began pacing his room, breathing deeply in an effort to control his jangling nerves. From downstairs the jovial noise that his family was creating filtered up. He should be down there with them sharing in the celebration but just couldn't bring himself to because he felt far from jolly. He looked at his watch. Just over an hour to go until he met his nemesis and the ticking seconds seemed suddenly to rev up, racing uncontrollably ahead. The jangling nerves in his stomach tightened into a gripping knot. His desperation for a drink threatened to consume him, but not the cheap sherry his mother was doling out. What he craved was being served over the counter of the Shoulder of Mutton.

Opening his bedroom door, he tiptoed across the narrow landing, descended the stairs, and as he got to the front door his mother came out of the kitchen, saw him and demanded, 'Where the bleddy hell d'yer think you're going?'

'For a walk. See yer in church.' And before she or any of his family could stop him he had let himself out and run off down the road.

Now totally oblivious of the congenial Saturday lunchtime atmosphere surrounding him, Ozzie held out his empty glass towards the gnarled landlord and demanded, 'Put another one in here, Gerry.'

Flapping the cloth he was drying glasses with across his shoulder, Gerald Gunn took the glass off Ozzie and positioned it under a pump dispensing Everard's best bitter. 'I thought you were getting married at one today?' he remarked.

'I don't need reminding,' Ozzie muttered in a maudlin way. 'Well, am I getting another drink or what?' he snapped.

Gerry pulled the pump. 'No need to jump down me throat, lad. I was just wondering if yer watching the time, that's all. Wouldn't be good leaving a grand gel like Lynnie waiting, would it?'

Ozzie flicked back his sleeve and looked at his watch. The hands showed ten minutes past twelve. Strange, he thought. A while ago time was racing by but now it seemed almost to have stopped. 'I've plenty of time,' he replied off-handedly, holding out the money for the price of his drink.

Gerry gave a shrug. 'If you say so.'

With an explosion from the rusting exhaust and a grating crunch from the gear box, Mr Bevins pulled his old Morris Minor 850 to a halt outside the church. Lynnie had been so grateful when their elderly neighbour had offered to act as chauffeur to take her to the wedding but then she had never been driven by him before and hadn't realised what she was letting herself in for. Mr Bevins was no driver and Lynnie had never been so glad in her life to reach a journey's end. The whole drive from the house to the church had consisted of non-stop jerks and jolts as Mr Bevins, his hand tightly gripping the steering wheel, had crunched the gears and continuously lifted his foot on and off the accelerator, causing the rusting vehicle to rev up and slow down, engine screaming in protest. Sitting beside her in the back, Ray had been convulsed in fits of mirth, finding the old man's attempts at driving hilarious, but Lynnie had been too scared to do more than clutch the door handle and keep her eyes fixed firmly ahead, willing the journey to come to an end.

As soon as the car stopped, she scrambled out before Ray had a chance to help her. 'I can't for a minute fathom how you found that in the least funny. As if I wasn't nervous enough about getting married! This hasn't helped me at all. I thought we were going to die, Ray, I really did. I'm walking back,' she hissed at him. 'There's no way I'm getting in that car again. Thank you, Mr Bevins,' she said to him, smiling as he looked at her through his window.

'My pleasure, ducky,' he said, beaming. 'Now I'll be waiting here ter tek you and yer new hubby back, so don't you fear.'

Before she could respond she heard her name being called and was confused to see her mother racing down the church path towards her. 'Go around again,' Avril was saying, gesticulating with her arms. She arrived level with them. 'Go around the block again, Lynnie.'

'Why?' she said, frowning.

'Anything wrong?' asked Ray.

Avril shook her head and said lightly, 'No, no. But the last wedding ran over a little and the Vicar isn't quite ready for you yet.'

'Oh!' Lynnie mouthed. The thought of getting back in a car with Mr Bevins behind the wheel terrified her witless.

'Right, back in yer get,' he urged them. 'I'll tek yer fer a slow drive around the outside of Braunstone Park. That should give the Vicar plenty of time to get himself together.'

Lynnie's eyes pleaded with Ray to do something.

He gave a shrug. 'Yer've no choice, Lynnie, unless yer want to upset the old geezer,' he whispered.

That was the last thing she wanted to do to the kindly old gentleman and so Lynnie had no choice but to get back in the car. Sighing resignedly and with Avril looking on, she gathered her dress around her and climbed back in while Ray got in the other side. Mr Bevins rammed the car into gear and, jolting and jerking, set off again.

Back in the Shoulder of Mutton, Gerry placed Ozzie's third pint of that morning before him, relieved him of his money, which he put in the till, then went back to drying glasses. After a while he looked at Ozzie, bothered. 'You all right?' he asked.

'Yeah, fine, top of the world, why yer asking?' he said irritably.

''Cos yer seem anything but, that's why I'm asking.'

Ozzie grunted as he took a large gulp of his drink. 'I'm a condemned man, that's why I look like this,' he muttered sarcastically.

Gerry's eyes widened in surprise as he stacked a pile

of clean glasses under the counter. 'Condemned!' he exclaimed, straightening up to look at Ozzie. 'You're hardly that.'

'Huh, yer don't think so, eh?'

'No, I bleddy don't. Just the opposite in fact. Good lord, man, there's half the males on this estate would give their eye teeth to be in your shoes today. How can you say yer condemned when yer've landed yerself someone like Lynnie? You're one lucky man, and if you don't realise that now then it's about time you did.'

Ozzie eyed him blearily. 'I'm getting married today, so how the hell can yer say I'm lucky? Lucky is staying exactly as I am. You're a married man, Gerry, so you know fine well what I'm talking about. All that responsibility. Bills ter pay. Never having any money of yer own. Having ter do things like, well ... decorating, gardening, and when kids come along ... I mean that's another worry, ain't it?' He looked at Gerry quizzically. 'Didn't you feel scared about taking the plunge?'

He laughed. ''Course I did, mate. Fucking terrified if yer want the truth, and if yer asked a million married men the same question they'd say they were too.'

'Then why did yer do it? Why does any man give up his freedom to land himself with all that?'

'Why? 'Cos deep down we want to, that's why. Well, the majority of us do if we're honest. Some men, I grant yer, get saddled with the wrong woman and try and make the best of it. Or they do meet the right woman but treat her badly so make their own life hell in consequence. Me, well I wanted to be with my

Sylvie, that's why I married her. I wanted to cuddle up to her every night and look at her face across the table each morning, and if I'm honest it was about time I left home. Don't get me wrong, I enjoyed being a single man, out with me mates most nights, lots of girlfriends and having me mam running around after me, but when I met my Sylvie I knew a good thing when I saw one and it was either marry her or lose her to someone else that would. She was a good-looking woman then, Ozzie. Well, I still think she is.'

Ozzie looked at him incredulously. 'But she nags yer.'

Gerry chuckled. 'Yeah, she does go on a bit sometimes, doesn't she? But then she wouldn't have ter if I gave her some consideration now and again and did what I had to before she got herself all worked up. But I don't, so the nagging's my own fault. I can be a lazy bastard when I want ter be. Most men try and get out of doing things until their women have reached a stage where they're threatening to cut their conjugals off or leave 'em. It's men's nature, is that. Like it's women's nature to rule the roost. But I tell you summat for n'ote, Ozzie, if it wasn't for my Sylvie pushing me on I'd still be plodding away on the factory line, having hardly anything ter show for all me years of work. Me going for the tenancy of this pub was all her doing, yer know, nagging me to make something of meself. Without her behind me I dread ter think what my life would be like. Oh, there's bin times when I could cheerfully have strangled her, but on the whole me and most men

201

wouldn't be where we are today if it wasn't for our wives.'

Ozzie thoughtfully stared down at his beer then brought his eyes back to Gerry. 'All me mam and dad do is snipe at each other. I'm worried me an' Lynnie will turn out like them.'

'And yer will if you treat Lynnie like yer dad treats yer mother, Ozzie. Your dad is one of those blokes that think wives are just around to wait on them while they sit on their fat arse doing nothing. I can't remember the last time he brought her in here for a drink, but he's always in here himself.'

Ozzie couldn't argue with that as he knew it was the truth. 'But me brothers never seem happy. As soon as they got married, I saw a change in them.'

Gerry laughed. 'Your brothers ain't happy! Ged off, Ozzie. All three of them are like pigs in shit. Trouble with you is, you don't want to think they're happy, so yer don't.'

'But they're always moaning about bills and things.'

The landlord laughed. 'All men moan when their wives ain't in earshot, it's what we do best. Have any of yer brothers left their wife and gone home to your mam?'

Ozzie looked at him blankly and shook his head. 'No.'

'Well then, knowing them as well as I do from them practically living in here before they wed, I'd say if they were as miserable as you think they are they'd have upped sticks a long time ago. The change in them you saw when they got married is called growing up, Ozzie, and we all have ter do that sometime, whether we get married or not.' He looked at the young man pityingly. 'I feel sorry for your type, Ozzie, I really do. Yer want a good woman around when it pleases you, but yer think that fooling around with yer mates is what life's all about.

'Listen ter me, lad, yer might live with yer mam now and have everything done for yer but that state of affairs won't last for ever. Sooner or later yer'd end up living on yer own, having to do everything for yerself. All yer mates would eventually have settled down so you'd have no single friends to muck about with then either. Fancy a lonely old age, do yer, Ozzie? 'Cos that's what yer heading for. But what I can't understand is why, if yer so against getting married, yer let it go this far with Lynnie? She of all people don't deserve being jilted at the altar.'

Gerry noticed a customer trying to get his attention and called over, 'Be with yer in a minute, squire.' He then leaned across the counter and looked Ozzie straight in the eye. 'Beds can be cold lonely places, mate, and sitting at a table eating by yerself ain't no fun either, after yer've cooked yer meal yerself that is. Okay, at the moment yer young, good-looking, getting a woman you can toss aside when yer fed up with her ain't a problem for you. But eventually we all grow old, and finding a woman that'll put up with your selfish ways will be hard then even for you.

'Marriage to the right woman is great, Ozzie, and to

my mind, knowing what I do of Lynnie, you couldn't have done better for yerself than her. Still, seems you've made your decision, I just hope yer don't live to regret it, that's all I can say. Now if yer'll excuse me, I've other customers ter see to.'

Ozzie stared at Gerry in shock as he moved away to serve another customer. These opinions of marriage from Gerry, a hard, no-nonsense man who had the ability to single-handedly see off the premises anyone causing the slightest trouble, however big they were or whatever state of intoxication they were in, were the very last Ozzie had expected and were forcing him to see the whole concept in a completely new light. He suddenly saw how stupid he had been to be frightened of taking this step with Lynnie, thinking that as soon as he did all he counted as important to him would be over. Gerry had made him realise that marriage was only the next phase of his life, and how good it was, would be up to him.

Instead of opposing Lynnie and causing himself strife, it was up to him to work alongside her as a partner should, embracing their future by helping her build a home and family together. Lynnie was no dictator who once she had a ring on her finger would want to control what he did every minute of the day or expect him to hand over every penny of his money for her to use as she wished, he having no say. She was fair and just, and wanted to marry him because she loved him enough to live out her life with him. He suddenly knew without doubt that that was what he wanted with her, had done all along but been too blinkered by his self-imposed belief that marriage was a jail sentence to admit it.

He knocked back what was left of his beer and put the empty glass on the counter. 'Thanks, Gerry,' he said gratefully as the man moved towards him. 'Thanks for making me see . . .'

'Sense at last,' he cut in. 'My pleasure, mate.' He glanced at the clock on the wall over Ozzie's head. 'Pity we didn't have this chat earlier then, ain't it? Another pint?'

Ozzie flicked back his sleeve and glanced at his watch. It read just after half-past twelve. He had time for another drink but suddenly didn't want one. He wanted to be at the church waiting for Lynnie to arrive. 'No, thanks. I think I've had enough for a man who's about to get married. And I tell you, Gerry, I can't wait to make Lynnie my wife.'

Gerry looked at him quizzically. 'I thought the ceremony was at one?'

Ozzie frowned at him questioningly. 'Yeah, that's right.'

'Well, unless me eyes are deceiving me the pub clock says it's just gone half-past one and I know it's right 'cos I set it meself only this morning before I opened up.'

'Eh?' Ozzie spun around and as his eyes caught sight of the clock on the wall behind him they blazed in shock. He jerked out his arm and looked at his wrist watch again. 'But . . .' He held it to his ear. 'Oh, bugger!' he exclaimed. 'Oh, hell, no, no! I must have been so drunk last night I forgot to wind it up and it's been slowing down all morning. Gerry, why didn't yer say something?' he furiously demanded.

'I tried but yer jumped down me throat. You kept looking at yer watch so I thought yer knew what time it was. I thought yer'd decided not to go ahead. That's why I had a go at yer about jilting Lynnie at the altar.'

Ozzie's face paled to a deathly white and contorted in horror. 'Oh, shit, I never realised that's what yer were getting at. Oh, God! Oh, God!' he cried, dashing out of the pub.

A few seconds later a man arrived at the bar. 'Was that Ozzie I just saw flying up the road like his tail was on fire? I thought he was getting married to Lynnie at one?'

Gerry ruefully shook his head. 'So did he. Now what can I get yer?'

Ten minutes earlier, a pale-faced Lynnie had exhaled in tremendous relief when Mr Bevins jerked the car to a halt outside the church once more. He turned his head and beamed at them. 'There yer go, safe and sound.'

She gave him a weak smile.

'Champion, Mr Bevins. Thanks very much,' said Ray, equally as relieved as he clambered out. He was just about to run around and help Lynnie when he stopped short on spotting his mother running towards them. She arrived breathlessly and pulled him out of earshot of Lynnie. 'Can yer go around again, son?' she urged.

He looked at her, astounded. 'What! You are joking, Mam? Why, yer'd have to chain and padlock me and Lynnie inside that car before yer'll ever get us to ride in it again with Mr Bevins behind the wheel.'

'I ain't joking, Ray. Just once more around the block, please, I beg yer.'

'What's going on, Mam?'

Avril spun round to face Lynnie who had now got out of the car and was making her way towards them, her face wreathed in questions. 'Oh, ducky, it's . . . er . . . it's that clumsy Vicar. He's . . . er . . . fell up the altar steps and sprained his ankle. We're just waiting for the doctor to get here to strap him up then we can get on.'

Lynnie's eyes narrowed, brow furrowing deeply. Her mother was extremely anxious, like a cat dancing on hot coals. All her instincts told her that the story about the Vicar was a ruse to cover the real reason why the ceremony was being delayed. A terrible feeling of foreboding filled her and her stomach churned. 'First the Vicar's running late, now he's sprained his ankle. Seems a bit far-fetched to me.' Then she spotted the Vicar heading down the church steps and hurrying across to them, and could see no sign of a limp. 'Seems the man in question has had a miraculous recovery. What's really wrong, Mam?' she demanded.

Avril turned her head and to her horror saw the Vicar heading their way. She looked back at her daughter, mouth opening and closing like a fish. 'Well, God really does look after his own, don't he?' she said, an innocent expression on her face.

'Mam, stop it,' Lynnie erupted. Suddenly the truth hit her and her heart thumped erratically. 'It's Ozzie, isn't it? It is, Mam. He's . . . he's not here, is he?'

Avril gulped, her brain whirling madly as it searched for something else with which to fob Lynnie off. Unfortunately nothing came to her. Sighing with resignation, she took a deep breath. 'No, lovey, he ain't arrived yet and his mam reckons she doesn't know where he is. He was all dressed ready and they were waiting downstairs for him to join them to toast his future happiness before they left for church but then she spotted him running out of the house, saying he was going for a walk and he'd meet them here.'

The Vicar caught up with them. 'I'm afraid I can't hold off any longer. The next party will be arriving soon.'

'Just give us five minutes,' Avril urged him. 'Please?'

He gave a deep sigh. 'Five minutes but no longer,' he said, hurrying back to the church.

'Has anyone gone ter look for Ozzie?' demanded Ray.

Avril shook her head. 'Well, no, 'cos . . . well, we told everyone that it's Lynnie that's late.'

'Why?' she demanded.

''Cos Ozzie's mam was worried his dad and brothers would go and look for him but end up supping in the pub, that's why. We women were just trying to keep the men where we could keep an eye on them.'

Lynnie's face screwed up. 'I bet that's where you'll find Ozzie.'

Avril looked at her, shocked. 'What, down the pub? No, he wouldn't. Not today, surely?'

Ray's face turned thunderous. 'I'll go down the Mutton and if Ozzie's there he won't know what's hit him, believe me he won't. How dare he keep my sister waiting?'

He made to dash off but Lynnie grabbed his arm. 'No, you won't. Take me home, please, Ray.'

'But . . .'

'Please. I'm not having my brother force Ozzie to do something he obviously doesn't want to.'

'Oh, come on, Lynnie, this is Ozzie all over. Yer might have guessed he'd be late. He's never on time for anything,' said her mother.

Lynnie was fighting back tears of distress. Her bottom lip trembling, she stuttered, 'I appreciate you trying to defend Ozzie, Mam. But this is our wedding day. If anyone has a right to be late it's me. He should have been here ages ago. He chose having a drink over marrying me.'

'Ah, now come on, Lynnie,' Ray piped up. 'Yer don't know that. He might not be in the pub. He might have had an accident or summat.'

'And pigs might fly, Ray! Ozzie's made a fool of me once too often.'

'Just give him another five minutes, Lynnie,' her mother begged.

'Mam, he's over half an hour late already and . . .'

Just then she heard her name being called and turned to see Ozzie racing towards her. They all stared at him as he drew up to them breathlessly.

'Where the bleddy hell have you been?' Avril shouted at him.

He ignored her, looking directly at Lynnie. 'Oh, God, I'm sorry I'm late, Lynnie, but me watch stopped.'

Her face devoid of any expression, she said, 'Your watch stops a lot according to you, Ozzie. You should see about getting yourself one that works.'

He grinned at her. 'You could get me one for Christmas. One of those ones yer don't have ter wind up. Are we going in then?'

Despite desperately wanting to rip into him, Lynnie fought to keep her dignity. 'You can if you like,' she said evenly. 'But I'm going home.' She spun round to face Ray. 'If you won't come with me, I'll go by myself.'

She made to get back into Mr Bevins's car but Ozzie, his face bewildered, grabbed her arm to stop her. 'But Lynnie,' he cried, 'I said I was sorry I'm late! Me watch has stopped, really it has.'

Facing him now, she gave a small laugh. 'You can't even think of a new excuse, can you, Ozzie? I forget how many times you've told me that one and like an idiot I've always forgiven you. But not this time.' She lost her composure then. Tears spurting, she hurtled at him, 'You've been in the pub, I can smell it on you! How could you do this to me, Ozzie? How could you?

How could you?' Then, gathering up her dress, she fled.

Ozzie kicked up his heels and chased after her, continuously calling out for her to stop. Avril made to follow but Ray held her back. 'Leave 'em to it, Mam.'

'Oh, but . . .'

'Mam,' he said warningly. 'Let them sort it out themselves.'

Avril wasn't happy but she did as her son bade.

Ozzie caught up with Lynnie as she ran across Braunstone Park. He managed to grab her arm and pull her to a halt. Gasping for breath, he blurted, 'Lynnie, please, listen to me. I'm sorry, really I am. I just popped into the pub for a hair of the dog and thought I'd plenty of time. Yer've got ter believe me, me watch stopped, really it did.'

She wrenched her arm free from his grasp and, gulping for breath, told him, 'There's a clock in the pub, Ozzie, and practically everyone in there including the landlord knew we were getting married today. Are you telling me no one mentioned the time to you? Don't bother spinning me a line, Ozzie, 'cos the truth of it is if you really wanted to marry me, you wouldn't have been in the pub in the first place.'

He looked at her awkwardly. 'I know. I know that, Lynnie, but . . . but, well, I was just . . . just . . .'

Her jaw dropped as sudden realisation filled her. 'You needed a drink because you were terrified of getting married to me, weren't you, Ozzie?' she uttered. Grief-stricken, she searched his face. 'It's all my fault. I

211

always had niggling doubts as to whether you would actually do it or not, but after we'd finally set the date, I thought, This is it. Ozzie really does want to settle down with me. But all the time you didn't, did you?'

He gave a shrug. 'Yeah . . . no . . . Oh, I dunno, Lynnie. I was just scared of all the responsibilities.'

Her face filled with hurt. 'This is not just about you being scared of responsibilities. Don't think I've not had a few sleepless nights, bothered about how marriage was going to change my life. But my love and need to be with you squashed those fears. No, love has nothing to do with it because I know you love me. What I've been stupid not to realise is that you simply don't want a wife, Ozzie. You want to keep your life exactly the way it is. That's the truth of it, isn't it?'

'It was, Lynnie,' he confessed. 'But not now. I want to get married, believe me I do. Gerry made me see . . .'

'Gerry? The landlord of the Mutton? You've been discussing this with him?'

'Well, yeah. I . . .'

'You never thought to talk to me so we could discuss this together? You didn't trust me enough to do that?'

Uncomfortably he scratched the back of his neck. 'It's nothing to do with not trusting yer, Lynnie.'

'Well, what then?' she snapped.

He pulled a face. 'I dunno . . . It ain't easy ter talk about things like this, is it?'

'Well, you seem to find it easy with Gerry. We've been together ten years and if you couldn't talk to me about your feelings after all we've been through, then you never will.'

A wave of acute pain crossed her face. 'Oh, why didn't I take notice of the signs? You using any excuse not to set a date, then when we finally did, leaving all the arrangements to me. I had practically to force you to go and see that flat, and don't think I didn't notice the relief on your face when it turned out to be so bad that we couldn't live there. It was you who persuaded me to leave looking for anywhere else until after we were married. And you haven't moved any of your belongings round to my mam's. You keep telling me that was because you were too busy but it wasn't, was it, Ozzie? It was because moving your stuff would've really brought home to you that you were doing the one thing you've fought tooth and nail against. But don't worry, I've finally taken the hint. What you did today has finally shown me what you think of me.'

His face twisted in confusion. 'What d'yer mean? All I've done is arrive a bit late.'

It astounded her to realise that he hadn't a clue just what he had done to her. 'Ozzie, without a thought for what I'd be feeling, you left me waiting at the church door while you stood at the bar, deciding over a drink whether to go ahead with marrying me or not.'

'It weren't like that, Lynnie. I told yer, me watch stopped. I only meant to have a quick pint to . . . well, yeah, okay I admit it . . . to give me courage.'

'Courage! If you really loved me and wanted me as your wife you wouldn't have needed that courage. Pete was desperate to make Shirley his wife and you laughed at him for being at the church an hour before the ceremony started. You more than anyone else took the mickey out of him, for showing us all how much he loved her. When anyone announced they were getting married your comment was always that they'd sealed their own doom. I thought it was just your way of having a joke but I was so wrong. You were describing what you yourself felt about getting married.'

He was looking at her, stupefied. 'Yeah, well, I was wrong to do that, I see that now. Look, Lynnie, why yer making all this fuss? I've said I'm sorry.'

'And that makes everything right, does it, you saying sorry?'

'Well, yeah, don't it?'

'In the past it might have but not now.'

'Well, what d'yer want me ter do then?' he snapped sarcastically. 'Get down on me bended knee?'

'You never even did that when you asked me to marry you,' she said, a hint of irony in her voice. Hurt and angry, she blurted, 'Go back to the pub and get drunk with your mates. Have a good laugh about this. Tell them all about your lucky escape.'

He looked at her, bewildered. 'Eh? But I don't understand!'

'Ozzie, I'm not spending the rest of my life knowing you only married me because the landlord of the pub talked you into it.'

'He never talked me into it at all. It wasn't like that. He just . . . well, he just made me . . .' He avoided her eyes before adding, 'See that I was wrong to think yer life's over when you tie the knot.'

'Oh, he made you see sense? Well, I'm glad someone has at long last. Maybe you won't be so quick to take the mickey out of anyone getting married in future.'

He ignored her jibe and said, 'Well, are we gonna get on with this then?'

'*Get on with this?* It's the most important event of our lives and you make it sound like a trip to the dentist. Something you want to hurry up and get over with 'cos it's so painful for you.'

He gave a long-suffering sigh. 'Oh, come on, Lynnie, we're quits now 'cos we're both to blame for being late after you throwing this little tantrum. You've made yer point and I'm getting fed up now.'

Her jaw dropped. 'A little tantrum! Is that what you think it is? And you're fed up, are you? I don't suppose you've given a thought to how I feel. Oh, Ozzie, you really haven't a clue, have you? After all I just said to you, you still think I'm just having a go at you for being late.'

'Well, yeah, that's what it was all about, ain't it? Come on, Lynnie, they'll all be waiting, and I don't know about you but I'm looking forward to the good do afterwards.'

She looked at him, astonished. 'It might surprise you to know, Ozzie, that I was the only one stupid enough to wait around for you. The Vicar will be conducting another wedding by now, and our families and friends will already be enjoying what should have been our reception, if they've any sense.'

He stared at her, shocked. 'Oh! What do we do now then, book another date?'

'Ozzie, you're not listening to me at all. You're not understanding what I'm trying to tell you.' Tears stung her eyes, a lump in her throat almost choked her, and she said the words she'd never thought to hear herself say and at this moment didn't know whether she meant or not. Regardless she still said it. 'I don't want to marry you any more.'

He looked at her for several long moments, then gave a snort of annoyance. 'Look, Lynnie, if yer trying to punish me, yer've succeeded. Now stop being daft. 'Course yer want to marry me. Christ's sake, yer never stopped going on about it. Besides, we've bin tergether for years so . . .'

'And that's maybe the trouble, Ozzie,' she cut in. 'We've been together that long you treat me like one of your mates, and I'm so used to it I accept it.'

He looked puzzled. 'I don't treat you like one of me mates.'

'Don't you? When was the last time you bought me any flowers?'

'Ah, don't, Lynnie. Soppy sods buy their women flowers. Besides I got you that bunch of daffys that time.'

'That you'd nicked from someone's garden! Don't think I didn't know that. And that was once in ten years. Other men buy their women flowers or choco-lates or just a little token now and again to show them how much they care, like I was always doing for you, to show you how much I loved you. You've never returned the compliment because the thought never crosses your mind that I might like a show of affection from you occasionally. But more importantly, the money those gifts would cost you'd sooner put across the bar of the Mutton.'

He raked his hands through his hair. This was all getting too much for him; he couldn't cope. He couldn't see the big deal. All he'd done was arrive a bit late for their wedding and now Lynnie was throwing all these insults at him. 'Look, I can't cope with you when yer in this mood. I'm off. I'll see yer when yer've calmed down.'

'And that's your answer to everything, isn't it, Ozzie? When anyone speaks the truth and you don't like it, you walk away. Well, go. But it's the last time you walk away from me.'

He looked at her contemptuously. 'Oh, stop it, Lynnie. How many times do yer want me to apologise for being late 'cos I was having the jitters? You're only making a big deal outta this to make me feel bad. Well, okay, I do feel rotten, but I've had enough now. As I said, I'll see yer when yer've calmed down.'

With that he turned and stormed off.

How long she stood staring in the direction he had gone in, frozen in shock, she had no idea. The next she knew she felt an arm being placed around her shoulders and heard herself being gently asked, 'Lynnie, are you okay?'

It was Sheila. Lynnie slowly turned her head and flashed her the briefest of smiles. 'Yeah, I'm fine,' she said tonelessly. 'Why wouldn't I be? My fiancé has just told me I'm making a big issue of the fact he left me waiting at the church while he propped up the bar deciding whether to marry me or not.'

Just then Shirley waddled up to them. 'Oh, God, I'm puffed out,' she said breathlessly. Arms hooked underneath her huge stomach as if holding it up, she uttered, 'I need ter sit down.'

She did look about to drop and Sheila removed her arms from around Lynnie and rushed over to her. 'I'm so sorry, Shirley,' she said apologetically. 'When I spotted Lynnie standing here all by herself, I just raced ahead and forgot about you. Come on, there's a bench over here,' she said, guiding her protectively over. 'Lynnie,' she called, 'come and give me a hand. Shirley's over-exerted herself. Lynnie!' she shouted.

Lynnie, who had lost herself again in a world of her own, looked over at them blankly. 'What? Oh!' she cried, realising what was going on and rushing over. 'Are you feeling all right, Shirley?' she asked, concerned now as she helped Sheila walk their pregnant friend over to a bench.

'Yeah, yeah, I'm fine,' she said, gently easing herself down. 'This little blighter weighs a ton. I think I'm having a baby hippo, I really do.' As soon as she was settled she asked, 'So what's happening about you and Ozzie? Yer mam came in the church and said summat about . . . well, I could hardly catch what she was saying but I heard the words "watch" and "stopped". Then everyone seemed to be piling out of the church and heading towards your house. Me and Sheila were worried about you and managed to catch hold of Ray. We had a job to get it out of him but he said you and Ozzie had headed off in the direction of the park to sort this out. We decided to come and look for you to check you were okay.' She suddenly stopped and, pulling a face, clutched her stomach. 'Ohhh!' she groaned in obvious discomfort.

'Are you all right?' both her concerned friends asked in unison.

She nodded. 'Just a testing pain, that's all. I've bin getting 'em for the last couple of weeks like the midwife at the 'firmary said I would. They were so bad last night I didn't get much sleep. Anyhow it's passing now.'

A shabbily dressed woman walking by laden down with shopping, several snotty-nosed, bedraggled children trailing behind her, looked at the three of them on the bench oddly.

Shirley giggled. 'She must think she's seeing things. A bride, a heavily pregnant woman, and you don't exactly look normal, Sheila, dressed up in yer best for a Saturday afternoon sitting in the park. Anyway what is going on, Lynnie? And where is Ozzie?'

She took a deep breath and, clasping her hands tightly, said, 'Probably down the pub with his mates, having a laugh over this. Or let's face it, he's brazen enough to turn up at me mam's house and join in with enjoying what should have been our wedding reception.' Her eyes filled with devastation. 'He never wanted to get married you know.'

'Oh, 'course he did, Lynnie,' Shirley said, aghast.

'No, he didn't. You know I had my doubts, Shirley, but I so wanted to marry him I ignored all the signs. Ozzie likes his life just the way it is and doesn't want to change it. He asked me to marry him when he was drunk and I should think he's regretted it ever since.' She looked stricken. 'Most couples meet, fall in love, court for a couple of years, then get married and live happily ever after. Well, hopefully. Ozzie just wanted to stay at the courting stage for ever only he hadn't got the guts to admit that to me.'

Both women were staring at her blankly.

'Guts or not, he should have told you how he felt before it had got this far,' said Sheila, annoyed.

Lynnie smiled weakly. 'He couldn't bring himself to, but he talked to Gerry down the pub though. Told him how he felt, and Gerry apparently persuaded him that he was wrong to feel like he did, so suddenly Ozzie wanted to get married.'

'Well, there you are then,' said Shirley. 'He *does* want to marry yer.'

Lynnie looked at her, astounded. 'Shirley, would you want to marry a man who was only doing it because the landlord of his local talked him into it?'

She gave a shrug. 'Yeah, I see yer point. I'd be a bit upset about that, so I suppose not.'

'And neither do I, and I'm more than a bit upset, let

me tell you. I want a man who wants to be with me so much he does just like your Pete did and starts pacing outside the church hours before the ceremony is due to start. And a man like your Everal, Sheila, who stood against everyone to marry the woman he loved. Ozzie would never do anything like that for me. Oh, I know he loves me in his own way but not enough to put me first. I come about fourth down the list. Mates, football and darts, then me.'

Shirley was frowning at her questioningly. 'Are yer saying it's over between yer then, Lynnie, for good?'

'I think Lynnie is too upset to know what she's feeling just now,' said Sheila. 'When they've both calmed down enough to think rationally, Lynnie and Ozzie need to meet and talk about whether they have any future together. We ought to get you home, Lynnie. It's very cold and you're going to catch your death in just your wed— in just your dress.'

'I can't go home!' she cried. 'I can't face all those people. Not at the moment. They're bound to want to know every detail of what went on between me and Ozzie. And he just might be there, and he's the last person I want to see at the moment.' She gave a violent shudder. 'Oh, this is so awful. All that work my mam and nan did. What everyone's done to make this day as special as they could. How am I going to face any of them?'

Sheila laid a comforting hand on hers. 'You don't have to until you're ready. You can come to my house and stay for as long as you like. I'll just let your mother know where you are.'

'Oh, God!'

Shirley's loud cry of anguish made both Lynnie and Sheila jump.

'What's wrong?' Lynnie demanded.

Her face was contorted in horror. 'I've pissed meself,' she uttered.

Both women glanced down to see the large puddle forming under Shirley's portion of the bench.

'Oh, she has!' exclaimed Lynnie.

Sheila tutted. 'No, she hasn't. Her waters have broken.'

Shirley gawped. 'Eh! Oh, yer mean . . .'

'Yes, your baby is coming. Those pains you've been having recently are labour pains, not testing ones. Lynnie, you stay with her while I run and telephone for an ambulance.'

'But Pete,' Shirley wailed. 'He doesn't know where I am. I never told him we were coming to look for Lynnie. I want him with me.' She suddenly grabbed Lynnie's hand and gripped it tightly. 'Oh, God,' she cried, her voice filled with terror. 'I'm getting more pains. Bad ones. Hurry, Sheila, hurry!'

Only moments after Sheila had run off, Lynnie heard Shirley's name being called and looked up to see Pete tearing across an expanse of grass towards them. Arriving breathless, he looked at his wife, still gripping Lynnie's hand but almost bent double, and panting heavily.

'What's going on?' he asked.

Before Lynnie could respond, Shirley screamed at him: 'Are you that stupid yer can't see your baby's coming? Ohhhh, fuck!' she bellowed. 'I'm getting another pain. Christ, I feel like me guts are being ripped open. Where's that fucking ambulance?' Eyes blazing furiously were fixed on her husband. 'This is all your fault,' she snarled. 'You did this to me. You come near me ever again and I'll kill you, you bastard.' Her face was bathed in sweat as she hissed at him, 'Don't just stand there like an idiot, do something!'

Lynnie was momentarily stunned by the fact this was all happening so quickly and shocked at the verbal abuse Shirley was directing at her husband. She gave herself a mental shake. 'Pete, Sheila's gone to tele-phone for an ambulance. Go and see if you can hurry it along,' she ordered.

'No,' cried Shirley. 'Don't leave me, Pete!' she begged him. 'Pete, don't leave me!'

He was staring at her, bewildered. 'What! But you've just said . . .'

'Pete, Shirley doesn't know what she's saying,' Lynnie cried. 'Go and see where the ambulance is,' she urgently ordered again.

His eyes danced wildly. He was in such a quandary he didn't know what to do. 'I can't leave, Shirl, Lynnie.'

'Okay, I'll go,' she said, making to jump up from the bench.

Shirley's already vice-like grip tightened on her hand. 'No,' she wailed. 'Don't leave me. Please don't leave me, Lynnie.'

Pete knelt down in front of her and took her other hand. 'We won't leave you, darling. We promise we won't.' He looked helplessly at Lynnie. 'What do we do?' he pleaded.

'Pray the ambulance arrives quick,' she mouthed at him.

'But we need towels, don't we, and hot water?'

'You stupid man,' his wife erupted again. 'Can't you see we're in the middle of a bleddy park? What you gonna do, sterilise the bench? Where the hell is that ambulance? Lynnie, Lynnie ... Ohhhhh, I'm getting another pain.'

Lynnie was at a loss. She'd never been in this situation before and had no idea what to do. 'Would you be more comfortable lying down?' she lamely asked.

'Yes,' urged Pete. 'Lie down until the ambulance comes, you'll feel better.'

'What would you know?' Shirley yelled back at him. 'Five minutes of fun for you and I go through nine months of lugging a baby elephant around and now this hell! I laid down once for you and landed up like this, I'll not lie down in a hundred miles of you ever again.'

'She doesn't mean it,' Lynnie said to him.

'I fucking do,' Shirley furiously shrieked. 'Oh, God, Lynnie, I want to push.'

Her mouth gaped in shock. 'But you can't, not yet! Labour goes on for hours.'

'Tell that to this baby. I want to push, I tell you.'

Lynnie's mind whirled frantically. Where was that ambulance? Her friend couldn't have her baby on a park bench in full view of everyone. Shirley's performance was beginning to attract the attention of several children who were congregating close by, straining to see what was happening, and she realised it wouldn't be long before others took an interest too and came over. Her head jerked around. At the back of them was an area of shrubs and trees. 'Pete, help me get Shirley into those bushes.'

'What?'

'Pete, just do as I ask.'

Lynnie prised her hand free from Shirley's grip, jumped up and placed the hand under her elbow. 'Shirley, we're just going to get you into those bushes over there so you can have some privacy while we wait for the ambulance to arrive.' She was mortally relieved that Shirley was in too much pain to protest.

Slowly and carefully, Pete and Lynnie supported Shirley, inching their way across to the shrubbery. Pete cleared the way through into a small clearing inside by pushing his weight against one of the bushes. Shirley, doubled over now, was intermittently shrieking out in pain and panting heavily and Lynnie knew she was also frightened. Gently they eased her down on to the hard ground.

Terrified eyes were fixed on Lynnie. 'I gotta push, Lynnie. Oh, hell, I can't stop.'

'Quick,' she ordered Pete. 'Help me get her knickers off.'

Ashen-faced, he looked at her, stupefied. 'Have yer delivered a baby before, Lynnie?'

She felt it best not to answer him. The nearest she'd seen to a baby being born was on 'Doctor Kildare' on the television, and then she'd never seen anything that would be of help now. None of the women in labour on the screen had screamed so loud or appeared to be suffering like Shirley was. Heart thundering, she demanded, 'Help me get her knickers off then go and look out for the ambulance. They'll need to know where we are.'

With a struggle as Shirley's writhing was not helping them they managed their task and immediately Pete shot off.

Shirley had drawn up her legs and Lynnie could see the top of the baby's head. She gulped in sheer terror, wishing she had gone for the ambulance. Sheila had had two children so was more equipped to handle this situation than Lynnie was. She had no choice, though. She had to deal with this as best she could, help her old friend deliver her baby safely. Despite her inexperience Lynnie's instincts told her that at any second now another contraction would come along, and with it an overwhelming desire for Shirley to push her baby into the world.

Then a thought struck her. Shirley needed

something clean under her for the baby to be delivered on. Her wedding dress! Without a thought for the dress's ruination, she jumped up, grabbed the hem at one side and, using all her strength, ripped it up to her thigh, then tugged with all her might until a wide strip of skirt was completely detached. As carefully and as quickly as possible she eased the piece of thick satin under Shirley's bottom. Just as she had finished, Shirley suddenly let out a scream so earth-shattering Lynnie almost jumped out of her skin. This was it, she thought. Shoving all her own fears aside, she shouted, 'Go on then, Shirl, push! Give it all you've got, gel.'

A few minutes later, Pete, Sheila and two ambulance men looked at the scene before them, choked with emotion. Lying on the hard ground in the middle of the bushes was a serene Shirley and nestling protectively in her arms, wrapped in what had been the bottom of Lynnie's wedding dress, was her baby.

A completely drained new mother smiled tiredly but lovingly up at her husband. 'We have a beautiful baby girl.'

'Oh, darling,' he uttered, falling down beside her, putting his arm gently around her, running a tender hand over her damp forehead, and kissing her lips. 'I love you,' he whispered.

She looked up at him. 'I love you too.'

Lynnie addressed the ambulance men. 'I'm sorry, I didn't know what to do about cutting the cord,' she said apologetically.

They both grinned at her and one said, 'Looks to us like yer should be extremely proud of what you've achieved already. We'll take it from here.'

A short while later, the ambulance along with the new baby and proud parents having departed for the maternity wing of the Royal Infirmary, Sheila and Lynnie were sitting next to each other on the park bench.

Sheila looked down at Lynnie's exposed legs and grinned. 'Good job minis are in fashion,' she quipped. Then her face grew serious. 'Are you all right, Lynnie?'

She took a deep breath and nodded. 'I can't believe what's just happened,' she uttered, her face filled with wonderment. 'Can you believe it, Sheila? I helped bring Shirley's baby into the world. I was terrified, I hadn't a clue what to do, but then suddenly I just sort of got on with it. Of course, I can't take all the credit. Most of that goes to Shirley, bless her. But the experience . . . Oh, Sheila, I'll never forget that, never, never. It really is a miracle, isn't it?'

She nodded, and remembering the emotional birth of her own beloved daughters said wistfully, 'You wouldn't think so much pain could bring so much joy.' She looked at Lynnie in concern then. 'It's been an eventful day for you, hasn't it? So how are you, Lynnie?'

She gave a shrug. 'I don't honestly know. While all this has been going on I forgot about my situation.' What had transpired with Ozzie – the ruination of her wedding day and the reasons behind it – suddenly hit her full force and her face crumpled, huge fat tears cascading down it.

Without further ado, Sheila put her arms around her and pulled her close. 'Come on,' she said softly, helping her up. 'Let's get you to my house.'

Chapter Eleven

The door of Mallin's Turf Accountant burst open and a dripping wet Ray shot through. 'Bloody weather,' he grumbled, hurriedly shutting the door and making a puddle on the wooden floor when he shook himself down. The shop was empty of customers, save for old Willy Noble who was perched in his usual spot on the bench underneath the Tannoy which at the moment was silent as there were a couple of hours to go before the first race of the day which started at two o'clock. Ray went across to the counter and in front of Lynnie put down a bulky time bag, something that all runners carried to record the time of the bets they took. 'Not a bad haul today, considering.'

Lynnie, who had been tallying some figures from bets she'd received earlier, looked up at him distractedly. 'Considering what?'

He gave a shrug. 'I dunno. The foul weather; not much spare money around; the fact people are saving up to put a good-sized bet on the Grand National in two weeks' time. It was just something I said, that's all,

I didn't mean anything by it.'

'Oh, I see,' she replied, picking up the bag which she put under the counter to deal with later, then immediately went back to tallying her figures.

Ray leaned on the counter and looked at her in concern. 'You all right, Lynnie?'

Continuing with her task, she replied. 'Yes, thank you. I couldn't be better.'

Ray knew by her brisk reply that his sister was not being truthful. She was far from her usual bubbly self and hadn't been since her ill-fated wedding day nearly six months ago. On returning to the bosom of her family, having spent what should have been her wedding night secreted at the Johnsons', Lynnie had made it very clear that what if anything the future held for herself and Ozzie, she wasn't prepared to discuss. She severely warned her family not to interfere in any way, however good their intentions. Regardless of her outward calm, Ray suspected his sister was still deeply distressed.

Despite her warning for them all to stay out of her business, his deep-seated brotherly protectiveness had come to the fore. Behind her back, several weeks after the cancelled wedding he'd squashed a great desire to attack Ozzie, both physically and verbally, and instead sought him out to see if he could do anything by way of healing their rift.

Ray hid his anger on finding Ozzie down the pub with his friends surrounded by several girls, noting that one in particular was paying great attention to him and that Ozzie seemed to be lapping it up.

'Not wasting any time, I see,' Ray snapped at the man whose thoughtlessness had cost his sister dear.

The shock on Ozzie's face at being found in such a compromising position had been most apparent. He'd pushed the girl away from him so abruptly she almost toppled over. 'Well, if yer expecting me to become a monk just 'cos Lynnie don't want me . . .' he snapped defensively.

'Do yer know she doesn't want yer then? Have yer even been to see her?'

''Tain't up ter me to go and crawl to her. I apologised, not once but several times, and she wouldn't accept it. She knows I love her. She knows where she can find me. So what more am I supposed to do?'

Ray could see his point but regardless felt it very remiss of Ozzie not to put up more of a fight to persuade Lynnie of his sincerity. 'Well, doing nothing ain't gonna sort anything out, is it? Lynnie needs more to convince her that you mean business, Ozzie.'

'Oh, yer mean flowers and chocolates, that kinda thing?'

Ray knew that it would take more than a bunch of flowers and a box of Dairy Milk to lessen the rift between this pair. 'It'll tek more than that, Ozzie. You let my sister down badly and she'll need concrete proof you ain't gonna do it again.'

'Such as?'

For a moment Ray was at a loss as to what to suggest. 'I dunno.'

'Well, if you don't, how am I supposed ter?'

'So you're just going to give up on my sister, are yer?'

'No. I've already told yer, I chased after her and begged her to go ahead with the wedding. She refused so it's up to her now.' He heaved a sigh and his face took on a hurt expression. 'Look, Ray, I pray Lynnie'll come back to me. Every time the doorbell goes, I hope it's her. Every time I come down the pub, I hope she's here. But it's obvious to me she's avoiding me 'cos I ain't seen hide nor hair of her since . . . well, yer know when. Now considering we only live a couple of streets away from each other, I think I've drawn the right conclusion, don't you? As I said, I apologised several times for being late. Me watch stopped and that's the truth of it. If she won't accept my apology I can't force her, can I? Besides . . .' His voice trailed off and his expression turned mulish, before he added, 'She told me she didn't want to marry me any more.'

'I ain't surprised in the circumstances! She was angry. Upset. Wouldn't you be if Lynnie had left you waiting on the church steps while she was supping at the bar in the Mutton?'

Ozzie hung his head. 'Yeah, well, I suppose so.' He lifted his head and looked Ray straight in the eye. 'But she hurt me an' all with some of the things she said, and I deserve an apology too. As I said, Ray, she knows where she can find me when she finally comes to her senses.'

Ray narrowed his eyes and looked at him darkly. 'And in the meantime you'll sow a few wild oats, eh?'

He flashed a look at the girl he had caught draped over Ozzie when he'd arrived and who was now hovering nearby. It was obvious to Ray she was waiting for him to leave so she could take up where she'd left off.

'There's n'ote wrong with having a bit of fun meantime, is there?' Ozzie said cockily.

'I hope fer your sake Lynnie doesn't find out.'

'Might do her good if she does. It might mek her realise how lucky she is to have me.'

Ray shook his head at him, fighting the urge to grab him by the scruff of his neck and drag him back to face Lynnie and sort this mess out. Fearing if he stayed longer he'd say or do something he'd severely regret, he turned and walked out.

Now Ray leaned his weight on the counter and looked at his sister. 'Why don't you go and see him, Lynnie?'

She raised her head and stared at him blankly. 'By *him* I trust you mean Ozzie?'

'Don't play games with me, Lynnie, you know damned well who I mean.'

'And why should I do that? He hasn't made any attempt to see me.'

'Because he's waiting for you to go and see him, that's why.'

She frowned at him quizzically. 'How do you know?'

'Eh? Oh, I don't,' he said hurriedly. 'I'm just guessing.'

She said knowingly, 'Despite me asking you not to, you've been to see him, haven't you? You have, haven't you, Ray?'

He eyed her sheepishly. 'All right, I admit it. If I hadn't have, Mam and Nan would have, and knowing how Mam feels about Ozzie he probably would have ended up in hospital and any hope of you ever getting back together would be gone fer good, so I thought it'd better be me.'

She looked at her brother for several long moments before flashing him a grateful smile. 'Mam and Nan have made it very plain they think I should have nothing more to do with him after what happened and I can't blame them for feeling as they do. But between them, Ray, they're driving me mad, constantly nagging me to go out and enjoy myself. They keep telling me there's plenty more fish in the sea. That's may be so, Ray, but meeting someone else . . . well, I know it's stupid but I feel that would be betraying Ozzie somehow. I just wish they'd leave me alone. I just wish you'd *all* leave me alone.'

'We're worried about you, Lynnie. We love you. All of us know deep down that yer unhappy.'

'Ray, I need to deal with this in my own way. I don't know how I feel at the moment, I really don't. Part of me misses Ozzie like hell and the other part is so relieved because I think I've had a lucky escape.' She looked at her brother for several long moments as she debated whether to ask him a question or not. Curiosity got the better of her. 'So . . . so what did Ozzie say when you saw him?'

'Just that he's apologised several times for showing up late at the wedding and if you won't accept it then he doesn't know what else to do. I know he's missing you badly, Lynnie, and wants to put things right between yer both.'

'Well, why hasn't he been to see me then?'

'As I've already told you, because you refused to accept his apology he feels it's up to you to go and see him. Come on, Lynnie, it's obvious yer still love him so why don't yer swallow yer pride before it really is too late?'

She looked at her brother, astounded. 'Me swallow my pride! What about Ozzie swallowing his? Just what is it with you men? You think you can treat us women any way you like and we'll love you enough to forgive you anything. That might have been the way of things in the past but this is the sixties, Ray, and we women have realised we don't have to bow down to men all the time. We have rights too. I've forgiven Ozzie so much in the past. This time he owes it to me at least to attempt to put things right between us. Do you have any idea how much he hurt me?'

'Yeah, 'course I have.'

She shook her head. 'No, I don't think you do or you wouldn't be telling me that I should go and see him and sort this out. As if you need reminding, he left me standing at the altar while he decided over a few pints whether he wanted to give up his freedom. It took a grilling from the landlord for him to make his decision. He then tried to fob me off with his usual excuse that his watch had stopped, and expected me to carry on like I should be grateful he'd eventually turned up.

Getting married is the most important thing in anyone's life, Ray. How would you feel if someone you had been courting for ten years, loved enough to want to spend the rest of your life with, did to you what Ozzie did to me, then expected you to go crawling round to them and pretend it didn't matter and have a good laugh over it?'

He gave a deep sigh. 'Yeah, I see your point, Lynnie, but for God's sake, gel, six months have passed since all that happened. Surely you've calmed down by now?'

'Calmed down!' she exclaimed, and gave a deep sigh of annoyance. 'Oh, Ray, just let's drop this subject, shall we? You're a man, you'll never understand. Anyway, you'd better go and dry off before you catch your death.'

He shook his head at her before he went.

Lynnie stared after him, her face set. She knew Ray was right and this situation between herself and Ozzie needed to be sorted out once and for all. She couldn't carry on jumping every time there was a knock at the door, her confused mood swinging between hoping it was Ozzie yet at the same time praying it was not. She couldn't keep taking the long route home, avoiding streets where she knew she might bump into him, yet part of her wishing she would. In reality since that dreadful day she had become for the most part a recluse, spending hours in solitude staring out of her bedroom window. Apart from going to work, when she did venture out socially it was only to visit Shirley or Sheila. She knew she couldn't go on like this or she'd go mad and life would have passed her by. She also knew her family were deeply worried about her. Even Dec and Jimmy, who were both usually too wrapped up in their own lives to notice much about any of the other family members unless it was forcibly pointed out to them, had asked her to go out to a night club with them, which she had politely but flatly refused.

She ran her hands wearily over her face. It seemed to her that her life had suddenly come to a fork in the road, two paths going in opposite directions. One led back to Ozzie, the other God knew where. It suddenly struck her that she would forever be stuck at that fork unless she faced him and found out if there was enough left between them to re-establish their relationship or else confirm it was definitely over. One way or another it had to be done. It was obvious from what Ray had told her that Ozzie wasn't going to come and see her, so she would have to go and see him. She made a decision. She would go tonight.

She jumped when she realised Ray had come back and was addressing her. 'Sorry, what did you say?'

'I asked if yer wanted some chips for yer lunch? Sid's just given me the money to treat us all.'

'Oh, that's nice of him. I'm not sure if I'm hungry or not. I've got an apple in my bag.'

'Oh, come on, Lynnie, an apple's not going to do yer much good. You've picked at your food since . . . since . . . You'll end up a bag of bones if yer carry on like this.'

'Okay, okay, stop going on. Just to shut you up I'll

have a tanner's worth of chips and a buttered cob, thank you.' She flashed a look at the pathetic figure of Willy Noble sitting on the bench. 'Get Willy some too, Ray.'

A while later, having had her fill of her lunch, Lynnie screwed up what remained in the newspaper and threw it in the bin. Leaving Ray in charge of the counter, she went through to the tiny kitchen next to Sid's office to mash a pot of tea for them all. As she walked past her boss's office she popped her head around the door. 'Cuppa, Mr Mallin?'

He jumped, startled at her unexpected appearance. 'God, you nearly gave me a heart attack,' he uttered, clutching his chest. Popping a chip in his mouth, he pointed to the rumpled sheet of newspaper they had been wrapped in and said, 'I was engrossed in reading about a bank robbery that took place in Birmingham last week. I don't often read the news in the paper, I'm only interested in the racing pages. News is depressing, ain't it? Ban the Bomb marches. Mods and Rockers beating each other to a pulp on Brighton Pier. Long-haired louts calling themselves pop groups wrecking rooms in hotels. The world's going mad, Lynnie.

'Anyway, I can't believe the nerve of the cheeky beggars what did that robbery. Seems they rented an empty shop next door to the bank, and during Saturday afternoon and into the hours of Sunday morning broke their way into the bank's cellar then up through the safe-room floor, blowing the safe before making off with close on sixty thousand pounds.'

'Blimey, that's a fortune!' she exclaimed. 'That amount would set anyone up for life. Well, it would me. Have the police caught them?'

'Dunno. This is just the initial report on the robbery. It ain't right but in a way yer've got to admire the gall of some people. That robbery must have taken some planning and nerve to carry out.' He popped the last of his chips into his mouth and screwed up the newspaper. 'That was grand. Good chips that Eyetie meks, for a foreigner. Cuppa? Yes, I'd love one, thanks, Lynnie ducky. Many punters out front?'

'Bit slow today, Mr Mallin, due to the weather as it's still raining cats and dogs and doesn't look like it's going to let up. But the runners have all come back and they seem to have done okay, especially our Ray.'

He leaned back in his chair, clasped his hands in front of his protruding paunch and smiled at her. 'I'm glad I took your advice, Lynnie, and gave your Ray a chance. He's turning up trumps. I know you'll understand when I say I watched him like a hawk for quite a while after he started here but not once have I had cause to regret taking him on. He seems to enjoy his mornings out and about collecting the bets, and he's picked up quite a few new customers. I'm actually thinking of asking him to come down to Leicester Races to stand with me at the rails taking the bets. Be an eye opener for him and then he can start to learn that side of things. Whaddya think, Lynnie?'

'I think our Ray would love to be given the opportunity and there's no one better to learn from than you,

241

Mr Mallin. Going back to those new customers Ray's procured from his running . . . did you know they're mostly women?' She gave a laugh. 'He says they can't resist his charms.'

'Well, yer can't deny your brother is a good-looking man, Lynnie. Pity betting shops aren't seen as places for the majority of women otherwise mine would be swamped when he's behind the counter. Shame really, it would up me profits.' And he added hurriedly, 'Not that I don't realise some of the men come in just to see your pretty face.'

'Oh, away with you,' she laughed. 'The only proposition I've ever had was from Wilf Warren and he's stopped that now . . .'

He eyed her quizzically as she suddenly stopped mid-sentence. 'Now what, Lynnie?'

She had been on the verge of saying since she'd stopped buying his knock-off meat. 'Oh, just since I threatened to tell his wife.'

Sid chuckled then looked at her meaningfully. 'It's my opinion there ain't any man comes into my shop that's good enough for you, Lynnie.' He paused and cleared his throat, looking at her tentatively. 'Er . . .'

Her instincts told her that Sid was going to ask her what the situation was between herself and Ozzie. She stopped him by saying, 'I'll go and put the kettle on.'

Later that night Lynnie pushed her nearly full plate of food away and made to rise.

'I'm getting sick and tired of you not finishing yer

dinner,' scolded her mother. 'You'll waste away carrying on like this, not to mention the waste of good food.'

'Yer mam's right, Lynnie lovey, yer'll end up with something nasty if yer don't eat yer greens,' chided her grandmother.

Lynnie felt it best not to say that in her opinion tinned processed peas could not be classed in the same light as fresh vegetables. 'You piled my plate, Nan, giving me far too much, but what I ate was lovely, thank you.' What she had said was not exactly the truth. Her grandmother, in an attempt to help out the family by cooking the evening meal, had burned the sausages, which being the cheap ones they were had had pieces of gristle in them and the gravy had been lumpy. But she was very conscious Freda had done her best and like the rest of the family always praised her for whatever she put before them. 'If everyone's finished, I'll make a start on the dishes,' she said, making to rise.

'There's pudding. Rice. Yer favourite,' said her nan.

Nan was right, a large bowlful of milky rice pudding topped off with a spoonful of red jam was Lynnie's favourite, but she was so nervous over her intended visit to see Ozzie that she couldn't even manage a spoonful even to please her grandmother. 'If our Colin doesn't demolish the lot,' she said, casting a glance at him, 'I'll have some later.'

'Yer seem in an awful rush to get away from the table,' her mother remarked.

'Yeah, yer do, Lynnie,' reiterated Ray, discreetly taking a piece of gristle out of his mouth and putting it on the side of his plate. 'Got something special on?'

Before she could check herself Lynnie erupted, 'What is it with this family? You're all watching me like beady-eyed old women scouring the stalls for a bargain at the church bazaar.'

Her mother gawped. 'That's hardly fair, Lynnie. We're all worried about yer, that's all.'

She sighed. 'Yes, I know. But there's worrying about me and stifling me. I'm not a china doll, I'm not going to break. I've got an errand to do, that's all.' She looked at Colin. 'Do the dishes for me and I'll give you a tanner?'

'A shilling and you've a deal.'

His mother leaned over and slapped his arm. 'Yer'll do it fer nothing out of the goodness of yer own heart,' she instructed him. 'Eh, and it's an early night for you, my lad, you've work in the morning.'

'I know,' he muttered, and added sulkily, 'As a working bloke I shouldn't have ter do chores like dishes no more. None of the other lads I work with do.'

'Oi, while yer under this roof yer'll pull yer weight like the rest of us. Unless yer wage as an apprentice gas fitter affords you the cost of yer own personal maid,' Avril added scathingly.

Colin realised he was heading for trouble and quickly changed the subject. 'Can I come with you and Jimmy ternight?' he asked Dec who was sitting at the side of him.

'Get lost,' he proclaimed. 'Where we're going they don't allow snivelling spotty youths.'

'That was uncalled for,' snapped Avril. 'Our Colin's got lovely skin, just like a baby's bottom,' she said, grabbing his cheek and giving it a pinch. 'And just where are you two going?'

'Oh . . . er . . . down the snooker hall,' he said as both he and Jimmy scraped back their chairs and dashed from the room, calling after them, 'See yer all later.'

'Those boys . . . I dunno,' mumbled Avril to herself. 'Too secretive for my liking.' She fixed her eyes on her daughter. 'Well, get off then and get yer errand done and I promise none of us will grill yer when yer come back. Unless . . . er . . . yer want ter talk about it, that is.'

Chapter Twelve

Lynnie hesitated just before the Matthewses' front gate.
She took several deep breaths to calm her jangling
nerves. She desperately wanted to rush back home to
the bosom of her family, but then gave herself a hard
mental shake. This situation had to be drawn to a
conclusion one way or another, and if she chickened
out today then she would only have to go through it all
over again or forever be stuck at her mental fork in the
road. Without further ado she moved towards the gate
and leaned over to undo the latch. As she pushed it
open, she jumped back in shock as it fell forward,
clattering on to the weed-embellished path that led up
to the Matthewses' front door. It was something she
had momentarily forgotten about, but for as long as
she could remember this gate had needed to be re-hung
on new hinges. During her six months' interlude from
calling here it still hadn't been done. Picking up the
gate, she propped it by the overgrown boundary hedge
and, with heart thumping, made her way up the path
to rap loudly on the door.

When no one answered she rapped loudly again and heard a disgruntled voice bellow from within, 'Fer fuck's sake, can't someone open the door?' Lynnie recognised the voice as being that of Ozzie's father who she assumed was as usual slumped in his chair in front of the television. Then she heard a shout from Ozzie's mother. 'Ozzie, fer Christ's sake get the door before yer dad has a seizure. I'm up to me eyes in soap suds.' Then she heard Ozzie voicing his disapproval before the front door burst open and he barked, 'Yeah, whadda yer want?' His face filled with shock. 'Oh! Er . . . Lynnie.'

As the eyes of the man she had loved with all her being and had been on the verge of marrying bored into hers, Lynnie's already thumping heart banged painfully and she had to fight mentally with all her might not to wipe out all that had transpired between them and leap into his arms. She needed to remember that it was not Ozzie's physical appearance that had caused their estrangement but certain traits in his character. It was those she must focus on now otherwise she would find herself back where she'd started and that she didn't want at any cost. She flashed him a quick smile. 'Can we talk?'

Still reeling from finding her on the doorstep, he said, 'Talk?'

'Yes. Something we never really did much of.'

'Yes, we did,' he blurted defensively.

'No, we didn't, Ozzie. Not the kind of talking I'm referring to. Besides, we need to decide what to do with the wedding presents.'

His face fell. 'Oh, I see. Yer'd better come in.'

The thought of coming face to face with Ozzie's mother and father she did not feel comfortable about. 'Not here, Ozzie. We'll have more privacy in the shelter on the park.'

'Oh, er . . .'

She had a feeling she knew why he was hesitating. 'If you've something else more important on then it doesn't matter. Another time.'

'No, no,' he said hurriedly. 'Hang on while I get me coat.'

As they walked in silence through the streets, over the park to the brick shelter, Lynnie was very conscious of the new awkwardness between them. Sitting on the park bench, she turned and looked at him, unsure how to start the conversation. She was saved by Ozzie blurting out, a cheeky grin splitting his face, 'I'm just glad yer've finally got around ter begging me forgiveness.'

'I beg your pardon?'

'Ah, come on, Lynnie. Yer've finally come to do the decent thing and accept me apology.'

She was astounded. 'And you don't think I deserve one from you?'

'You've already had more than one apology from me, Lynnie. Several, in fact. Look, it's okay, I accept yours, so let's forget about it all, eh? I've missed yer. You've missed me too, I know yer have.'

She bristled from this seemingly nonchalant disregard of the serious incident that had caused the cancellation of their wedding. Regardless she said, 'Yes, I have, just a little.'

'Just a little!' he exclaimed. 'Ah, playing hard ter get, are yer? Come on, Lynnie, we've known each other too long to be like this with each other. Ain't yer gonna give me a kiss?'

She was far from ready for any intimacy between them and moved up the bench to create a distance. 'So, what have you been up to?' she asked, hoping she sounded casual.

Her moving away from him had been most notice-able and he looked hurt for a moment, before giving a shrug. 'Nothing much.'

An awkward silence fell and her mind raced franti-cally, looking for something to say. 'Still in the darts team?' she asked him.

His eyes lit up. 'Oh, yeah. I've improved no end.' He puffed out his chest proudly. 'I'm in the team perma-nently now.'

She gave a small laugh. 'I'm glad your performance hasn't suffered any.'

He looked at her, confused. 'Why would it?'

'Because of us breaking up?'

'Well . . . yer have to put these things out of yer mind when a good placing in the darts league is at stake and yer mates are relying on yer. Yer have to get on with things, don't yer?'

Lynnie flashed him a brief smile. 'Yes, I expect you do.' She looked at him for several long moments. It was most apparent to her that during their time apart Ozzie hadn't changed his attitude to life one bit, not having learned anything from what had driven them apart, and it struck her that sitting here with him now was pointless. It was time for her to journey down the road leading away from Ozzie. She made to rise.

'Where yer going?' he asked, looking at her in confusion.

'Home. We'll sort out the wedding presents and whatever else another time.' She gave a deep sigh. 'This is a waste of time, Ozzie. You haven't changed. You're still putting everything else before me.'

He jumped up to join her. 'How d'yer make that out? You ain't been around for me to put you before everything else, Lynnie. I wanted ter get married, remember. It was you that called it off.'

She wanted to remind him that it was his late arrival at the church that really put a stop to the wedding, so his claim that she had called it off wasn't true.

'Lynnie, sit down,' he urged, sitting back down and patting the bench beside him. 'Yer must have wanted us to get back together being's yer came to see me. The sorting out of the wedding presents was just an excuse, I know it was. Come on, sit down.'

She hesitated before she did so. For several moments they sat in silence before she asked a question that was niggling away at her. 'So . . . er . . . have you been seeing anyone else?'

'What, another woman, yer mean?' He looked deeply offended that Lynnie could even think such a thing. 'No, 'course I ain't.' Then he remembered Ray had caught him red-handed with a girl and might have told Lynnie. 'Well, I've . . . er . . . took a couple for a drink. But there was nothing in it. Nothing at all.'

The bolt of pain that shot through her at the thought of Ozzie with another woman, however innocently, shocked her enough to remind her that she still had very deep feelings for the only serious boyfriend she'd had. 'So you were too busy to be pining for me then?' she said lightly.

''Course I was pining for yer, Lynnie. I love yer, for Christ's sake. But what was I expected to do? I thought you didn't want me any more. Sitting around the house doesn't do any good, does it? Drive yerself mad, especially in my house. Yer know yerself what it's like with me dad ruling the roost like he does and me mam fannying around him to keep the peace. At least being with me mates, I had a laugh. But yer here now, ain't yer, so everything is all right.'

She knew that to agree would make him a happy man, but she couldn't. In doing so she would be agreeing to carry on exactly as they had before. If ever there was a time for her to give Ozzie a chance to address the sides of his character that she knew would eventually cause problems between them it was now. She gave a sigh and looked at him hard. 'I'm not sure.'

'Whadda yer mean by that?'

'I mean, I'm not sure everything is okay. I'm not sure how I feel about us getting back together, Ozzie. I don't know if it would work.'

'What? But I don't understand. It worked before.'

'On your terms, yes. You doing whatever you liked and me going along with it.'

'It weren't like that.'

'But it was, Ozzie.' She clasped her hands together and lowered her head to study her feet. Her voice low, she told him, 'You used to be my world, Ozzie, and I loved you so much I wasn't aware how badly . . . no, that's the wrong word, how much you took me for granted. I can't blame you entirely for that. It was my fault you felt you could treat me like one of the lads, but I wasn't one of the lads – I was your girlfriend . . . fiancée.

'I was so wrapped up in you that I just accepted your excuses for whatever you'd done to upset me and we carried on. I should have made it plainer how much you hurt me and then maybe you might have thought twice about what you were doing. Anyway, that's all in the past. During our time apart I've had time to think. If we do get back together I can't return to the way things were between us, Ozzie, coming third or fourth down the list in your order of importance. I want to come first, and if I don't then I'm sorry but I don't see we have any future together.'

He was looking at her, dumbstruck. 'But yer did come first, Lynnie.'

She shook her head. 'No, I didn't. Your friends, football and then darts came before me. On more occasions than I care to remember I've arrived as we arranged at the pub and you've been so involved with your mates, it's been ages before you even noticed I was there. If I came first, Ozzie, you'd have been looking out for me and immediately I arrived you'd have broken away from your friends and greeted me. Bought me a drink at least.'

'Well . . . yer could have let me know yer'd arrived,' he responded, a hint of defiance in his voice.

'You don't get it, do you, Ozzie? I shouldn't have to. As the supposedly most important person in your life, you *should* have been looking out for me, like I would have you. If I've ever said I'd call for you at a certain time, I did everything in my power to make sure I was there when I said I would be. I never let you down unless I really couldn't help it, Ozzie, because you were the most important person to me.'

He gave a shrug. 'Well, yeah, I admit I ain't the best time-keeper, but I always came eventually.'

'Eventually, Ozzie, like you did the day we were getting married? Eventually isn't good enough for me any more.'

He narrowed his eyes. 'Who's turned yer head? Yer never used ter think like this.'

'No one's turned my head. Maybe I've grown up, Ozzie. Maybe I don't want to act like a teenager any more, like I don't want a teenage kind of relationship. I want a grown-up one.' He was still looking at her non-plussed and she gave a wan smile. 'You don't understand what I mean, do you? Look, when you asked me to marry you, whether you meant it or not, you led me to believe you wanted to spend the rest of your life with me. Even so, you still wanted to be one of the boys and do all the things you enjoyed. I didn't expect you to give your friends up, far from it, but what I did expect you to do was put our future together first.

'Be honest with me, Ozzie. That bank account for the deposit on a house you were saving for ... I suspect that if you had a choice between a few shillings in it for us or buying a new shirt for yourself for a night out with the lads, your own priorities won every time. That's why you went on about us renting instead of buying, because you knew you hadn't managed to put away nearly enough for the deposit and fees. I'm right, aren't I?'

He lowered his head and his silence gave her her answer.

She sighed. 'I should have taken charge of that, I know, had you hand over a weekly amount and put it in the bank myself, but I felt that would be wrong of me, like I wasn't trusting you, and we had to be able to trust each other if we were going to build a future together. It was me who got all the stuff together for our bottom drawer, apart from gifts that is. I didn't mind that at all, I really enjoyed seeing the pile grow, imagining what we'd collected being used in our home, but it would have been nice if just occasionally you had made some sort of contribution. And we never talked, Ozzie, not really talked like couples who are planning to spend the rest of their lives together should do, making plans, that sort of thing. If we had done, I'd have known about your fear of marriage and could have helped you.'

'Well, I'm over all that now.' His face took on an earnest expression. 'I will start saving properly, I'll hand over the money to you every week if that's what yer want. I want to get married. I really do, Lynnie.'

She gazed at him and said softly, 'But I don't know if I do, Ozzie.'

His face fell. 'What, yer mean yer don't love me any more?'

'Oh, I love you, Ozzie, but that's what I've been trying to explain to you. It's not enough, being in love. There's more to marriage than that. Both sides need to be equally as committed to make it work. In truth it was only me in our case, wasn't it?'

He grabbed her hands, his face pleading. 'I am committed now, Lynnie. Honest I am. I'll marry yer tomorrow. We'll go and see the Vicar and sort it out. I'll do anything yer want. I'll . . .'

'Ozzie, please,' she interrupted. 'If we're going to try again, I need to be sure this time you're not just saying all this.'

'But I ain't! I swear I ain't,' he exclaimed. 'Please, Lynnie, yer've got ter give me another chance to prove I mean what I say. Please, Lynnie, please. There's no one else for me but you. You're my life, Lynnie. I ain't half missed yer. Sure I took a couple of other gels out for a drink but they meant nothing to me. All the time I was with them I was thinking about you.'

He sounded so sincere she knew she owed it to them both to give him another chance. She took several deep breaths before saying, 'Then if we are to get back together, you'll agree to take things slowly so we can both be sure?'

'But I *am* sure of you, Lynnie.'

'Well, I need to be of you.'

He gave a bewildered shrug. 'How do I make you sure?'

'By proving it to me, Ozzie. You could start by courting me properly. That means making arrangements and sticking to them and us doing more things together, not you larking about with your mates while I sit and watch.'

'That's fine with me, Lynnie. Anything . . . anything yer want, I'll do it. So what do we do now then?'

Her hopes soared. If Ozzie was agreeing to her terms and appearing so eager to do so, then maybe they did have a future together. 'You could start by asking me out on a date.'

'A date! A date, eh?' He looked at her for a moment before nodding fervently. 'Okay, Friday night. I'll tek yer somewhere nice.' He grinned at her cheekily. 'I'll act all grown-up, I promise yer.'

She smiled. 'All right. But Ozzie, remember, one step at a time. Okay?'

'Great. So do I get a kiss now?'

'No. I want us to treat Friday as our first ever date together.'

'Oh! Okay, if that's what yer want, I'm game. What time do yer want me to call for yer?'

Her eyes lit up mischievously. 'As this is supposed to be our first date, you have no idea where I live, have you? I'll meet you at Timothy White's on the clock tower at eight.'

He looked disappointed. 'Oh, all right then. So where do yer want to go?'

She gave a chuckle. 'Ozzie, you said you would take me somewhere nice so it's up to you to decide and arrange it. And please, don't even be a minute late because if you're not there bang on the dot of eight, I'll go and that's it.'

'I'll be there,' he said firmly.

'And I think it's best we keep this to ourselves for the moment.'

'Why?'

'Well, for a start my mam is still after your blood and she's going to take some convincing that what happened between us last time isn't going to happen again.' Lynnie rose. 'So I'll see you Friday then?'

He stood up to join her. 'I'll walk with yer.'

A look of amusement lit her face. 'Oh, I never let a man walk me home until I know more about him.'

He gave a heavy sigh. 'You really do mean business, don't yer, Lynnie?'

'I do,' she said resolutely and added, 'and I hope you do too.'

Chapter Thirteen

Mid-morning Friday found Lynnie wondering what to do with herself. Since opening time at ten a steady stream of regulars had been in to place their bets which she had now entered into the book as well as completing several other menial tasks. All was now in order for her to cope with the lunchtime rush. Excitement was building for the pending Grand National due to be run the following weekend, and trade in respect of this special race was particularly brisk. Large amounts of money – or large to the types who frequented Cigar Sid's establishment – had been placed, and Lynnie had had a good few laughs with the punters as they had relayed to her what they proposed to do with their winnings.

It wasn't unusual to have a lull mid-morning and usually when it happened she would find menial tasks to do to while away the time. This particular morning she needed something more taxing in order to keep her mind from dwelling on her date that night with Ozzie. As the day had drawn nearer, to her own surprise she found she was looking forward to meeting him with great optimism, sincerely hoping that their break had taught him a valuable lesson and he would indeed now leave her in no doubt of his commitment to her. The problem she faced was avoiding probing questions from her family when they saw her all dressed up for a night out.

After looking around she found nothing else that needed doing and glanced across at Ray who was standing on a small step-stool at the chalk board that spanned half the far wall, writing up the runners and the odds of the first race of the day. 'Would you like a cuppa?' she asked him.

Without taking his eyes from his task, he replied, 'No more for me just yet. You've forced at least six on me this morning. Yer've some thirst on yer, gel. What's the matter with yer?'

'Nothing,' she said lightly. 'I'm just looking for something to do, that's all. Anyway you exaggerate. It wasn't six but four.'

He turned and looked across at her. 'Why don't you pop in and see if yer can help Sid with anything?'

'Oh, he's busy ringing around hedging his bets at the moment.' She looked at Ray enquiringly. 'I know a lot about this betting lark from what Sid's explained to me and what I've picked up by working here, but I've never quite understood what "hedging your bets" means?'

'Oh, it's simple. When a bookie takes on a big bet, for instance a thousand pounds on a horse with a starting price of ten to one, well, it might just win and for him to stand the loss of ten grand is not something he's really prepared or can afford to do, especially if he gets several big bets at the same time.'

'He could refuse to accept them,' said Lynnie.

'Ain't good business doing that. A bookie's reputation would stink if he stipulated limits on what he was prepared to accept. Besides, don't forget his odds on keeping the original wager far outweigh those of the punter – unless that punter has concrete inside information that the race is fixed in some way. Usually bookies are astute enough to know when something ain't quite right, or more than likely they're tipped off by the bookies' grapevine. Then the tic-tac men down on the rails or Tattersall's reduce the starting price before the race starts.'

She looked confused. 'It's mind-boggling all this.'

Her brother stopped what he was doing and turned to look across at her. 'That's what I mean when I say that to be in this game you've got to know what you're up against, keep one step ahead of all the scams punters try. Anyway, what the bookie does when he gets a large wager he isn't prepared to take on fully himself is to split the bet with other bookies. That way, should the horse lose, which they pray it will, they all get a share of the original thousand-pound stake. Should it win they all suffer a smaller loss on the payout, not one huge one.'

'A bet of a thousand! You'd have to be rich or just plain stupid to risk losing that amount,' Lynnie scoffed.

'Some people are though, and they do risk it. Not the sort we deal with over the counter here. Most of them ain't got the price of a loaf of bread, let alone money for a decent wager. But all their shillings, half-crowns, the occasional ten bob and quid, add up to make bookies sizeable profits at the end of the day. It's the small bets that make them their living, Lynnie, not the big ones. It's a good way of earning a living, provided yer know what yer doing.' He knew by the look on his sister's face just what was going through her mind and scowled at her scornfully. 'Don't be daft, Lynnie. Women don't become turf accountants.'

'I don't see why not! I probably know nearly as much as you do, and what I don't I could learn if Sid would teach me.'

'I grant you you could, but knowing the game inside out is only part of it. For a start you need enough money behind you as a fallback in the unlikely event that your losses are more than your profits. It wouldn't matter then if you were a man or a woman, you'd be dead as far as the punter was concerned if you couldn't pay them out.'

'Mmm, I suppose. It's a nice thought, though, isn't it? Having yer own business. I love working for Sid but I'd prefer it much more working for myself.' A thought struck her. 'His father came from a poor background so he couldn't have had that much money behind him when he started off.'

Ray eyed her narrowly. 'I'd stop this train of

thought, if I were you. Things were different in Sid's father's day. Apart from needing to know every runner's details intimately by constantly studying form, it took him years to build up enough behind him to do it full-time. In the meantime he slogged his guts out in the factory from seven until six, gradually building up his collateral from pennies and halfpennies gained from the paltry copper bets his workmates could afford.'

She laughed. 'Sid's told you the family history, I see.'

He nodded. 'Not once, several times. He's very proud of the way it all started off and the least I can do is listen to him.'

'Yes, me too,' she agreed. 'Like you I've learned a lot from his reminiscing, but he seems to go more readily into technical details with you than he does with me, unless I prise it out of him.'

'That's 'cos I'm a man and turf accounting is a man's world, Lynnie.'

She sniffed haughtily. 'Mmm, so it seems. But we women will have our day, you'll see, and then you men will need to watch out. By the way, has Sid told you he's thinking of taking you to the track with him to learn how bets are handled at the rails?'

'Yes.' Ray's face lit up excitedly. 'I'm going with him next week. That track is where it all happens, Lynnie, and I can't wait to learn it all, believe me. 'Course, yer've got to have yer wits about yer 'cos there's some real dodgy things go on down the track. You've got to be able to spot the scams, and I couldn't hope to be taught by anyone better than Sid. He knows all there is to know.'

Lynnie pulled a face, remembering his refusal to take her to the track despite her appreciating the reasons why. 'Ah, well, a woman like me would have no chance down there, would she? I don't suppose you men think we have so much about us up top as you do. And of course it's rough, isn't it? Not the sort of place a respectable woman should be seen in,' she said sardonically.

Her irony was lost on him. 'Yer right, it's not. Look, I can't stand here idly chatting, I've work to do and the lunchtime rush is nearly on us. If yer that desperate for summat to do, you could tidy under the counter. It's a tip under there, I can't find anything when I want it.'

'It was tidy enough before you started here,' she accused. 'If you learned to put things back in their rightful place it wouldn't be such a mess now.'

He grinned at her cheekily. 'I could, I suppose, but then you'd have nothing to do, now would yer?' he said as he turned his attention back to chalking up the latest information on the board.

She was just about to respond to this when the door opened and a man entered. He approached the counter and said to Lynnie, 'I wanna see the boss.'

She immediately wondered what this shabby-looking man, who judging by his appearance didn't look to have much to his name, could possibly want with Sid Mallin who only saw clients in private when they had money to gamble away on big bets and wanted to keep their business to themselves. So she said, 'I can take your bet for you,' pushing a blank betting slip in his direction. 'If you write it down, I'll deal with it. Or tell me what it is and I'll fill in the runner that you want to back and its odds before I time and date your bet.'

She thought she was being helpful but what he did next made her realise that he didn't think so.

The man leaned over the counter and thrust his unhealthy-looking face at her, screwed up warningly. 'I said, I wanna see the boss.'

'Who shall I say wants him?' she responded tartly.

'Me. I do.'

She tutted indignantly. 'I'll see if he's free.'

She popped her head around Sid's door. 'There's a bloke wants to see you, Mr Mallin. He wouldn't give his name and I haven't seen him before.'

He lifted his head from the racing pages of the *Daily Sketch* and smiled at her. 'Oh, all right, show him through, Lynnie, thank you.'

She went back into the shop and lifted the counter flap. 'Mr Mallin's office is just through the back,' she said, standing aside to allow him past.

Without acknowledging her, he pushed by and disappeared through the door leading to Sid's office. She returned to her work. It was nearing twenty minutes later and she had dealt with several customers before the man came out of the office again. Without a word to Lynnie he lifted the flap, passed through and left the shop.

Just then Ray came over. 'That's the board updated.

Time for a cuppa now, I think, Lynnie. Are you going to do the honours?'

'Can't you see I'm busy?' she snapped. 'Oh, I'll do it in a minute.' Then she looked at her brother enquiringly. 'What do you think that man wanted with Sid? He was in his office a long time and Sid hasn't been out to ask me to log a bet in the book, which he usually does.'

'What man?'

'The one who just left. Didn't you see that shifty type who came in about half an hour ago? Well, he looked shifty to me. He kept looking around him, like he was worried anyone would see him.'

Ray shook his head. 'I never noticed, and anyway lots of our customers could be described as shifty. Are yer gonna make that tea, before the lunchtime rush?'

Just then Sid emerged from his office and approached Lynnie. 'Can you manage on yer own for a bit, lovey? I just need a quick word with Ray.'

She glanced over at the crowd of punters in a haze of smoke, gathered in groups, discussing the form while they waited for the first race to start at two. She looked back at her boss and knew that it wasn't her imagination: he looked like a man who was deeply disturbed by something. 'Yes, sure I can, Mr Mallin. Is everything all right?'

He flashed her a smile. 'Yes, of course it is, Lynnie. I just want to speak to Ray about coming down the track with me next week, that's all. Oh, and . . . er . . .

make sure we're not disturbed unless it's desperately urgent.'

'Yes, of course I will.'

It was a good half an hour later before Sid and Ray came back and they were both dressed for outdoors.

'Lynnie, do yer think you can manage for the rest of the afternoon by yerself? I'm off to visit a couple of my turf accountant friends and I'm going to take Ray along and introduce him to them.'

She smiled and nodded. 'Yes, 'course I can.'

For the rest of that afternoon her thoughts were centred on the most important matter to her: her evening out with Ozzie.

Chapter Fourteen

Lynnie stole a surreptitious glance at Ozzie across the table and a warm glow of hope filled her. He had obviously taken great care with his appearance for their date, when in the past, on more than one occasion he had been known to turn up at her house in his old leather jacket and the jeans he wore for work or messing around in, saying he couldn't see the point in changing as they were only sitting around. She couldn't remember him ever looking so smart. He was wearing trendy light blue trousers, a multicoloured striped shirt and a dark blue Beatles-style collarless jacket. He'd had his hair restyled in a Paul McCartney mop which suited him. She could tell he had shaved carefully and he was smelling enticingly of Brut by Fabergé, the up-to-the-minute aftershave that all hip men wore.

She had dressed very carefully herself, mindful that in view of their fresh start this should be treated as their first outing together. She had questioned herself as to what she would wear in such circumstances to look as good as she could, in the hope of the man she had agreed to meet asking her out again. After great deliberation, and by cheating a little as she knew very well what clothes Ozzie preferred a woman to dress in, she chose a black and white checked mini-shift dress and knee-length white plastic boots. Her hair had been washed and brushed, and fell softly to her shoulders. Her makeup was pale, her white-shadowed eyelids thickly edged with black eye pencil, while several layers of black mascara emphasised her long thick eyelashes to their fullest.

She had arrived at their designated meeting place at five minutes before the hour and had been almost shocked to find Ozzie already waiting for her. Without attempting any undue intimacy, he had taken her arm and led her off to a popular pub called the Tavern in the Town where for a couple of hours they'd chatted amicably over their drinks while listening to the latest sounds pouring from the juke box. Lynnie's particular musical leaning at this moment in time was a new sound from America called Tamla Motown and she had popped several shillings in the juke box so she could listen to Smokey Robinson and the Miracles singing 'Tracks of My Tears', the Temptations' 'Beauty Is Only Skin Deep' and Marvin Gaye's 'I Heard It Through the Grapevine' plus several other of her favourites.

At a quarter to ten Ozzie had taken her completely by surprise by announcing that he had booked a table for them at the new Chinese restaurant that had opened for business at the bottom of Belgrave Road.

The food – sweet and sour pork, and egg fried rice – had been delicious, and as she pushed her plate away she had given a satisfied sigh. 'That was fabulous,' Lynnie said appreciatively.

'I prefer sausage and chips meself,' responded Ozzie, pushing his own plate away. 'But as long as you enjoyed it, that's the main thing to me.' He looked at his watch. 'Better get you home as you've work in the morning and Saturdays are your busiest day, ain't they? I don't want you falling asleep on the job 'cos I kept yer out too late,' he added jokingly.

She was taken aback at this most unusual thoughtfulness. Then an awful thought struck her. 'Oh, Ozzie, we'll have missed the last bus!'

He smiled at her winningly. 'That's no problem.'

'But a taxi will cost a bomb.'

'Who mentioned a taxi?'

Lynnie assumed that meant they were walking home and it was a good two miles which she wasn't looking forward to.

He summoned the waiter and asked for the bill.

Lynnie retrieved her handbag from the side of her chair and took out her purse.

'What are yer doing?' Ozzie asked.

'Just giving you my share,' she said, offering him a ten-shilling note.

He waved it away. 'Put yer money away, this is my treat,' he ordered.

As she put away her purse it crossed her mind that although his act of unexpected chivalry had been most

271

welcome, it was hard to see how he was managing to afford all the expense of his new clothes as well as their night out. She wanted to ask him how he was doing it but felt that right now it wasn't quite her place. This was their 'first' date together and such intimate questions weren't asked in those circumstances.

Having paid the bill, Ozzie accepted Lynnie's coat from the polite Chinese waiter who had brought it over. 'Ta, mate,' he said as he held it out for her to put on. Outside in the street he took her arm and immediately steered her down a side road at the back of the Chinese restaurant. Her face was wreathed in surprise when he stopped beside a parked car.

The Rover 3000, judging by its ramshackle condition, had obviously been driven for a good few years by a not very caring owner or succession of owners. It was several different shades of red, blue and a rather murky brown due to replacement doors and wings being fitted to replace the original rusting or damaged ones, and it seemed to Lynnie in the gloom of the evening and from where she was standing that the exhaust pipe was being supported by a length of wire wrapped around it and the mudguard.

'What d'yer think then?' Ozzie asked her.

'What do I think? Oh! This is yours?'

'Ours now, Lynnie. I bought it from a bloke I know. He wanted a tenner but I beat him down to a fiver,' he said proudly, pulling the door open.

She wanted to tell Ozzie he had been robbed even so but thought better of it and said instead, 'Do you know anything about cars?'

He gave a shrug. 'Enough to get me by. Kelvin, me mate, knows a fair bit through tinkering with his dad on a few old bangers they've restored and sold on. Between us we got this baby going,' he said, giving the roof of the car an affectionate pat. Then he glanced it over. 'She needs a bit more work doing on her body, but with the few parts we salvaged from the scrap heap we got her purring like a kitten and she can certainly motor when yer put yer foot down, considering when I first got her we couldn't even get her started and had to push her to Kelvin's dad's lock-up.'

'Mmm,' Lynnie mouthed sceptically. 'Is it safe?'

''Course it's bleddy safe,' he proclaimed, hurt. 'I wouldn't risk yer life, would I? Give me some credit, Lynnie.'

She felt ashamed. 'I'm sorry. No, of course you wouldn't. Your own neither. I didn't know you'd passed your test?'

He flashed her a look, then glanced out of the window before replying. 'Well . . . I ain't, not yet, but I've only got to put in for it. Kelvin's been teaching me to drive and I'm practically an expert now. Passing the test will be a doddle. Driving is easy, Lynnie. All yer need to do is get yer foot co-ordination between the accelerator and the gear pedals, the rest is child's play. Well, are yer gonna get in or not unless yer fancy walking?'

She didn't. 'Okay.' Just then a thought struck her. 'The car was unlocked, Ozzie. Shouldn't you have locked it up when you parked it earlier? What if someone had stolen it?'

He shrugged. 'I can't exactly lock it up.'

'Why not?'

"Cos I ain't got any keys. I musta dropped 'em somewhere when we were pushing her home after I'd bought her. I just wanted to impress yer tonight, Lynnie, so I took the risk.'

'Oh, Ozzie, you don't need to impress me,' she scolded. Then a thought struck her. 'How do you get the car started without keys?'

He grinned. 'Kelvin showed me how to hot wire. He's a good mate to have, I can tell yer. Opened me eyes to lots of things he has. Come on then, let's be off.'

Reluctantly Lynnie slipped inside on to the long leather bench seat which was torn in places and watched in fascination as Ozzie took hold of two wires from under the dashboard. While he pressed his right foot onto the accelerator, he touched the two wires together. They crackled and sparked. The car exploded into life and Lynnie had to admit, despite her limited knowledge of vehicles of any description, that the engine, after Ozzie's initial few hard revs to ensure it was fired, did sound like it was purring like a cat, unlike Mr Bevins's old jalopy which had seemed to scream in agony.

Hand on the door handle, she braced herself and they were off.

Despite her watching Ozzie's every movement like a

hawk, the drive home was exhilarating and Lynnie found she was enjoying every minute, her sensible side temporarily forgetting that Ozzie was breaking the law, not having passed his test. Finally he drew the car to a halt by stalling the engine in a small cul-de-sac off the street where he lived.

She eyed him questioningly. 'Why have you parked here and not outside your house?' she asked. 'Oh, in case your parents catch us out together and ask questions, I suppose.'

'Er . . . yeah, Lynnie, that's right. I'll tek yer out in it again, if yer like?'

'If you don't mind, not until you've passed your test. I don't fancy being stopped by the law for any reason and them finding out you're not licensed to drive and . . . well . . . I don't know whether I could be charged with anything if I was with you, and considering my family's drive to keep out of trouble that wouldn't look very good, would it?'

He looked at her, shocked. 'Good God, Lynnie, you ain't all still carrying on that malarkey?'

'Yes, absolutely. We were deadly serious when we made our pact, Ozzie. You were there when we did, you were part of it, remember?'

'Yeah, yeah. So . . . have yer enjoyed tonight, Lynnie?'

She nodded. 'Yes, I have, thank you very much.'

'So you'll come out with me again?'

She smiled at him warmly. 'Yes, I'd like to. What about the pictures on Sunday?'

'Sounds good ter me. I'll meet yer at the Odeon and you can choose what film we see. And just for you, I'll even see a sloppy one, how about that?'

She was impressed. 'You really are making a great effort, aren't you, Ozzie?'

'I'm doing my best ter keep yer, Lynnie, believe me I am. Can I get a kiss now?'

Before she could stop him he had grabbed her to him and his lips were on hers. It felt good to be back in his arms again, his hungry kiss flooding her with an answering desire to take matters further. But in her quest to make sure Ozzie was in no doubt this relationship was his number one priority, she pulled away from him.

'I'll see you Sunday then. Half-seven, okay?' she said, sliding across the seat to open the passenger door.

'Oh!' he exclaimed, extremely disappointed. 'One kiss. Is that it, Lynnie?'

She nodded. 'I'm afraid so. One night out is not proof positive you're putting us first, Ozzie. But you've made a good start.'

He took several deep breaths to cool his ardour. 'Phew, yer a hard woman, Lynnie – but yer worth it,' he added, grinning at her wickedly.

She got out of the car and jauntily set off to walk the short distance home.

Her hope of getting to bed unobserved and escaping probing questions about where she had been all evening proved futile. She opened the front door and found, to her dismay, her mother in the passageway waiting for her.

'Oh, thank God, yer home safe and sound, our Lynnie. When yer didn't arrive on the last bus I was worried. Dec and Jimmy ain't home yet either, but I don't worry about them like I do you. Well, they're blokes, ain't they, and can look out for each other. I was just about to get our Ray up to go look for yer. Where yer bin until this time?'

It immediately struck her how tired her mother looked. It was obvious that labouring at two jobs in order to help the family's finances and keep them all to their vow was taking its toll on Avril. Lynnie already did more than her fair share around the home but wished she could do more financially. As it was she handed over as much as she could from her wage and hadn't that much left for herself. She would speak to Ray as soon as possible, ask him if he could think of something that all the Downs offspring could do jointly to ease their mother's load.

She smiled affectionately. 'With a friend,' she said lightly, which was true. 'After we got off the bus we chatted for a bit, that's why I'm late.'

'Oh, I know this friend then, do I, if they live around here?'

'Er . . . I'm not sure. It's a friend from my youth club days. If you don't mind, Mam, I'm so tired so I'll go straight up. You look to me as though you could do with a good night's sleep yourself.'

'Yes, I am rather tired tonight. I was just making yer

nan a cuppa cocoa as she reckons she can't get to sleep, then I'm going up meself. Oh, Lynnie, before yer go . . .'

She paused on the stairs and turned to face her mother, knowing instantly by the look on her face that as well as her tiredness something else was bothering her. 'What's the matter, Mam?'

'Oh, it's summat and n'ote, I'm sure, but I just wondered if 'ote happened at work today to do with our Ray?'

Lynnie shook her head. 'Not as far as I know. Why?'

'Oh, just that he was very quiet tonight and you saw fer yerself that he never ate his dinner. Just picked at it. He went to bed just after you went out at eight. I can't remember the last time he went to bed that early.'

Lynnie frowned thoughtfully. 'Maybe he's sickening for something?'

Her mother shook her head. 'No, I'd know if he was. Could it be girl trouble, d'yer reckon? Has he mentioned any woman to you?'

'He's seeing a couple at the moment, neither of them seriously enough to cause him to go to bed early if something had happened between them. Maybe he was just tired, Mam.'

Avril flashed her a brief smile. 'Maybe yer right. Now I'd better get yer nan that cocoa before she starts bellowing for it.' She leaned over and kissed her daughter on the cheek. 'Nighty night, lovey.'

Lynnie responded by kissing her back. 'Nighty night, Mam.'

★ ★ ★

Lynnie lay in bed unable to sleep, her thoughts dwelling on her night out with Ozzie. Aside from her disapproval of his driving around in an unlicensed vehicle, which she felt after her strong words to him he would quickly resolve, she'd had a wonderful night in his company. He'd been attentive, fun to be with, even seemed to listen to her when she was talking – unlike in the past when she had been fully aware that his mind was on other things, usually involving his mates and nothing to do with her. If tonight's performance was anything to go by then she felt there was a good chance that sometime in the future she and Ozzie would be walking back down the aisle together as a married couple. She was so glad now she had taken Ray's advice, had gone to see Ozzie and given him another chance.

Chapter Fifteen

The evening out at the pictures was a great success. True to his word, Ozzie had uncomplainingly sat through *Doctor Zhivago*, despite hinting at his own preference for watching Clint Eastwood in *The Good, The Bad and The Ugly*, and had not even ridiculed Lynnie for sobbing at the sad ending. With high expectations that their renewed relationship was just going to keep improving, Lynnie pushed open the door of Mallin's, looking forward to her day's work.

As she entered a movement behind the counter made her stop short and stare open-mouthed at the strange man staring back at her. As their eyes momentarily met Lynnie gave a shudder as a bolt of sensation shot through her so strongly she was temporarily struck speechless. As his startlingly blue eyes bored into hers, for an instant she thought she knew him, that they were connected somehow, then mentally shook herself. She had never seen this man before in her life, and after scrutinising him closely decided that neither did she particularly like the look of him.

In appearance he was almost theatrical, like a character from a B-rated Ealing black comedy. His age she guessed to be around thirty, he was about five foot eleven and of slender build, dressed very loudly in a badly fitting Prince of Wales checked suit, glaring red shirt and gaudily patterned kipper tie. His dark hair was heavily greased and slicked back. His facial features, although far from ugly, could not be classed as handsome but would no doubt benefit greatly if he readdressed his taste in hair styles. To anyone who asked her she would describe him as an over-the-top wide boy.

'Who are you?' she demanded. 'And just what do you think you're doing behind that counter?' She glared at him menacingly. 'There's no money in the till, if that's what you're after.'

With a hint of a grin twitching his lips, he said, 'You're Caitlyn Downs, I assume. I'm your new boss, Alfie Manners.'

She had expected his voice to match his clothes and was taken aback by his firm tone and politeness. Nevertheless what he had announced caused her to stare at him. 'New boss!' she uttered. 'What do you mean, you're my new boss?' Then she looked around. 'Where's Mr Mallin?'

'Your brother not with you?' he asked.

'Eh? Oh, he's just coming. He went into the tobacconist for cigarettes. I asked you where Mr Mallin was.'

Just then Ray entered. He took one look at the

stranger behind the counter then at Lynnie and asked, 'What's going on?'

She spun round to face him. 'This man reckons he's our new boss, Ray.'

Before he could say anything, Alfie said, 'Ah, so you're Ray Downs. Would you like to come through to the office? I'd like a chat.' He cast a glance at Lynnie. 'You carry on opening up and when I've finished with Ray, I'll have a chat with you. A cuppa wouldn't go amiss. Not too strong with a spot of milk and two sugars.'

She stared at him speechless as he ushered Ray into the privacy of Sid's office and shut the door firmly behind them. Despite being frantically worried about Sid Mallin's whereabouts, with many questions she desperately needed answers to, she was also seething at this man's treatment of her. She deserved to be kept informed as much as her brother about what was going on, and especially considering she was the longer serving employee of the two and far more experienced.

She tiptoed across to the office and put her ear to the door. All she could hear was the low murmur of voices. Her temper rose as well as a great desire to burst into that room and demand to be told what was going on. She quickly quashed the urge, realising that apart from risking making a complete fool of herself, if this man were indeed now in charge then he could dismiss her for doing such a thing.

There was nothing she could do but be patient until

her turn with Mr Manners came and then she would make it very plain what she thought of his handling of this situation.

She went into the tiny kitchen and mashed a pot of tea which she put on a tray along with a small jug of milk and basin of sugar. Putting the tray on the floor outside the office, she rapped loudly on the door to announce its presence before scooting off behind the counter to get on with her work. A small feeling of satisfaction rose within her. Whether her small act of defiance in making Alfie Manners pour the tea himself would have any effect on her new boss or not remained to be seen, but she had made a small stand and felt better for it.

Her desperate need to fire questions at Alfie Manners and have them answered made the time drag laboriously. It seemed hours later when the office door finally opened and Ray came out.

'Oh, God,' she exclaimed, slipping off her counter stool and rushing up to him. 'You've been in there ages! Just what have you been talking about? What's happened to Sid, Ray? Why's he suddenly gone off like this and put *him* in charge? Ray, what's . . .'

'Oh, fer God's sake, give it a rest, will yer, Lynnie?' he snapped at her abruptly.

She stepped back, shocked at his attitude. 'Eh?'

'Well, yer throwing all these questions at me when Mr Manners is the one you should be asking,' he said, grabbing his overcoat from the peg on the door.

'Where are you going, Ray?' she asked, confused.

'I don't work here any more, Lynnie.'

His unexpected announcement shook her rigid. 'What!'

'You heard me right,' he said, pulling on his coat.

'But you love working here. And what about the round you've built up?'

'I *did* like working here. As for the round, split it between the other runners. I'm sure they'll be over-joyed at the prospect of earning more money.' He looked at her tenderly. 'Look, don't worry, Lynnie, this is just something I have to do.'

'But Sid's been good to you, Ray, he deserves . . .'

'Lynnie, please,' he cut in. 'You won't understand, but what I'm doing is in Sid's best interests. Look, I'll see yer at home later.'

With that he pushed past her and before she could stop him he'd left the shop. Next thing she knew she felt a presence by her side and spun around to see Alfie Manners looking at her strangely.

When he realised she was looking back at him he seemed mentally to shake himself before saying, 'I take it your brother has told you he's terminated his employment?'

'Yes, he has. But why? Why has he done that? He loves working here, it doesn't make sense that my brother would do such a thing.'

'He has a right to decide where he's going to work and made the choice that it wasn't going to be here. Now, young lady, Sid Mallin spoke very highly of you. Said you were a hard worker and very loyal. I hope you're going to show me the same loyalty?'

'That remains to be seen, Mr Manners. After you've explained what's going on!' Lynnie said sharply.

Their eyes met and as they did so she gave a violent shudder as the sensations she had earlier experienced were repeated.

'Are you all right?' he asked her.

'I'm fine,' she said hurriedly. 'Or I will be when you explain to me why Mr Mallin left in such a hurry. I know him very well, and regardless of anything I know he wouldn't just up and leave his business to any Tom, Dick or Harry. And especially someone . . .' She stopped short of saying 'someone like you', realising she would be severely jeopardising her own position. 'Especially someone he hadn't introduced to us. He was fine on Saturday night when we closed up the shop. His going off like this without any explanation doesn't make sense. Mr Mallin wouldn't do that, I know he wouldn't.'

'Just accept that he has,' Alfie said matter-of-factly. 'It was all very sudden.' He held out an envelope. 'Sid asked me to give you this in the hope it might make things clearer. If anyone asks for the boss, I'll be in my office.' He turned away and walked back to it, shutting the door behind him.

She stared after him then was shaken out of her stupor by a loud voice bellowing, 'Eh up, Lynnie, are yer ever gonna serve us? Goodness, gel, the race will be over before we've placed our bets if yer don't hurry up.'

With a start of surprise she saw several customers

milling around the counter waving their slips at her. Thrusting Sid's letter into her pocket, she rushed over to serve them.

'Who's the diamond geezer?' asked Ronnie Jakes, a cockney who had lived in Leicester since being evacuated there as a child during the war and had never lost his original accent.

'Pardon? Oh, that's Mr Manners who's standing in for Mr Mallin. Apparently he's been called away urgently.'

Ronnie grimaced. 'Really? You watch yer back, Lynnie. I'm surprised the likes of Sid Mallin is trusting the likes of *him* with his business. For a start someone should mention his tailor ain't doing him any service. Are you sure he's kosher, Lynnie?'

Loyalty to her boss flared. 'If Mr Mallin has put Mr Manners in charge, then of course he is.'

'Okay, okay. I only ask 'cos my dad had many dealings with that type down the smoke and none of 'em could be trusted. Of course, that was before a bomb blew me dad to smithereens while he was sleeping off one of his binges. He never knew what hit him, poor old bloke,' added Ronnie, laughing.

'I take it you didn't think much of your dad?' she said, pushing his slip back across to him.

'Let's just say that his type should never have bin allowed ter father kids,' he said, putting the slip safely back in his pocket. 'I've got a feeling in me water I've backed a dead cert this time, Lynnie. What say you come out with me on me winnings?'

She stared at him blankly. 'Let's see if you win first then we'll talk dates. Will you be bringing your wife along too?'

'Ah, Lynnie, now yer've spoiled it. I was hoping you might have forgotten I'd got one. See yer later.'

She smiled at him. 'Tarra, Ronnie.'

During the next half an hour she worked mechanically, desperate for a free few minutes in which to read Sid's letter. Hopefully afterwards she would be wiser as to what was going on, and then she'd see what Alfie Manners had to say for himself. Meanwhile if she was asked once by a customer where her brother was, she was asked a dozen times, and on each occasion politely told them that Ray was attending to business on Sid's behalf, not wanting it spread around that he had walked out of his job until she saw him that night and discovered why he had decided he couldn't put up with Alfie Manners until Sid returned. It was all very baffling. Ray loved his job, saw this line of work as where his future lay. Maybe she could persuade him he had acted hastily and change his mind.

It was nearing noon before she got her few minutes of peace to read Sid's letter. Her hope of a full explanation was not to be fulfilled. The letter was brief.

Dear Lynnie,

I have been called away on urgent family business and have no idea how long I will be gone. Alfred Manners has kindly agreed to look after the business during my absence. I hope you will give Mr Manners

*your unquestioning support and show him the same
loyalty as you have always shown me. Mr Manners
has full control over my business interests and whatever decisions he makes have my full backing.*
    Yours sincerely, Sidney Mallin

Lynnie read the letter over twice before folding it up
and putting it in her pocket. It told her no more than
Alfie Manners had himself. A feeling of uneasiness
stole over her. Something about this whole situation
didn't quite ring true, especially Alfred Manners himself. She couldn't fathom for the life of her how Sid
Mallin had come to trust him with charge of his
business, no matter how urgently he'd been called away.
He must have been desperate. She and Ray could have
managed, and she was upset to think that Sid hadn't
considered that.

She made her way to the office and knocked on the
door, entering when she heard Alfie call out.

Before she could utter a word he said, 'I take it
you've read Mr Mallin's letter? I hope everything is
clear to you now.'

'Well, no, not really . . .'

'Isn't it? Oh. Well, it's quite simple, Miss Downs. Mr
Mallin was called away urgently on Saturday night on
a private matter and asked me to look after things
meantime. Luckily I was free to do so. I'm sure we'll
rub along together nicely until he returns. Now,
another cuppa wouldn't go amiss. Send any visitors
through, won't you?'

'Oh, but . . .'

'That tea, Miss Downs.'

It was most apparent to her that Alfred Manners thought any further information on the matter was none of her business. Her anger mounted at his high-handed attitude towards her. On this showing, how on earth was she going to tolerate this man as her boss until kindly Sid returned? She had absolutely no idea. No wonder her brother had walked out if this was how Alfie Manners had treated him. She just prayed that Manners was better at running a business than he was at handling people. She stalked from the office and banged the door behind her.

To her bewilderment she never clapped eyes on Alfie Manners for the rest of the day, except for the couple of times he popped his head through the back shop door and asked for more tea. Just after six, she had cashed up and updated the book. Physically and mentally exhausted, she knocked loudly on the office door and waited until she heard him call her in.

She found him sitting back in Sid's chair, feet propped on the desk, thumbing through a magazine. Her hackles rose. In all the time she had worked for Sid Mallin, never had she found him in such a situation. From the minute he arrived at work until the moment he left, which at times was long after his employees had gone home, he would be beavering away, poring through the racing pages studying form, keeping his records up-to-date, or dealing with his private clients via the telephone. And no matter how busy he was, he would never have left her on her own all day to cope with the counter without even a dinner break.

'That the takings?' Alfie said, looking at the bulky bag in her hands.

She fought to keep herself from showing the anger she was feeling but regardless her tone was clipped. 'Yes, including what the runners took today. I've updated the book. The betting slips are all paper-clipped together for you to go through.' She placed everything on the desk then couldn't stop herself adding, 'I expect you'll want to check that everything is in order, but I can assure you there are no discrepancies.'

'I don't expect there to be. Mr Mallin told me you were very thorough. In fact, he said that you were quite capable of handling most matters on the counter by yourself.' He eyed her enquiringly. 'No one came in and asked to see the boss, I take it?'

She shook her head. 'No. I would have informed you if so. Were you expecting anyone in particular?'

He stared at her blankly. 'I'll see you tomorrow then. Goodnight, Miss Downs.'

'Oh! Goodnight.' She made to leave then stopped. 'Er . . . before I go, Mr Manners. I've managed the counter all by myself today but . . .'

'Yes, I appreciate that,' he cut in. 'I'll . . . er . . . see about getting you some help. I trust you'll do your best to manage meantime?'

'Yes, of course, but . . .'

'Goodnight.'

She stared at him open-mouthed for several seconds

before deciding it was best just to leave.

In her desperation to get home and tackle Ray on what had taken place in the office to make him walk out like he had, the journey seemed to take for ever. To make matters worse it was pouring with rain and several already overflowing buses had driven straight past her at the bus stop. By the time she arrived home she was sodden.

As soon as she stepped into the kitchen it was immediately apparent that something was dreadfully wrong. Dec, Jimmy and Colin were gathered around her mother who was sobbing uncontrollably. Nan was sitting at the table and her aged face was grim. No one seemed at all concerned about the pans on the stove that were bubbling away, lids rising and falling, spitting boiling water on to the gas flames below.

'What's wrong?' Lynnie cried.

They all turned and looked at her.

'It's our Ray,' blurted Colin.

'Ray? What about him?' A great surge of foreboding went through her. 'What's happened to him? Dec, Jimmy, for God's sake, tell me what's going on!'

'He's gone,' said Jimmy.

She was bewildered. 'Gone? What do you mean, he's gone?'

It was Dec who responded. 'Nan came home from visiting one of her cronies this afternoon and found a note propped on the table. It just sez he's decided to go and stop with a mate for a while and that we're not to worry, he'll be in touch soon.'

Her mother erupted then. 'Why's he done this, Lynnie? He seemed so settled working at Cigar Sid's. Why has he done this?'

She shook her head in disbelief. 'It's obviously something to do with what happened there today. Ray walked out on his job.'

'He's what?' Avril cried, astounded. 'But why?'

Lynnie sighed heavily. 'You'd all better sit down and I'll tell you. Well, what I know anyway.'

They did as she said and she told them what had happened at work, finishing by saying, 'So I'm as much in the dark as you. I never got a chance to speak to Ray after he came out of his interview with the new boss. Mr Manners . . . well, I can't say as I've taken to him at all. He's nothing like Sid in any way. I can only hope Sid comes back soon. But why our Ray couldn't just put up with the new boss until Sid returns is beyond me.'

They all sat in bemused silence.

It was Dec who spoke first. He gave a shrug of his shoulders and said matter-of-factly, 'Well, our Ray's old enough ter tek care of himself so I don't know what all the fuss is about. He's given up his job and gone away to stay with a mate for a bit. So what?'

'Yeah, so what?' Jimmy echoed.

'So what? So what!' their mother exploded. 'Have you two brainless idiots got any idea what it's like for a mother when one of her kids buggers off without a word? Have yer? Well, have yer, eh?'

Dec looked at her blankly. 'But our Ray ain't gone

off without a word. He left a note.'

'Yeah, he left a note,' said Jimmy.

Avril jumped up from the table and screamed, 'Oh, get out, the pair of yer. Go on, get out me sight.'

'Mam, don't,' cried Lynnie. 'They're right. Ray obviously wants some time to himself. He'll be back before you know it.'

'Listen to the gel, Avril,' said her mother. 'Yer getting yerself all worked up over nothing. Ray left you a note telling yer what he was up to, so what more d'yer want?'

'I want him here, that's what I want.'

Her mother gave her a warning look. 'He's not a kid any more, Avril, and the sooner you loosen those apron strings, the better you'll be for it. You can't keep yer kids tied to you for ever. Now there's other members of this family besides Ray and I don't know about you but this one is famished. D'yer want a hand dishing up the dinner?'

Avril stared at her mother and reluctantly saw sense. Freda was right. Her children, except for Colin, were all of an age when they could decide for themselves how they conducted their lives. She had in fact been lucky up to now, considering their ages, that her elder children still remained under her roof, apart from Ray's year in prison and Dec and Jimmy's few months down in London. It suddenly hit her that this situation could not go on for ever. She ought to start getting used to the fact that sooner rather than later they would all leave home. She felt a lump form in her throat. That was a time she wasn't looking forward to. But then she consoled herself by thinking that for the time being at least she had them all here and would make the most of that. Her eldest son had not left home. All he'd done was go away for a short while. Hopefully he'd be back before she knew it, just like Lynnie had said. In the meantime the rest of her brood needed her motherly attention.

'Set the table, Colin,' she ordered. 'Dec, you mash the tea. Jimmy . . . mek yerself useful. Lynnie, get out of those wet things before yer catch yer death, and hurry up about it. I don't want yer dinner going cold.'

Before she busied herself with her task she flashed a loving smile at her own mother.

Later that evening, along with Shirley, Lynnie sat at Sheila's kitchen, nursing a mug of tea.

'So hopefully,' Shirley was saying, 'fingers crossed, we'll get a house soon. Mind you, I have no idea where. Yer get a choice of two apparently and have to pick one of them.'

'Around here, though?' said Sheila.

Shirley looked at her apologetically. 'I requested not to have one round here 'cos I want to be away from me mam, Sheila. If I get one within walking distance she'll never be off me doorstep, ordering me about like she does. Me and Pete want a fresh start and to be allowed to run our own lives. I can't even mek me own daughter her dinner without me mother sticking her oar in. I wouldn't mind if she had a clue what she was talking about, but she hasn't, and the last thing I want is my kids being dragged up like I was.' Sheila smiled in understanding and Shirley continued, 'The council said they'd see what they could do, so we might land up on either the Saffron Estate or New Parks. I prefer New Parks to the Saff. At least I'd be not too far away from you two to visit, but far enough away not to have me mam popping in every five minutes.'

'Well, we'll keep our fingers crossed that you do get offered New Parks. That's great news, isn't it, Lynnie?' Sheila enthused. When she received no response she turned to look at her, 'Isn't it, Lynnie? Good news about Shirley hopefully getting a house of her own soon?'

Lynnie had been only half-listening to the conversation, her mind dwelling on what had transpired during the day. 'Pardon? Oh, yes, it certainly is. You need a place of your own. It doesn't matter how far away you end up, Shirley, I'll come and see you even if I have to catch a dozen buses.' She took a sip of tea and asked, 'So, how's my beautiful god-daughter Jenny since I saw her last week?'

Shirley's face lit up. 'Oh, she's a bit of a misery at the moment as she's teething, bless her. I can't grumble though as on the whole she's a good little soul. I can't believe she's six months old already. I just wonder what she's going to say when she finds out she was born in the middle of Braunny Park in a clump of bushes.'

'If she's anything like her mother she'll see the funny side of it,' said Sheila.

Shirley guffawed. 'Yeah, she will, although it weren't exactly funny at the time.' She nodded a greeting at Everal as he came through. 'All right?'

He nodded back. 'Yes, thanks.' He smiled broadly, displaying his perfect white teeth which seemed to sparkle against his dark skin. He smiled affectionately at his wife. 'Don't mean to disturb you, darlin', just getting meself a bottle of beer. I've checked on the kids and they're both fine.' He opened the pantry door, took out a bottle, then returned to the living room to watch television.

As the kitchen door closed Sheila gave a sigh.

'What's up?' Shirley asked her.

'Oh . . . nothing really. I just wish Everal could find two such good friends as I've found in you, that's all. He's happy enough, I know he is, me and the girls are his life. But, well . . . it's not just us women who need friends, men do too. He seems to get on well enough with his mates at work – not all, some still give him a hard time because of his colour, and I know that upsets Everal. Not that he says much, I just know. But I also know he would just be delighted to have another man to share his love of music or to go for an occasional drink with. He had lots of friends before he married me. If only . . .'

'If only what?' prompted Shirley.

'Well, I just think it would go a long way towards Everal being accepted back into his own community if only his parents would mellow towards us. Hopefully then others would too. We aren't the first mixed marriage and I'm damned sure we won't be the last. Everal misses his parents terribly, especially his mother and brothers. For that matter, I miss mine. I dread the girls starting to ask questions about having no other family but us. How do I explain to them that we have lots between us, but because their father is black and their mother is white and they are a mixture of us both, we've all been ostracised?'

Lynnie patted her arm reassuringly. 'It'll all come right, Sheila, in the end, I'm sure it will.'

She gave a wan smile. 'You've more faith than me, Lynnie. As time passes, I lose hope.'

Lynnie sighed thoughtfully. 'I wish there was something I could do.'

'Oh, Lynnie, you and your family between them have done more than enough. It's because of you that we've been accepted around here. Yes, I grant you, we still get stares in the street and people nudging and pointing. There's still abuse occasionally. I hope with time that will lessen, but at least we get invited by the locals whenever there's an occasion going on and, touch wood, no bricks through the windows or dog muck through the letter box any more. I'm grateful for that, really I am.' She rose. 'I'll mash another pot of tea.'

Shirley stood up and took her coat from the back of the chair. 'Not for me, Sheila. Best get back and see Pete's coping with our Jenny okay. She was fast off when I left and he insisted I come to see you both but . . .'

'It's okay, Shirley,' Sheila cut in. 'We understand.

We'll see you next Monday, all being well.'

She grinned. 'You bet. Coming here for a couple of hours, having a natter with you two is what's keeping me sane at the moment.'

'I'll pop by later in the week as usual,' said Lynnie. 'Take care now.'

Sheila went to see her out. On returning, she filled the kettle and lit the gas beneath it, then turned to face Lynnie. 'Both Shirley and Pete have taken to parenthood like ducks to water. Little Jenny is so cherished by them. Right, you've listened to me and Shirley rattle on. Now it's your turn.' She sat down opposite Lynnie and looked at her in concern. 'I know a woman with something on her mind.'

She sighed. 'I wasn't going to bother you and Shirley with it. You two have enough to cope with as it is.'

'Lynnie, I know I speak for Shirley too when I say that as your dearest friends both of us have time for your troubles whatever we're dealing with ourselves, the same as you do for us. And you are troubled, I can tell.'

She nodded. 'You're right, I am.' She took a deep breath and before she could stop herself everything poured out.

'Well,' Sheila exclaimed when she had finished, 'I'd better mash that tea, hadn't I, before the kettle boils dry?' Minutes later, she put the pot on the table and sat down again. After pouring them both a fresh cup, she said, 'I shouldn't worry about your Ray, Lynnie. He's a grown man and quite capable of looking after himself.'

'That's what Dec and Jimmy said. But what about his job, Sheila? He was so lucky Sid gave him a chance when no one else would because of his criminal record. He loved working in that bookie's so much. He'd built up a great round, had at least twenty collections from firms on his patch each morning, and Sid was going to teach him everything to do with the betting world. Ray had a great future ahead of him, Sheila. I can't understand why he would give it all up just like that without even trying to get along with Alfie Manners until Sid comes back. What he did doesn't make sense to me. And now he's gone off like this to God knows where. It's like he's gone away to nurse his wounds.' She paused before saying, 'Alfie Manners must have said something to Ray to make him do what he did. I don't know, made it impossible for him to work there any longer.'

'Why would he want to do that, Lynnie? The man's only temporary, it's not like he's taken over permanently, and to my mind it would be in his own best interests to keep good employees happy. They know the workings of the place so it makes his life much easier for the time he's there.'

'Mmm, yes, I can see your point.'

'Have you thought, Lynnie, that maybe Ray was upset Sid put someone in over him? Maybe he felt insulted, left because his pride took a battering. You know what men can be like when it comes to their pride.'

'Oh, yes, I never thought of that.'

'There you go then. That could be the answer. Look on the bright side, Lynnie. By the time Ray comes back from staying with his mate, Sid could be back too and then any misunderstandings can be cleared up, Sid will give him his job back and all will be back as it was.'

A smile lit Lynnie's face. 'Oh, I so hope you're right, Sheila.' Then she added, 'If, that is, Sid has a business to come back to.'

'What makes you say that? Don't you trust Alfie Manners?'

She pulled a face. 'It's not that exactly. Sid obviously trusts him so I should too. But there's something odd about him. I suppose it's going to sound daft when I say this but he doesn't go with his clothes.'

'What do you mean?'

'Well, Alfie Manners dresses very loudly and you'd expect his personality to be the same, but it isn't. It's like the clothes and the man underneath clash with each other. Oh, it's so difficult to explain. Anyway, I've caught him a couple of times looking at me in a funny way.'

'What sort of funny way?' It was obvious to Sheila that Lynnie was having difficulty explaining herself. 'In a way maybe that gives the impression he thinks you're up to something? Like he's watching you, to catch you at it?'

'Well, now you come to mention it, yes, I think he could have been. Oh, I dunno, Sheila, it's probably only my imagination like it was when . . .' Her voice tailed off and she stared thoughtfully into space.

'When what, Lynnie?' Sheila prompted.

'Pardon? Oh . . . well, it's strange really what happened and I expect you'll think I'm barmy, but the very first time I clapped eyes on him behind the counter I got this funny feeling that I knew him. But that couldn't possibly be true. I'd never seen him before in my life.'

Sheila was looking at her thoughtfully. 'You've probably just seen him out somewhere. Is he good-looking?'

'He could be, I suppose, if he hadn't such appalling dress sense and did something about his hair.'

Sheila laughed. 'If I'd judged Everal by his dress sense, I would never have accepted a date with him.'

'Why, what was he wearing when you first met?' Lynnie asked, intrigued.

Sheila laughed. 'Brown trousers, a brown shirt and sleeveless pullover, and an overcoat that was too big even for Everal – and he's definitely no midget. That was brown too. Oh, and a brown pork pie hat. You can imagine what those clothes did for him with his skin colour.'

Lynnie laughed at the vision her mind's eye was conjuring up. 'I can imagine. If he'd been standing against a brown wall, you'd never have known he was there at all.' She looked at Sheila enquiringly. 'If he looked so bad, what was it about him that attracted you?'

Sheila looked at her dreamily. 'It was his smile.'

'His smile?'

'Yes. I'd gone to the Palais with several of my girlfriends. Everal was there with his mates. We were making our way to the dance floor and I had to squeeze past him. As I did so he smiled down at me and I was mesmerised. I think I knew then and there that I had met the love of my life. Don't ask me how, I just knew.' She laughed. 'I think he asked me to dance because he was so embarrassed by me standing staring at him like the idiot I must have looked. I can't even remember saying yes. I just remember this big firm hand taking hold of mine and leading me off. Next thing I was in his arms and it felt so right. Anyway, the rest is history. But I soon changed his dress sense, I can tell you,' she said, chuckling. 'Anyway Alfie Manners's appalling clothes aren't important, Lynnie. Getting along with him until Sid returns is.'

'Yes, I suppose you're right. Sid asked me in his letter to show the same loyalty to Mr Manners that I show to him, and the least I can do is honour that. He's been good to me has Sid.'

'That's the spirit, Lynnie. Seems to me as though you have more important things to be concentrating on than your job. You and Ozzie back together! You're a dark horse keeping quiet about that.'

'I didn't mean to be secretive, it's just that I wanted to make sure first before I said anything. Especially to my mam and nan. I've a fair idea how they're going to react if . . . when I break the news to them.'

'Well, their attitude is understandable. They witnessed how much he hurt you, and don't want to see it happen again. Yes, you're right to keep this from them until you know for definite. Mind you, I think it will be *when* you do, Lynnie. From what you've told me Ozzie seems to have learned his lesson and is trying hard to prove himself to you.'

'Yes, he is, I'll give him that. I can't fault his efforts. The first night we went out he took me to a Chinese restaurant and the food was lovely. He wouldn't let me pay anything towards the bill. We've been out since and he's been . . . well, just great. He hasn't been late when we've arranged to meet or given me any reason to think he's shoving me aside for his mates.'

'So everything is going swimmingly up to now?'

'Yes . . . yes, it is, and I've no reason to think it won't continue. I have to keep pinching myself, it all seems too good to be true.' Lynnie stood up and grabbed her coat which was draped around the back of her chair. 'I feel so much better for speaking about all of this to you, Sheila,' she said, smiling affectionately at her. 'Thanks for listening to me and for your advice. Now I'd best get off. I've a busy day tomorrow considering I'm manning the counter alone until my temporary boss sorts out some help for me. I just pray this situation doesn't last long and everything returns to normal soon.'

Chapter Sixteen

The following Friday morning Lynnie sighed with relief after seeing off the last of a long queue of desperate punters and was just about to make a start logging each individual transaction in the book when suddenly she jumped as she felt a presence by her side. She turned her head to see Alfie Manners staring at her. 'Oh!' she exclaimed, feeling unnerved by his close scrutiny. This wasn't the first time she had caught him looking at her. 'Er . . . is there anything I can do for you, Mr Manners?' she said tartly.

He held a mug of tea towards her. 'I thought you could use this.'

She stared at the mug in his hand, the gesture coming as a total surprise to her. This was the first time since he had announced himself as her temporary boss five days ago that he had done anything of the sort. 'You made the tea? Oh, thank you, Mr Manners.' She then mentally scolded herself for sounding so grateful. Making her a mug of tea was the least he could do considering she was working so hard.

He then thrust a sheet of paper at her. 'Here are the odds for the next race for you to chalk on the board.'

She had to stop herself from snatching it off him. How on earth did he expect her to look after the counter as well as chalk the board, plus taking note of the results of each race as it was announced over the blower? She had been coping all week now and the strain was beginning to tell. It appeared he did, though. 'Er . . . any joy in getting any help in for me?' she asked.

'I'm working on it,' he said, and added, 'I haven't interviewed anyone suitable yet.'

As she had not witnessed any candidates arriving to be interviewed and would have had to let them through the counter, she wondered how he could make that statement. Maybe he saw people after hours? Though why he would choose that over daytime was beyond her. To her, though, at this moment anyone would be suitable; she would even welcome Madge Crane back, she was so desperate for assistance. She saw him reach into his pocket and pull out several small brown envelopes which he handed to her.

'The runners' wages, plus your own.'

Sid usually handed out the wages himself and she wondered why Alfie Manners was giving her the additional responsibility. She accepted them. 'Thank you. Oh, Mr Manners, it seems a lot of punters are backing Sunny Afternoon in the three-fifteen.'

He looked at her blankly. 'And?'

'Well, the odds are rather long and . . . do you not

want to shorten them? I mean, at the outside chance it does romp home it means a big payout for us, and that could risk wiping out today's profits.'

'Oh, yes, right. We'll shorten them then.'

'To what, Mr Manners?'

'Oh, I'll er . . . study form and let you know.'

With that he turned and disappeared back into his office.

She stood for a moment staring at the closed door, her thoughts whirling. From his manner she had received the distinct impression that Alfie Manners didn't know much at all about the betting business. Then she mentally shook herself. Her impression must have been wrong. Sid Mallin would never leave his precious business in the hands of someone who didn't know what they were doing. She did wonder, though, if the man possessed another change of clothes as up to now she had yet to see him in anything other than that loud checked suit, red shirt and heavily patterned kipper tie.

She returned to her work and several minutes later Alfie came out and addressed her. 'Reduce the odds against Sunny Afternoon to fives. Oh . . . er . . . and thanks for bringing it to my attention.'

You should have known, like Sid would have, she thought. He had enquired constantly how the betting was proceeding, and she felt annoyed that Alfie Manners was heaping the responsibility for this on to her when it was his job as the manager to do such things.

The rest of the day passed quickly. After finishing off that evening, as usual she gathered everything together to take through to Alfie Manners. She knocked on the office door and as she waited for his response, could hear him speaking and realised he must be on the telephone. Despite branding Madge Crane an eavesdropper her own curiosity got the better of her and she put her ear to the door. Although his voice was muffled she felt positive she heard him say: *'No, not a thing yet. Look, I have to go . . '* Then she heard the handset being replaced and Alfie's shout of, 'Come in.'

As she entered her thoughts were confused, trying to work out who he could have been speaking to. Certainly not a punter, because she couldn't reason out why he would say what he had to a punter. Just what had he meant by *'No, not a thing yet'*?

She laid the day's business on the desk. 'Everything is in order, Mr Manners.'

'Thank you,' he said.

She saw him look hesitantly at her. 'Is there anything else, Mr Manners?'

'Er . . . no.' He turned his head to look out of the window. 'I expect you want to get off, being's it's Friday night. To go out with your . . . er . . . boyfriend?'

'Yes, I do,' she replied and wondered if it was her imagination that a brief look of disappointment crossed his face. 'Goodnight, Mr Manners.'

He turned to look at her. 'Goodnight.'

She couldn't help but notice that his tone had a sharper edge to it.

She had just shut the shop door behind her when a car drew up, simultaneously the horn blasted and Ozzie's head appeared out of the driver's side window. 'Come on, Lynnie, hurry up,' he called over, grinning at her broadly.

She ran across to him. 'Ozzie, what are you doing here in this car? I told you I wouldn't get in it until you'd passed your test.'

'I have,' he announced. 'I passed it this morning.'

'You did? Oh, you did! Why, Ozzie, that's great. Congratulations!'

'Come on, get in,' he urged. 'I just thought I'd surprise yer by giving yer a lift home.'

The thought of not having to stand and wait for a bus was a welcome one. 'Oh, thanks, Ozzie, I appreciate it.' As she got into the car, she said, 'I've not spoken to my family about us yet so best you drop me off at the corner of the street.'

'Yer gonna tell them soon, though, ain't yer, Lynnie? 'Cos we're all right now, ain't we?'

She smiled warmly at him. 'Yes, we are, and I will soon, I promise,' she assured him despite the thought of her mother's reaction filling her with dread. If only Ray would come home she could have asked him to try and smooth the way for her; as it was she would have to do this by herself.

As they drove off, she happened to turn her head to address Ozzie and out of the corner of her eye caught sight of Mallin's shop door. She could have sworn Alfie Manners was peeking behind the blind looking out at them. But before she could confirm this Ozzie had driven the car off down the road.

Her mother looked at her in surprise when she walked in the back door. 'You're sharpish tonight, our Lynnie. Since that new bloke took charge it's bin gone seven before you've arrived home.'

'Oh, I . . . er . . . got a lift from a friend, Mam,' she said, taking off her coat and hanging it on a hook at the back of the door.

'A lift from a friend? One with a car? Oh, our Lynnie, you are coming up in the world. Ain't she, our Mam?' she said, turning to look at Freda who was mashing a pan of potatoes at the table.

Nan nodded. 'I expect yer going out again tonight too,' she said, adding milk and a knob of margarine to the pan. 'Nice to see you starting to go out and enjoy yerself after getting rid of that cretin.'

'Cretin! Oh, Nan, Ozzie's no cretin.'

'Oh, defending him now,' said her mother as she put plates on the table. 'You've changed yer tune.'

'No, I've not, Mam,' Lynnie sharply responded. 'I might have said some nasty things about Ozzie when I was angry with him for leaving me standing at the church, but I've never called him a cretin. What is a cretin anyway?' she asked her grandmother.

'Eh? Oh, I haven't got a clue,' said Freda, vigorously thrashing a fork around the potatoes. 'I just heard someone call it to someone else once and thought it sounded a good word to use about someone who doesn't appreciate a good thing when he's got it.'

'And Ozzie certainly never appreciated just what he'd got in you, Lynnie,' piped up her mother. 'He was always putting his mates before you and leaving you standing around waiting for him. And you, like a clot, always forgave him. A' yer finished mashing the spuds yet, Mam?' she asked Freda.

'People change. They learn their lesson. Maybe he wouldn't treat me like that now,' said Lynnie.

Avril eyed her shrewdly. 'You ain't thinking of giving Oswald Matthews another chance, are yer?'

Lynnie took a deep breath, choosing her words very carefully. 'Would you be angry if I was?'

'Angry? I wouldn't be angry, I'd be . . . well . . .'

'What yer mam's trying ter tell yer, Lynnie,' Freda interjected, 'is that she'd be very surprised a gel like you would want to go back down that path. And so would I. Ozzie's not a bad lad by any means, and he'd make some woman a good enough husband, but . . .'

'But you don't think he would me?' cut in Lynnie.

'Well, if his sort is what yer really want, me and yer mam will stand by yer. You'd go along with it, Avril?'

'I suppose I'd have to like I did when yer was courting him,' she responded gruffly as she strained a pan of cabbage over the sink.

'But people *do* change,' Lynnie reiterated.

'So you keep saying,' her mother snapped. 'And I agree with yer, some people do. We have, ain't we? Our Ray's experience in jail certainly made us all see the light. But Ozzie . . . well . . . I'm not sure if he's the sort to manage to keep it up for long. You might be convinced that he has, 'cos yer want to think so, and when he starts to make small lapses you'll make excuses for him. But if yer weren't careful, before yer know it yer'd be back where yer started, him fobbing yer off with his cock and bulls to cover up boozing with his mates, playing darts or snooker, while you're left at home looking after the babies and it'd be too late for yer to get out of it then.'

'Listen to yer mam, Lynnie,' Freda advised. 'In fact, listen to both of us. We've seen how a man can put on an act when he badly wants something. We both thought the sun shone out of yer dad's arse when he was courting yer mam and seemed so eager to do the right thing when she fell pregnant. It wasn't until after the wedding, when he didn't need to play the part anymore 'cos he'd got what he wanted, that his true nature came out and we found out what a bastard he was. I ain't saying Ozzie's anything like yer dad but you've seen his true colours and suffered from them, Lynnie. His shortcomings were enough to mek you weep buckets more times than I care to remember. So, unlike yer mam, yer forewarned. If you are thinking about giving Ozzie another chance, just try and be as sure as yer can that he ain't putting on an act to get yer back, that's all we're asking, lovey.'

Before she could respond there was a knock at the front door. 'Who the hell is that at dinner time? Colin!' Avril shouted. 'Get the door. So, Lynnie,' she continued, 'just think twice before yer do 'ote yer might regret. And if yer do tek him back, well, we'll both know it's what you really want and we'll be happy for yer.'

Colin arrived. 'It's Piss Pot, Mam. She wants ter see yer. Is dinner ready? I'm starving.'

'I've never known you when yer ain't. I bet I can guess what that old bag wants. Lynnie, help yer nan dish out the dinner. Colin, get yer brothers through. This won't take a minute.'

They were all sitting at the table tucking in to faggots and mash when Avril returned. 'It was as I thought,' she said, her eyes dancing wickedly. 'She came to suss me out, hoping that I'd reconsidered my decision and was in the market for her knock-off stuff again. I bleddy gave her what for! Sent her away with a flea in her ear. We Downses stick to our word. Ain't that right, you lot?' she said, casting her eyes around each in turn.

Freda fixed hers on Dec and Jimmy. 'Squeaky clean,' she said, looking at them meaningfully. 'That's us, ain't it? All of us. Or we know what's in store.'

They stared at her fearfully. 'Yeah, we do, Nan,' they both said in unison.

As she put a forkful of food in her mouth, Lynnie looked at her grandmother then at Dec and Jimmy. She had caught the warning behind Nan's words, and the look of fear in her brothers' eyes. She was distracted then by her mother announcing, 'Now yer all together, I've summat ter yell yer.'

They looked up, intrigued.

Her face split into a happy smile. 'I had a letter from our Ray today. Not much of one, I grant yer, and no address on it either so any of us can write back or visit, but at least he bothered to write and that means everything to me.'

'So what does the letter say, Mam?' urged Lynnie.

'Oh, just that we're not to worry about him 'cos he's fine. That he's getting on all right with his mate, whoever this mate is as he doesn't give him a name, and has decided to stay put a little longer since he's found work.'

'What kinda work?' asked Dec.

She shrugged. 'He didn't say. Whatever it is, it obviously pays well 'cos he enclosed a five-pound note and said he'd send me one every week 'til he got back. Bless our Ray, he knows this two pound above what he normally gives me for his board will mek such a difference.' She beamed in delight. 'With all your board money and my wages and Ray's extra, we ain't so badly off now, I'm relieved ter say.'

Lynnie gave a sigh of relief. With all that had gone on recently and what she was being forced to contend with, it had temporarily slipped her mind that she had been going to try and rally her brothers together to see if they could come up with a way to ease their mother's burden. Ray's thoughtfulness could go some way to doing that until they could all contribute more. Lynnie wouldn't be entirely happy until it was possible for her mother to give up at least one of her jobs.

'Does Ray's money mean we don't have to have those rotten sausages no more?' said Colin.

'There was n'ote wrong with those sausages,' snapped Avril.

'Yes there was,' said Freda. 'They were full of fat and gristle.'

Avril sniffed. 'Well, yeah, okay, they were bleddy awful, but they helped fill a hole which is better than starving. Yer right, Colin, this means we can get our meat from a better butcher for as long as Ray's extra money keeps coming. Anyway, I'm happy to know me eldest lad's all right so all I have ter worry about now is you lot. Right, anyone for jam tart and custard?'

Dec scraped back his chair. 'Not for us, Mam.' He motioned to Jimmy. 'Come on, we've things to do.'

'What things?' asked Avril, looking at them enquiringly.

'Oh, we're helping a mate out.'

'Helping him do what?'

Dec gave a shrug. 'Just helping him.'

'Yeah, just helping him,' said Jimmy, leaping up to join his brother.

Before anyone could question them further, they both grabbed their coats and shot out.

Avril's face was screwed up with worry. 'I hope those lads . . .' Her voice trailed off and she gave a deep sigh.

'Hope those lads what, Mam?' asked Lynnie.

Avril gave herself a mental shake. 'Nothing. So who's for jam tart and custard?'

Lynnie's thoughts whirled. She knew her mother had

been going to say she hoped her lads were not doing anything they shouldn't be. They had all solemnly promised to keep on the straight and narrow and the rest of them had striven hard to do so. She prayed Dec and Jimmy weren't breaking their vow. At first breaking the habit of practically a lifetime and managing without their illicit extras had been a hard-fought thing for all of them. They had struggled and gone without but together they had come through. Now they had turned the corner and their money problems were easing enough to up their standard of living a little. If Dec and Jimmy were up to no good it could divide the family. It suddenly struck her that they went out most nights and were never forthcoming over where they were going. Were they hiding something? She knew she must speak to them, satisfy herself that her mother's fears, and her own now, weren't justified. If they proved to be . . . well, she hadn't a clue what she would do then.

Chapter Seventeen

Worry that her brothers had lapsed back into the world of petty crime, something Ray had fought so hard against because of his great fear of any of them suffering the atrocities he had in prison, was responsible for Lynnie spending a fitful night. It clouded her thoughts as she worked the next day.

Trade had been brisk, and made hectic for her by the fact she was still doing the job of two, or even nearing three as she was also having to do tasks that Sid had previously taken care of, such as keeping an eye on the way the betting was going. Alfie Manners had still not produced any help for her, something she was starting to doubt he was actively seeking, and neither did he offer to pull his weight when it was obvious to anyone that she was struggling to cope.

To make matters worse for her that day, it was abnormally hot for May and the shop was stuffy. Enhancing the bodily odours emanating from the punters gathered around the Tannoy waiting for the first race to start was the increasingly thick

317

swirl of their cigarette smoke.

After dealing with a long queue, mortally glad when it seemed for a couple of minutes at least that no one was demanding her attention, Lynnie used the lull to concentrate her thoughts on the best way to approach her brothers with her suspicions. She could offend them badly if she was wrong, but there was good reason to think she was right. So consumed by her thoughts was she that she didn't realise anyone else had come in until she heard a voice demand:

'I said I wanna see the boss.'

She jumped. 'Pardon?' Then she recognised this man as being the same one who had demanded to see Sid previously, the day before his sudden departure. 'Who shall I say wants him?'

She received the same blunt response as before. 'Me. I do.'

Fighting to keep her annoyance at his attitude from showing, she took a deep breath and said evenly, 'I'll see if he's available.'

Without thinking she opened the office door and marched straight in and then, realising just what she had done, she stopped short. Alfie was scribbling something down on a piece of paper whilst talking on the telephone and was saying: 'No, no, nothing yet. Have patience . . .' He almost leaped out of his chair when he realised Lynnie was staring at him. 'Oh, God, Miss Downs. Er . . . er . . . I'll have to go, call you back,' he blurted down the telephone which he then slammed back into its cradle. He grabbed up the piece of paper he had been writing on and thrust it in her direction. 'The latest odds for you to chalk up.'

She took them from him and it was on her mind to say as she had enough to do it wouldn't hurt him to help her by doing it himself, but she thought better of it. 'There's a man called to see you. Well, he never asked for you by name, just asked to see the boss. He won't give his name.'

Was it her imagination or did a look of excitement briefly cross his face? She watched, puzzled, as hurriedly he bundled up a pile of magazines and thrust them in a drawer then grabbed up that day's newspaper which had been folded neatly on the edge of the desk. He opened it at the racing pages, spread it quickly across the desk then, pen poised, looked at her and said: 'Well, show him in.'

It struck her he was setting the scene to give the appearance of being a busy man. Huh! She turned on her heel and did as she was bidden.

Twenty minutes later the shabby man emerged from the office and left the shop. Lynnie did notice he seemed happy about something. Immediately after him Alfie came out and made his way over to the shop door. Lynnie watched curiously as he inched aside the blind and appeared to be watching the man as he walked off up the road. She wondered what was so interesting about that particular punter that made him do that. Then she remembered thinking that the night before Alfie Manners had been watching her and Ozzie in the same kind of way. Mr Manners, it seemed, had a habit of secretly watching people.

As usual before she left for home, Lynnie – remembering this time to knock on the office door before she entered – took the day's dealings through to Alfie, placing them on the desk in front of him. 'Everything is in order, Mr Manners.'

He smiled at her. 'As usual then.' He seemed to pause, eyeing her hesitantly. 'Er . . . off out with the boyfriend again tonight?' Then he added hurriedly, 'It's just that you look tired. I thought you might be best off getting an early night tonight, that's all.'

She felt the urge to say to him that what she did out of working hours was her business and nothing to do with him, despite the fact that he was right. She was extremely tired and had already begun to wish she hadn't arranged to meet Ozzie this evening for a drink in town. How she wished now that she had taken her chance when the subject of Ozzie had come up the night before to come clean about them both. She loved her mother and grandmother, respected their views, had listened to their advice on being cautious before she did anything she might later live to regret, and she knew they had meant it well, had her best interests at heart, but she was now convinced Ozzie was a reformed character. He'd done nothing to make her feel otherwise, and she was sorry for going behind their back now that she and Ozzie were back on as an item. Had she taken the opportunity to get this problem over and done with then she and Ozzie could both have curled up on the settee tonight and watched some television together, instead of spending the evening in some noisy pub costing them money that would have been better saved towards their future together.

She looked at Alfie meaningfully. 'With all due respect, Mr Manners, I wouldn't be so tired if you would see your way to getting me some help.' And she couldn't help but add, 'I do appreciate your concern for my welfare but what I do with my evenings is really my business. As a matter of great interest, have you had any news on when Mr Mallin is expected to return?'

'You'll be the first to know when I do, Miss Downs.'

He was angry with her, glaringly so. It was obvious to Lynnie that Alfred Manners didn't take kindly to women who spoke up for themselves. In a small way the pleasure she derived from this fact compensated for his laziness. She hid a smile as she said, 'Goodnight, Mr Manners.'

She gave a toss of her head and walked out of the office.

Later that evening Lynnie felt a hard nudge in her ribs and jerked up her head to see Ozzie shaking his at her.

'Goodness, Lynnie, I thought yer'd drifted off then. Look, if yer didn't want to come out ternight because yer too tired, you should have said summat. I'd have been upset but I'd have understood.'

A warm glow filled her at his genuine show of concern for her welfare, one of the things that had been seriously lacking previously. Not that he had never showed he cared, but had never openly showed it without her prompting him. 'I'm sorry, Ozzie. I'm not much company, am I?'

'There's plenty of other jobs, yer know, and you'd be snapped up. I don't know why yer standing for being treated like a galley slave.'

'Ozzie, this situation is only temporary until Sid comes back. It would be totally different if it was permanent. I can assure you, I would definitely be looking for other employment if so.' She gave a worried sigh. 'But I've no idea what could be keeping Sid from his business for so long. It must be something terrible that's happened.'

'Yeah, but even so that bleddy temporary manager shouldn't be relying so much on you. I've a good mind to come down and give him a piece of me mind.'

'And that's the last thing I want, Ozzie, so don't you dare. You doing that could get me the sack. Oh, Alfie Manners isn't so bad really. He never bothers me apart from now and again on small matters. He even makes the tea sometimes now which he never thought to do when he first took over.'

'And leaves you to do practically everything else.'

'Well, as I said, hopefully it won't be for much longer. My mam always says that a bit of hard work never killed anyone.' She looked at him searchingly for a moment, then took his hand. 'Look, Ozzie, I know this news will please you. It's getting difficult for me to cover up where I'm going and who I'm with when I'm seeing you, and I hate lying to my family. So I'm going to tell them about me and you. I'm going to do it tonight when I get home.'

His face lit up in delight. 'You are! Ah, Lynnie, that's great. I know we ain't been back together long, but I did wonder how long this trial period would last.' He squeezed her hand tightly. 'You mean everything to me, Lynnie. You have ter believe, I'd do anything it takes to make you happy.'

'I believe you, Ozzie,' she whispered softly.

He let go of her hand, thrust his own into his trouser pocket and pulled out a small box. 'Here,' he said, holding it out to her. 'I never got yer one before because I never had the money. Well, I suppose I could have saved but that's past history now, ain't it? My days of not pulling me weight money-wise are over. This is a new start for us, Lynnie, and you're never gonna regret it – never. I wasn't meaning to give this to you tonight, I wanted to take yer somewhere for a nice meal and propose proper, but what the heck? Yer might as well have it now and we can go for a meal to celebrate another time.'

She took it from him. 'What is it?'

'Why don't yer look?'

She opened the box and gave a gasp when she saw the tiny solitaire diamond twinkling back at her. 'Oh, Ozzie,' she whispered. 'It's beautiful.'

'Are we engaged then?'

She laughed, her eyes shining with love. 'Oh, Ozzie, what a proposal! How could any woman refuse an offer like that?'

He grabbed her to him, crushing her. 'I'm gonna get you the world, Lynnie. A big house, four bedrooms at least, and nice furniture . . .'

'Ozzie, stop it! Stop getting carried away. We don't have the kind of jobs to pay for all that. A little terrace will do us fine, and until we save up enough for the deposit I don't mind where we live . . . but not that terrible flat we saw. I draw the line at something that bad. Besides, this ring must have cost a fair bit. You must be skint at the moment.' Then an awful thought struck her. 'Oh, Ozzie, you haven't borrowed the money to pay for this, have you?' she asked worriedly.

'No, 'course I ain't,' he scoffed. 'What, and pay those sharks their extortionate interest rate? I saved the money up,' he said proudly. 'I've bin doing lots of overtime on the nights I ain't been seeing yer.'

Her eyes widened in shock. 'Oh, Ozzie, and I thought you were out with your mates.' She gazed at the ring. 'And you did all that extra time at work to pay for this for me?' She brought her eyes back to rest on him, her face tender. 'What can I say? You have changed so much. I can't believe it.'

'Well, I'm doing me best to be the kinda man you want. So . . . er . . . are yer gonna put it on or what?'

She looked at the ring longingly for a moment then shook her head, handing it back to him. 'I want to tell my family first then we can have a proper engagement get together with everyone there and you can put it on my finger officially.'

'If that's what you want, my darlin', then that's fine

with me,' he said, returning the box to his pocket.

She fought to stifle a yawn. 'I know it's still very early but would you mind taking me home now? I'm that tired I could sleep on a clothes line. That's if I can now, after all this excitement.'

'Yeah, sure.' He grabbed her hand and pulled her up. 'Come on then, the future Mrs Ozzie Matthews.'

Giggling together, they left the pub to collect the car where Ozzie had left it earlier in a deserted side street, tucked behind an old disused building.

On the journey home, relaxed and happy, Lynnie dozed. Her dream was a wonderful one. She and Ozzie were walking back down the aisle serenaded by church bells, all around beamed the happy faces of their family and friends. Suddenly her sleep was shattered as the church bells seemed to get louder and louder. She struggled to open her eyes and sit upright, not under-standing why she could still hear bells ringing in her ears. 'Oh, I must have dropped off. I had a lovely . . .' Her drowsy voice trailed off, face creasing in bewilder-ment when it suddenly dawned on her that Ozzie was driving the car very fast and erratically.

'What's going on?' she asked. Then she realised that the bells had not been those of a church but were in fact the sounds made by a police siren. Automatically she turned her head to look out of the back window and gasped in shock to see a police car behind them, obviously giving chase. She jerked round to look at Ozzie.

'Why is a police car chasing us? And for God's sake,

slow down! You'll kill us both,' she cried as she grabbed hold of the door handle for support, gripping it tightly as the car sped faster, swerving dangerously as Ozzie weaved through the traffic. 'Oh!' she screamed as they sped straight through a red light and Ozzie narrowly missed a woman crossing the road. 'For God's sake, slow down!' she shouted. 'What the hell has got into you?'

It was then that she saw the fear in his eyes, the sheer panic on his face, and terror ripped through her.

The police car passed them to pull up just ahead and across the road, blocking their route. In an effort to avoid it Ozzie slammed his foot on the brake as simultaneously he pulled hard on the wheel. The car careered up on to the pavement and came to rest with a crunch against a low front garden wall. The impact caused Lynnie to lurch forward, banging her head on the windscreen so hard she was temporarily stunned.

Two policemen got out of the squad car and came over. While one walked around their car, looking over it, the other tapped on the driver's side window.

Ozzie wound it down. 'I'm sorry about that, officer,' he said breezily. 'I don't know what got into me. I was going a bit fast, wasn't I?' He gave the policeman a winning smile. 'I suppose yer'll give me a speeding ticket and then we can be on our way?'

'No hurry, is there, sir?' The policeman took a notebook and pencil from his top pocket. 'Is this your car?'

'What, this old thing?' Ozzie laughed. 'No, definitely

not, it's a mate's. I borrowed it for the evening.'

'And what's this mate's name?'

Ozzie gave a shrug. 'I'm not sure. I don't know him that well. Well, hardly at all. He very kindly offered me his car when he overheard me telling another mate that I would love to take me girl out for a drive, if I had a car that was. Well, yer don't refuse an offer like that, do yer?' He looked politely enquiring. 'There's nothing wrong, is there, officer?'

'That remains to be seen. And your name is?'

'Er . . .' He flashed a quick glance at Lynnie who was looking around, obviously still dazed from the knock she had received on her head. Quickly he turned his attention back to the policeman. 'It's Roger Wilson. I suppose yer want me address? It's twenty-six Caladine Road, New Parks Estate.'

'Thank you, sir,' said the policeman, jotting it down. 'Can I see your driving licence?'

'Oh, I ain't got it with me. It's at home. I can drop it down the police station for yer later, if yer like?'

'Would you get out of the car, sir?'

Lynnie regained her full faculties then. 'Oh, my head . . . Ozzie, are you all right? And why have the police stopped us? Why were they chasing us?'

'Yer know what the rozzers are like, Lynnie. They pick on anyone when they ain't got n'ote better to do.'

'Oh.' Her thoughts whirled. 'But I'm sure I heard you telling the policeman that this was a mate's car and your name is Roger and you live in New Parks. Why did you lie to them?'

'Oh, Lynnie, fer God's sake, you know as well as I do that yer never tell a copper yer true identity 'cos the bleeders will find summat to pin on yer, especially if they find out you come from the Braunstone Estate,' he hissed. 'Now, you stay here while I sort this out.' He pushed open the car door and got out. 'All right, officer, what else do yer want to know?'

The other policeman opened Lynnie's door and she looked up at him, confused. 'I'm sure this is just a misunderstanding, officer. My boyfriend didn't mean to drive so fast. I think you must have panicked him when you put the siren on.'

'Yes, I'm sure you're right. You are Miss Caitlyn Downs?'

She looked at him, mystified. 'Yes, but how did . . .'

'Would you like to get out, miss?'

Mind whirling as to how the policeman could possibly know her identity, she did as he asked and automatically followed him to the back of the car where Ozzie and the other policeman were standing.

The policeman with Ozzie said, 'Would you like to open the boot, sir?'

Ozzie's face paled alarmingly and he blurted, 'Why? You caught me speeding, okay I'm guilty. Give me a ticket and then I can get my fiancée home. She's had a bang on the head, she's probably got concussion. She might need to see a doctor. In fact, I should really get her to the hospital. Can't we deal with this later?'

'Just open the boot, sir.'

'No, I told yer, I won't. It ain't my car. Besides, I ain't got a key for the boot.'

'Judging by the wires hanging down from beneath the steering wheel you don't appear to have a starting key either. Mind you, that doesn't surprise us, sir, considering this car was registered as scrapped over four months ago and should not be on the road at all. According to our records it isn't registered to anyone and has no tax or insurance. And this isn't the first time you've driven this car, is it, sir? You've been seen driving around in it quite regularly. Well, certainly on three occasions to our knowledge during the past week, late at night. Can you explain that, sir?'

Lynnie's mouth dropped open. 'Ozzie, what's going on?' she demanded.

'Ozzie? Now would that be a nickname for Oswald Matthews by any chance?' the policeman with the notebook asked.

He froze rigid as a look of pure terror filled his face. 'How . . .'

The policeman smiled condescendingly at him. 'I'd strongly advise you not to mess with us any longer, sir. Quite a clever idea using an unregistered car as a vehicle in which to transport stolen goods before selling them on.'

Lynnie's mouth gaped even wider. 'What's he mean?' she demanded.

'I dunno what he's talking about,' exclaimed Ozzie, his voice revealing an edge of hysteria.

'Oh, I think you do, sir. A man answering to your

description and an accomplice bought this car from a scrapyard, using the excuse they wanted to use if for spare parts. We now know that your real intention was to fix it up enough to use it as a pick up and drop off vehicle for the boxes of shoes you've been buying from colleagues at British Shoe, who risk bringing them out concealed on their persons. In the event you were stopped for any reason, you thought you could lie your way out of it like you tried with us tonight. Or more than likely your hope was to abandon the vehicle and scarper before we actually caught up with you.'

'That's a lie,' Ozzie spat furiously. 'I've told yer the truth and you can't prove otherwise. This is a mate's car. I borrowed it. I don't know what's in the boot. If there is 'ote it's nothing to do with me,' he shouted frantically.

'And we might have had no choice but to take you at your word on that, sir, but we've actually witnessed you in action. Last night, for instance. You were watched from the minute you left your house to when you got home, making sure you parked the car some streets away as an added precaution. We saw you again tonight picking up a load before you met Miss Downs, and after you had dropped her off for the night we have good reason to believe you were intending to pay a visit on the man you are in cahoots with who runs a stall on the market. Well, that *was* your intention before we decided to pull you over and have a word, wasn't it, sir?'

Ozzie was staring at them in a frenzy. 'Who tipped you off?' he demanded.

'That's our business, sir. But if you'd like a chance to prove us wrong, just open the boot. Tell you what, to save us wasting any more time, let me do it for you,' the policeman said as he pressed the boot button and the lid shot up.

Ozzie said desperately: 'I did it all for you, Lynnie. Yer've got to believe me.'

She froze in horror as her eyes fell on the stack of boxes inside the boot. The policeman's account of Ozzie's illicit activities struck her full force.

'Oh, Ozzie!' she screamed at him. 'How could you? How could you do this to me after you know how strongly me and my family feel about this sort of thing now? How hard we've worked at keeping ourselves straight. You paid for the ring from the proceeds of stolen goods, our evenings out too, and all the time I thought you were being careful with your wages. How could you lie to me like that, so convincingly? You said you'd never let me down again. What do you call this?'

He looked at her, mystified. 'But I never let yer down, Lynnie. I was never late. I put you before me mates, like yer asked me. You complained I spent all me money on meself and it was you that was getting all the household stuff together. Well, I thought it'd make you happy, me chipping in and buying you nice things.' He looked at her questioningly. 'Oh, come on, Lynnie, how the hell did yer think I was managing to pay fer nice meals and whatever else out of the miserable

331

amount I get from me job as a warehouseman, even if I did all the overtime God sends? You musta realised that I was topping up me wages somehow? I wasn't going to keep doing it for long, Lynnie. Just long enough to get us the deposit for a house and a few bits and pieces.'

'Oh, so what you're trying to make me believe is that you've only been doing this since we got back together? This policeman says the car was bought from the scrapyard *four months ago* so what you say can't be true. We weren't back together then. Admit it, Ozzie, you've been planning this a long time and more than likely been at it for ages too. Do you seriously expect me to believe you would have stopped as soon as you'd made enough for a deposit on a house and some furniture? How much of a fool do you take me for? As long as you were getting away with it, you'd have carried on.'

He hung his head in shame. 'Lynnie, I'm sorry. I won't do it again. You will stick by me, won't yer? Please, Lynnie, please.'

She shook her head, stupefied, not understanding how he could be asking her to stand by him after such a mindless betrayal. 'How do you ever expect me to trust you again, Ozzie? You not only lied but blatantly risked my life by driving me around in a car that rightly belongs in a scrapyard crusher. You've no road tax or insurance, and I bet you never passed your test either. How do you think my family are going to react when they find out about all this?

332

'We vowed to each other, Ozzie, and you were with us and included, not to do anything like this ever again. Not only have you broken that promise, I've broken my vow to my family by associating with you, even though I didn't know anything about what you were up to.'

The policeman took her arm. 'Best go home now, miss. Can you find your way all right? We need to get Mr Matthews down the station so we can charge him.'

'Go home?' she uttered, shocked. 'But I thought you'd be charging me too? You caught me with Ozzie, didn't you? You must think I'm his accomplice.'

'Just go home, miss.'

She stared at him, perplexed. 'Oh! Oh, all right.'

Eyes filled with devastation, she looked at Ozzie. 'I never want to see you again.' Then she turned and walked off in a trancelike state.

It wasn't until she was halfway across Braunstone Park that what had just happened finally sank in. Tears flowed then, great torrents of them pouring down her face. She rocked with grief for an age, sobbing hysterically.

An elderly man out walking his dog spotted the distraught woman and immediately went over to her.

'You all right, me duck?' Which he knew was a bit of a daft question as the woman before him was clearly far from all right. When she didn't answer he repeated his question.

Lynnie's head jerked up and she looked at him blindly. 'What? Oh, yes, I'm okay,' she blubbered, wiping her wet face with the back of her coat sleeve.

'That yer ain't, me duck,' he said, taking her arm. 'Look, let me get yer home. D'yer live around here?' he asked.

She froze. Home. Sheer panic seized her. She couldn't go home. She couldn't let her family see her in this state. They'd immediately demand to know what was wrong. And what would their reaction be when she tried to explain what had happened? Would they understand why she had kept her renewed relationship with Ozzie secret from them? Would they believe she hadn't knowingly been driving around with him in a car that had been registered as scrapped, with a boot full of stolen shoes? Would they think her stupid enough not to have questioned his lies or even considered how plausible his stories were? Would they think she had never taken their vow seriously and had always been aware Ozzie was up to no good, and gone along with him? No matter how hard she tried to convince them of her innocence they might never trust her again. That possibility was unbearable to her.

Her mind whirled frantically as she fought with her conscience. Half of her wanted to be truthful with them, knowing that they loved and respected her enough to believe her innocence in all this, but the other part was terrified just in case they didn't. That terrible fear was enough to sway her decision. She must keep this to herself. Hope that her involvement with Ozzie and the fact that she was actually present at his arrest would never come out. That the police hadn't taken her along to the station to charge her as his accomplice, or even to question her to satisfy themselves that she wasn't, was something she still couldn't quite understand. But for some reason they hadn't and she was so thankful for that. Hopefully her recent reassociation with Ozzie would never come to light and her family and everyone else need be none the wiser.

She knew she must look awful. It was very apparent that something dreadful had happened to her. Before she went home she needed to compose herself in order to give no one any reason to question her or she might break down and tell them everything and she couldn't risk that. Where could she go to find some privacy to freshen up and compose herself before she faced them? Then it struck her. The shop. She carried the emergency key that Sid had entrusted her with on the key ring she always kept in her handbag. In total privacy there she could bathe her face in cold water from the kitchen tap and rest for a while until she felt sure all her family had retired to bed and she could slip in unobserved.

Taking several shuddering breaths, she looked at the kindly old gentleman who had come to her aid. 'Thanks for your concern. I'm fine now, honest.'

He eyed her knowingly. 'Had a row with yer chap?'

A bolt of pain shot through her as she wiped her tearful eyes with the back of her hand. 'Yes, something like that. I'll get myself off home now.'

'I'll come with yer,' he offered. 'It's dark and getting kinda late for a pretty gel like you to be wandering about on yer own. It wouldn't be right of me to abandon yer.'

He made to take her arm to escort her.

'No, honestly,' she insisted. 'I'm grateful for your offer but I can manage, thank you. I only live across there,' she fibbed, pointing over to a row of houses that edged the park.

'Oh, okay, if yer sure. Tek care now,' he said as he pulled on his dog's lead and together they set off again.

As soon as he had gone a short distance, she kicked up her heels and raced off in the direction of the Hinckley Road which would take her to the shop.

Despite all her efforts her distress was still so great she could not stem the constant flood of tears and by the time she reached her destination she knew she must look even worse than when the old man had approached her.

Fumbling in her handbag for her key ring which she finally unearthed tucked at the bottom, she let herself in. Due to hardly any light being allowed into the shop to afford punters their privacy the room was almost pitch black. Conscious that to put a light on at this time of night could be to risk attracting unwanted attention, she felt her way over to the counter where she lifted the flap and let herself through. In the square of passageway which held two doors, one of which led to Sid's office, the other into the kitchen, she was just about to switch on the kitchen light when she suddenly froze rigid. She could have sworn she heard a door being shut. Her eyes flashed down to see a shaft of light coming from under the office door which in her traumatised state she hadn't noticed before.

Her heart leaped and started to race frantically as realisation struck: Mallin's was being burgled. The burglars must have broken into the premises by the back entry which was in the office. It must be the contents of the safe they were after. Then it struck her that she couldn't remember Alfie Manners making any trips to the bank since he had taken over, a task which Sid had always carried out himself as he'd felt it too dangerous for a young woman like her to be out alone carrying a large amount of money on her person. In view of everything else she was coping with work-wise she had never given a thought to it this week. The safe must be holding at least five days' profits plus cash for any payouts which hadn't yet been collected. Oh, God, her mind screamed as loyalty to Sid and desire to protect his business flooded in. What was she to do? By the time she fetched the police the culprits could have long departed, their haul along with them. There was only one thing she could do. She would have to tackle them herself. Somehow she hoped that her sudden appearance would be enough to scare them into fleeing empty-handed. And there was no time to lose.

Without a thought for her own safety she grabbed hold of the door handle. She threw the door open and burst in, shouting, 'I've called the cop—' Her voice trailed off, eyes widening in utter amazement to see Alfie Manners with his hand on the back door knob, staring back at her. It was very much apparent he was

337

just as shocked as Lynnie was.

Alfie was the first to gather his wits. 'Good God, Miss Downs, you scared the hell out of me. What on earth are you doing here at this time of night?'

'What are you?' she blurted.

'Eh? Me! Oh, I suddenly got it into my head I hadn't locked the back door properly after I left tonight so I came back to check. I needn't have worried, I had.'

Her hand clutching her chest, she cried, 'Oh, God! I thought we had burglars.'

'Well, as you can see you were mistaken. But you still haven't explained why *you're* here?' he said, making his way across to her. It was then that the evidence of her recent trauma struck him. 'Why, whatever is the matter?'

'The matter?' This sudden reminder of what had brought her to the shop in the first place took her by surprise and before she could even try and control herself her face crumpled, huge fat tears spurted from her eyes and her whole body shook as she wept uncontrollably.

Alfie stared at her, shocked for a moment, before mentally shaking himself. He grabbed the chair in front of the desk and, taking her arm, guided her into it. Then he shot off into the kitchen, took the towel from its roller and went back into the office.

'Wipe your face and blow your nose on that,' he instructed. He stared at the hysterical woman, seeming unsure what to do next. A thought struck him. 'You need a drink. With a bit of luck the off licence will still be open on the corner. Sit tight, I won't be a tick.'

Lynnie was far too distraught to protest but by the time Alfie returned, brandishing a bottle of brandy and two mugs from the kitchen, she had managed to compose herself slightly. As he sat down behind the desk she sniffed hard and croaked, 'I'm sorry about that. I . . . I didn't mean to break down in front of you.'

He smiled at her kindly. 'Oh, that's all right.' He unscrewed the bottle and poured out two measures, pushing one of the mugs across the desk towards her. 'Knock that back, it'll do you good. Help calm you anyway,' he said, picking up the other and taking a gulp of the contents.

She wanted to say she didn't like brandy but felt a dire need for something stronger than tea and as this was the only thing on offer she picked up the mug and swallowed the contents back, shuddering violently as the fiery liquid hit the back of her throat.

'Feel better now?' he asked her.

The brandy had done nothing as yet to help ease the terrible physical pain that was gripping her stomach or the continuous throbbing in her temples. Her body felt limp, like a floppy rag doll. She was having great difficulty understanding how she had been taken in so completely by Ozzie's lies. She had really believed they had a serious future together. Suddenly she gave a loud mournful cry, buried her face in the towel again and before she could stop herself, wailed, 'Oh, I can't believe how stupid I've been. You think you know someone, and you love that person for what you think they are, then you find out they aren't that person at all, that they've been conning you even though they didn't realise they were but convinced themselves that what they were doing was for your benefit . . . Oh, I know I'm not making any sense, it's all such a mess.'

Alfie squatted down beside her chair and slid one arm around her shoulders. 'You're talking about your boyfriend, I take it?' he said gently.

'Yes,' she cried. 'He promised me he wouldn't let me down again, and I believed him. I really believed him.'

'Well, you had no idea what he was up to so you were bound to, weren't you?'

'No, I hadn't. I would never have got back with him if I'd had any idea what . . .' She stopped suddenly, sniffed hard, raised her head and looked at Alfie quizzically. 'How did you know what Ozzie was up to?'

'Eh? Oh, well.' He gave a shrug. 'It's obvious he was seeing another woman behind your back. I'm right, aren't I?'

'Yes,' she hurriedly agreed, 'that's just what he was doing. Can I have another brandy, please?' she asked, dabbing her eyes.

'Yes, sure,' he said, rising to pour her one. He handed it to her and while she sipped it, perched on the edge of the desk. He looked at her sympathetically. 'I'm sure when you're feeling better you'll be thankful you found him out before it was too late.'

'Yes, I'm sure of it too,' she said flatly. She finished off her drink and handed him the mug. 'Better get off.

I expect you'll be wanting to go too. If you don't mind I'll just wash my face first.' She made to rise and the effects of the drink made her stumble. Automatically he reached out to grab her and the next thing she knew she was in his arms. Her head jerked back and as their eyes met strange sensations shot through her. She realised then with a feeling of shock that she wanted him to kiss her, the desire so strong it made her gasp. She stepped backwards as if struck by lightning and mumbled, embarrassed, 'I'm sorry . . . I'm so sorry.'

He looked bemused. 'For what?'

'For . . . for . . . stumbling like that. It was so clumsy of me. Excuse me.'

She dashed out and just made it to the kitchen before she was violently sick in the sink.

The contents of her stomach emptied, she swilled her face several times with cold water then raised her head to look at herself in the small mirror fixed to the wall above the sink. The face staring back at her was a haggard one, drained ashen, eyes puffy and red, dark hair limp and straggly. She straightened up and turned to lean back against the sink, thoughts all over the place. What on earth had made her want Alfie Manners of all people to kiss her when she had found herself in his arms? It didn't make any sense to her. There was nothing about him at all that appealed to her. But, thank God, she hadn't done anything about it and made a complete and utter fool of herself. It must have been a combination of shock at finding out the truth about Ozzie and her consumption of drink, there was no other explanation. But then, that did not explain the electric sensations that had tingled through her when their eyes had met. That had happened before as well and she had not been traumatised then or touched a drop of alcohol. She suddenly thought she was going mad.

She needed to get home to bed, to try to fall into a deep sleep and for a few hours at least put all this out of her mind. Maybe tomorrow she might make sense of it.

Taking several deep breaths, she emerged from the seclusion of the kitchen and found Alfie hovering inside the office door. 'I was just about to come and check on you, see you were all right. How are you now?'

She found she couldn't look at him. 'I'm all right, thank you. It's amazing what a splash of water can do. I'll . . . I'll see you tomorrow, Mr Manners.'

'Hold on,' he urged. 'I've called you a taxi. It'll be here any minute. It's too far for you to walk by yourself, and it's so late.'

She needed to walk to help clear the jumble of thoughts in her head. 'I appreciate that but I'd prefer to walk. I'll be fine.'

And before he could respond further, she turned and dashed out.

By the time she arrived home the house was in darkness save for the hall light which her mother must have left on for her. Slipping in as quietly as she could, she tiptoed up the stairs and thankfully arrived inside her room without disturbing any of the others. Stripping off her clothes, she dived under the covers, gathering them all protectively around her. As soon as she closed her eyes a vision of Ozzie rose up and in the still of the night she broke her heart over her lost love for the very last time.

Chapter Eighteen

Lynnie arrived for work the next morning knowing she looked far from her usual well-presented self. She had spent a terrible night, half crying, half tossing and turning as she fitfully slept, and had woken with a start to find that she had forgotten to set the alarm and was badly late. She then dressed hastily, aware that the colour of her turquoise skinny-rib polo clashed badly with her red mini-skirt, but she had no time to do anything about it. She was also aware that her hurriedly applied makeup did little to disguise her puffy and blotchy skin or eyes which were red-ringed and felt gritty.

But her appearance was hardly the most important thing. Showing a brave face to the world and getting through the day ahead in one piece was imperative to her. She knew if she managed that today then hopefully from here on it would become easier. In order to achieve it she must somehow push all thoughts of Ozzie to the back of her mind. With a great effort, up to now she had managed to do that.

Much to her relief she had managed to slip out of the house as she had arrived the previous night, undetected. She had reached the kitchen prepared to make excuses for her obvious state but was relieved to find it was empty. She knew Dec and Jimmy would already have left to do their shift on the building site but where the others had gone was not apparent. She guessed her mother had decided to do the shopping earlier; Colin was still in bed as, new to his apprenticeship, he had the luxury of not having to go in on a weekend at all until he'd gained more experience; her grandmother was probably round at a neighbour's, catching up with any gossip. After pouring herself a lukewarm cup of stewed tea, Lynnie gulped it back and left.

She had decided to walk to work, feeling this would help to prepare her for the ordeal she knew was facing her. For the first time since Alfie Manners had so unexpectedly arrived on the scene she was thankful that his way of running the show meant her workload had substantially escalated. She had more than enough to occupy her mind, hopefully leaving no room for anything else.

The main race of that day was the Two Thousand Guineas at Newmarket and the atmosphere promised to be lively. She knew from experience that betting would be ferocious, the punters' excitement building to fever pitch as the horses reached the course; the punters praying their favoured ones would fulfil their dreams of a large win, which in most cases would be shattered.

As she arrived behind the counter Alfie came out of the office and she stopped short, praying her embarrassment was not apparent. She hoped he would not make any reference to it. As he approached her the memory of her own wanton desire for him to kiss her when she had landed in his arms flooded back and she felt a hot flush begin to creep up her neck. She just thanked God he had no idea what she had felt or there was no way she could face him.

'Good morning, Miss Downs.' His tone was brisk and businesslike. 'I've no doubt you're going to be busy today what with the Two Thousand Guineas. As far as I know all the other races are still going ahead so I promise I'll keep out of your hair as much as possible. I'll bring the sheet of odds for the first race out to you as soon as I've formulated it. Right, when you're ready, you can open up and . . . er . . . right, I'll leave you to it.'

As he returned to the office and shut the door she stared after him, puzzled. A thought suddenly struck her. The side of Alfie she had witnessed last night had been thoughtful and caring, so unlike the persona he displayed at other times. But then she supposed last night she had been far from her own usual self, and it would have to be a callous man who would turn his back on any woman in obvious need. It had been pure coincidence that he had been in the shop when she had arrived so late, and then all he had done when he had seen the state she was in was lend her a sympathetic ear and offer a drink of brandy, for medical purposes, as any man with a shred of decency would have.

As she turned to begin readying herself for the constant parade of punters she knew would soon descend, something on the edge of the counter, tucked between a large ashtray and the far wall, caught her eye. She went over to investigate. It was a posy of flowers, only small, nothing elaborate, and with great surprise she realised that Alfie must have put them there when she wasn't looking. Totally unexpected, this small gesture of kindness touched her deeply. It helped to ease the weight of desolation that gripped her. With a hint of a smile on her lips she went in search of a receptacle in which to put the flowers so she could display them on the counter.

The day passed like a flash with Lynnie constantly on the go. At lunchtime she only had time to gobble down a sandwich and gulp back a cup of tea, but that's how she had hoped the day would be and she had got her wish. Exhausted and very thankful it was over, Lynnie finally locked the front door after herding out the last straggling punter, distraught at the fact he'd lost a good portion of his wage on a horse that had stood little chance of coming third let alone first past the winning post, and he had yet to face his wife. After finishing off, as usual she gathered everything together and took it through to Alfie. She wished him good-night and left for home. It had been on her mind to offer her thanks for the flowers but she had decided against doing that on the outside chance that it hadn't been Alfie who had left them there and she would therefore make a fool of herself. This decision was reached regardless of the fact that it could not have been anyone else.

She arrived home to be greeted by a grimace from her mother as she bustled about the kitchen preparing the tea. 'Corned beef salad tonight. Hurry up and get yer coat off, I'm just about to call the others through,' she said, putting a plate of bread and margarine on the table. She then placed her hands on her hips and fixed her eyes on her daughter. 'You were late in last night?' she said accusingly.

'Er . . . was I?' Lynnie said evasively as she rinsed her hands under the cold tap and grabbed at a towel to dry them. 'I didn't think it was that late myself.'

'Yes, yer were,' piped up her grandmother who was cutting up tomatoes at the table. 'I didn't drop off until after twelve last night and you wasn't in by then.'

'Oh, well, it wasn't much after that then. I was just chatting to my friend and didn't realise how late it was.' Her lie came off pat and she justified it by reminding herself that her decision to keep the family in the dark over Ozzie had been made with the best of intentions.

'That's all well and good when yer ain't got work the next morning, but have yer seen the state of yer, gel? You looked fair whacked out. Death warmed up is how I'd describe yer. An early night wouldn't go amiss for you tonight, me lady. But then I expect yer going out?' Her mother's statement was more of an accusation than a question.

'Mam, you did everything you could to get me to go out after . . . well, you know after what, and now you're complaining because I am. I can't win, can I?'

'I'm not complaining 'cos yer going out, Lynnie, I'm complaining about the fact that I expected yer home on the last bus last night, considering Sat'day is your busiest day at work. Usually if yer think yer might be back late, you tell me before yer go out, *that's* why I worried. Yer might be past the age of consent, Lynnie, but that still don't stop me worrying about yer when yer out late and I don't know where yer are or who yer with for that matter. You seem to spend at least three or four nights a week with this new friend of yours and yer've never brought her back here to meet us. Are yer ashamed of us or summat?'

'No, of course I'm not,' she said with conviction. 'I was going to suggest she came for tea to meet you all, but . . . well . . . she's got herself a new boyfriend and seems pretty smitten by him so I doubt I'll be seeing so much of her, if anything in fact, in the future.' She hurriedly decided to change the subject. 'Actually, I'm not going out tonight. I might pop and see Sheila, see if she fancies a natter and a cuppa, but that's about it. And I won't be late in, I promise you.'

'Oh, right, well, I'm glad to hear it. I think a natter with Sheila might be a good idea. I might have got it wrong but I thought she didn't look too happy when I saw her getting off the bus just after twelve as I was coming home after doing the shopping. But by the time I caught up with her she'd gone inside and shut the door and I needed to get home and put the groceries away.'

Lynnie stared at her, bothered. 'Oh? I wonder what she'd be upset about? I hope she hasn't had any more abuse.'

'Well, yer can ask her when yer go round, can't yer? Me and yer nan are going to settle down to a bit of telly tonight. Max Bygraves and Tommy Trinder are in a variety show.'

'I'm looking forward to it,' said Freda enthusiastically. 'I like that Tommy Trinder, he meks me laugh.'

'But are you not going out, Mam?' Lynnie asked her. 'It's been ages since you went for a drink down the Mutton. Since we made our pact to go straight, in fact.'

'Well, I know we've turned a corner but money still don't quite stretch far enough to be spending it willynilly at the moment,' Avril replied as she collected knives and forks and put them on the table.

'Oh, surely a couple of halves isn't going to bankrupt us? Tell you what, I'll sub you and Nan to a couple of stouts.'

'But you already give me over half yer wages as it is and that's enough. You more than need the rest for yerself.'

Lynnie hoped she didn't show any tell-tale signs of her still terrible distress when she said, 'Well, it's not like I'm saving to get married or anything. What I have is more than enough to pay for all I need at the moment and I still manage to put ten bob in my Post

Office savings book most weeks.'

Avril's face lit up. 'Ah, well, when yer put it like that, our Lynnie. How d'yer fancy a wander down the local, Mam?'

Just then Dec appeared. 'Tea ready yet, Mam? It's gone seven and me and Jimmy are gonna be late.'

Avril looked at him enquiringly. 'Late? Late for what?'

He gave a nonchalant shrug. 'Just late, Mam. If yer must know we've booked a table at the snooker hall for eight-thirty and if we ain't there on time the table'll be given to someone else, that's all.'

'Oh, I see.'

Colin appeared at the side of Dec and before he could utter a word Avril shot at him, 'And I expect you're going out too?'

'Eh? Yeah, I'm off over Terry's. He got the new Rolling Stones LP for his birthday and we're gonna listen to it.'

Avril glanced at her youngest son scathingly. 'Listening is one thing but that don't mean ter say yer have to look like one of them Stones. Scruffy bunch of tykes is my opinion. It's about time you got yer hair cut, son.'

Colin pushed a thick clump of almost-black hair out of his face. 'It's the fashion, Mam. Short back and sides went out ages ago.'

'Oh, not being able to see where yer going through yer fringe is the latest craze, is it? Get it trimmed, lad, before I tie yer to a chair, stick a basin on yer head and do it meself. It's a wonder to me yer boss at the gas board ain't docked your wages for it. And what the hell the customers must think when yer turn up at their houses to help sort out their gas supply . . .' She shook her head. 'Considering how tall and thin yer are, and with that head of hair, they'll take you for a mop, I should think. And where have you been all day, I want to know? When I went out to do the shopping this morning yer bedroom door was shut so I gather yer were still in bed. Just 'cos you're lucky enough not to have to do a shift on Sat'day morning like lots of people do doesn't mean ter say yer can laze half the day away. Anyway, when I came back I checked and you'd gone out. Now yer didn't get back 'til just gone six and don't deny it 'cos I heard yer sneaking in the front door while I was busy in here. You was hoping I wouldn't notice. Well, bad luck for you, son, I did. So . . . where have yer bin all day?'

He flashed a look at his elder brother before saying, 'I've just bin messing about with some mates. And it ain't fair, Mam. Yer don't question our Dec and Jimmy's every movement like yer do me.'

''Cos they're much older than you. Besides, it'd be a waste of time because I know for a fact they only tell me what they want me to know.' She was looking at Dec accusingly now. 'That's right, ain't it, son?'

He just looked back at her blankly as if to say he hadn't a clue what she was going on about. 'Are we getting our tea or what?'

'Yes, yes,' she snapped, irritated. 'Now our Lynnie's in we can all sit down.'

During her mother's exchange with her brothers, Lynnie had been listening and observing, especially Dec's manner. When he had told Avril where he was going tonight there had been a definitely shifty look in his eye and she had received the distinct impression he wasn't being truthful. If she was right, what was he hiding? Where were Dec and Jimmy really going? And if her worries over them weren't enough, now it seemed that Colin was being evasive too. She had seen that quick look he had given his elder brother before he replied to his mother about his own activities today. And it wasn't just that. If she wasn't mistaken he looked too tired for a young lad of his age who had lain in bed late that morning, spending the rest of it, so he said, messing about with his mates. Her thoughts were suddenly shattered by her mother shouting at her and she jumped.

'Sorry. What, Mam?'

'I said, will you mash the tea? Colin, fetch our Jimmy through. Dec, you sit down and start tucking in.' She suddenly paused and laid a hand on her mother's shoulder. 'So what d'yer feel about popping out for a bit tonight, Mam?'

Freda nodded vigorously. 'Everyone else is so we might as well. Hurry up and get the tea past and we can go and get ourselves ready.'

Just after eight Lynnie knocked on Sheila's back door and despite the enthusiastic welcome she received from her, Lynnie knew it wasn't her imagination that her friend didn't seem quite her usual bright sunny self.

She wondered if her mother's observations had been right and Sheila had been upset about something earlier. If the opportunity presented itself she would enquire. 'I'm not interrupting anything, am I?' she asked as she entered the kitchen.

'Not at all,' her friend said sincerely. 'Me and Everal are always glad to see you, aren't we, Everal?'

His smile was broad and Lynnie could appreciate just how it had first attracted his wife. 'We always pleased to see you and anyone else from yer family, Lynnie, and don't ever forget that. You the only true friends we both have, and my wife couldn't have found a better woman friend than you,' he said, glancing lovingly at her. 'Nor forgetting Shirley, of course.'

'Everal's right, Lynnie. Your friendship means everything to us. I'll always owe you a debt of gratitude for helping the neighbours to accept us.'

Such sincerity touched her deeply and she had to fight back tears. How glad she was that she had found it within herself to fight their cause. The result had been worth every risk she had taken, and most importantly as far as she was concerned had brought about a close and valued friendship between herself and Sheila. It was growing stronger as time passed, and was particularly welcome when Shirley, caught up in the joys and ties of new motherhood, did not have much time to spend with her friends. Lynnie was pleased to have it confirmed that both Everal and Sheila felt the same way she did.

'Now,' he continued, 'it always amazes me what you

ladies find to talk about for hours on end, so I'll leave yer to it. I'll be in the living room playing me music but I promise not to be too loud so I don't disturb yer. I'll check on our girls, Sheila, so you can relax.'

'He's a good man,' Lynnie said after he had retired to the front room for the duration.

'He's the best. Now tea, or a drop of Everal's rum?'

'Oh, tea, please.'

Sheila picked up the kettle, shook it to check there was enough water in it, and lit the gas underneath. Pulling a chair out opposite Lynnie's, she sat down and looked at her knowingly. 'You surprise me, refusing a tot of Everal's rum. You look to me like a woman in dire need of a drink.'

Lynnie gave her a wan smile. 'I obviously can't fool you like I've managed to do the others. Oh, Sheila, my bubble's not just burst – it's exploded.'

Her friend eyed her. 'Would you like to explain what you meant by that?'

So she did, and a while later Sheila shook her head. 'Oh, Lynnie, what can I say? Except that I'm so sorry.'

'So am I,' she uttered. 'I can't believe how stupid I was to be taken in so completely by Ozzie.'

'Oh, come on, don't be hard on yourself. Despite Ozzie telling you he was just trying to get money together for your future, he knew full well that what he was doing was against your principles or why did he not take you into his confidence? You had no idea what he was up to because he was careful to make sure you didn't. Deep down he knew just what your reaction would be. You have to see that none of this was your fault, Lynnie. Ozzie used your justified criticism of the way he failed to provide for your future together to excuse his illicit activities. In a way he was trying to put the blame on you and that was most unfair of him, Lynnie.' She leaned forward and placed a hand affectionately on Lynnie's arm. 'Are you sure you're doing the right thing in not telling your family any of this? You're going through such a terrible time at the moment and they could help you through it.'

'As much as I want to, I just can't, Sheila,' she said with conviction. 'I can't risk them ever thinking for one minute I knew anything about what Ozzie was up to and turned a blind eye. Or that I was helping him in any way.'

'But, Lynnie, they think far too much of you ever to believe anything like that.'

'I still can't risk it, Sheila. We've all struggled damned hard to keep on the straight and narrow, even though sometimes it's been touch and go. I'm so proud that none of us has lapsed. But I do worry that if any of them thought I had, it could just make them think, What the hell? I might as well too. Then before we know it we're back where we started, risking our freedom and liberty for the sake of a few extra bob. I still shudder when I think of all the time I was in danger of that.

'Ray put the fear of God in me when he explained what he'd gone through in prison. I tell you, Sheila, when those coppers were breathing down our necks last night, despite how demented I was over finding out what Ozzie had been up to behind my back, I was also absolutely terrified that any minute the scuffers were going to clamp me in handcuffs and cart me off to the cells. I still can't understand why they didn't charge me with anything, considering I was with him when they caught him, or even question me.'

Sheila pulled a face. 'Odd that, isn't it? You could have been the brains behind it for all they knew. I wonder who it was tipped the police off to him? I don't suppose we'll ever find out. Just be grateful for small mercies, Lynnie, and leave it at that.' She smiled kindly at her friend. 'Look, now you've fully explained your reasons to me, I can understand why you don't want to mention a word of this to your family, but remember I'm always here if you need someone to talk to. Getting over Ozzie isn't going to happen overnight. You loved him for the man you thought he'd turned into, and that's a loss you'll be mourning.'

She smiled appreciatively. 'Thanks, Sheila. But to be honest, I think I've talked and cried enough over Ozzie. I have to push him to the back of my mind now and . . .'

'Make room for another man to come into your life,' Sheila cut in.

'That's not what I was going to say. I think I'll give men a rest for a while. I'm very lucky to have a great family and such good friends around me, and for the moment they're all I need.' Lynnie noticed an envelope lying on the edge of the table, obviously containing a card. 'Oh, someone's birthday?'

Sheila looked at the envelope for a moment before saying, 'Yes, Everal's mother's.'

By her tone Lynnie knew that this fact distressed her. 'I take it you still wish all was well between you, and then you'd have been invited to celebrate it as part of the family?'

Sheila gave a deep sigh. 'Yes. Oh, Lynnie, I had another go at trying to break the ice between us this morning. I didn't tell Everal what I was up to as I didn't want to build his hopes up. I dressed the girls up in their best and took the card over in person.'

'That was a brave thing to do, considering the way you've all been treated before. I gather your appearance didn't exactly go down well. So what happened, Sheila?'

'As soon as she saw who it was she slammed the door in our faces. I had hoped if I took the girls along she'd see for herself just what she was missing out on, but I don't even think she noticed them. And I so badly wanted to tell her that, no matter how unwelcome I might be, the least she could do was let her son visit her. As it was I didn't get to utter one word. I can't tell you how upset I feel. I wish I hadn't bothered now.'

'Oh, Sheila, I am sorry. I can't believe you just sat there and listened to my tale of woe when all the time you were so upset yourself!'

'Oh, that's all right, Lynnie. In a way listening to you took my mind off it for a while.'

'Did you tell Everal what happened?'

'We have no secrets between us, Lynnie. I would have got round to telling him. But as it was, as soon as he walked in from his Saturday morning shift he knew I was upset. Bless him, he was just grateful I'd taken the trouble to try and sort things out. He said not to bother again as he hates to see how much her rejection upsets me. But, rightly or wrongly, I've decided to post the card like I've done in the past, as I do when it's any of my family's birthday or at Christmas, and as I shall continue doing, whether they like it or not. I don't know if any of them actually opens the cards as they're bound to know they are from us, that is their choice, but I feel better for doing what I'm doing.'

Lynnie lapsed into thought. How she wished there was something she could do herself to bring about a reconciliation between all the families but, like Sheila, she felt any such effort would be a waste of time. Both families' feelings on their offspring's choice of partner were evident. Sheila had tried almost everything in an effort to resolve matters but both sides had remained uncompromising. Then a thought struck her. But had Sheila tried *everything*? Maybe there was still something Lynnie could do. Her own life might be in chaos but that didn't mean she couldn't bring a little cheer to someone else's. And having something else to concentrate on besides her own misery would help her put what had just happened behind her.

She picked up the card and before Sheila could stop her had stuffed it in her handbag. 'I'll post it for you on

Monday at the Post Office near work.'

'Oh, I wouldn't put you to the trouble, Lynnie. I could have posted it on my way home today, but I was so upset I forgot.'

'It's no trouble.' She smiled brightly at Sheila. 'Let's talk about something other than our problems. Oh, I'll tell you something I've often wondered – just where was it you grew up? You don't mind me asking, do you? Only we've become such good friends, and unlike Shirley who I've known since I was twelve I don't know much about your background. Tell me if I'm being nosey.'

Sheila smiled. 'I don't mind you asking at all. It's nice for me to know you're interested enough to care.' She leaned back in her chair and folded her arms. 'I grew up on Knighton Road. In fact, my parents still live there.'

'Oh, Sheila, I didn't realise you came from somewhere so posh. Those houses are big. It must be some comedown for you, landing up on this estate.'

'Lynnie, all that matters to us is being happy and allowed to live in peace. And the house I grew up in wasn't that big, compared to others.'

'Oh, but they are compared to the ones round here. We originally lived in a two-up, two-down that my nan rented off the local landlord when she and my grandad first got married. It was never up to much, but it was all they could afford. By the time I was born it was only fit to be pulled down, which of course is what eventually happened when the council cleared the slums. That's why we landed up where we are. What number?'

'Number?'

'The number of the house you lived in.' Lynnie shrugged innocently. 'I don't know why I asked really. It's of no importance.'

Sheila laughed. 'Well, since you did, I'll tell you. Number seventy-five. My father was . . . still is as far as I know . . . in a good position in the Town Hall. Mind you, he could be retired by now.' She paused and gave a wistful sigh before adding, 'Well, I wouldn't know, would I, being's they won't have anything to do with me. Anyway, my sister and I had a very happy childhood. We girls never wanted for anything. My mother never minded how many friends we brought home, they were always made welcome and we insisted they stay for tea. We went for holidays in Wales every summer where my grandparents had a little chalet in a place called Clarach Bay, near Aberystwyth, and June and I spent hours playing on the rocky beach, collecting shells in our little tin sandcastle buckets. We used to cover my father up in sand and he'd pretend he was stuck so we had to dig him out. My mother would take a picnic . . .' Her voice trailed off and she gave a sad smile. 'Oh, such halcyon days.'

Lynnie looked at her nonplussed. She didn't want to embarrass herself by telling Sheila she had no idea what that word meant but judging from her friend's face she assumed it meant 'good'.

'So what did you do after you left school?'

'I went to secretarial college and became personal assistant to a chartered accountant.'

'Oh, goodness,' Lynnie said, impressed. 'Your parents must have been so proud of you.'

Sheila's face turned grave. 'They were, but I doubt they are now, Lynnie.'

Her own face clouded. She was mortified that an innocent remark could have been such a painful reminder, but before she could even begin to apologise for her lack of thought they both jumped at a knock on the back door. The next thing they knew it burst open and Shirley charged in.

'Oh, good, yer both here,' she cried, then began jumping up and down, clapping her hands in delight. 'You'll never guess what's happened! Oh, I couldn't wait ter tell yer both. I don't know how I've got through the day. As soon as I got Jenny off, I rushed over so I could tell yer.'

'For goodness' sake, tell us then,' Lynnie cried, excited as it was obviously good news.

'Yes, please do,' urged Sheila.

'We got a letter this morning. We've got a house.'

'A house!' they both exclaimed in unison.

'Oh, that's great,' cried Lynnie. 'Where?'

'On Bird's Nest Avenue on the New Parks Estate. Oh, it's lovely! Just lovely! Pete and I got notification last Tuesday that our name was top of the list to see two houses and his boss was kind enough to give him a couple of hours off so we could go to view. We didn't need to see the other one, we fell in love with this one as soon as we walked through the front gate. And that was hanging on its hinges, not like many round here that's hanging off. Anyway, we said we'd tek it and then had to wait until we got confirmation in writing that it was definitely ours. I can't tell you how slowly them days went! I daren't let you in on it. In fact, no one knew anything until we were sure as I was terrified summat would happen to put the blight on it. And you'll never guess what it's got . . .'

'What?' they both cried.

'A bathroom! A proper bathroom. With a bath in it. And hot and cold water.'

'Oh!' Lynnie exclaimed. 'What luxury.'

'I lay in it, Lynnie,' Shirley said, as if she had committed an illicit act. 'I did, Sheila. Pete thought I'd gone barmy, but I just wanted to know what it felt like to lie in a bath. My own bath. Oh, I can't tell yer what it felt like. I can't wait to have a proper bath with boiling hot water up to me chin. Eh, and yer don't have to boil the water in no copper either, it's got an emergency heater thingy. Yer just flick a switch and after about an hour yer've enough scalding water to fill the bath right up to the brim. And it's got two lavvies, one outside the back door under a porch-like thing and the other in the bathroom. You can come and have a bath anytime yer like, Lynnie. You too, Sheila, and Everal and the girls.'

'That's very good of you. I might take you up on that offer,' Sheila said enthusiastically.

'I definitely will. I've never had a bath in a proper bath either,' said Lynnie.

Sheila declined to comment as obviously she had when she had lived with her parents.

'It's got three bedrooms,' continued Shirley. 'Can yer believe it? Two big ones and a smaller room that's called a box room. I've no idea why it's called that unless yer supposed to put boxes in it, though why anyone 'ud want to do that don't mek sense to me. And a big garden. Pete says he gonna turn the top bit into a vegetable plot and he's gonna grow me some flowers edging the grassy bit for Jenny to play on.'

'Oh, it sounds wonderful,' sighed Lynnie. 'So when do you move in?' she asked.

'It's ours from the end of June. Just think, in five weeks we'll not be sleeping on our living-room floor no more with our Jenny in her cot at the side of us, and all me family driving me daft and giving us no privacy. Yer know, I couldn't believe it when we broke the news to me mam and dad this morning. Me dad didn't say 'ote, I don't think he was listening as he was too interested in the telly. "Grandstand" had just started. Me mam, though, well, she weren't happy at all. Oh, not 'cos of the fact we'd got a house, but she was upset it was a good distance away and that I won't be able to pop around every day to do chores for her while she lazes around. I can't believe her, I really can't. As if I won't have enough to do, looking after me own house and family, without looking after hers too. She had the nerve to suggest we cancel this house and wait until we got one around here. Next door would suit her best.'

Lynnie and Sheila declined to comment.

'Oh,' Shirley suddenly erupted, 'you ain't heard all me good news yet.'

'There's more?' asked a shocked Lynnie.

Her friend nodded. 'To top it all, as if I wasn't on cloud nine already, Pete's been promoted at work. Got a foreman's job. That means more money so we can manage the bills and possibly I won't have to get a part-time job, but we'll see how we go. So now I'm on cloud ten and yer can't blame me, can yer?'

'I think this definitely calls for a drop of Everal's rum,' said Sheila, rising to fetch the bottle and glasses.

'Did someone mention my name?' asked Everal, entering the room. 'Actually I came to see what all the excitement was about. You were so loud it was drowning out me music. Oh, and it's such lovely music by Rachmaninov.'

Shirley grimaced. 'Rack who? Is that a new group? I thought you were into that scab music, or raggie, or whatever it's called that they play back where yer come from?'

He laughed loudly, a deep throaty sound that was so infectious that within seconds they were all laughing too, although Shirley wasn't quite sure why.

'Ah, you English! You have no taste,' Everal chuckled. 'And for future reference, Shirley, my lovely young lady, I do appreciate all sorts of music but my favourites at the moment are ska and reggae as they remind me of home. So what was all this jubilation about?'

Shirley repeated her news again, word for word.

When she had finished Everal beamed. 'I can see why you were so pleased now. I will be glad to lend a hand when you move, and I am sure these ladies will too.'

'You will? Oh, that's great. Not that we'll have much to move as such, but there'll be plenty to do. Mind you, I don't care if I end up sleeping on the floor and we have nothing else. Me and Pete have our own four walls and that's all we've ever dreamed of. I nearly fell off me chair when me mam said I could take the mattress as a moving in present. That was good of her, weren't it?'

None of them was sure if she was being sarcastic or not as they knew from Shirley's description of the mattress she and Pete slept on that it wasn't exactly up to much, so they all just nodded.

Lynnie stared at her thoughtfully for a moment. 'Our Colin might be able to help with a cooker.'

'A cooker!' Shirley exclaimed. 'Really? Oh, d'yer think he can, Lynnie? It would be a Godsend if he could.'

'Well, I can't promise anything 'til I speak to him, but as you know he works for the gas board and told us one night around the dinner table that when a cooker goes wrong some customers insist on a new one being fitted even though the old one just needs a few new parts to bring it up to scratch. And also some of the gas fitters tell a customer they need a new cooker just because it's easier for them to fit a new one in than fix the old one up. So when that happens some of the blokes take the old cookers home, fix them up themselves and sell them on to their mates and such like. Apparently the gas board bosses know that some of the old cookers don't end up being scrapped as they're supposed to be, but tend to turn a blind eye. I suppose it saves the company money on paying the scrappy to collect and dispose of them. Mam said that when our cooker finally packs up then she wants another this way. But don't build your hopes up, please, Shirley, until I find out more.'

'Oh, I'll try not to, Lynnie, but a cooker . . . well, that's one of the things I was worried about as they cost such a lot and what we've managed to put past won't go anywhere near enough to pay for one. I was trying to persuade Pete to get one on tick but yer know what he's like when it comes to things like that. He doesn't approve at all and I was bothered I'd end up trying to cook for us on a primus stove. Well, hopefully now I won't have to, eh? And if we've got summat proper to cook on and summat to sleep on, then it's just summat to sit on we'll be needing and the rest can wait, can't it?'

'Oh, I might be able to help you out there,' said Everal. 'Well, at least until you manage to get a suite of your own.'

'As long as it's summat to park me backside on then I don't care and neither will Pete,' Shirley responded excitedly. 'So how can you help us?'

'Well, I know where I can get hold of two old deckchairs. They were propped at the side of the house where we went to do some repairs last week. As we left the old lady who lives there asked if any of us wanted them as her husband had passed on and she'd no use for them any more.'

'Oh, Everal, they'd be just the job.' Shirley turned and looked at Lynnie, her face ecstatic. 'Ain't life grand, Lynnie?'

She was glad that it was for some, and nodded and smiled in agreement.

Shirley then decided it was time she went home and Lynnie did too as it was now well past ten o'clock. She knew she ought to do what her mother had suggested and have an early night, although whether she would sleep or not remained to be seen. Certainly, though, her talk with Sheila and Shirley's good news had gone some way to help lift her depressed mood and make her realise that no matter what life threw at you, it didn't just stop, it went on and you had to go on with it.

She had just stepped into the kitchen and was in the process of taking off her coat when her mother came out of the living room and launched a verbal attack.

'Oh, I'm glad yer back, Lynnie. I can't wait ter tell yer what a flipping lucky escape you've had.'

She said, taken aback, 'And what lucky escape is that?'

'Not getting back with that Ozzie is what! Well, I know you was considering it from what yer said the other night, but I'm so glad yer never. It's all round the pub. Seems he got arrested yesterday evening by the coppers after a high-speed chase involving several police vehicles. He was driving around in a stolen van with a cargo of loot in it. Jewellery and all sorts, it's said. Oh, Lynnie, the mind boggles at just what that lad's been up to since you and him split. Completely gone off the rails, it seems. I mean, nicking the odd box of shoes is one thing but jewellery raids are another, 'cos according to the gossip that's what everyone in the pub seems to think he must have been involved in. It's reckoned he'll get put inside for a long stretch, and if gossip's right on what he was up to then he bleddy deserves all he gets in my opinion.'

Without pausing for breath Avril continued, 'And I don't tek kindly to the fact that Oswald Matthews sat in our living room next to you on the settee that night we made our pact ter go straight and promised along with all of us that he would. Bleddy liar obviously had no such intention! Well, I'm glad you and him ain't together any more, that's all I can say. Some life he'd have led yer, lovey. Yer well shot of him.

'Cuppa cocoa? I was just about ter mek yer nan and me one. Oh, we had a great time down the pub, thanks fer subbing us, ducky. Although to be honest the Mutton ain't really my scene any more. Not that they're a bad lot and you do get a laugh, but all yer hear 'em talk about is what so and so is up to and whether we're back in the market for knock-off stuff again 'cos so and so knows someone who's got this or that for sale. It don't interest me at all now we've moved away from that kinda thing and I much prefer to sup a stout around me own fireside. Yer nan feels the same.'

Mortally glad that no mention of her own involvement in Ozzie's arrest had come to light, Lynnie smiled warmly at her. 'Cocoa would be lovely. You go and sit back down, I'll make it.'

Chapter Nineteen

A week later, immediately after finishing work, Lynnie was hurrying down Uppingham Road on the other side of town from where she lived. Her mind was totally absorbed in the mission she was about to perform. Spotting her destination, she stopped abruptly to steel herself before she went inside, and as she did so a person collided with her from behind.

'Yer should watch where yer going,' a disgruntled male voice said gruffly, and she saw someone bending to pick up the evening newspaper which he had dropped.

She turned around to apologise for her carelessness but the man had already continued on his way. She saw him turn into the pub further down the road and vanish inside. What had caught her interest was that this was the same man who had come into Mallin's on at least three occasions now to her knowledge and demanded to see the boss without giving his name. The public house he had entered looked as rundown as he did. She was curious as to what he could possibly have to discuss in private first with Sid and then on two separate occasions with Alfie. Then it struck her. He was obviously being paid to act as go-between for someone who had the money to place a large bet, but for whatever reason did not want to risk being seen themselves entering a turf accountant's in order to do so. It was probably a prominent person well known in Leicester, she decided, as she knew Sid had several of that kind on his books. But then, they didn't usually use as gofer such a shabby-looking character as that little man. It was usually someone like their chauffeur.

She suddenly remembered she had a pressing matter to attend to and hadn't time to waste mulling over something that wasn't important. Taking a deep breath to prepare herself, she turned into a café doorway and entered.

Before she had time to enquire at the counter whether anyone was waiting for her, two middle-aged women sitting at tables at opposite ends of the room rose and came across to her.

The first one to reach her said, 'Excuse me, are you Miss Downs?'

'I was just about to ask the same,' said the other woman who had by then joined them.

The two women eyed each other with expressions of disgust.

Before either of them could speak again Lynnie, her heart pounding with trepidation, said, 'Shall we sit down?' She walked ahead of them to a vacant table she had spotted.

The first woman who had approached her arrived ahead of the other and didn't look at all happy. 'Look, I have no idea at all why you could possibly want to see me. For a start, I don't know you. And the letter I received from you wasn't very informative. All it said was you had something to tell me that would be to my advantage. All very cloak and dagger, I must say, and I wasn't going to bother only my curiosity got the better of me. But what could you know to my advantage that could possibly involve *her*?' she hissed as she flashed a look of disdain at the other woman who had now joined them.

'I was t'inking that meself,' said the newcomer, flashing her a contemptuous look. 'I got der letter too, saying the very same.'

Lynnie smiled at them warmly. 'Would you both care to sit down? I can assure you there is something you both have in common that would be very much to your advantage, if only you would let it be.'

She knew that she had roused their interest further and sat down, watching as both women stared warily at each other before sitting down as far apart as possible.

'Can we just get on with this so I can go home?' the first woman urged sharply, sitting ramrod straight on the edge of her chair, clutching her handbag as if to make a quick getaway as soon as she had heard what Lynnie had to say. The other woman was doing likewise.

Now she was facing them both Lynnie was nervous and unsure of herself, but should she back out now her one chance of helping two people she was very fond of to achieve their hearts' desire would be gone. She took a deep breath.

'I've asked you to come here tonight hopefully to make you both see sense. What you have in common is that you're both mothers. I know you must love your children deeply yet you've both cut off all association with them because you didn't approve of their choice of partner. They didn't fall in love with each other on purpose to upset you, it just happened, and when it did they both knew they couldn't live the rest of their life without each other. They hoped their families would understand and be happy for them, but instead they were ostracised.'

She knew both women were beginning to realise what Lynnie had brought them here for. Praying neither left abruptly before she had said what she had come to say, she hurriedly continued. 'Mrs Johnson, Mrs Miller, each of you expressed your disapproval of the fact that your child married someone of a different colour, not the actual person underneath. If you would only agree to meet up and get to know your son- or daughter-in-law, your mind would be changed, I know it would. By not doing so you're robbing yourselves not only of your own children but of their children too, who whether you both like it or not are your own flesh and blood.

'From what Sheila and Everal have told me about you both and how close they were to you before this happened then I am sure you're missing them as much as they are you. Can't either of you find it within yourself to set aside your prejudices and at least give your respective children's spouse a chance to prove themselves to you? You might even get to like them. In fact, I know you would. You might even get to like each other, if you'd only give yourselves the opportunity to find out.' She smiled at them both. 'All I'm asking is that you think about what I've said before you both miss out on any more of your children's lives than you already have done. Thank you for listening to me.'

Leaving the two women staring at her, and praying her words had hit their intended mark, she left.

As Lynnie was making her way home, in the public house just down from the café a barman wiping up spilled beer looked at the man who'd just walked up to the bar. 'Usual?' the barman asked.

Glancing around him, the man leaned on the counter and nodded. 'Quiet in here tonight,' he casually remarked.

As he pulled a pint mug of bitter, the barman replied, 'It might pick up later. You never can tell in here.'

The man looked the barman directly in the eye. 'I like it here. It's my kinda pub, if yer get me drift.'

The barman put the brimming pint mug in front of him. 'Sorry, sir?'

'Yer know, the kinda place I might get a job,' the man said.

'Oh, sorry to tell yer but there's no jobs going here.

There's only one full-time barman and a part-time barmaid also comes in lunchtimes, and of course the owner. Have yer tried the Labour Exchange?'

The man laughed. 'The kinda jobs they have on offer ain't for me. The hours don't suit me for a start, nor does the miserly pay packet. No, I'm . . . er . . . looking for the kinda jobs that pay well.' He took a sup of his drink and eyed the barman over the top of his glass. 'I don't suppose you get any snifters in here, do yer?'

The barman looked at him nonplussed. 'Snifters, sir?'

'Yeah, yer know, a sniff of anything. Certain people coming in on the lookout for a useful man like me.'

The barman shrugged his shoulders. 'I don't know what yer mean, sir.'

The man tapped the side of his nose. 'Oh, I'm sure yer do. Anyway, just so yer know, in case you do happen to get a whiff of anything, I don't mind what I do. You understand me, don't you?' he said meaningfully. 'Always been a barman, have yer?'

'I have.'

'Can't pay much?'

'I manage.'

'It's not easy doing that when yer've not long come out.'

'Come out? Oh, I see what yer mean, sir. No, I don't suppose it is.'

'It's a case of getting yerself back around, letting people know yer available again. I know, though, that once they do, I'll be snapped up. Good at what I do if I say it meself. And very trustworthy. If yer get a chance you'll put in a word for me, won't yer? Oh, I ain't introduced meself, have I?' he said, holding out his hand. 'Ray. Ray Downs.'

The barman shook his hand.

Ray smiled at him as he withdrew his. 'I've got a feeling we're going to be good friends.'

The barman looked at him without expression. 'Excuse me, sir, I've customers to see to.'

As he picked up his mug and took a sip of beer, Ray watched the barman closely as he went about his business. He was hoping his words had had the desired effect. Now he'd just have to wait and see.

Chapter Twenty

'Doing anything tonight?' Avril asked her daughter as she dried her hands after washing the dishes.

Lynnie picked up the last of the cutlery, giving it a wipe and placing it in an old tin at the side of the wooden draining board.

'No, nothing special. I think I'll go and tidy up my bedroom, and I've some washing to sort out, then I'll come and join you and Nan to watch a bit of telly before I go to bed.'

'Oh, that'll be nice,' said her mother. 'I expect the lads are going out so it'll be just the three of us. I suppose there's no news of when Sid Mallin's expected to return or yer'd have said summat?'

'No, nothing yet. If Mr Manners knows any more about what's keeping him away so long then he's not letting on to me. It's getting on for four weeks now.'

'Mmm, and just about the same length of time yer brother's been gone too.'

'Oh, Mam, don't worry. You know our Ray's fine.

Yer've had a letter from him every week since he's been gone.'

'Letter! Huh, nothing more than a hurried note with a fiver attached to it. I've still no idea where he is.'

Lynnie sighed. That was puzzling and she hoped the fact that Ray hadn't let them in on his actual whereabouts was just a lapse of memory on his part and didn't have any other significance attached to it, like for some reason he didn't want them to know where he was. But then she reasoned that it could just be her brother wanted peace and quiet in which to make decisions on what he proposed to do with his life without his family constantly badgering him about it. He was certainly taking his time to reach a decision, though.

'Look, at least he's found time to send you the fiver every week like he said he would, Mam, and the scribbled note just means he's busy, that's all. He'll be back soon, I bet you he will. He won't half be missing your cooking.'

'He'd better be. Well, go and get yer jobs done and I'll finish off in here, then we can all sit down together.' There was a knock on the door. 'Oh, before yer go get that, lovey, me hands are wet.'

Lynnie opened the back door and almost froze in shock to find Sheila standing there. She didn't know what to think about this visit. Had her friend come to berate her for what she had done just the day before? Had she maybe come to tell her the plan had worked? Or was she in fact still unaware of what Lynnie had done? She wasn't quite sure how to react to this sudden arrival.

'Well, don't keep Sheila on the doorstep, Lynnie. For goodness' sake, what's the matter with yer, gel? Ask her in.'

'Oh, yes, I'm sorry,' she said, standing aside. 'Is this a social visit, Sheila?' she warily asked.

Her friend eyed her quizzically. 'Have I ever called here for any other reason, Lynnie?'

'Er . . . no,' she said, shutting the door behind her.

'So why would you think otherwise now? Or . . . is there something you haven't told me? Maybe because you don't know whether what you did was right or wrong, would work or not.'

'What the hell are you going on about, Sheila?' Avril asked, thoroughly confused. ''Cos that was all double Dutch to me.'

'Er . . . I know what Sheila is referring to, Mam. You know what I've done, don't you, Sheila?'

She looked at Lynnie gravely. 'Yes.'

Lynnie knew by the look on her friend's face that what she had done had failed badly.

'Oh, Sheila, please forgive me . . .'

'Forgive you?' she cut in. 'Why ever would I want to forgive you for performing a miracle? You deserve thanks.'

Lynnie stared at her, bemused. 'I'm sorry, I don't understand.' Then the truth hit home. 'Oh, Sheila, don't tell me it worked?' she cried, jumping up and down in excitement.

Sheila's face was mischievous now. 'Lynnie, I shouldn't have done that to you but I couldn't resist it! I can't tell you what it felt like when I opened the front door early this afternoon and found my own mother and Everal's standing on the doorstep together. My mother just said, "Well, don't I get a kiss? And aren't you going to ask us in? We could do with a cup of tea. I'm sure Bethina wants one, don't you, Bethina?" And Everal's mother said, "That would be very nice". Well, I was dumbstruck. I couldn't say anything. It was as if my throat had seized up. Like a zombie I just stood aside and they walked in together. They even sat together on the settee. We've all just had the most wonderful afternoon. We talked and talked and they played with the girls, and I know they both fell in love with their grandchildren. They stayed until Everal came home from work. He nearly collapsed when he walked into the living room and found them both sitting there. He almost fell into his mother's arms. Oh, Lynnie, it was so touching! I came round as soon as I could to tell you.'

'Oh, Sheila, really? So everything is all right then?'

She nodded. 'Very much so. I know we have a way to go yet, both mothers have to talk to the rest of our families, but it's a start, isn't it? At least now we have our mothers back. And for that I have you to thank, Lynnie. Believe me, I haven't a clue how to begin doing that.'

'Sheila, you're my friend, and friends try to help each other. I just wanted to do something.'

'And whatever yer did was obviously right,' said Avril, looking at her daughter proudly. 'This news definitely calls for a celebration.'

'Oh, don't worry, Mrs Downs, that's already been organised by Everal. He's asked if you'll all come round on Saturday night, and boy, are we going to throw a party. The party to end all parties. Everal's going to make his special rum punch.'

Avril grinned. 'Then yer can definitely count me in, and Nan too.'

'Oh, good, because it wouldn't be a celebration without you all. Right, I'd better be off as he and I have so much to talk about. If I don't see you before, about eight on Saturday?'

As she shut the door Lynnie gave a deep sigh of relief. 'Oh, Mam, I took a huge gamble and thank God it paid off.'

'The whole of life's a gamble, Lynnie. It'd be against the odds if we all won through. Well done, lovey. You can tell me and Nan later what exactly it was that yer did do, but first go and get yer chores done.'

A couple of minutes later, upstairs on the landing, Lynnie was just passing the bedroom her brothers shared on her way to her own when she heard Dec say loudly, 'That much, eh? It's building up, ain't it?'

Her curiosity got the better of her. Wondering what they could possibly be referring to, she pressed her ear to the door to listen for more. And what she heard next made her gasp in shock. '*So how much did you mek last night, Colin?*' Lynnie's mind raced frantically, her fear that her brothers were up to no good horrifyingly confirmed. And to make matters worse they had roped in Colin. Well, she wasn't going to allow it to continue. She'd put a stop to their antics, just see if she didn't! Face wreathed in fury, she burst through the door, hurriedly shut it behind her and hissed, 'After all we vowed to each other, how could you?'

They sat staring at her, frozen.

It was Dec who gathered his wits first. 'Could we what?' he snapped.

'Don't, Dec. Don't take me for a fool. I heard you asking Colin what he made last night, and that can only mean one thing. You're all at it. Go on, admit it. And shame on you for roping in our Colin. This is going to break Mam's heart, not to mention how Ray's going to take it after all he did to keep you out of trouble. You've let him down. You've let all of us down.'

'Ah, Lynnie, this ain't what yer think,' Jimmy interrupted. 'Tell her, Dec, tell her she's got the wrong end of the stick.'

'Oh, pull the other one, Jimmy.' She pointed to the shoe box on Dec's bed half-filled with coins of all denominations plus several notes. 'My eyes playing tricks on me, are they? Don't tell me you managed to save up all that out of your wages.'

'No, yer right, we didn't, Lynnie,' said Dec, looking at her cockily. 'But we've earned it all the same.'

'I bet you have! Well, I'm telling you all, no more. Is that clear? Else I'll . . .'

'You'll what?' snorted Dec.

'Tell Mam,' she warned.

He gave a nonchalant shrug. 'Tell her then. Saves us the bother. Although we'd have preferred to wait a while before we did.'

She gasped, mortified. 'What's become of you, our Dec? Have you lost all respect for your family as well as yourself? You as well, Jimmy. And, oh, Colin! We had such high hopes of you, what with you getting your apprenticeship and having such good prospects for the future. I can't believe this of you all, I really can't, not after what we've achieved so far. How long have you all been at it? Have you ever *not* been? Come on, I want to know.'

'Oh, tell her, Dec,' implored Jimmy. 'Fer God's sake, put her out of her misery then hopefully we can still surprise Mam.'

'No. Let her suffer, serves her right for being so nosy.' He gave a sigh. 'Oh, all right. This ain't anything like what yer think, Sis, regardless of what it looks like. We've earned this money and it's all bin done honestly, believe me it has.'

'It has, our Lynnie, really,' piped up Colin.

'Will yer shuddup and let me finish?' Dec hissed at him. 'We've all got work to do tonight, and if we don't hurry up and get this explanation over with we'll miss out on a chance to add to our coffers.'

'Sorry, our Dec,' muttered Colin and sat back on the bed.

Returning his full attention to his sister, Dec took a

deep breath. 'Look, I have ter be truthful and say that when we first made our family pact to go straight me and Jimmy . . . well, more me really . . . didn't take it seriously. Yer can't really blame me. This family turning itself around . . .' He gave a shrug. 'Considering our past it were a bit far-fetched to me and I thought it'd only be a matter of time before everything was back to square one. Only Nan didn't quite agree with my way of thinking.'

'Nan?' queried Lynnie.

'Yeah, Nan. She overheard me and Jimmy talking about playing you all along that we'd gone straight but behind yer backs carrying on just as we were, and she threatened us.'

'Threatened you? With what?'

He looked at her awkwardly. 'Well, she overheard us discussing why we scarpered from London back up here, which I ain't prepared to tell you about so don't ask, but Nan threatened to tell Mam and the police if she saw us put a foot wrong in future. Now, you might not believe we think much of our family, Lynnie, but it might surprise yer to know that actually we do. After Nan's words, well, it really struck home that we could lose you all if we weren't careful. So we decided to make as much of an effort at keeping to the straight and narrow as you all were.'

'Really?' uttered Lynnie, shocked to realise that her brothers had such a deep regard for them all when she had always been of the opinion that Dec and Jimmy only really cared for themselves.

'Yeah, really, Sis. Anyway, after a bit we saw how tired Mam was, doing two jobs as well as looking after us, so we wondered how we could help out more so she didn't have to do so much. But we already gave her as much as we could out of our wages as it was, and sometimes we got laid off 'cos there was n'ote for us to do on site or the weather was bad. Labourers are the first to be laid off, ain't they, and yer don't get paid for sitting around. So me and Jimmy put our heads together to try and come up with an idea for making some extra money and decided to ask around, see if anyone wanted odd jobs doing, like fixing up walls or fences, clearing rubbish, that sort of thing. Some people will pay well for a few hours' labouring work, especially in posh areas.

'Well, I don't think anyone was more shocked than me and Jimmy when it took off, and within a week or so we had so much on that we had a job fitting our normal day job in. But we liked doing it, didn't we, Jimmy, and it felt great when people thanked us for a job well done. Some even gave us more than we'd asked as a thank you. It was then it struck us that maybe we could make a good living out of doing this full-time. Set ourselves up as odd job men. Well, anything's gotta beat working for someone else, ain't it? And we thought maybe we could do more for Mam in the long run that way. Sounds ambitious, I know, but we could even do well enough that she'd be able to give both her jobs up. Anyway, that's when Colin went snooping around and found our shoe box. The little sod demanded to know what we were up to, said he'd tell Mam otherwise. Well, we had no choice but to let him in on it, and when he heard what we were trying to do he wanted to be part of it too.'

'I did,' erupted Colin, who couldn't keep quiet any longer. 'I was fed up with me old mates ribbing me whenever they got the chance, saying we were all soap flakes – yer know, cleaner than clean. So I thought, Let 'em laugh the other side of their faces when they hear my brothers are businessmen. That'd show 'em, wouldn't it? So I've bin doing what I can after work and on Sat'days. Mowing lawns, dog walking, that kinda thing.'

'Mowing! Dog walking!' uttered Lynnie, astounded. 'You?'

'Pays half a crown a time. Look, a bloody dog bit me ankle last week and it flipping hurt, I can tell yer,' he said, pulling up his trouser leg and showing Lynnie his scabby wound.

'And I'll give the lad his due,' said Dec, 'he handed over every penny that he'd earned this way for us to add to the fund.'

Lynnie was staring at them all. 'So . . . why didn't you let any of the rest of us in on what you were up to instead of letting us begin to have suspicions that you were up to no good? You knew we were beginning to think that, didn't you?'

''Course we did,' said Dec. 'But we just let you carry on 'cos we didn't want any of yer to argue this was some hare-brained scheme before we could prove it wasn't. We wanted to have made enough to rent our own little yard and buy a stock of materials. That looks more professional, dunnit, than asking fer money up front for them. And then yer'd have all seen for yourselves what an effort we'd made and that we were serious.'

'You really have thought this all out, haven't you?'

Dec grinned. 'Shocked you, ain't we? I can tell by yer face we have. What's up, Sis? Didn't yer think we had the brains to make 'ote of ourselves?'

'No . . . Yes. Oh, yer've shocked me all right. I'm . . . well, I'm just lost for words.'

Jimmy laughed. 'That meks a change, Sis. So are you going to tell Mam and spoil our surprise?'

She shook her head. 'No, I'm not. But I'll tell you what I am going to do.'

They all looked at her warily.

'Oh, and what's that?' Dec asked.

'I've some money in the Post Office. I'm going to give it to you. Well, the least I can do is help the Downs Empire off the ground.'

Their faces lit up. 'Really!' they all cried.

She nodded. 'Yes, really. I'll sort it out the first chance I get. Oh, I can't tell you how proud I am of all of you. Mam's going to be over the moon when you let her in on it, I know she is. What Nan's going to say I've no idea. Ray . . . well . . . he'll be flabbergasted. Oh, you daft lot!' she cried, rushing towards them all and gathering them to her in a big hug. She released them and said, 'Well, yer've work to do, so get to it. Come on, no time for idling now, not when time is money.'

Chapter Twenty-one

'You look happy with yerself today, Lynnie. Meks a change from last week. Bit down in the mouth then, weren't yer?'

She smiled at her customer. 'Yes, I was a bit. But I'm happy today.' And she had every reason to be. When all else had failed, she had helped her friend and her husband be reunited with their respective families; her other friend had got her dearest wish and now had her own house so she could get on properly with married life; her youngest brothers had thrilled her beyond words with their plans for a business venture which hopefully would lead to the easing of her mother's financial burdens; and she herself was slowly coming to terms with Ozzie's betrayal of her, beginning to realise she had indeed had a lucky escape from the life he would have led her if they had married. As a consequence the pain of her loss was easing. All she needed now was for Ray to come back home and Sid Mallin to return, which would hopefully be soon in both cases.

She took the betting slip from her customer, checked it and handed it back to him. 'I'll keep my fingers crossed you're lucky, Mr Warren.'

'Oh, let's hope so, ducky. I ain't had a winner for weeks now,' he said, putting the slip safely in his pocket which he patted as if to help bring him luck before turning to leave.

She had no more customers to deal with for the moment and before she tackled anything else thought she would seize the moment to mash a pot of tea. Before she did she looked across at old Willy Noble who was sitting in his usual spot under the Tannoy, peering through his thick milk-bottle-lensed spectacles as he studied the runners in the racing pages, making his mind up which one might be worth the risk of a shilling or two.

'Fancy a cuppa, Mr Noble?' she shouted across.

Without lifting his head, he vigorously nodded.

As she made her way into the tiny kitchen next to the office to put the blackened kettle on to boil, she giggled to herself. Willy might be old and decrepit but his hearing was still acute. Assuming Alfie Manners wouldn't say no to one either, as he never did, she set out three mugs, added milk and sugar as well as tea to the chipped brown pot, and made her way back behind the counter while she waited for the kettle to boil, which always took ages.

On returning, the shock she received when she spotted Willy Noble collapsed in a heap on the floor made her cry out. 'Oh, my God! Mr Manners, Mr Manners!'

She dashed out from behind the counter and over to the old man, bending down to look at him.

Alfie Manners arrived behind the counter. 'What? Oh!' he exclaimed as he saw for himself what had happened and immediately rushed over. Kneeling down, he took the old man's wrist.

Lynnie, who had never been in a situation like this before, asked what he was doing.

'I'm checking for his pulse. Found it. He's not dead, thank God. I think he's had a heart attack. Stay here while I go and telephone for an ambulance. Don't move him whatever you do. Talk to him, reassure him that we're getting help. I won't be a minute.'

Lynnie was taken aback by Alfie's medical knowledge and also the way he was taking control of the situation. He'd obviously had experience of this kind of thing before. 'Right. Yes, okay, I will.'

Ten minutes later the ambulance arrived. After getting Willy inside one ambulance man jumped behind the wheel while the other prepared to climb into the back to take care of the patient. Before he did he looked at them both and said, 'Someone will need to come with us to deal with the formalities while the old chap's being dealt with by the medical staff. Who called for the ambulance?'

'I did,' said Alfie.

'Then would you come with us, please, sir?'

Was it Lynnie's imagination or did a horrified expression flash across his face? Before he could protest, as she got the distinct impression he was about to do, the ambulance man had herded Alfie inside, shutting the door behind him. Siren blaring, it raced off down the road.

Returning to the shop, Lynnie was greeted by the shrill whistle of the kettle boiling its lid off. Rushing straight into the kitchen, she turned off the gas. As there were no customers requiring her assistance she decided she may as well make herself the pot of tea she had been in the process of doing just before Willy's collapse. She certainly felt the need for one.

She had just finished pouring herself a mug when she heard a thump on the counter top. Someone was banging for attention. Putting down the mug, she went out to them.

It was the shabby little man. 'I wanna see the boss,' he said, his tone more of an order than a request, as usual.

'He's not here,' she replied, fighting to keep her voice from showing her annoyance at his manner.

'What d'yer mean, he ain't here? He's expecting me.'

'He got called away urgently.'

'When will he be back then?'

'I don't know. Depends how long it takes for him to deal with what he has to.' She was becoming agitated now. She was worried about Willy and this man's attitude towards her wasn't helping. 'Look, can I help you?' she said tartly. 'I assure you, I can deal with anything Mr Manners was doing for you. There's nothing I don't know about or can't take care of.'

By the look on his face he seemed totally shocked to

hear that she was fully conversant with every aspect of bet-taking. Did he think her a fool or something?

'Oh, you're in the know, are you? Well, I've come to collect the betting slip. The one Mr Manners said would be waiting for me to collect when I telephoned earlier this morning.' He winked at her knowingly.

She had no idea what he was talking about but wasn't about to let him know that. And she didn't like the way he had winked at her either. 'Oh, I see. It's probably on his desk then. I'll go and check. What race is it for?'

He looked at her quizzically. 'What race?'

'Yes, so I know I'm giving you the right slip.'

He gave a shrug. 'How am I supposed to know that? Mr Manners never told me what he'd made it out for when I phoned to confirm he'd done the business. Look, I ain't got time to be wasting, can yer just go and get it? It'll be in the name of Brown.'

She looked at him for a moment, thinking she must have misinterpreted his reply. But she didn't like this man and wanted rid of him, and the only way to do that was to deal with his request. Hopefully then he'd be on his way and would leave her in peace to drink her much-needed mug of tea. 'I'll ... er ... just go and check if there's one on his desk with that name on it,' she said, disappearing off.

There was only one filled out betting slip she could find, tucked inside the flap of the leather binder holding the blotting pad. She eased it out and glanced it over to check it was indeed the right one. It was made out for a Mr Brown. Then she gasped, realising that not only was the stake for the enormous amount of one hundred pounds with high odds of winning at twenty-five to one, but this race had actually taken place the previous day and she remembered that the horse named had come in first.

She blew out her cheeks in surprise. Whoever this man was go-between for had won himself over two thousand pounds after betting tax had been deducted. Not only did she hope that when Alfie Manners had accepted this bet he had hedged it around other turf accountants, but also that there was enough money in the safe to pay it out now until Alfie had split the huge loss between those he had hedged it with. She noticed a bunch of keys on the desk. Thank God they hadn't been in Alfie's pocket and were now down at the hospital with him. At least when the man demanded his payout she wouldn't look stupid having to tell him she hadn't got access to the safe, considering she had already told him she practically ran the business in the manager's absence. If there wasn't enough money in the safe to cover it, which she thought more than likely, then he would have to come back later and Alfie could deal with it.

She took the slip through and handed it over.

He snatched it off her, studied it with a satisfied smile before thrusting his hand inside his shabby jacket and pulling out a bulky envelope which he slapped down on the counter in front of her. Before she could ask him if he wanted to collect the winnings, he had spun on his heel and rushed out.

Lynnie stared after him, mystified. She couldn't understand why he had not insisted on being paid out. That was the whole idea of betting. Take a gamble on backing a horse, pray it came in, and when it did, jubilantly collect the spoils. She could never remember any of Sid's other lucky punters failing to collect at the very first opportunity.

Then something else struck her. What was in the envelope he had slapped down in front of her? She picked it up, saw it wasn't sealed and inquisitively flicked open the flap. There was money in it. Why was this man giving her money? Surely the betting wager had already been settled when the bet was actually placed? She counted the notes. They totalled two hundred pounds. Two hundred? Why would this man be handing her such a fortune? Oh, unless it was payment for another large bet Alfie Manners had agreed to take. But if so, why hadn't the man given her a completed betting slip for her to date and time along with this wager payment, or asked for the one Alfie Manners would have completed on his behalf when he had agreed the bet which she assumed had been done over the telephone, like he told her the other one had been?

None of this made any sense. Not one bit of it.

She stood gazing into space and the more she pondered over what had taken place, the more puzzling it became to her. It was all probably perfectly innocent, she tried to tell herself. But the more she tried to believe that, the more the feeling that it wasn't filled her.

Several customers came in together then and she was forced to forget her worries for a few minutes while she dealt with them. As soon as they had gone, she returned her thoughts to the problem.

Why hadn't that man made any mention of his winnings? They were after all the most important thing of all in the betting world. And why had he given her an envelope containing two hundred pounds and not asked for anything in return? Then slowly an idea began to take shape. It seemed absurd, but could it possibly be that Lynnie *had* given the man what he had come in for? The betting slip. The more she thought about it, that was what he had seemed most interested in. But why was that slip so important to him? Just what was its significance? And why hadn't he even known the name of the horse he was backing?

Slowly it began to dawn on her just what was going on, and her conclusions were so awful they didn't bear thinking about.

Alfie Manners must be accepting a backhander to make out betting slips after the outcome of a race was known. That was why the man had looked at her oddly when she had asked what horse's name was on the slip he was requesting. He wouldn't know what he was backing, would he, until Alfie Manners had sifted through all the winners, biding his time until something with decent odds against it was first past the post. Although that conclusion still didn't explain why the man hadn't collected the payout, it did explain why he had just paid over two hundred pounds. It was Alfie's payment for what he had done, it had to be. Or just a small token maybe? Could it be they would meet up at some prearranged place later where no one could witness them split the winnings equally?

She was furious with Alfie. Sid had trusted that man with the care and protection of his business and Alfie Manners had seized his opportunity to wangle himself a fortune. How many times had Alfie done this before? That obnoxious man had come in three times to see him in private to her knowledge, so that was three times at least, and if the 'winnings' from the last bet were anything to go by then that could mean the scam had already netted them six thousand pounds, possibly more. Whatever Alfie Manners's cut was it would mount up to a tidy sum, and that money had to be coming out of Sid's profits. Alfie Manners was in the process of bankrupting him.

Her mouth felt dry and bile swirled sickeningly in her stomach as she thought of Alfie sitting in Sid's office, feet on the desk, thumbing through magazines all day, probably laughing up his sleeve at her as she beavered away trying to run the business single-handed, only tackling those jobs he couldn't get out of and condescending to make the odd cup of tea to keep her sweet. The bastard! she fumed.

She had never taken to Alfie, always had the impression he was not quite right in some way. She had been correct. So that was why she'd had that strange feeling when they had first met, and again later. She had recognised that this was a man she should be very suspicious of but she hadn't listened to her own instincts. She shuddered, not believing she had actually felt a great desire for him to kiss her when he had saved her from falling. God, she must have been in some state to have wanted that!

Memories flooded back then of little things that had happened while he had been here. That night of the trauma with Ozzie, when she had sought the sanctuary of the shop to compose herself, she had thought she had heard the back door shutting and in her shocked state had taken his word that he had thought he'd left it unlocked and come back to check. Maybe in fact that horrible man had just left by it after an update meeting over their crooked scheme.

She had also overheard Alfie on the telephone though his conversation hadn't made any sense to her at the time. Maybe it did now if he had been talking to that man and not, as she had assumed, one of Sid's telephone account customers. What had Alfie been saying: '*no, nothing yet*' and '*have patience*'? Had he been saying he hadn't come across a horse that had won with high enough odds against it as yet? Had he been advising his fellow con artist to have patience while he waited?

Oh, God, her mind screamed. This was all so terrible. It had been going on under her nose and she hadn't had a clue. Thank God she had found out now for Sid's sake. He was in danger of being ruined and she had to put a stop to it. But how?

If only Ray were here, he'd know what to do. But he wasn't so it was up to her to act.

She forced herself to concentrate. She had nothing to go to the police with. As matters stood, she could not prove that Alfie had written out any betting slips after the results of a race were known. She couldn't prove he had been given money for doing so either.

She needed to get evidence somehow. Think, she ordered herself. What do the police do when they suspect someone? Oh, of course, they followed them to catch them out. Like they had done Ozzie. Then a memory struck her. She had seen the shabby man entering a pub near the café where she had arranged to meet Everal's and Sheila's mothers, several nights before. Maybe that was his local. If so she could follow him from there to see where he went next and who he met. If she could manage to discover the meeting place where he and Alfie divided their illicit gains then she could have the police waiting there the next time.

That was where she would make her start, the public house.

The door opened and Alfie came in. Her mind whirled frantically. She couldn't face him. He'd know immediately by her attitude towards him, which she hadn't a hope in hell of concealing, that something was wrong with her and would demand to know what it was. He might even guess she was on to his part in the scam and could make a run for it. She couldn't risk that, not until she'd found out something concrete she could go to the police with, because come hell or high water she wanted Alfie Manners to pay for his betrayal of Sid Mallin's trust in him.

Jumping off her counter stool, Lynnie rushed into the kitchen where she made a grab for her coat and handbag. When she came back into the shop Alfie had just lifted the counter flap and was about to walk through it himself. He stared, dumbstruck, when she pushed him aside and stepped through it herself. Heading towards the outer door, she called out, 'I have to go out. Be back when I can.'

After making her way across town on two buses, Lynnie spent the next two hours hiding in an alleyway across the road from the public house, constantly reminding herself she could not afford to lose her nerve in what she was about to undertake. She was doing it for Sid, she kept telling herself.

Two minutes to six found her waiting with a few others – after making sure that her prey wasn't one of them – for the pub's doors to open. She was hoping she could slip inside and find herself a vantage point from which she could keep a lookout for the man to appear and discreetly watch his movements.

At precisely six o'clock the doors opened. Walking in behind a large man, she hurriedly looked around her. The bar was much smaller than she had expected, square, with no alcoves for her to hide in but plenty of tables and chairs to sit at. They weren't an option for her though as she would then be in full view of everyone.

She quickly realised that just inside the dimly lit passageway to one side of the bar counter was her best option. A door led off it on the same side as the bar, but further down. She could stand there and have a clear view of whoever entered the pub while hopefully no one, not even the burly-looking barman at present busy serving drinks to those customers she had arrived with, would notice her.

Drinks!

She ought to buy one. Why else would she be in a pub if she wasn't having a drink? She started to make her way across to the bar when suddenly she froze as behind the bar the shabby-looking man appeared. Her mind raced frantically. So he was a barman. He worked here. She couldn't go over to the bar now and buy her drink as he might be the one to serve her, and if she stood here for much longer he might look over and spot her. What should she do? She had to get across the room unobserved into the dimly lit passageway, forget about the drink and hope no one noticed her there.

Quickly pulling up her coat collar and hunching her shoulders, head hanging low, she walked across and sighed with deep relief when she reached the dim passageway. She had just concealed herself against the door to the back of the bar when she heard the loud voice of the burly barman addressing someone.

'Ah, there you are, Neville, I thought you were never coming down. I did shout yer and I banged on yer door.'

Neville. So that was his name.

405

'Sorry, boss, I fell asleep. It won't happen again.'

Oh, so he lived on the premises. Maybe he went to meet up with Alfie Manners after work, to split the winnings between them?

'Bleddy right it won't. You're employed to start at opening time, not five minutes later. We need some bottles of light ale fetching up from the cellar. But before yer go and fetch 'em up, serve that customer.'

'Okay, boss. Yes, mate. Usual, is it?'

The cellar? Lynnie thought frantically. Where was that? She looked hurriedly around her. She could try and find somewhere to hide further down the passage-way but was not sure where it led, and besides the cellar could easily be down there and with no escape route Neville would soon discover her presence. She looked at the door beside her. It had a key in the lock. Maybe it wasn't used and she could hide inside until she felt it was safe to slip out again. She heard the counter flap being lifted and Neville say, 'Just ales, boss? Anything else while I'm at it?'

Quick as a flash, she unlocked the door and pushed it open. To her horror she saw steps leading down into near pitch darkness. This was obviously the cellar and the last place she wanted to be. Any minute now Neville would be behind her. She had no choice, how-ever: she had to go down. Panic gripping her, she shut the door behind her as quietly as she could, and with her heart in her mouth put her hand on the wall to help guide her and made her way down as fast as she dared, constantly aware that at any second now Neville could come through the cellar door, put the light on and immediately discover her. Then her only chance of finding evidence to convict him and Alfie would be gone. She almost cried out in relief when she reached firm ground.

Now where could she hide? She couldn't see a thing except for dark eerie shapes looming around her. If she bumped into anything the noise could alert him to her presence. Then it struck her – under the stairs. She just had to hope she could find enough space there for her to crouch down in, and hopefully something to hide behind.

Heart hammering painfully, she felt her way around the cellar steps until her hand encountered air, then kicked out with her foot, praying she would find enough space to hide herself. It was her only hope. Thank God, there did seem to be an empty space which she just might fit into with a bit of a squash. Almost bending double so as not to hit her head on the edge of the stairs, she backed her way into the space as far as she could. She had just crouched down to make herself as small as possible when she heard the cellar door open, and then – which she thought rather odd considering he would have his hands full holding the crate of ale when he went back up the steps – shutting again, and then the flick of the switch fractionally ahead of the light coming on. She listened as his footsteps descended the stairs. They were getting louder and louder as he passed directly over her. She still worried he would see her if he looked her way.

She glanced rapidly around. To the side of her were several barrels, one which had an old length of thick cloth draped over it. Grabbing the cloth, she pulled it over her head and around her just as she heard his footsteps reach the bottom of the stairs. Holding her breath, she listened to the sound of his steps against the stone slabs moving away from her across the room. Then she heard something being scraped across the floor, and a grating noise, and wondered just what Neville could possibly be doing. Lifting a crate of ale off the floor wouldn't make that noise. Curiosity got the better of her. Gently inching down the cloth just enough for her to peer over the edge, Lynnie looked across to see what he was up to.

He was over at the far end of the cellar, squatting down beside the wall and taking something out of his pocket. It looked like a piece of paper. Although he had his back to her, it seemed to her that he looked at it and kissed it before reaching over to put it inside the wall. There had to be a hollow niche in it. Then he took something else out of his pocket, it looked like a book of some kind. He then did the same with that as he had with the piece of paper. He then stood up, put his hands on the sides of a heavy barrel and, with the scraping noise she had heard before, heaved it over to cover his hidey hole.

Then a voice shattered the silence. 'What yer doing down there, Neville?'

'Just coming, boss. Saw a mouse and was trying to catch it.'

'The cellar's full of bleddy mice. Just get back up here, will yer, with that ale? We've customers to deal with.'

Lynnie froze as near hysteria rose within her. Mice! She was terrified of mice. She had to get out of here. She mentally shook herself as she realised Neville had turned around and was about to make his way across the cellar. If he happened to glance at the stairs he might spot a pair of eyes watching him. Quick as a flash she pulled the cover back across the exposed part of her face and held her breath. Seconds later she heard the chink of bottles and his laboured footsteps going back up the stairs. Then she heard the crate being put down on the top step straight after the door being opened, the click of the light switch seconds later, the clink of bottles again and then the banging of the door as she assumed he'd kicked it shut behind him with his heel. Her ears pricked hopefully. She hadn't heard the key turning in the lock. Hopefully he had forgotten to lock it in his haste to get back behind the bar.

She waited for a while before slowly easing the piece of cloth from over her head. Now what did she do? Her thoughts raced wildly, torn between her need to get out of the cellar for fear she was discovered and her desperation to find out just what Neville was hiding. It could be all she needed to bring him and Alfie Manners to justice. But to see what she was doing she would need to put the light on, and while she was searching for clues Neville could return and catch her in the act.

What was she to do?

A scratching sound made her freeze. Mice! Or, worse, rats. Oh, God, she had to get out of here. She couldn't think straight with the threat of mice or rats crawling all over her. Without another thought she removed herself from her hiding place, felt her way around and almost ran up the stairs. On the top step she paused long enough to make up her mind that if anyone spotted where she'd come from and tried to question her, she would kick up her heels and make a run for it.

Taking hold of the door handle, she pulled the door just far enough open for her to slip through and quickly shut it behind herself. Thankfully no one was in the passageway. So far so good. Now all she had to do was get out of the pub without Neville spotting her. She would then wait across the road hidden inside the alleyway and keep a lookout to see if Alfie turned up, or if not when Neville himself went out after the pub shut she would follow him.

She flashed a look ahead. A couple of feet before her, where the passage wall ended and the bar began, a man was perched on a bar stool, leaning on the counter. Several others stood around with pint mugs in their hands. All she had to do was ease her way through them and make her way to the door. Hunching her shoulders and lowering her head, she stepped out. She had to turn sideways to pass between the man on the stool and another standing behind him. She was just in the process of doing so when the standing man stepped backwards, knocking Lynnie into the man on the bar stool, who lurched forward in turn, splashing beer over the counter top.

Automatically they both turned their heads to look at each other, the man on the bar stool to see who had knocked into him, Lynnie to apologise hurriedly for causing him to spill his drink.

As soon as their eyes met they both froze in horror.

Before she could stop herself Lynnie blurted, 'Ray! What on earth are you doing here?'

Neville, who was in the process of pulling a pint nearby, looked over at them and gawped in shock when he recognised Lynnie. His eyes flashed questioningly to Ray, then back to her.

Ray let out a loud defeated groan. 'Oh, shit,' he uttered. Jumping off the stool, he grabbed Lynnie's arm and unceremoniously dragged her through the drinkers and out into the street where he thrust her away from him, shouting, 'You've blown it! Now he knows we're connected somehow. For God's sake, Lynnie . . . How? . . . What . . .? Oh, bugger. Now we'll never find who the hell is behind all this. Just when I thought I might be getting somewhere.' He glared at her menacingly. 'Where the bleddy hell did you spring from?'

'Me?' she shot back at him. 'What were you doing in the same pub as *him*, that's what I want to know?' Then her face filled with horror. 'Oh, no – no. Please don't tell me you're involved with them in some way? No, I can't bear it, Ray.'

'Oh, shut up, Lynnie,' he cried furiously. 'The only way I'm involved in this is trying to find out about that chap in there. Now I'll never get close. Blast! Blast! Blast!' He shook his head at her in disbelief. 'Oh, go home, Lynnie. I've got to go and tell Alex that thanks to you we've just wasted a month of our time for nothing. I'll deal with you when I get back.'

She was staring at him, confused. 'What do you mean? Er . . . who's Alex?'

'Alfie Manners to you.'

'Alfie Manners? *Alfie*. Oh, Ray, listen! He's in on it with that Neville. He's taking bribes to . . .'

'I know.'

'You *know*? That Alfie is in the process of bankrupting Sid? That's if he hasn't already. If you do, why haven't you got the police involved?'

'Because Alfie . . . Alex, *is* the police.'

'What! But . . . but . . . I don't understand.'

'I don't think I do at the moment, Lynnie, at least what you're doing here. Oh, go home, I'll explain later. And I'll definitely want to know what you were doing in that pub tonight.'

He made to rush away from her but she ran after him and grabbed his arm, pulling him to a halt. 'What shall I do about the hiding place, Ray?'

He turned and looked at her. 'What did you say?'

'The secret hiding place where I saw Neville putting something while I was down in the cellar.'

'You were where?' His face suddenly lit up and he grabbed her shoulders, shaking her hard. 'Where exactly was the hiding place, Lynnie?' he demanded.

'In the wall at the back of the cellar. Near the bottom, I think. If you moved the barrels aside . . .'

'Oh, Lynnie,' he cut in. 'Lynnie, Lynnie, Lynnie! I don't know what the hell you were doing down there but you might just have discovered something. It's worth checking out anyway. Now go home and I'll see you later.'

With that he hared off, leaving her standing behind him stupefied.

Chapter Twenty-two

Lynnie woke with a start to find Ray leaning over her. 'You're back,' she cried, struggling upright.

'Where is everyone?' he asked, sitting down on the settee beside her.

She glanced across at the clock. 'Where do you think? In bed. It's five o'clock in the morning, Ray. I came straight home like you said and immediately went to bed, telling Mam I had a headache. But I was really watching out of the window for you to come in. As soon as I knew they were all in bed asleep I came back down to wait for you and I must have fallen asleep myself. I had to do that or they'd have known something was wrong and started asking me questions. And how could I answer them? If I told them any of this they'd be as confused as me! So why don't you put me out of my misery? Ray, what the hell is going on?'

He shook his head. 'You ain't gonna believe what I'm about to tell yer.'

'Ray, I'm going mad here. Will you just tell me, and I want to know it all?'

He sat back on the settee. 'It all started when Neville Brown turned up to see Sid and asked if he was willing to supply him with a few winning betting slips for a horse at good odds if he was paid. Neville Brown didn't want the winnings, though, it was just the betting slips he was interested in. Well, you know how honest Sid is, won't have anything to do with any monkey business. He was just about to send Brown packing when he realised there was obviously a money-laundering scam going on or about to be. What better way to prove how you'd got hold of a good deal of money if anyone questioned you than to say you'd won it on the horses, and to back up your claim, produce winning slips to cover the amount? No one could do anything about it then. Obviously this money that had to be accounted for was illegally come by, or else why bother? But you'd only to look at Neville Brown to see he hasn't much to him, so he must be working for someone else. Maybe a big-time criminal who needs to launder the proceeds from a major job like a bank robbery.

'Sid felt the least he could do was alert the police to his suspicions and then what they did about this information was up to them, but he decided to ask me what I thought about it all first. I was really honoured he did that. Meantime he told Neville he'd think about his proposition but gave him the impression he was very interested and told him to come back. As soon as he'd gone Sid called me into his office and told me what the man had asked him to do, and what he felt it could all mean. I agreed with him that it had to be a money-laundering scam and said he was right to inform the police. He asked me to accompany him because he was worried that given my background they might other-wise suspect I was involved in some way. Sid wanted me to tell them myself I wasn't.

'The police were very interested in what he had to tell them. There was now a chance to uncover the whereabouts of stolen money. They asked Sid if he would be willing for them to put an undercover man in his place, one who would appear ready to accommo-date this plan if there was money in it for him and at the same time try and befriend Neville Brown. The plant would make out he was up for anything else the boss might need doing, might hopefully get an intro-duction set up to meet the man behind all this. In the meantime the police would have Neville followed to see where he led them.

'Sid was happy to agree, but the police asked both of us not to tell anyone else about any of this as they didn't want Neville spooked in any way. They wanted everyone to act as normally as possible. That's why you were kept in the dark about all this, Lynnie.'

She was too amazed by his story to protest at this.

Ray continued, 'After our meeting with the police I could think of nothing else. On Monday when Alfie . . . Alex first introduced himself to us as our "new boss" and called me into the office to ask me privately to help him out as he knew hardly anything about betting, I put a proposition to him. To nail this gang or whoever was behind it, to my mind the police would need inside information. Someone would have to get in on the scam, someone who would fit in thanks to his background. Well, if these blokes we were dealing with were worth their salt then a copper's cover would be blown before they could get all they needed to bring the gang to justice. But should I be checked out they wouldn't find a flaw in my background. I was an ex-con and would have far more chance of convincing them. I told Alex that you'd be able to manage the counter meantime, Lynnie, and Sid could help him with whatever he couldn't manage over the telephone, like the latest odds and such like. He'd run the business from home until he opened the shop, so it wasn't really a problem.

'Alex was against it at first, said it could be dangerous for me as we weren't at all sure what kind of men we were dealing with. I told him I was prepared to take the risk. I think . . . I know . . . I saw this as a way of proving to everyone who still had doubts about me that the old Ray Downs was dead and buried. Anyway, eventually I persuaded Alex to have a word with his boss and they gave me the go-ahead and sorted me a place to stay that'd be in keeping with the part I was playing. Sid agreed to pay my wages while I was doing it and as I had no rent to pay I was able to send Mam that fiver every week.

'Crouching down behind a wall over the road from the shop, lying in wait for Neville to show up again, was . . . well, summat I don't want to have to do again. I'm sure some people thought I was a suspicious character casing the joint or something. Anyway, as soon as Neville did finally turn up and found Alex explaining that the boss had been called away and he was now in charge and quite open to what was on offer, I was on his tail. I followed him across town and into a pub. It looked seedy enough for a secret meeting. I hung back for a minute or two then slipped in and sat in a corner. When I looked around I couldn't understand it because there was no sign of Neville. The pub's an old one, only got one bar, so if he wasn't in there, where the hell was he? Then it struck me that this pub could be the gang's headquarters. Maybe they had a room out the back where they met. I was getting really excited now. This was going to be easier than I'd thought. So I just sat and kept me eyes peeled to see what happened next.

'Come closing time I still hadn't seen hide nor hair of Neville or anyone I thought he could be working for. In fact, no one went down the passageway or came out of it except customers to go out into the back yard to the toilet and then back again. I had to leave the pub as it was shutting so I went back outside and hid in an alleyway across the road to keep an eye out for anyone leaving after hours. But nothing. No one went into the pub and no one left it. Then it struck me that there must be a back entrance. I went to check and a gate at the back led into an alley. I was cross with meself for not thinking of that before. That's how Neville and whoever else he'd arranged to meet had managed to give me the slip. I decided next time I followed him anywhere, I'd be more alert for things like that.

'I telephoned Alex as we'd already agreed beforehand, to update him on what had happened. He told me that when he broke the good news to Neville that he was willing to help him, Neville asked if he could collect the betting slip the following Monday morning. He said that he would telephone earlier that morning to confirm everything was in order before he came, when he telephoned he wanted to know the total amount of the winnings on the slip. We reckoned I could follow him again then. Meantime Alex said there wasn't much I could do and best I keep a low profile.

'The next Monday I was waiting across the road from the shop to follow Neville when he came out. From the direction he was going I knew he was making his way to the pub again, but this time he didn't go straight there but stopped off first at a bank. I followed him in and pretended to be filling out a form. I saw Neville depositing money, and what struck me as really odd was that he showed the betting slip to the bank clerk dealing with him. It took me a couple of minutes to work out why he had done that. I realised it must have been to justify to the clerk him putting such a large amount in.

'The clerk wasn't suspicious, but I was. Let's face it, Lynnie, yer don't give yer bank book to just anyone to deposit money with, and especially such a large amount. The person could just abscond with it – unless of course that person was highly trusted. Which either meant our Neville was more than just a gofer in this gang, or that he was working alone. The only way I was gonna find that out was to keep as close to him as I could.

'As soon as he left the bank he went straight to the pub and this time I wanted to find out where he went next so I followed him in immediately, trying to make myself as inconspicuous as possible as I didn't want to make his acquaintance just yet. I was surprised that when he passed the bar a woman behind it shouted across to him, "Hiya, Neville. Bin out for a stroll? Well, enjoy the rest of yer day off. On tonight, a'yer?" He replied, "As usual. Can't remember the last night I had off. Just gonna pop down the cellar to mek sure the delivery arrived okay." Then he entered the passageway, unlocked the first door he came to and disappeared inside. He was down there for at least ten minutes. Now we know what he was doing, thanks to you, Lynnie. Anyway, I couldn't believe it. He actually worked in the pub, must live on the premises. The first time I'd followed him back he'd obviously gone straight up to his room because he'd nothing to hide in the cellar then, had he?

'I watched his every movement like a hawk during the following week but he passed no more than the time of the day with any customer and never went out except to pop down to the newsagent's just after seven and get an evening paper for his boss. The next Monday he did exactly as he'd done the previous week.

'This was starting to get a bit puzzling. Surely Neville would need to report back to whoever he was working with or for? Or was I correct in now guessing that he worked alone? Maybe his pub job was cover for his real occupation, but then he didn't seem to have much time off to plan or carry anything out that would substantiate the amount he seemed to want to justify with the betting slips. To date the two betting slips Alex had provided him with amounted to over three thousand pounds. Where the hell do you get money like that? A big enough job to bring that kind of money in needed thorough planning, and his one day a week off from his bar job didn't give him enough time for that.

'I kept a close eye on his movements all the following week but he never left the pub at all and no one that I saw came in to see him 'specially. The same again on his next day off. He visited the shop, collected the betting slip from Alex, paid over the sum indicated on it after making the same arrangements for the following week.

'Alex, who'd tried his best during Neville's visits to hint that he was very interested in becoming more closely involved, wasn't having any luck so I decided it was my turn. Instead of huddling in a corner keeping a watch on him in the pub, I sat at the bar. Boy, that man is hard work! I hardly got him to pass the time of day, let alone 'ote else. A couple of nights ago I finally got my chance to hold him in conversation, such as it was, though it was practically all on my side. I did manage to keep his attention just long enough to let him know

I was the kinda chap who was available for a certain kind of work. I hoped that might bring some results. But nothing. The next couple of nights conversation between us was no more than it had been before, him asking if I wanted my usual and making absolutely no reference to what I'd said to him. I was getting desperate. I seemed to be getting nowhere and neither was Alex.

'So now we've arrived at what happened today – well, yesterday now, isn't it? I usually arrived over the road to lie in wait for Neville about half an hour before he was due, just in case he was early and I missed him. But I was delayed when the bus from my bedsit didn't show up and I had to run across. I just saw him going into the shop bang on eleven like he always had done before. God, I was out of breath but I managed to have a breather while he was being dealt with by Alex – so I thought. My hope of Neville doing something different then was a waste of time. After collecting his betting slip, he did exactly the same as before. Bank to deposit money, then back to the pub. Only difference this time was that when he went to go down the cellar the woman behind the bar told him the boss was down there, still checking off the delivery because it was late in arriving, so he went straight through to the back where I presume stairs lead up to his room.

'It was then I made up me mind that I was going to take the bull by the horns and get something moving. This could go on for weeks otherwise and us none the wiser where this money was coming from. I suppose I should have talked over with Alex what I proposed to do, got his advice first, but I thought, what the heck. Someone has to do something and I haven't the patience the police have. I decided that as soon as I could catch Neville on his own without any other customer or his boss overhearing, I would bluff him into believing I was on to him. All I had to say to him was, "I'm on to you, mate." Then just sit back and smile smugly, as though I knew everything. I thought that was bound to make him do something. Hopefully put the wind up him enough to take me into his confidence in the hope he could bribe me into not doing anything further.

'I'd not long taken my place at the bar and was awaiting my opportunity when someone nearly knocked me off my stool and I got the shock of my life to see it was you. Good God, Lynnie, what a flipping fright you gave me! But all I could think of was that he knew you from the betting shop, and now he knew we knew each other, and . . . well, to me that was it. I was furious. He wouldn't use our betting shop again and so we'd lost all hope of finding out anything. Just what the hell were you doing there, Lynnie?'

She had been totally mesmerised by what her brother was telling her and was desperate to hear the outcome. 'Eh? Oh, Ray, I've *got* to know what happened after you left me at the pub. Just what was he up to? You must have found something in that hiding place? Please, Ray, please?'

'Okay. After leaving you, I wasn't sure where I'd find Alex. As it was getting on for seven I didn't know whether he'd have left the shop and gone down to the police station to update his boss, but I decided to try there first anyway. I managed to get a taxi and was glad to find him still in the shop. He was still there because apparently as soon as he managed to return from the hospital after making sure Willy Noble was in good hands, you flew out and left him to it and hadn't been back. When he found the betting slip gone, and the envelope of money, he didn't know what to think. Anyway, I hadn't time to listen to all that. Neville could be in the process of clearing out for all we knew. I quickly told him what had happened, about Neville seeing us together which had probably put the wind up him enough for him not to use our shop again. I'd been sitting at the bar for a fortnight. He could have decided I was the police by now. But at least we knew his hiding place.

'Alex telephoned his boss, quickly explained to him what had gone on and asked if we had got enough to go and tackle Neville. His boss thought so, said he and a couple of others would pay Neville a visit and search the cellar. He told Alex and me to come to the station and await the outcome.

'About an hour after we got there they brought Neville in. Seems he was still serving behind the bar when they turned up and nearly collapsed in shock when they asked to speak to him in private. When he was told that he was suspected of laundering the proceeds of a theft of some kind, he broke down and confessed.'

'And Ray? And?' Lynnie urged excitedly. 'How did he get it? Was it from a big bank job? Was he working for a gang? What? What?'

Her brother scraped his hands through his hair and said, 'No, nothing like that. He'd found it, he said.'

'What! Found it?'

'That's what he's claiming. He told the police that just over a year ago he'd gone to bed in the pub when he remembered he'd not put the rubbish out so he got up and went to do it. Outside in the yard he'd put the rubbish in the bin and was just about to go back inside and lock up when he noticed something by the wall. It was a canvas bag which obviously had something in it. He knew the boss hadn't got a bag like that and neither had he, so he opened it and got the shock of his life to find a stack of money inside. How much it was then he hadn't a clue.

'He panicked. Didn't know what to do. Someone must have thrown it over the wall. Who he had no idea. Where this money had come from was a mystery to Neville. His first thought was that he should tell his boss about what he'd found. Then he thought he should give it to the police. But this was like a dream come true for him. He'd never had anything in his life and didn't look likely to. This money could change things completely. It was like a gift from God. He took it up to his room and counted it out. Nearly ten thousand pounds. He could buy his own pub if it was his. Tell the landlord where to stick his job. Then he worried what if whoever had thrown it over the wall turned up and asked questions about the bag, and they found out he had left the pub more or less straight away after working there for years, they'd put two and two together, know it must have been him that had found it. They would come after him then and heaven knows what they'd do to him.

'He decided to put the bag in the bottom of his wardrobe and sit tight and see what happened. If anyone came into the pub and started asking questions about its whereabouts he'd make out he'd been keeping the money safe as he'd no idea who it could belong to. So he put the bag in the bottom of his wardrobe and went to bed. Then he couldn't sleep, knowing all that money was so close to him. He also knew that the woman who worked behind the bar sometimes came up to his room when he was out. He was worried she'd snoop around and find it. He couldn't lock the door as he had no key. Then he remembered that years previously part of the cellar had been bricked up because of damp or something, and behind the newer wall was a cavity. He got up there and then, taking the bag with the money in it. It took him nearly all night to remove two bricks and stash the money inside the cavity then replace the bricks and stack the barrels back in front of it. The dustbin men were due early that morning so he stuffed the empty bag in a dustbin.

'Next day he did his best to carry on as normal, but he said every time someone unfamiliar walked into the pub he just about leaped out of his skin. But no one asked any questions about a bag. He scoured the local paper for days for any report of a robbery taking place nearby on that night. There was nothing. He decided to sit on the money for a year, and if nothing happened within that time he would feel it was safe to use it. The year passed and still no one came in to ask about the bag. Then he started to worry that if anyone asked him how a barman earning the pittance he was on came into a good amount, how could he explain it? He'd no relatives that he could say had left him an inheritance, and besides, if his story was checked out it would be found to be untrue. He'd always be watching his back. Then an idea came to him. If he said he'd won it on the horses and could prove it, no one could say a word. They'd just think he was a lucky man who'd had a winning streak. His boss didn't know what he did on his days off so he could make out he'd always had a flutter but had kept it private. All he had to do was get a turf accountant to give him enough betting slips to cover the amount he'd found and then he was free to do just what he liked with it. He felt sure someone would do such a simple thing for him if he paid them to, and it wouldn't harm them anyway as he wasn't claiming the winnings. His only mistake was in approaching Sid. Another turf accountant might have been tempted, but Sid prides himself on his absolute honesty.'

Ray took a deep breath. 'So there you have it, Lynnie. A man who found a bag of money that no one seemed to want to claim, and tried to make out it was his by producing winning betting slips'

'Well!' she exclaimed. 'What's the odds on finding something as valuable as that?'

'Phew! You tell me!'

'Do the police believe him?'

'Well, if they can't tie this money back to anything positively illegal then it looks like they'll have no choice.'

'Will he get to keep it?'

'Finders keepers, ain't it? Now, I've told you all my story. What were *you* doing down that cellar?'

Lynnie explained. 'Well,' she finished off, 'what would you have thought in my position? I didn't know Alfie . . . sorry, Alex . . . was a policeman and I still can't take that in. I knew something wasn't right about him but him being a policeman never crossed my mind. Anyway, I just thought him and this Neville were ruining Sid's business between them. What would you have thought and done in my place?'

He grinned at her. 'Probably the same as you, Lynnie.' Then his face clouded over. 'But what you did was so stupid. Didn't you stop to think what could have happened to you?'

'No. I just knew I had to do whatever I could to put a stop to it.'

He leaned over and kissed her cheek. 'I'm proud of you, Sis.'

She kissed him back. 'I'm proud of you, too.'

He rose and yawned loudly, stretching himself. 'I've

got to get some sleep. I am absolutely shattered. I'll have to go over that whole story again tomorrow with the family, and you can be damned sure they'll want to know every last tiny detail.'

'And I think we've a few stories to tell you, too, about what's been happening while you've been away.'

'Oh?'

She gave a tired smile. 'They'll keep until tomorrow, Ray.'

She rose and hooked her arm through his. 'Come on, let's go to bed for what's left of the night.'

Chapter Twenty-three

'Quiet, isn't it?'

Lynnie turned her head to see Sid Mallin standing beside her. 'I'm not complaining. I'm still recovering from the shock of all that happened last week and the exhaustion of running this place single-handed while it was all going on.'

Sid smiled at her and patted her arm affectionately. 'Yer did a grand job, Lynnie. But yer do understand now why we couldn't get you any help in, and why we had to keep yer in the dark?'

'Yes. Actually I rather enjoyed the extra responsibility, if you want the truth.'

'I'm glad to hear that because ... Oh, I might as well tell you both now. Ray, come over here for a minute, will you?'

He clambered down off the stool he'd been standing on while updating the board. 'Yes, boss?' he asked, arriving beside them.

'I've decided it's about time I took a back seat. I actually enjoyed being at home with me wife, and she enjoyed having me there with her. She reckons she's seen more of me in that month than she has in nearly forty years of marriage. We need to spend more time together, so I'll have to appoint someone to run this place for me.' Their faces dropped and he laughed. 'And what better people than you two? You can do it between yer, and if there's something you can't handle I'm just the other end of the telephone. 'Course, I'll remunerate you both accordingly. I was thinking in about a couple of months' time. That gives us plenty of time to get you both up to scratch, with visits down the track, et cetera.'

'You'll take me down the track too?' cried Lynnie, astounded.

He nodded. 'Yes, you too. I still don't think it's quite the place for a woman like you, Lynnie, but then times are changing, ain't they? This is the middle of the sixties after all. Who knows? Yer might be the first woman turf accountant, Caitlyn Downs.'

'Oh, don't give her any ideas,' laughed Ray. 'She gets above herself enough as it is.'

'Oh, you,' she chided, giving him a playful slap on the arm.

'So what do yer think then?'

They both looked at each other, then at Sid, and enthusiastically cried, 'We think it's a great idea.'

'Good, that's settled.'

Just then the door opened and a man entered. He approached the counter and Lynnie automatically smiled at him. 'Good morning, sir. Want to place a bet, do you? Oh! Alfie . . . Alex.'

He nodded a greeting to Sid and Ray, then focused his attention on Lynnie. 'My Alfie Manners character was that good, eh, Lynnie, that you never recognised me?'

She looked him over. She couldn't compare this man with wide boy Alfie Manners. Gone was the loud attire and the greased-back hair. He was smartly dressed in a pair of casual slacks and an olive green jumper with a crisp white shirt underneath. His hair was ungreased, slightly ruffled where the breeze had caught it, and strands were flopping over his forehead. She swallowed hard, feeling unnerved by his intense gaze. 'Well,' she said, finally finding her voice, 'you do look very different.'

'You didn't like Alfie Manners much, did you, Lynnie?'

'No, I can't say as I did. So have you come to give us an update?'

'An update?'

'Yes, on the situation with Neville Brown? I presume that's what you've called for?'

'No, that wasn't what I came for but being's you asked, I'll tell you. As yet there's no trace of where the money could have come from so it looks like we'll have no choice but to let him keep it. He found it, after all. Morally, he should have handed it over to the police but, regardless, I don't think we can charge him with failure to do so, as no one has reported the money missing.'

'Lucky man,' said Lynnie. It suddenly struck her that her heart was racing and she felt hot, and she wondered if she was coming down with a cold or something. 'Er . . . so what did you come for?'

'I'd like a word, please. In private, Lynnie.'

'You can use my office,' offered Sid. 'I'm sure I can make meself busy out here meantime.'

'Thanks, Mr Mallin,' said Alex as he walked behind the counter. 'This won't take long.'

Wondering what on earth he could want to see her about privately she followed him through into Sid's office. He shut the door behind them, made his way over to Sid's desk and leaned back against it.

He looked at her for several long moments before saying, 'I've come to make a confession to you, Lynnie.'

She felt, confused. 'Oh?'

Looking at her full on, he took a deep breath. 'I put my colleagues on to Oswald Matthews.'

'You did!' she exclaimed.

He nodded. 'I saw him pick you up from work one night. I didn't like the look of him, Lynnie, and I certainly didn't like the car he was expecting to drive you around in. It looked like a death trap to me. So I asked my colleagues if they'd keep an eye on him. I just had the feeling he was a bad 'un, and I was proved right, wasn't I? I'm sorry for the way he was finally picked up, but I couldn't do anything about that.' He paused before adding, 'For myself, I'm not so sorry.'

'Is that why I wasn't charged with being in collusion

with him? But how did you know I wasn't? I could have been behind it, for all you knew.'

'I just knew you weren't, Lynnie. Besides, any time he did anything you were never around. It was just unfortunate you happened to be with him when he was nicked.'

She looked at him for a moment as she digested this information, then her face clouded over. 'What did you mean when you said you weren't sorry for yourself?'

'I wasn't sorry to see Oswald Matthews out of your life, because . . .' He paused, looked down at his feet, then brought his gaze back to rest on her. 'Well, because it means that you're a free woman now and I can ask you out.'

She gave a sardonic laugh. 'And after what you've just confessed to me, what makes you think I'd go out with you?'

Alex took another deep breath. 'I live in hope you will. I knew immediately, you see.'

She frowned, puzzled. 'Knew? Knew what?'

Straightening up, he walked towards her and looked deep into her eyes. 'That you were the one for me, Lynnie. The woman I've been waiting all my life to meet. It's hard to explain but all I can say is that as soon as I saw you it was like a thunderbolt had struck me. It was like we were connected somehow. Sounds so stupid, I know, but that's how it felt and I just hoped with all my heart that you felt the same, or something similar. I can't tell you how hard it was for me not to dash over to you there and then, sweep you up in my arms and declare my true feelings, but I couldn't as I was on an undercover job and couldn't jeopardise it for anything, but once the operation was over there was nothing stopping me.

'When I found out you had a boyfriend, I was jealous . . . insanely. I watched you from behind the blind when Oswald met you from work. I wanted to see what the man looked like who held your affection. That night you turned up here so upset after Oswald's arrest, it took every ounce of my will power not to comfort you in the way I really wanted to, Lynnie. What on earth took me to the shop that night, God only knows. I lied when I told you that I was worried I'd left the premises unsecure. I was always very careful to make sure I'd locked up at night. I can only now put it down to my intuition telling me that the woman I secretly adored needed me. You caught me shutting the back door after arriving'. He paused and looked at her tenderly. 'You know the rest, Lynnie.'

Alex's look of tenderness turned to one of uncertainty. 'So, will you agree to go out with me now? For dinner? Saturday night? We can get to know each other at last. I hope you'll like Alex Goodwin better than Alfie Manners. So, will you, Lynnie? Please?'

She was reeling from his confession and amazed that the feeling that had shot through her when they'd first fixed eyes on one another was not her instincts telling her he was a crook but simple recognition of the fact that this was the man she had been destined to meet, her soul mate. She looked searchingly into his eyes. She knew without a shadow of doubt that Alex was sincere. She also knew without him actually saying the words that he loved her, would never ever wittingly let her down. She suddenly felt an overwhelming desire to throw herself into his arms and kiss him and how she stopped herself from doing so she didn't know. 'Er . . . no, I can't go out on Saturday night. Very dear friends of mine are having a party to celebrate a big family reunion. But . . . you're welcome to come, Alex,' she added, with a look of expectant hope in her eyes.

His face lit up in pure joy. 'I'd be delighted. Until Saturday then.' With that he walked out of the door and left her standing staring after him. Next thing she knew Sid was beside her.

'Everything all right, Lynnie? Alex looked pleased with himself when he left just now. Nice bloke that.' A twinkle of amusement sparkled in his eyes. 'You rather like him, don't yer?'

She took a deep breath. 'I might. Just a little,' she said cagily. 'Well, better get to work.' She walked towards the door, then paused and looked back at him. 'Sid, what do you think the odds are on me becoming a policeman's wife?'

He stared at her knowingly. 'Oh, I've no doubts about that. Got a good eye for a safe bet, I have. Dead cert.'

A Cut Above

Lynda Page

For Kacie Cooper, life in Leicester in 1959 is almost perfect. Jobs are plentiful, shops are filled with the latest fashions and dance halls are packed with people jiving to rock 'n' roll hits. Kacie is the top stylist in a reputable hair salon and her machine-mechanic husband Dennis is dreaming of the big time with his band, Vernon and the Vipers. Only one thing mars her happiness: her parents' constant disapproval that she doesn't have a 'proper' job or a more respectable husband, like her sister Caroline.

But when Caroline turns up on Kacie's doorstep, asking to stay for a while, it's clear that her sister's marriage has been far from idyllic. It is a revelation that plunges Kacie's own life into chaos and threatens everything that matters . . .

Don't miss Lynda Page's other sagas, also available from Headline.

'Cookson/Cox aficionados who've missed her should grab this. Romantic and gripping' *Peterborough Evening Telegraph*

'It keeps the reader enthralled from start to finish' *Hull Daily Mail*

'It's a story to grip you from the first page to the last' *Coventry Evening Telegraph*

'Full of lively characters' *Best*

0 7472 6674 3

headline

madaboutbooks.com

. . . the

Hodder Headline

site

for readers

and book lovers

madaboutbooks.com

Now you can buy any of these other bestselling books by **Lynda Page** from your bookshop or *direct from her publisher*.

FREE P&P AND UK DELIVERY
(Overseas and Ireland £3.50 per book)

Out With The Old	£6.99
A Cut Above	£5.99
All Or Nothing	£5.99
In For A Penny	£5.99
Now Or Never	£6.99
Any Old Iron	£6.99
At The Toss Of A Sixpence	£6.99
Just By Chance	£6.99
And One For Luck	£6.99
Peggie	£6.99
Josie	£6.99
Annie	£6.99
Evie	£6.99

TO ORDER SIMPLY CALL THIS NUMBER

01235 400 414

or visit our website: www.madaboutbooks.com

Prices and availability subject to change without notice.

News & Natter is a newsletter full of everyone's favourite storytellers and their latest news and views as well as opportunities to win some fabulous prizes and write to your favourite authors. Just send a postcard with your name and address to: *News & Natter*, Kadocourt Ltd, The Gateway, Gatehouse Road, Aylesbury, Bucks HP19 8ED. Then sit back and look forward to your first issue.